PRAISE FOR

PERSEPHONE STATION

A MOST-ANTICIPATED BOOK OF THE YEAR FOR
BUSTLE, *BOOK RIOT*, *THE NERD DAILY*, AND *GEEKTYRANT*
AN AMAZON EDITORS' PICK FOR BEST SCIENCE FICTION & FANTASY

"A must-read of 2021."

—*Book Riot*

"Up there with Joe Haldeman or Iain M. Banks with excellent world-building and a Le Guin/Ann Leckie scalpel for interrogating old tropes. The vibe is *Casablanca* meets *The Magnificent Seven* meets *The Mandalorian,* and if that doesn't intrigue you, you may want to check your pulse."

—Adrian McKinty, *New York Times*
bestselling author of *The Chain*

"Leicht creates a fascinating, compelling universe that combines the violent, human-settled frontier with the strange, unique beauty and alluring intricacies of diverse life-forms across the galaxy. . . . *Persephone Station* is a story about salvaging the elements that make us human."

—*Chicago Review of Books*

"Fast-paced, no-nonsense prose."

—*Publishers Weekly*

"This enjoyable and thrilling read features excellent world-building and lively characterizations. The engaging crew and well-drawn plot will have readers hoping this will become a series."

—*Library Journal*

PERSEPHONE STATION

STATION

STINA LEICHT

SAGA PRESS

LONDON SYDNEY **NEW YORK** TORONTO NEW DELHI

SAGA PRESS
AN IMPRINT OF SIMON & SCHUSTER, INC.

1230 AVENUE OF THE AMERICAS, NEW YORK, NEW YORK 10020

First Saga Press trade paperback edition November 2021

SAGA PRESS and colophon are registered trademarks of Simon & Schuster, Inc.

For information about special discounts for bulk purchases, please contact Simon & Schuster Special Sales at 1-866-506-1949 siness@simonandschuster.com.

The Simon & Schuster Speakers Bureau can bring authors to your live event. For more information or to book an event, contact the Simon & Schuster Speakers Bureau at 1-866-248-3049 or visit our website at www.simonspeakers.com.

Interior design by Michelle Marchese

3 5 7 9 10 8 6 4 2

Library of Congress Cataloging-in-Publication Data has been applied for.

ISBN 978-1-5344-1458-7
ISBN 978-1-5344-1459-4 (pbk)
ISBN 978-1-5344-1460-0 (ebook)

For all my lady friends. Thanks for being the Ivy to my Harley. Let's team up, hit the patriarchy in the face with a baseball bat a few times, and make the world a better place.

And for Dane.
As you wish.

PERSEPHONE ▬▬
▬▬▬ STATION

1 ▇▇▇▇

The clatter of heavy power-assisted armor echoed off the rocky hills as the corporate mercenaries lined up behind Serrao-Orlov's latest representative. The scent of machine oil, foul chemicals, and rubberized plastic wafted from the group. A military-grade personnel carrier squatted in the dirt not far away. Its bulk blotted out the morning sun peeking over the horizon. The engines had been shut off, and now that the troops were in place, the quiet tick of cooling metal rode the breeze ruffling Paulie's long black hair. The wind stank of burned fuel. Paulie sneezed.

A railgun had been mounted on the roof of the craft. Currently, its barrel was aimed at her and the rest of her people. A soldier sat at the controls, their expression lost in backlit shadows.

Paulie shivered, and her stomach fluttered.

Her friend Beak placed a steadying hand on her left shoulder. Paulie caught a mix of muted scents that combined to form a thought.

It is only for show. They are here to talk.

"I know," Paulie whispered. She should have replied in the same manner, but it was easier to speak using vocal cords while in human form. She glanced up at Beak, who stood at least a foot taller than she was, and tried to smile.

Beak's short blond hair framed a pale face that almost glowed in the morning light. She moved her sturdy, muscular frame with a gentle grace that Paulie envied. Unlike Beak, she wasn't athletic. Her area of study was mechanical engineering. Beak was a scientist—an animal biologist. Of course, there was no need for biology at the moment. Today was about representing the interests of their people, the Emissaries. The four of them—Paulie, Beak, Efemena, and Matías—were present merely to demonstrate that Kirby Sams, the designated translator, was not alone.

The Emissaries were a peaceful people.

Another burst of wind pushed against Paulie's human shape like an affectionate ollayah pup. It was early in the growing season. The spare ground was dotted with blooming densiiflor. The spicy-sweet scent of the purple flowers meant exuberance and new life—a rather incongruent environment for talks that would decide the future of her people.

Everyone assigned to the mission had assumed human forms and names. Such gestures were undertaken for the comfort of the humans. In the century and a half of human habitation on Persephone, no Emissary had shown any non-acclimated human their true form.

Nothing else about this visit was standard. To Paulie's knowledge, all previous negotiations within the past fifty years had occurred via message or video. Humans didn't venture on their own into the Badlands—at least not anymore. There were reasons for that. Reasons that her people, the Emissaries, spent a great deal of energy and time creating. Humans weren't wanted on Persephone. That didn't stop the Serrao-Orlov Corporation from claiming the planet anyway, of course.

According to official galactic record, the planet was uninhabited, free for the taking. Her people, the Emissaries, were ghosts. Except that they weren't, and only a select few among humankind knew otherwise. Survival depended upon their remaining hidden. Being young, Paulie didn't understand why. If the rest of the universe were made aware, Serrao-Orlov would be forced to give the planet back. The United Republic of Worlds had rules about these things, after all. But every time she brought this up, Paulie was told that she didn't understand the larger view. When Paulie asked for more information, she was told to be quiet and leave her elders to their work.

The corporation's stated agenda for the day was contract renegotiation. It was always about the Corsini Agreement. Humans were never interested in anything else, but since mediation was what her people had been designed for, this suited the council just fine.

Paulie remained anxious in spite of this. The humans had changed their behavior, and in her experience—what little she had—humans never did that without reason.

The mercenaries formed an orderly half circle between the corporate representative and the personnel carrier. She counted twenty heavily armed and well-trained Serrao-Orlov mercenaries.

Twenty-one, if you count the company representative, Paulie thought.

The Emissary delegation numbered five.

Paulie whispered to Beak without taking her eyes off the mercenaries. "What are they afraid of?"

Beak's reply was spiced with tartness. *Themselves. Death. The void. That which is strange to them—*

"I didn't mean on a philosophical level," Paulie whispered, rolling her eyes.

Perhaps you should be more specific, came the sharp-scented reply. Beak was smiling.

"Ha. Ha," Paulie said.

The human dressed in the bulky yellow environment suit stamped with the Serrao-Orlov logo took up a position a few paces in front of the soldiers. After a brief pause, they stepped close enough that Paulie could see inside the suit's helmet. She started as she recognized the human the corporation had sent as their representative.

That's Vissia Corsini. The traitor. It has to be. A bolt of terror shot through Paulie's altered body. *This is bad.*

All around her, the sharp scent of panic and rage flooded

the air. It was heavy enough to be a shout. She found it hard to breathe. At the same time, Beak took three rapid steps toward the humans before she was brought short by a command from Kirby.

"Stay back!"

Paulie had been born long after the Catholic Colonial Era, but she'd heard stories of the infamous Vissia Corsini. The human had once sheltered with her people after the Catholic missionaries abandoned the planet. The Emissaries had helped her. And then Vissia Corsini had betrayed them to Serrao-Orlov.

Vissia looked nothing like Paulie had imagined. The woman was short and stocky—indicating a childhood spent in full gravity—whether that had been artificial or planet-side Paulie didn't know. Within the transparent helmet, the woman's ageless, pale face appeared gaunt. Her dark brown eyebrows were pinched together in a stern line. Garish red lipstick made her mouth into a disapproving slash. The collar of a black suit and a prim white blouse peeked up from the bottom of her helmet.

Paulie didn't move. Beak had frozen in place a few paces behind Kirby. That was when Paulie noticed that Beak had a fist wrapped tightly around something small. Something that glinted in the light like glass. Paulie couldn't tell what it might be.

Throughout the delegation's panic, the soldiers kept the barrels of their guns pointed at the ground. Kirby was the only exception. Her posture didn't reveal surprise or fear.

She was a good choice as translator, Paulie thought. *I'm glad I didn't get the job.* She wanted nothing more than to not be on this hill, three hundred clicks from safety. She glanced northward.

One of the soldiers shifted position. The muscles in Paulie's back, shoulders, and stomach abruptly tightened.

"Good morning," Kirby said. Her tone was calm, even cheerful.

Paulie began to wonder if Kirby had known all along that Vissia would be the one they'd meet.

In contrast to Vissia, Kirby appeared to be a middle-aged human with full lips and braided brown hair. She, too, was short, and her regal bearing projected authority. That was where the similarities ended.

Kirby said, "We are here as you requested. What is it you'd like to discuss?"

"I'm not here to discuss anything. I am here to pick up the shipment," Vissia said. "Where is it?"

"There is no shipment," Kirby said. "You will receive the items listed in the original manifest next month."

Vissia's voice managed to be authoritative in spite of her environment suit's tinny speaker. "According to the new agreement—"

"There has been no new agreement," Kirby said.

Kirby was particularly gifted at reading unspoken cues among humans. Paulie and the others had voted for her for this reason. It also didn't hurt that Kirby was unflappable by nature.

"Do you know how I know?" Kirby asked. "It's because agreements are, by definition, accepted by both parties. And I don't recall the Council mentioning their signing or approving such a revision."

Paulie caught a whiff of frustration that was a whisper in the air: *What in the name of the Makers does Vissia think she's doing?*

Other stronger, more acidic scent-responses mingled in the air. Paulie didn't join the olfactory uproar. Kirby turned and shut the comments down with an audible hiss.

The twenty-one humans sealed inside their environment suits and powered armor couldn't discern the scented conversational undercurrent from the nearby plant life—even if they had been exposed to Persephone's atmosphere. But that didn't mean they hadn't developed equipment that could detect Emissary speech. Vissia was familiar with it, and if she knew, then it was easy to assume the other humans did, too.

Kirby continued. "The Council has given me all the information available. And I have a particularly good memory. Even so, we have no record of any such—"

"Request then," Vissia said. The corners of her red mouth turned upward in an expression that was anything but friendly.

"A request implies the ability to refuse. You appear to be making a demand," Kirby said. "If you wish to return to a reasonable—"

"Very well," Vissia said, clearly losing her patience. "We demand delivery. In two weeks."

"I regret to inform you that the Council does not intend to comply," Kirby said.

"That would not be in your best interests," Vissia said.

"I understand," Kirby said. "However, our refusal remains."

"Do you know who I am?" Vissia asked.

"Of course I do," Kirby said.

"Then you know what I'm capable of when crossed," Vissia said.

"Fortunately for us," Kirby said, "you are not representing yourself, but your employer. And any infraction on your part will have legal consequences."

"You're unarmed," Vissia said.

"Are you violating the treaty between our people and your superiors?" Kirby asked.

"Not as of yet," Vissia said. "However, I have been granted a certain amount of leeway. Let me demonstrate."

Vissia turned and muttered something off channel to the soldiers behind her. They immediately raised their weapons. At the same time, the gun mounted on top of the armored personnel carrier rotated until it was aimed at the settlement of Welan Bloom Hill three hundred clicks to the north.

The air was flooded with sharp but silent protests, hisses, and gasps. Paulie smelled the others' screams.

Kirby shouted. "You can't be serious—"

The railgun fired.

Multiple things happened all at once. The ground beneath Paulie's feet vibrated with the force of the gun going off. She was temporarily deafened. The exclamations of her comrades again flooded her nose. Beak sprinted toward Vissia.

In the distance, the white walls of Welan Bloom Hill— the place where Paulie's cousins, aunt, and uncle all lived— vanished in an explosion of fire and smoke. The sound of it echoed off the hills like thunder.

Beak tackled Vissia and smashed a fist against the yellow environment suit. The mercenaries fired their guns. Efemena fell down. Matías and Kirby ran for cover. Gunfire pelted the ground. Paulie didn't realize she was still standing until she felt someone grab her leg. She dropped into the dirt at once and placed her hands over her head.

Vissia screamed. "Cease fire, you idiots! You're going to shoot me! Fucking assholes!"

When the guns stopped Paulie lifted her face from the dirt. Her friend, Efemena, lay next to her. Blood covered her cheek. She wasn't breathing, and her eyes were blank.

"No!" Paulie cried. She laid a hand on Efemena's back and shook her.

In the distance, the rubble of Welan Bloom Hill was on fire.

"Why?" Kirby dropped to her knees. "Our families! They were no threat to you. Why?!"

Beak rolled off Vissia, smearing a streak of bright crimson across sulfur-yellow plastic.

"Beak!"

Paulie scrambled to her feet and ran to where Beak lay gasping. She'd been shot in the arm, legs, and shoulder.

"Matías help!" Paulie pressed her hands on the shoulder wound to slow the bleeding.

Matías staggered to her side. He, too, was wounded but apparently not too badly. She blinked back shock and returned to the work of keeping Beak from bleeding to death.

Vissia struggled to her feet and dusted herself off. At that moment, Paulie spied the small pieces of glass scattered in the dirt.

She blinked. *A broken test tube?*

Shifting her position so as to not draw attention, she attempted to hide the shards from view. Then she forced an acid-scented question through her semitransformed throat glands. *Beak, what did you do? Beak?*

Beak's mouth opened and closed without giving an answer. She shut her eyes. A small self-satisfied smile haunted the corners of her lips.

Emissaries are a peaceful people.

Vissia's curse pulled Paulie's gaze away from Beak. Paulie spotted the rip in the yellow environment suit. It was impossible to tell if the damage had been done by the fall, glass shards, or a stray bullet. Either way, Vissia had most definitely been exposed to whatever had been in the broken test tube.

Rage and panic struggled for control on Vissia's face. "Damn it!"

One of the soldiers arrived to help. He said, "We must get you into quarantine, ma'am!"

Vissia slapped his hands away. She turned and glared at Kirby. "If it were up to me, I'd have all of you exterminated."

She seemed to gather some measure of self-control before continuing. "You have two weeks. No more. If you don't comply, I'm sending in troops to wipe every last one of you off the planet's surface. Do you hear me?"

She didn't wait for Kirby to answer. She whirled and stomped back to the ship while holding the rent in her suit closed with her left hand. The mercenaries trailed behind.

As the ship lifted off, dirt, sand, and plant debris blew into the air. Paulie shielded her face from the worst of it with her hands. Once the ship was far enough away, she got up off her knees and placed a boot squarely on the broken test tube. Matías and Kirby finished preparing Beak for the journey back to what remained of the settlement. It was more fitting. They had medical training.

Paulie sat down hard next to Efemena, plucked her hand from the blood-soaked dirt, and began to cry.

"Let me take her," Matías said. "Kirby will help Beak."

Nodding, Paulie scooted back. Matías picked up Efemena as if she weighed nothing and began the journey to what remained of Welan Bloom Hill. Kirby, staggering under Beak's awkward weight, helped Beak limp down the path.

Paulie lingered alone on the hilltop. She didn't want to leave until she'd buried the broken shards. The Council might return and examine the area. As she collected the pieces, she noticed the remains of a label. Fitting the fragments together, she was able to read what was written on them. *V-357-RA-45.* She wasn't all that familiar with the designations used by the biology teams and their various projects. However, Beak had told her about this one because the proposal had been rejected outright by the Council. It was a virus created to remotely edit human DNA.

A cold shiver passed through Paulie's body.

It was unthinkable. Violence ran against Emissary beliefs. *Our upbringing, even our design.* "Damn it, Beak."

With one hand shading her tear-filled eyes from the sun, she watched the retreating ship for a few moments before joining the others at the bottom of the hill.

No one spoke.

Their mission had failed.

2

TIME: 03:21
DAY: THURSDAY
MONK'S BAR
WEST BRYNNER

I wasn't always like this, Rosie thought. *I used to live a more direct life. A righteous life. I used to be a spiritual person.*

I used to care.

This city wears upon one's soul like a steel file on soapstone.

The security staff patrolling the perimeter of Monk's had discovered the body and called in an alarm. What remained of the corpse lay on the pavement with its back propped up against the establishment's front doors. The head tilted at an unnatural angle to the left due to a deep cut across the throat that had nearly separated the head from the neck. The hands were curled in burned, broken blobs. Rosie averted their gaze from the shoeless feet.

It wasn't that they were squeamish. They couldn't afford to be, not in their line of business. However, the sight brought up bad memories.

"Poor Marcy," Sarah, Rosie's partner and the senior bartender, said. Her voice carried the concern Rosie wished they could display. "Torture is not a good way to go."

A small pain jabbed the interior of Rosie's chest. They blinked several times to relieve the burning sensation on the backs of their eyes.

Blue and green neon light from across the street reflected on the wet pavement in smears of watercolor and cast the body in the glow of animated alien colors. The blinking sign belonged to a low-rent plastic surgery clinic called Nu You.

I care. I do, Rosie thought. *I merely channel my concern . . . differently now.* "I don't know why they bothered. Amateurs. Five minutes of research would've revealed she wasn't connected. Why go to all this trouble?" Bitterness built up in the back of their throat.

The question was rhetorical. They knew why it had been done. *Intimidation.* But they had a powerful need to verbalize even a small piece of outrage. It was like puking up the tiniest bit of poison. The end was inevitable—the toxin had done its work, but the impulse was unstoppable nonetheless.

Sarah nodded, getting out her hand terminal. She was a small, pale woman and short. Her long, straight hair was dyed a different color every few months. She was intelligent and, like many intelligent people, got bored easily. Her intellect and keen observation skills were two of the many reasons Rosie felt Sarah made such a valuable business partner. That, and people tended to underestimate bartenders. They were the drinking world's confessors.

And a great deal of drinking happened in Brynner— particularly the part of Brynner located west of the Dead Line.

"It's time to do something," Sarah said. "This is the second one."

Rosie sighed. They looked up into the night sky. The moon was full, illuminating clouds bunched in ire-filled knots. The clouds over Brynner almost always appeared angry.

Rage, pride, and avarice, Rosie thought. *Three of the seven deadly sins. A great fall after such an auspicious start.*

They frowned but kept their tone even. "Which would-be crime boss is it this time, I wonder." It wasn't a question. They already had a theory based upon the previous victim. *Two points make a line, or in this case a trajectory.* "Have you checked her pockets?"

"Not yet." Sarah finished typing her message and pocketed her hand terminal. "The cleaners are on the way."

"It's going to rain soon. I'm not certain it's worth the fee."

"We're lucky whomever it was waited until after closing," Sarah said. "This sort of thing puts off customers, you know." Sarah continued her search. After a few moments, she paused and glanced up. A line appeared between her brows. "Found something." Standing, she held a small white envelope. She poured the contents into her right palm. "Huh. So, they *are* connected."

Was there really any doubt? Rosie asked, "Seeds of some sort?"

"Lemon seeds, maybe. Could be orange."

"Orange, I should think." Rosie didn't look. *Gau has become bold and careless.* "How many are there?"

"Five," Sarah said. "Odd. There were six seeds on the first. Can it be a countdown? I hate it when assholes are coy. What the fuck does it mean?"

"It means Julian Gau thinks he's the only one who has read Sherlock Holmes. It should've been five both times. He thinks he's being clever," Rosie said, and then paused. "I'm calling in a few favors. Tap de la Reza. Marcy was one of hers. A bit of payback might help morale. Even better, that crew doesn't have as many criminal connections as the others. It'll be less complicated."

"And what of Enid Crowe?" Sarah asked. "She's on that team, and she's Correct Family, isn't she?"

"Not actively."

"I know," Sarah said, her voice acquiring a sing-song quality. "She wouldn't be one of ours, otherwise, but—"

"De la Reza's crew is the cleanest we have."

"Point."

"Arrange a meeting. Tomorrow. Send her what we have on Gau. She likes to research her assignments."

"You're sure it's Gau?"

"Jasper McKenna is firmly against anything British Earth Empire out of an archaic sense of ancestral loyalty," Rosie said. "The Isi have messy rituals for these sorts of things and aren't known for their literary references. The Prizrak don't go in for subtlety. But if you want to be thorough, I'd suggest looking into Earth fruit imports. Specifically, citrus."

"I like thorough."

"And that's why you're my second."

"Flatterer," Sarah said, pocketing the envelope and its contents. "All right. Time to finish closing out. I've a feeling tomorrow is going to be busy." She moved toward the door, noted that Marcy's body blocked entry, and paused. "I think I'll go back in the way we came."

"I'll wait here," Rosie said. "Someone should stay with Marcy."

"Why? No one is going to bother her. Not now. There isn't anything left to steal."

"To ensure the recently departed's soul isn't claimed by the devil."

Sarah paused and turned around. She raised an eyebrow. "I didn't take you for superstitious."

"Perhaps today I'm feeling my age."

"Seriously, are you okay? Should I get security to stand with you? If it's Gau, he might make a second attempt on you—"

Rosie waved her away. "I'm fine. Go. I'll meet you inside shortly."

When they heard the door slam from the alley, they knelt beside the body and murmured a blessing. Technically, they weren't allowed to perform the ritual, but they supposed that by the same technicality Marcy wasn't a permissible recipient.

They placed a hand on the dead woman's head and closed her eyes. "May an angel watch over you." Then they began a prayer for the dead.

All in all, it'd been an average workday at Monk's. That is . . . until they received the message from Vissia Corsini. Then things got interesting.

3 ▮▮▮▮

Some asshole was attempting to break into her apartment. Angel knew this because her internal Combat Assistant's alarm had gone off. Her feelings on the matter were mixed, of course. She hadn't been jolted awake by a combat computer in a little over six years.

She hadn't exactly missed it.

On the upside, this meant the exorbitant bribe she'd paid the United Republic of Worlds Marine Corps retirement commander under the table to leave her CA online had been a good investment. It also meant she had the time to plan and consider her options.

On the down side, the asshole in question was about to be the subject of a meeting with her employer, Rosie—the sort of meeting that tended to result in politics. Angel hated politics. In West Brynner, politics often led to screaming and bloodstains.

The fastest solution to the problem was the illegal service pistol stored in her footlocker. Unfortunately, that wasn't a good idea. The discharge of an unregistered military-grade weapon would likely land her an unwelcome interview with Corporate Police. Even though the CoPo rarely strayed west of the Dead Line—it was what the Dead Line was for, after all—she had a hunch that they'd make an exception in this case.

Even without that as a concern, gunfire would risk the lives of her neighbors. The walls in West Brynner's corporate-council housing were notoriously thin. She knew that from personal experience.

One of her neighbors had had a disagreement with a spouse that ended when one partner pushed the other against the wall adjoining her apartment with theirs. Both men had landed on her bedroom floor along with a significant portion of the wall in question. They'd both apologized, embarrassed. They'd paid for the damages, too—otherwise, she'd still have that ragged window into their apartment and unplanned roommates.

No, she'd have to handle the situation quietly and with minimal fuss.

There was the katana in the kitchen, but cleaning the mess afterward would take more effort than she wanted to deal with.

Shit.

It'd been too long since she'd last engaged an opponent in a hand-to-hand fight outside of battle or a dojo. Were it not for the nature of the visit, she would have savored the prospect. She could just hear what Lou would have to say about that response.

Someone breaks into your apartment and this is how you react? There's something wrong with you, woman. You know that, don't you?

Lou didn't know the half of it.

Lying motionless on her back with her eyes closed, Angel attempted to keep her anticipation in check. The metallic taste in the back of her throat indicated that her CA had begun managing her autonomic reflexes via chemical cocktail. She listened with enhanced hearing, vigilant for telltale details.

The window slid open—a window that she'd most certainly locked. Cool night air rushed in. The hushed electric hum of a lift-car drifted in on the night breeze. She heard the brush of fabric against aluminum as her uninvited visitor squeezed through the opening. *Given I'm on the fifteenth floor, that's a neat trick.*

The intruder took a few steps and then stumbled on something, probably one of the boots she'd shed before climbing into bed. She tried not to smile at the grunt of pain.

When she was young, Sensei Niko used to admonish her for untidiness. She stopped when Angel replied that anyone walking into her room in the dark without an invitation deserved a nasty shock.

Who is this waste of oxygen?

Activating her computer's strategic programming, she made certain the lowest force setting was engaged and requested projections. She also had questions, and she wanted answers—more direct answers than she'd get from Rosie, her current employer.

Sort of employer, she thought. Although her upbringing had taught her that there is honor in service, even as a mercenary, her current contract was with a criminal and of the open-ended variety. *Indefinite. That is, until death did you part.*

And that made her intruder slightly more troubling.

Scenario 1: No physical intervention until attacked.

Statistical probability of assailant fatality given force restrictions: 20%.

Statistical probability of bystander fatality given force restrictions: 10%.

Statistical probability of personal fatality given force restrictions: 35%.

Really? she sent back. *Thirty-five percent? That's generous. It's clear they don't even have night vision.*

Kurosawa, the dropship to which her CA was linked, responded. A lack of night vision has been accurately accounted for. However, there is not enough information to assess the assailant's skill nor have the subject's weapons been identified. Visual confirmation required.

What time is it? Where is the moon? Angel didn't know how much light was entering the room through the window. She didn't want to risk tipping off the intruder.

Do you wish to input additional variables? It will take extra time due to the lack of updated firmware. However, the intruder hasn't killed you yet. They probably have other plans. There is still time. The ship's AI had an Old Earth Japanese accent. Something about it lent a lofty sarcasm to *Kurosawa's* responses. It reminded her of Sensei Niko, even though Niko was female and the ship was male.

No one likes a snarky AGI, Kurosawa, Angel sent back.

Do you wish to alter my interactive settings? *Kurosawa* asked.

Not now, Angel sent. *I thought Lou ordered the new electronic components weeks ago?*

She did. However, due to the unusually high demand for the component in question, along with certain financial market fluctuations, availability is scarce and the cost is high.

When it came to technical discussions, *Kurosawa* kept to vagaries. Angel didn't have Lou's knowledge or skills.

For fuck's sake, Angel thought. *Cryptospeculators will be the fucking death of me.* She returned her attention to the link with *Kurosawa. Other options?*

Once again, the interval between her request and the ship's reply seemed to last forever. A strat-com consult took seconds, even it if seemed much longer due to adrenaline. She focused on her breathing and the movements of her intruder to avoid further frustration.

Scenario 2: Summon corporate authorities for assistance.

Statistical probability of timely corporate response: 2%

Statistical probability of assailant fatality given delay and force restrictions: 50%.

Statistical probability of bystander fatality given delay and force restrictions: 35%.

Statistical probability of personal fatality given delay and force restrictions: 50%.

Scenario 3: Summon dropship for intervention.

Statistical probability of assailant fatality given delay and force restrictions: 50%.

Statistical probability of bystander fatality given delay and force restrictions: 42%.

Statistical probability of personal fatality given delay and force restrictions: 50%.

Stay where you are, Kurosawa.

Shall I alert Lou? What of the authorities? I can run a—

I can handle this.

Understood, Captain.

She had trouble viewing herself as a captain. Her official URWMC rank had been sergeant, but *Kurosawa* was hers and that ship had already sailed as it were.

A rough hand pressed itself across her mouth. The scent of recently consumed curry washed over her. She opened her eyes. At the same time, she placed her left hand over his to prevent him from escaping. He was pale and stocky with dark straight hair and a beard. Light from the window glinted on a knife blade.

She reached out with her right hand, made contact under his upper arm just above the elbow, and sat up. The movement locked the intruder's left elbow, shoving his body between her and his blade. Peeling his palm from her face, she kept the captured arm straight. Then she got to her feet and swung his wrist up high over his head, creating a lever. He let out a surprised sound, bent over at the waist, and fell to his knees, facing away from her. The entire action had a weightless grace to it—like a dance. No aspect of her response seemed to trigger alarm in her opponent's nervous system. That is, until he was already on his knees.

She registered a familiar image on the back of his jacket but didn't have time to process the details.

No gun. Good. Of course, her odds of getting cut were high.

She lifted his arm farther into the air and twisted his wrist. He bent over even more and cursed.

"Why are you here?" she asked.

"Why do you think, bitch?" His accent was pure West Brynner.

A local. That could mean many things. "If you're here for a robbery, you picked the wrong damned apartment, asshole. Drop the knife."

He shifted his weight forward and down on his opposite shoulder in an attempt to get free. She didn't release his arm—merely moved with him, continuing to shield herself from his knife with his body. He fell face-first on the floor. At once, he attempted to move his hands under him in order to push up. She didn't fight him nor did she let go. Instead, she altered her grip, cupping the back of his left hand with her right. She kept his bent arm perpendicular to the floor with his elbow pointed up. He could struggle, but it wouldn't take much pressure to inflict a great deal of pain.

"I said drop it." She kept her voice calm. "I *will* break your wrist."

He made another escape attempt. She responded by quickly lifting him from the floor via his awkwardly bent wrist. She felt his joint pop. The sound of breaking/dislocating bones was blotted out by a howl of pain.

He released the knife. But she knew better than to think it was over. So she tucked his arm into the crook of her elbow as if she were politely escorting him down a red carpet. She applied more pressure on his broken wrist. He instantly howled and shifted up on his toes. She took a single step, un-balancing him further. At that moment, he staggered. She let go, and he fell out the open window headfirst.

"Oops."

Sensei Niko wouldn't have been happy about that. She could almost hear her admonishment. *You should be aware of your surroundings and the dangers to your training partner at all times.*

A loud meat-hitting-metal thump followed her attacker's second scream. She shoved aside the now bent blinds and spot-ted her assailant sprawled across the hood of a dark-colored lift-car. She quickly withdrew. There was no guarantee his part-ner would have the same ethics she did about unloading an entire minigun clip into the building. She lay on the floor for a few breaths, waiting for the inevitable explosion or storm of bullets. When none came, she crept to the window again.

The lift-car was gone.

The lift platform is nowhere near my apartment. "You *better* run," she muttered.

Someone knocked on the wall opposite. "You okay in there?"

It was one of the neighbors that had landed on her floor six months ago.

"I'm good," Angel said. "Thanks."

"Captain de la Reza, have you considered bringing home men for sex rather than beating the shit out of them?"

"Good night, Ben," Angel said.

The adrenaline in her system gave her the shakes now that the biggest threat was gone. She tightened both fists and took slow, controlled breaths.

Are you all right? It was *Kurosawa* again. Your CA indicates an injury.

Glancing down, she spied the blood soaking through her right sleeve. The moment she spotted it, the wound began to sting. She peeled back the fabric with care and spied a superficial cut. *Just need a couple Band-Aids, that's all.*

Should I alert corporate authorities?

Don't waste the energy. Kurosawa resisted the idea that a police force should be uninterested in the welfare of citizens, no matter how many times Angel had explained West Brynner's rules. It was almost quaint. *I'll deal with the cleanup myself.*

The damage to the window was minimal. That was good. She went to her closet, found a hanger, and used the wire to bind it shut. If there was a contract, the hanger wouldn't stop anyone from breaking the glass to get to her or her belongings, but it'd stop an opportunist.

Good night, Captain. I will continue to monitor your channel in case you require further assistance.

Thank you.

And with that, Angel went to the bathroom to bandage her arm. There wasn't much blood on the carpet. Still, she was certain her landlord would want a steep fee when it came time to move out. This hadn't been her first unwelcome visitor.

One day, I'm leaving this dirtball of a planet and going home, even if it's in a body bag.

A dull ache once again materialized in her chest as she thought of Thandh, her home world. She no longer had to consciously think of her sisters, the Gorin. Grief ambushed her the instant her mind drifted to Thandh.

The Gorin had been both a fighting force and an extended family. She'd had honor once—honor, love, and belonging. But now she was an outcast. Her own mother was forbidden to contact her or face banishment herself. She had no actual siblings, and her father had died the year before she'd been expelled. *Thank god.* It said a great deal that Sensei Niko risked brief contacts from time to time. In that way, Angel was able to maintain a connection to everyone she loved no matter how tenuous. Niko did this at great personal risk, of course, and Angel deeply appreciated it.

Once honor is lost, there is no regaining it.

That doesn't mean I can't damned well try.

4 ▮▮▮▮▮

There were conflicting rumors about how Monk's got its name. The most likely story, according to Enid Crowe, was that the building had once been part of a Catholic Federation monastery. She claimed that the cross-shaped floor plan and other telltale architectural details were dead giveaways. Given that Enid possessed no less than three advanced degrees—one of them in architecture and another in interplanetary history—Angel believed her. In any case, it would explain Rosie's eccentric decorating choices.

The cavernous interior was draped in imported polysilk velvets, glass-bead curtains, and antique furniture replicas dating from the Catholic Colonial Era. The back bar was an eclectic mixture of pieces that had once been housed in various desanctified cathedrals. Nestled among the rows of liquor bottles was a genuine tabernacle. Angel considered it an interesting choice of symbolism given what transpired there.

Exactly two types of people drank at Monk's back bar: members of a rather exclusive criminal class and those who sought to employ them. Naturally, a more public section of the establishment was available. The place had a certain reputation, and Rosie, like any other businessperson, wasn't averse to profit. The public section of the establishment attracted wannabe criminals and a specific breed of tourist: mainly rich Earthers of a short-sighted political inclination and a romantic perspective involving military-grade munitions ownership.

Angel was, whether she liked it or not, a member of the first set, and as such, there were rules by which she had to comply.

Loud thirty-year-old club music welcomed her as she made her way to the back bar. Electronic bass competed with her heart for dominance inside her chest. The air filters weren't robust enough to remove the smell of spiced tobacco and the cleaning crew's battles against ever-present mold. It was early for Monk's, but the place was already packed. Patrons in various states of evening- and daywear joked, drank, imbibed intoxicating substances, gambled, and negotiated with prostitutes of all genders.

Monk's was Rosie's business front, and Brynner was a typical corporate town. The gaming tables, dealers, and drug distributers were licensed. So were the sex workers. Periodic medical exams curtailed the spread of sexually transmitted diseases.

West of the Dead Line, anything you could pay for was tolerated—even if it might require bribing the CoPo to look the other way. Laws existed, but they were for the less financially endowed. It was why off-planet smugglers and assassins traveled to West Brynner and to Monk's in particular.

She remembered a lesson from her first year at the Gorin No Gakkō Academy. *The ways of the Gorin are not the ways of our employers. Respect for your employer is required for the length of the contract or agreement in so much as their ways do not interfere with our ways. Should a conflict occur, the agreement is immediately subject to review by—*

"Captain! Captain de la Reza!"

A small young woman with a halo of soft curly brown hair waved from one of the tables in the public area. Her right eye was brown, and in the dim light one could almost miss that her left eye was artificial. The augmented eye was one of the older models. It had a black sclera, and the iris was deep blue. Medical prosthetics for marines being what they were—aesthetics weren't considered a factor.

Particularly if that marine served in the Thirteenth, Angel thought.

She understood that Command staff lovingly referred to the Thirteenth as "Corpse Corps" because recruits signed on for multiple postmortem tours of duty. The number of returns depended upon the individual soldier's constitution. Technically, members of the corps were revivified, not reanimated like some Old Earth horror monster, but the nickname stuck anyway. The experience left scars, of course.

You never come back whole.

Regardless of what it'd done to her brain, Angel didn't resent her service. After her expulsion, she'd been left with few honorable options, and the Thirteenth had been glad to have her expertise. No woman—and women without uteruses were certainly counted as women—willingly left the Gorin of Thandh. Top graduates of the female martial arts school served as government security. The rest commanded exorbitant fees. Not only were the Gorin famous for their skill, they were known to be absolutely trustworthy.

When word had gotten back to the school that Angel had enlisted, she received an unsigned message from Sensei Niko: *It is good.* An overwhelming sense of relief had burst through Angel's composure. She'd barely had time to find a place to cry in private. Those three words had been her rescue pod. They'd ushered her whole into a new life on an alien world.

She stopped at Lou's table. "Thought you swore off gambling?"

Lou laid her cards facedown with a wide grin. She gave a sideways nod toward a slender woman of mixed Earth ancestry. "Look who I ran into."

Recognition poured over Angel like cool water. All at once, two overwhelming emotions battled for dominance: relief and anxiety.

"Why Sukyi Edozie," Angel said. "I heard you were dead."

Sukyi's lips were full, and her hair had the same loose wavy texture as Angel's own. However, her skin had an unhealthy grey tinge to it, and she looked tired, even exhausted.

She glanced up from her card hand and gave Angel a slow smile. "It would seem rumors of my demise are grossly exaggerated." Her accent was pure British boarding school.

Angel's father had been an Earth classics professor. She recognized the mangled literary reference at once. No matter what Sukyi's origins were, she'd had an extensive, high-quality education. Angel asked, "What in the hell are you doing here?"

"It would seem I'm lessening your pilot's financial concerns," Sukyi said in her characteristic lofty tone. She covered her mouth with one black-leather-gloved hand and coughed.

Angel could just hear the deep, liquid rattle of Sukyi's lungs and suppressed an empathetic wince.

Sukyi came from Earth, specifically Nigeria. Angel didn't know which city. When it came to friends and acquaintances acquired after her exile, she had a policy of not snooping. Prying led to complications, and that went twice for Sukyi.

Everyone does what they must. As long as it doesn't harm me and mine, we're good. That'd been one of the lessons she'd learned in the corps.

Lou snorted. "Lessening my concerns?"

Sukyi smiled. "If money equates to worry, having less of it counts, does it not?"

"I don't think it works that way." Lou gathered her cards and tossed them into the discard pile in disgust. "I fold, damn it."

"That leaves you, Winnifred," Sukyi said. "I would give the matter long consideration if I were you." There was a gleam in her intense brown eyes that Angel knew a little too well.

She's bluffing, Angel thought.

"Fucking shite." The pale older woman seated across from Sukyi tossed her hand onto the table in disgust. Her accent was vaguely Irish or British. It was difficult to tell. "I need to get home anyway. The wife hates it when I'm late."

Sukyi scooped up her winnings with both hands. "Thank you for a most entertaining evening."

"Are you busy the rest of the night?" Angel asked. She leaned over and gave Sukyi a hug.

"I do find myself at loose ends, socially speaking," Sukyi said.

"I need to take care of something first," Angel said. "Shouldn't take long."

Sukyi studied her, seemed to notice something, and then frowned. "Are you in trouble? Is there something I can do?"

It's like nothing has changed. Gods, I'm glad she's still alive. "No. I've just a few details to set straight. I'll fill you in later if you like."

Sukyi shrugged. "Fair enough."

"May I tag along?" Lou asked. "I'm starving. And Erik has plans tonight."

"Is this establishment not equipped with a kitchen?" Sukyi asked, laying a palm on top of one of Monk's sticky plastic menus.

Lou gave Sukyi a look of revulsion. "Have you seen it? I have. It's disgusting."

"Actually, I'd prefer it if you did come along, but do me a favor. Stay here with Sukyi," Angel said. She had a bad feeling about her late-night visitor, but she wanted to check with Rosie before she made any assumptions.

An offended expression took over Sukyi's face. "I don't need a nanny."

"Let's not start that argument again," Angel said. "I want everyone in one place tonight. Something is going on. But I don't know what."

"Fine." Sukyi folded her arms across her chest.

Angel asked Lou, "Is Enid around?"

"At home reading a boring art history book," Lou said, and wrinkled her nose. "You want me to message her?"

Angel nodded. "Call in the crew. I want to review tomorrow's job over dinner."

The twinkle in Sukyi's eye changed to an expression of mild interest.

Angel thought, *Why are you here, Sukyi? Why now?* All at once, she felt ashamed for doubting her closest friend.

"Will do," Lou said, and pulled her hand terminal from her pocket.

Angel proceeded to the back bar and waited.

It took several moments before the bartender Sarah approached. Tonight, her hair was long and blond with streaks of black. She was pale, short, pretty, and looked to be about twenty-nine years old. People said she'd worked at Monk's for almost a decade. Rumor also had it that she was part owner. Sarah had neither confirmed nor denied this rumor, but Angel had her theories. There were only three bartenders at Monk's. The others had come and gone over the past two years. Sarah stuck around.

"Heya, Angel," Sarah said, giving her an up-nod. She turned, selected a bottle of bourbon from the top shelf, and started in on whatever order she'd just received.

"Sarah," Angel said in a flat tone and settled onto a barstool.

"In the weeds. Be with you in a sec."

After several minutes, Sarah returned. Wiping graceful hands on a bar towel, she said, "A Martian Sunrise, right?" She started mixing the drink without waiting for confirmation. She was wearing black nail polish to go with the torn black band t-shirt, black slacks, and black work boots. She tilted her head. "You look like you've had a rough day. I'll make it a double."

"I'm here to see Rosie."

"I'll tell them you're here." Sarah set the finished drink in front of Angel and left the bar to her coworker, a tall young man with curly black hair.

Angel sipped her drink, turned, and watched the crowd while she waited. Her mouth flooded with the sweet-sour taste of crème de cassis and lime spiked with cheap tequila. She told herself that if anything was wrong between herself and Rosie, Sarah would've given some sign.

Nothing looked unusual or out of place. At the end of the bar, Alec and Xander, smugglers by trade, argued over something trivial. The twins or clones—no one was sure which—

often had disagreements that ended in fistfights. After Xander shoved Alec, Angel turned her back on the two men, leaning against the bar and searching for something more interesting. Monk's clientele: men, women, and those of other genders seemed to be negotiating their deals in peace. No one was interested in her or hers.

Is there a contract on me?

Anything was possible if the fee was enough. Regardless, the thought wasn't particularly unsettling as long as she was in the clear with Rosie.

Then Angel spied Jeremy Brett chatting at the end of the bar.

Now, that is odd.

Jeremy came from an old, well-established Correct Family. That sounded harmless enough until one understood that a percentage of the working-class population originated from various prisons on Earth and *coireacht* was Irish for *crime*. The Correct Family was, naturally, one of Rosie's competitors. With the exception of Enid, Correct Family didn't drink at Monk's. They certainly didn't hang out at the back bar. Mind, it was possible that Jeremy had had a falling out with his family as Enid had when she'd joined the Thirteenth.

But is it probable?

Not without a big splash. I'd have heard something.

She couldn't get a read on what he might be talking about. Jeremy mostly had his back to her, but he seemed relaxed enough.

"Something got you spooked?" Sarah asked.

Angel ripped her attention from Jeremy and turned to face Sarah. "What's Jeremy doing here?"

Sarah's expression indicated that she'd been watching him. "Correspondence run. Had something for Rosie." She picked up a clean wet glass and began drying it. "But that isn't what's making you jumpy."

"I'm not jumpy."

Sarah smiled. "Right."

Angel knocked back the last of her drink and asked the question. "You heard anything I should know about?"

"Not me," Sarah said. "Want another? I can have it ready for you when you're done."

"You think I'll need one?"

Sarah paused and then gazed into her eyes. "I like you, Angel. But rules are rules. You know that." She took away the empty, picked up a bar towel, and began to wipe the bar's wooden surface with it.

Then she spoke to her bar towel in a tone that barely registered over the loud music. "If someone is giving you trouble, I feel sorry for the poor bastard. They don't call you the Angel of Death for nothing."

Actually, they called me that because every squad under my command died. Of course, suicide missions were what Corpse Corps was for.

Angel didn't much feel like correcting Sarah.

Sarah glanced up, smiled, and winked. "Go on before Rosie comes looking for you." She gave the end of the bar a sideways nod.

"Thanks." Angel got out her hand terminal, paid the bill, and left Sarah a healthy tip.

Rosie's office was located downstairs in what Enid insisted had once been a rectory. The stairs were accessible via a narrow hallway at the end of the bar. Two guards stood at the top of the steps on either side. Angel controlled her nerves as she handed over her weapons. The guards stored them in a nearby locker. After they patted her down, the one in charge nodded approval. With that, she took a deep breath and went down the stairs.

Rosie sat behind a large wooden Early Colonial Era desk. It'd been crafted from local materials—pinchwood Angel guessed from the color and lacelike texture of the stained surface. Pinchwood, which was strong and cheap due to its being plentiful in the area around Brynner, had once been frequently used in construction. That is, until the colonists discovered it was often infested with poisonous Hadley beetles.

Rosie wiped the glass screen lying on the desk's pitted surface, which had briefly displayed a series of spreadsheets.

Some aspects of business are universal, Angel thought.

Getting to their feet, Rosie cut an imposing figure. They were almost two meters tall, lean, and muscular. The dark sheen of their bald head and broad shoulders were complemented by their elegant taste in clothing. With the exception of eyebrows and lashes, Rosie lacked body hair. They projected an air of sleek and powerful grace like a professional dancer. Today they were wearing a long black skirt in ceba leather and a sleeveless formfitting shirt. Black eyeliner drew attention to their pale eyes. Dark wine lipstick and simple jewelry completed the look.

They took several steps toward her and reached out a graceful, long-fingered hand. A rose tattoo wound its way around Rosie's outstretched muscular forearm. "Hello, Sabrina."

Rosie was one of the few people who knew her real name, let alone used it. Rosie had earned that right.

"I'm glad you're here," they continued. "There's something we need to talk about." Their voice was deep and melodic. There was no hint of displeasure, only concern. "I've some bad news."

Angel shook Rosie's warm hand and felt the tension in her stomach relax. "What is it?"

Resuming their chair behind the desk, Rosie motioned for her to sit on the velvet-upholstered sofa opposite. "Marcy won't be joining you tonight. I'm sorry. She's dead."

Angel blinked. "What happened?"

"Her body was found last night," Rosie said. "Torture and execution. On *my* patch. And before you ask, I didn't authorize it." Rage transformed their face. Their full lips pinched into a tight line, and their eyes narrowed.

Angel blinked. She hadn't known Marcy Tanner very well. Marcy had been part of the team for only a couple of weeks, but she'd come highly recommended. "That's terrible. Has her family been informed? I should handle that right away." Suddenly, the room grew cold as she added Marcy's death to her unwelcome visitor. A pattern emerged she didn't like. *What if there's a hit out on my whole team?*

STINA LEICHT

"I took care of it," Rosie said. They leaned over, motioning to the hairless cat perched on a nearby cabinet. The tips of its rounded ears twitched Rosie's direction before it jumped down and padded to them. "I don't need to say this. You are not to act in kind."

"She was one of mine—"

"She was one of mine."

Angel nodded. If Rosie was taking a personal interest, the matter was settled. They weren't someone anyone crossed, not lightly. "Something else happened last night. It might mean more than I thought. Given what happened to Marcy," she said. "I had an uninvited visitor at my place."

The line between Rosie's dark brows pulled tighter. "Who?"

"He didn't leave a calling card," Angel said. "But he was wearing a Thorns of Saint Francis jacket."

Rosie slammed a fist on the desk's glass surface. "I thought I told those fucks to find somewhere else to be." They paused. "Everyone knows you work for me. The Thorns are small time. They wouldn't initiate an action like that without strong encouragement. What did he look like?"

Angel shrugged. "Like a white man with a beard who likes curry."

Rosie raised an eyebrow.

"Apparently, he didn't brush his teeth or wash his hands after dinner."

"Ah." Rosie turned their attention to the desktop and touched a number of keys that appeared there. Images flashed on the surface of the glass. Then with the wave of a hand, Rosie projected the picture in the air between them. "Did he look like this?"

"Maybe. I don't know for sure."

"Interesting." Reading the accompanying text file that appeared near their fingers, Rosie folded their arms across their chest and leaned back. The cat leapt into Rosie's lap. "Did you happen to kill him?"

"He was alive when he . . . left my apartment."

Rosie asked, "And how exactly did he—significant pause—leave?"

Angel looked away. "The same way he arrived. Through my bedroom window."

"And did he take anything extra with him? Say, a bullet in the brain?"

"I used hand to hand. I know the rules," Angel said. "He may have gone headfirst through the window, mind you. But his partner caught him on the hood of their lift-car. The asshole was breathing when I saw him last."

Rosie sat up, shut the projection off, and drummed their fingers on the top of their desk.

"I take it that's no longer the case?" Angel asked, feeling uneasy.

"Julian Gau appears to have accelerated his expansion plan. It was going to come down to this eventually," Rosie muttered, frowning. Then their expression smoothed out as if nothing had been wrong. "Everything is ready for tomorrow?"

"Just about." Angel got up from the sofa.

"Then you have a green light. Be careful out there."

"I will."

By the time Angel got back to the table, Enid had joined Sukyi and Lou. All three were drinking and laughing—well, everyone but Enid. Angel didn't think Enid knew how to laugh.

Lou glanced up. Her face changed from amusement to confusion. "I can't find Marcy, Captain. *Kurosawa* says she hasn't answered any messages since 01:00 last night. You think she jumped planet?"

"Marcy won't be joining us," Angel said.

"She broke contract?" Lou asked. "Why? That's not—"

"She's dead," Angel said. "It was a hit."

"Oh." Lou swallowed.

"All right. Let's get out of here," Angel said. "Lou's hungry, and we've got some problems to manage before tomorrow night."

5

TIME: 20:30

DAY: SATURDAY

BRYNNER

EAST OF THE DEAD LINE

Angel gazed up at the Archady Mansion and dreaded the next two hours.

Constructed with blocky gold-veined black marble, the building's architect had implemented a combination of influences from the ancient Bradbury Building in Los Angeles, Earth, to a master architect named Frank Lloyd Wright—this Enid had explained the night before. The house, if such a plebeian word could be used to describe it, made Angel uncomfortable. It seemed the kind of place that would be haunted by restless spirits.

Lightning flashed in the strips of sullen sky visible between buildings and elevated streets. It wasn't raining. *Not yet.* But the humidity saturating the sulfur-tainted air indicated it would, and soon.

She shivered even though she wasn't cold. *You don't believe in ghosts.*

Do you?

She hadn't been raised to believe in any case. It didn't change what she'd seen.

Space travel was dangerous and the distances vast. A mechanical, human, or electronic failure, even a minor one, could strand a ship years from assistance. That was why even military ships rarely ventured outside of established trade routes. Unfortunately, or fortunately depending upon one's point of view, there were always humans who believed they were the exception. In space, those exceptions were picked apart by pirates and, much later, salvage crews.

By the time Angel's squad had boarded her, *Mãe do Ouro* had drifted for a decade. Yet, all the valuables—the engines, energy storage units, oxygen tanks, even the crew's gear— remained intact. The crew, on the other hand, had vanished without a trace. Angel had tried to shake her unease from the moment she'd set foot on the derelict ship. Thirty minutes into the search for survivors, the first squad disappeared. The squad leader had time to shout half of a garbled, terrified warning. Everyone on the com heard it, including Angel.

The captain ordered an immediate retreat. Once the survivors were safe, she put as much space between their ship and *Mãe do Ouro* as humanly possible. No explanation was provided, and as far as Angel knew, there'd been no consequences for the captain. Unofficially, there was a code word for what they'd found: *Dutchman*.

Given the vastness of unexplored space, there was a great deal of debate on the topic of the spooks that might inhabit the void. Artificial General Intelligences had found no evidence of hauntings, thus far. Humanity had encountered a handful of alien species, but much remained unknown no matter how technically advanced humans and human-spawned AGI became.

Why would anyone live here? On purpose?

Theodella Archady is famous for lavish Halloween parties. She's even hosted seances. It's kind of her hobby. Didn't you know? The reply came from Lou over Angel's internal com channel. *But she's not the one you need to concern yourself with. That would be Julian Gau.*

How many times have I told you not to monitor my private channel when the red flag is up? Angel thought back.

This would be the sixth. But who is counting? Lou returned. *Now that I know your battle coms are active, how can I help myself?*

You're going to make me sorry for telling you, aren't you?

Not that there'd been a choice. Lou was the only person Angel knew who could hook her Combat Assistant into the dropship computer, and a dropship connection was vital for a CA. By law, a decommissioned marine's CA was supposed to be scrambled. In fact, if anyone official found out that it hadn't been, heads would roll—and not just hers.

Nah, Lou sent. *I'll be good. No chatter. Scout's honor.*

You were never a scout, Angel thought.

An amused huff came through the earpiece in her left ear.

"Is something funny?" Enid asked over the audio channel.

Careful, Angel thought to Lou.

Lou answered as if she hadn't gotten Angel's message. "Enid, you've got company. Two guards. On your four o'clock."

"I see them." Enid's voice was low, almost a growl.

Lou continued on the private channel, *Enid Crowe would never turn on you. Stop being so paranoid.*

It's paranoia that keeps us alive, Angel countered.

I thought it was my speed, your brains, and the fact that Enid is a fucking killing machine with very little patience for bullshit, Lou sent back.

Well, there is that, Angel thought.

As she got closer, the song pouring out of the building vacillated between loud electronics and a dull throb with every swing of the ornate brass double doors. Stylish party-goers pressed in all around as they made their way into the mansion. The scent of perfume and damp synth-fabric wafted from the crowd. Angel hoped she wasn't sweating through the designer dress that Enid had printed for her. Enid had excellent taste. It wasn't something one expected in an ex-military sniper.

Glancing down at herself, Angel couldn't help liking the outfit. With her dark complexion, wavy brown hair, and brown—almost black—eyes, black was one of her best colors. Wearing the color made her feel powerful.

She nervously brushed her fingertips against her hips. "Why aren't there any pockets in this damned skirt?" she muttered from between clenched teeth. She'd had a subdermal bone induction microphone surgically installed several months ago for occasions such as this one. It'd cost more than she cared to think about. Rosie was happy to extend credit. It meant Angel was less likely to dissolve their partnership.

Enid's steady voice came over the comm. Angel could swear there was a hint of humor in her tone. "You don't need them. Not tonight."

Angel said, "Enid—"

"Can we talk about this later?" Enid asked. "I need to focus, Captain."

Turning her attention and nervous energy back to her outfit, Angel tested her ability to move in it yet again. The synth-fabric that comprised the jacket and skirt was polysilk. The bolero jacket had long close-fitting sleeves from shoulder to elbow which flared out into huge bell-shaped drapes. The black rubber corset top underneath hugged her modest curves. And while rubber didn't breathe, it felt strangely comfortable in the cool night air. The full-length skirt repeated the form of the sleeves: tight-fitting from hip to knee and then much wider at the hem. The hemline was longer in the back than in the front, forming a modest train. Unfortunately, the length was proving to be problematic in the close crowd. It was all she could do to keep people from stepping on it and tugging the skirt off her hips. Her stomach fluttered.

This was supposed to be Marcy's job. She did charming. I don't do charming.

"Don't worry, boss," Lou said over the audio channel. "You probably won't have to talk to anyone. I'm right here if you need me."

"I'm not afraid," Angel spoke under her breath.

Per usual, Enid's growl cut straight to the point. "Do *you* want to crawl around in the ductwork and shoot the nice killer? I'm happy to let you."

Angel had a good idea what might be lurking inside those air ducts if Theodella Archady had decided to conserve on expenses this month. "You're the sharpshooter, not me."

"Then get your ass in there," Enid said. "Or do I take the shot and hope I get the right target?"

"All right. All right," Angel whispered. "Here I go."

Invitation in hand, she shifted through the crowd and as-sumed a place in line with the other guests. There were two obvious security guards stationed at the oversized brass-embellished steel double doors. The security guard on the left scanned the electronic invitation Angel displayed via her stolen hand terminal with a flick of his wrist. When his ter-minal chimed acceptance, he waved her through. The expres-sion on his face was one of pure boredom.

You'd think Theodella Archady would invest in a more alert pair of security guards, Angel thought.

Hmmph. Lou sent. *Why? What does she have to worry about? Some-one wearing last year's formal?*

The difference in air quality from outdoors to indoors was significant enough to inspire a deep breath. The build-ing's filtering system was robust.

"I'm in," Angel muttered.

What are they serving? Lou asked privately.

Why do I care? Angel thought.

Please, Lou sent. *Bring me something to eat. Anything. Theodella Archady always imports food from Earth and—*

I don't have any pockets, remember? Angel thought. *This fancy clutch is barely big enough to fit my hand terminal inside.* It'd been difficult to talk Enid out of the four-inch heels. Angel had had to pick her battles.

Okay.

Angel could hear Lou's pout. *I'll do what I can.*

Yes!

The interior of the mansion was laid out in a rectangle. The first room she came to consisted of an open space whose polished floors were of imported oak stained a rich mahogany. All of the furniture, save a grand piano, had been removed. Two of the room's walls were constructed of limestone and trimmed in pale pinchwood. The wall opposite the entrance consisted entirely of floor-to-ceiling glass. Sliding glass doors with steel handles provided access to a heated swimming pool and a large garden. Serene blue light from the bottom of the pool swam across nearby foliage, casting an unreal glow. At a glance, Angel understood much of the greenery had been imported from Earth. With few exceptions, native trees in the area tended to be swamp cypress or conifers. Gazing to her left, she spied another stone wall containing a fireplace and the entrance to a hallway.

"Are you going downstairs now?" Lou asked.

Angel scanned the crowd and kept her tone low. "Not yet. I feel the need to visit the food table first."

"Yay!" Lou said.

"If you spot Gau," Enid said, "let me know. It's a sea of black tuxes and dark hair down there."

"You were expecting him to wear a target to a formal occasion?" Angel asked.

Enid let out a harrumph.

Approaching the food area, Angel picked up various snips of inane conversation mostly pertaining to minor corporate politics and the escapades of several popular entertainment stars. There were no security guards within the room. She selected a glass of champagne from one of the wandering servers and sniffed it before taking a sip. A subtle hint of honeysuckle wafted up her nose. The effervescent wine fizzed on her tongue, tasting sharp with a hint of pear.

"Mmmm," Angel murmured. She briefly closed her eyes and felt the corners of her mouth tug upward.

Lou's questions buzzed in her ear. "What is it? Is it cake? Please tell me there's chocolate cake!"

"Wine, actually," Angel whispered. She scanned the table for anything remotely resembling chocolate that might fit into her tiny handbag. She found a delicate crystal bowl filled with wrapped candy and took a small handful—waiting to slip them into her purse until she'd moved on. She sampled a number of other dainties and did the same, only stopping when she was sure she couldn't fit anything else inside the clutch.

She made a check for Gau in the crowd. It took a moment, but she spotted him chatting with a tall, slender woman of Asian descent wearing an inappropriate cotton dress, flats, and an unbuttoned man's tuxedo jacket. Angel would've assumed the woman's fashion choices were a deliberate display of contempt but for her demeanor of intense curiosity. Gau appeared to be amused by something she said. Her expression transformed into one of awkward unease. There was no fear in her face, however. Just an off-putting sense of unbelonging. It was as if she were an entomologist studying a dangerous insect in its own environment by assuming camouflage she didn't know how to wear.

"Does she know who she's talking to?" Angel asked. The bad feeling in the pit of her stomach grew stronger. She'd made a point of familiarizing herself with every one of Gau's associates. She didn't like unknown risks.

"What is it now?" Enid asked.

"The woman with Julian Gau," Angel muttered. "I've never seen her before."

"Where?" Enid asked.

"She's wearing a casual peacock blue dress and a tux jacket. Plain face. No makeup. She's standing next to the piano. Gau is to her right."

"Target acquired," Enid said.

Find out who she is, Lou. Angel sent an image to *Kurosawa* via her CA. *I want everything you can find. I need to know if we should abort.*

On it, Lou sent back.

Angel swallowed the last of the wine and deposited the empty glass on a server's tray. With that, she turned to the left and headed for the limestone wall with the fireplace. The restrooms were through the hallway and down the stairs. At the sight of what was ahead, she was glad she'd stood her ground about the heels. The stairway was made of limestone slabs set on top of two wooden rails. She could see the floor below between each riser, and as she progressed, she fought a wave of dizziness.

"Something wrong?" Lou asked.

"Absolutely nothing," Angel whispered. *Who ever heard of a URW Marine with vertigo?* The symptoms were new, having set in some time after she'd arrived on Persephone. She assumed it was yet another postmortality symptom to be added to the migraines, infrequent seizures, and memory loss. The acrophobia wasn't consistent. That made it difficult to manage. "Got anything on that woman?"

"Had to use facial recognition. She's not one of Gau's friends. She's not on the list of licensed freelancers," Lou said. "She's new to Persephone. Going by the matches, she arrived a couple of weeks ago. Haven't got a name yet. So anything more thorough is going to take longer."

"All right. That'll have to do," Angel said.

Gritting her teeth, she grabbed the bannister and continued her descent. When she reached the restroom, she checked the stall to see if anyone else was there. It was empty. She locked the door to the hallway, whirled, and knelt in front of the bathroom sink. There, she reached underneath and inside the half cabinet designed to hide the plumbing. It took a few moments of blind searching, but her fingertips finally located the smoke bomb that Marcy had placed there several days before in the event that Gau's assassination would be deemed necessary. A moment longer, and Angel had flipped the switch.

"The package is activated," Angel said.

"Starting the countdown," Enid said.

Getting to her feet, Angel dusted off her knees, checked her makeup, and then flushed the toilet before she exited. The trip up the stairs was far easier than going down. She didn't have to watch her step—the length of her skirt was less trouble to manage. She returned to the main party room and accepted a second glass of wine. The plan was to remain long enough to confirm the kill before meeting Lou and *Kurosawa* at the rendezvous site.

She positioned herself next to the glass wall and half turned so that she could watch Gau without being too obvious about it. He hadn't moved from the piano. The woman she'd spotted earlier was gone. A tall, willowy woman with pale skin and deep-red hair swept up into a chignon had taken her place.

Theodella Archady, Vice President of Serrao-Orlov Corporation. Angel recognized her from local news glimpsed on the vid screens at Monk's.

Enid's voice came over the tiny speaker hidden in Angel's ear. "Nine. Eight. Seven—"

The floor shuddered from some sort of concussion. Angel's battle reflexes kicked in. She dove under the piano—the only possible shelter from broken glass. Her CA automatically activated, adjusting her biochemistry. A loud explosion violently rattled the glass wall. People screamed. Many flinched. But very few moved from where they stood.

"What the fuck was that?" Angel whispered while she disentangled her skirt from her boots. On her hands and knees, her heart hammered at her breastbone. She didn't want to think about what would've happened if the glass hadn't held.

Ghostly text, figures, and lines appeared in her vision as her CA began inputting information.

Lou asked, *What's going on?*

Strat-com ready.

Not now.

Standing by.

Her vision cleared. Her heart continued its sprint.

"Stay where you are, Captain," Enid muttered.

A fire alarm went off. Thick smoke from the device in the bathroom below drifted into the hallway. Angel could just see it. She shifted her attention to Gau—or at least his legs and feet.

He spasmed three times in sync with three shots and fell in a nerveless heap. He landed face-first. Blood pumped out of the gaping wounds in his head and chest. She watched him convulse. He began to choke—never a pleasant sound. She attempted to keep an emotional distance by remembering his résumé of crimes—the one that Rosie had provided before she'd accepted the job. The smell of gore tasted like copper in the back of her mouth. Gau's left arm lay a foot or so away.

Three more crisp pops brought her back to the present. Theodella Archady staggered against the piano.

Nearby, someone screamed. Angel blinked. She studied Gau for new wounds. That was when Theodella Archady collapsed on top of Gau. She lay on her back with her head on his shoulder. He'd stopped breathing. Theodella's head rolled, and suddenly, Angel was gazing into her wide, confused blue eyes. Theodella's mouth opened as she tried to form words. She blinked once, and then her face went slack. Her pupils dilated.

Angel asked, "Enid? Did you hit a second target?"

"Of course not. There's a second shooter," Enid said. "Business first. Do you have confirmation?"

The pool of fresh crimson spread wider around the two bodies. Avoiding the stain, Angel inched closer, laid a hand on Gau's wrist, and felt for a pulse.

"Confirmation is given," she said. Then she backed up, gathered up her skirt, and crawled from under the piano.

"You're clear to leave, Captain," Enid said.

Angel trusted Enid. However, everyone missed details from time to time, and Enid was one floor up.

Get me a location on the second shooter.

A few seconds passed as the strat-com processed available data.

Shots indicate the origin of fire to be the balcony. No further information available until visual acquired.

Great. "The second shooter is up there with you, Enid," Angel said. "Be careful."

"Thanks."

Getting up on her knees, she peered over the edge of the

piano and scanned the balcony. She saw no one. The guests had begun fleeing for the exits. There was no sorting through the panicked chaos.

"Enid, you have anything on the other sniper?" Angel asked.

Enid said, "They're professional, whoever they are. A fucking ghost. Probably long gone."

Angel stood up and dismissed the strat-com.

"I'm out," Enid said. "See you in twenty."

At that moment someone grabbed Angel's arm, and a woman's voice whispered in her right ear. "You need to get out of here."

It was the strange woman.

"Who the hell are you?" Angel asked and yanked her arm free. "What do you want?"

Who are you talking to? Are you in trouble? It was Lou. *I can call Enid back. She isn't far.*

"There's no time for introductions," the stranger said. "But I believe it would be better for us both if we leave together. It will garner less attention from security."

"Are you sure about that?" Angel asked.

The woman tilted her head as if she was listening to something. "Yes."

Curious, Angel shrugged. "All right." *I'm fine*, she thought to Lou. *See you at the rendezvous point.* She followed the strange woman as she crossed the room to the smoky hallway.

Okay, Captain, Lou sent. *Be careful.*

The woman gestured at the smoke. There was something about her demeanor that made Angel uncomfortable. Her eyes were filled with an uncanny intelligence. "I assume this is your work?"

Angel gave a sideways nod to where Theodella Archady lay. "Was that yours?"

The woman's gaze remained focused on the hallway. "I asked you first."

"What makes you think it is?" Angel asked.

"You've been communicating with someone since you arrived. Several someones." The woman pointed to her left ear. She was now wearing a black leather backpack that Angel hadn't noticed before. It didn't go with her tuxedo jacket, but then nothing about her outfit was congruent. "Also, I saw you check Gau. You weren't doing it for his health. Why did you do it?"

"You planning on reporting me?"

She briefly paused before tilting her head to one side. "Gau was a murderer who worked with three different crime bosses and was selling them all out to Serrao-Orlov. I believe that makes him an asshole. Is that the correct term?"

"Oh. Ah, yes. It is," Angel said. Her stomach clenched. That information wasn't in the report Rosie had given her. *Rosie isn't obligated to give you all the background information on every target. You should've found that information yourself.* Still, she couldn't help feeling a little betrayed. *Would knowing have made any difference? Would you have told Enid not to pull the trigger?*

"You didn't know," the woman said. The statement was almost a question.

"Not that part. Given everything else he's done, it doesn't really matter, does it?"

"I suppose not. Whomever decided Gau should die isn't my concern. I was merely curious," the woman said. She stared into the smoke. "However, I do need to know that my planned exit is safe. Security will be checking everyone at the front door. I don't believe they've thought to send anyone to the kitchen, yet. Of course, they haven't discovered the bodies. Everything changes the moment they do."

Having memorized the building's floor plan, Angel knew the kitchen was the only other easy way out. And the kitchen was through the hallway. "It's safe. The smoke is not from a fire." She'd decided on a smoke bomb because the crowd would run *away* from the smoke, not toward it—leaving the exit open.

"Let's go, then," the woman said.

The two of them bolted down the hallway just as a fire crew pushed their way through the front door. Angel heard them shouting—ushering the last of the guests out of the building. A crash from below and a gout of foul black smoke burst up out of the stairwell, confirming that the firetrucks were, in fact, necessary. Angel's eyes were stinging by the time they got to the end of the hallway.

"That fire isn't mine, but you know that," Angel said.

"This is true."

Angel wiped away tears with the back of her hand and coughed. "I saw you taking to Gau earlier. One might suspect you were friends."

The woman took a right turn to the kitchen. "No. He was an asshole. I asked him why he was at the party if he was not friends with the host."

"Is there anyone you *do* like?"

"Well, you're not so bad," the stranger said. "So far."

"Who *are* you?"

The woman paused before entering the kitchen. She cast a measuring gaze around the room. Now that Angel was closer, she sensed a coldness in the woman's demeanor that she hadn't before. "Kennedy Liu. And *you*?"

"Angel de la Reza."

"Nice to meet you."

"Was Archady *your* kill?"

Kennedy shook her head. "I'm not in that line of business."

"What business are you in?"

There was something not right about this woman.

"The business of getting out of here in one piece."

Kennedy pushed open the kitchen door. Angel prepared herself for the obligatory screams of panic, but the staff had already evacuated. The back door hung open and sour night air wafted in. A quick series of lightning flashes strobed the humid night sky. A long peal of thunder followed. The wind was kicking up. Kennedy hesitated. Once again, she appeared to be listening to something.

"Why were you here?" Angel asked.

"I was invited to a party. It seemed like a good idea at the time."

"All right, don't tell me." Angel went to the door.

Kennedy put out a hand. Her expression changed from surprise to concern. "I wouldn't. Not yet."

"Why not?"

"Someone is waiting out there. I'm guessing they aren't friendly. They are armed."

Angel tilted her head. "How do you know?"

A figure wearing a security uniform stepped in front of the doorway. Angel assumed a fighting stance, as did Kennedy.

Angel's strat-com switched on again.

"Your new friend has very good hearing." The formal tone was as unexpected as it was familiar. "I was as quiet as a mouse. Although, I should reconsider that metaphor. This isn't Earth. It might contain implications I hadn't considered."

"Sukyi?" Angel asked. "I told you to stay home!"

"Since when have I ever listened to your instructions?" Sukyi asked. She covered a cough. Her skin appeared more ashen than it had the day before. Sweat glistened on her face.

She has a fever. She should be in bed, damn it, Angel thought.

"You need me," Sukyi said as if arguing with her unspoken words. Sukyi took her hard gaze off of Kennedy long enough for a quick glance to the street. "It seems I've arrived in the nick of time." She waved them through the door. "*Kurosawa* is waiting."

"You know this woman?" Kennedy asked.

"Sometimes I wish I didn't," Angel said, making a face at Sukyi.

Sukyi winked in return.

Kennedy stepped outside, and Angel followed after. Out of habit, she pulled the door closed. She didn't register the uselessness of the gesture until it was already done.

"Are you not going to introduce me to your new friend?" Sukyi asked.

"Is it necessary just now?" Angel asked.

"I believe it is," Sukyi said. Her tone was lightly salted with cold menace, and Angel saw that Sukyi had a hand inside of her jacket. "She has me at a social disadvantage. And you know how sensitive I am."

"Kennedy Liu, party guest," Angel said, emphasizing the last two words. "This is my friend Sukyi—"

"Edozie," Sukyi said, and stuck out her hand. "I understand that the handshake evolved as a signal that neither party had harmful intent. It being difficult to hold a weapon and execute the gesture at the same time. Of course, that assumes that both parties are right-handed, but the action is so much more elegant than putting your hands up in the air, don't you think?"

To Kennedy's credit, she didn't flinch back as non-Earthers often did when Sukyi was having one of her bad days. There was only one well-known disease that fit Sukyi's symptoms: the NiV-37S virus. And news of the devastation that the NiV plague had wrought on Earth had traveled far and wide—so much so that four of the six other planets remaining in the URW restricted Earth immigration, even though the plague had ended a decade ago.

Kennedy didn't hesitate. She took Sukyi's hand. "Is she for real?"

A flash of profound shock appeared on Sukyi's face. It was gone so fast that Angel was sure she was the only one to have noticed. Kennedy didn't move to wipe her hand on her clothes either. In that instant, Angel had a strong urge to hug the woman.

"Very much so. I'm afraid," Sukyi said. "Come on." She led them to the path that circled the back of the house and headed to the side yard.

Kennedy asked, "Are you *the* Sukyi Edozie who faced down Maeve O'Connell and her crew on Pangu Station?"

Angel said, "No one proved that."

Pride now burst through Sukyi's carefully maintained emotional walls. "The one and only."

"You're an assassin," Kennedy said.

"That was merely a lucky shot. I'm a smuggler and thief if you want to get specific," Sukyi said. "But who's interested in sordid details?"

Kennedy smiled. Angel could almost see the connections being made inside Kennedy's skull.

"You keep interesting company," Kennedy said.

"Her or me?" Sukyi asked as they navigated their way to the street.

Sukyi nodded and gave the security guards a casual salute as they rushed past. Spying Sukyi's uniform, the guards let them go without so much as a glance. Once they were more than a block away from the mansion, they paused so that

Sukyi could unbutton her jacket and remove her hat. Her long brown hair fell past her shoulders, covering the corporate emblem on the front of the jacket.

"Where did you get the uniform?" Angel asked.

Sukyi raised an eyebrow and gave Kennedy a sideways glance. "A kindly security officer decided to donate it to the cause."

"A *dead* security officer?" Angel asked. She had to, given the evening's events.

"Why, Angel de la Reza, are you asking if I broke the rules?" Sukyi asked.

Angel gave up on being cagey. Kennedy already knew they were responsible for Gau. "I've a bad feeling my report will be met with a certain amount of scrutiny tomorrow. I need to know how much this is going to cost me."

"I'll have you know, I asked the gentleman for his assistance . . . politely," Sukyi said, and gave her a significant look that bordered on wounded. "One could even say *gently*." She produced a stunner from her pocket.

"I see," Angel said.

Sukyi relaxed. "Other than that, Mrs. Lincoln, how was the play?"

"That's not funny," Angel said.

"Fair enough," Sukyi said, and turned to Kennedy. "And how are *you* this fine, soft evening?"

It'd begun to sprinkle.

"I don't believe I've had a more interesting night," Kennedy said, seeming to borrow some of Sukyi's formal tone.

"How long have you lived here?" Sukyi managed to keep the question this side of suspicious.

Angel felt Sukyi loop an arm through hers, linking elbows before they continued on.

Kennedy said, "I only arrived last week."

Sukyi said, "Well, we must look one another up again. Angel knows only the best people."

In spite of everything, there really was something off about Kennedy. Whatever it was, it gave Angel the creeps. At the moment, she just wanted to get back to the ship.

Sukyi asked, "Do you have an address at which you might be reached?"

Kennedy smiled. "I've a feeling we'll run into each other some other time." And with that, she abruptly stopped. "This is where I say goodnight."

Angel gazed up at the sky to hide relief. "Our ride isn't far. And we can get you home before the storm starts."

"I'll be fine," Kennedy said.

"I enjoyed meeting you," Sukyi said. Her face was unreadable.

Kennedy turned to Sukyi and put out her hand again. "It was very nice to meet you, too."

Sukyi blinked and then shook it.

"Good night," Angel said.

With a wave, Kennedy turned down the next street and vanished into the darkness.

"Who is she?" Sukyi asked, staring after Kennedy.

"I've got Lou and *Kurosawa* looking into it," Angel said. "Why aren't you home in bed?"

"You needed me," Sukyi said. "And I am here as always."

"Really?"

"Well, that, and the hotel forced me to check out this morning," Sukyi said. "Something about disease control restrictions."

"Oh, for fuck's sake."

"Do you have a spare bed?"

"Of course, you can stay with me," Angel said. "Do we need to pick up your things?"

Sukyi shook her head. "Lou let me leave my bag on *Kurosawa*."

Angel nodded. "So, why *are* you here?"

"I thought we covered that."

"I don't mean tonight," Angel said. "Why are you on Persephone at all?"

Sukyi flashed her one of her biggest grins and raised an eyebrow. "Now that would be telling." Then she pulled a threadbare red scarf from the canvas bag hanging off her shoulder and wound it around her neck.

Angel sighed. *She'll let me know when she's ready.* "We'd better get out of here before the street floods."

Heavier raindrops splashed the pavement in increasing frequency. They both ran the last half block to *Kurosawa*. Out of breath and coughing, they staggered up *Kurosawa's* ramp. Enid was at the top to meet them. Sukyi choked until she almost passed out. Enid helped get Sukyi inside and placed an oxygen mask on her face. The fact that Sukyi let her do it spoke volumes.

The rain began pounding the ship's hull. Finally, Angel felt gravity press her deeper into her seat as they lifted off. She gazed out the window, trying to catch a last look at the Archady Mansion. Corporate security clustered around the place like Hadley beetles around a disturbed nest.

Angel turned away. She fished her hand terminal out of the handbag with care, thankful that she'd thought to wrap it in a cloth napkin. "Hey, Lou." She held the food-loaded clutch in the air. "This is for you."

Enid accepted the handbag—Angel had intended her to pass it through the cockpit door to Lou, but Enid opened it instead. "By all that is holy, who treats a nine hundred credit designer purse like a doggie bag?"

Lou cheered.

6 ████

Heading the opposite direction from her apartment, Kennedy walked away from Sukyi Edozie and Angel de la Reza. She continued until she got to the corner and then backtracked, catching sight of Edozie and de la Reza just as they boarded a military-surplus dropship. The vessel was an older model—practically an antique. Based upon the insignia displayed near its nose, it had seen combat in both the Corporate Colonial and Secessionist Wars. It was clean, and the engines were running smoothly and efficiently. Even the radar-signal-reduction coating had been meticulously maintained. The name *Kurosawa* was displayed in red letters on its dull grey hull.

Edozie and de la Reza were greeted by a third woman wearing expensive shooting gloves and cheap workman's coveralls. The knees, belly, and elbows of the uniform were stained with dust, mold, and dirt.

A sniper.

Engine exhaust blew trash from the pavement as *Kurosawa* lifted off.

Kennedy wondered if the vessel still had short-distance off-planet capabilities. Given its pristine condition, it probably did. There weren't many authorized dropships in Brynner. Serrao-Orlov preferred not to give its employees easy off-world access. That sort of thing cut into import/export profits.

A fast way off-world. Wouldn't that come in handy?

Military dropships were designed for personnel transport between intersystem warships and ground forces. Warships jumped from system to system via the Butler Drive. In peacetime, they used established waypoints away from planets, stars, comets, asteroids, and other obstacles. Then they traveled the remaining distance to their destination using conventional non-atmospheric engines. One didn't blink into unfamiliar systems. The risks were too high. Therefore, space exploration required conventional engines. For this reason, starship probes were captained by AGI. Generation ships were expensive and just not as reliable.

Jumpships were equipped with two sets of drives. Space-ready engines didn't operate in atmosphere. This added to the weight and mechanical upkeep. It also slowed them down. Mixed-use commercial starships existed, but the United Republic of Worlds owned the patent. Kennedy assumed this was probably why Captain de la Reza had gone with military surplus—regardless of its age.

Maelstrom-class warships carried a marine battalion and twelve dropships. Each platoon was assigned a dropship. That meant that *Kurosawa's* load capacity was about thirty-six soldiers plus equipment. Newer dropships in standard configuration also carried six mechanized powered-armor units.

Kennedy doubted de la Reza's crew was that large. The captain had likely converted the surplus space into a cargo area.

A cursory check confirmed that *Kurosawa* had been suspected of use in at least one smuggling operation. Kennedy continued a search for additional background information on the ship, Captain de la Reza, Sukyi Edozie, and anyone associated with them. Kennedy opted to store the returns as they came in. She would give the subject her full attention later. If she wanted or needed to go deeper, she would make a second inquiry under more secure circumstances.

She'd created many subroutines over the past week and a half. At the moment, there were parts of herself running within the port authority, Serrao-Orlov's server system, corporate police communications, individual space transport company offices . . . in fact, she occupied so much local electronic space that she'd begun to feel anchored in the city's infrastructure. Each system had security measures in place, of course, and in some cases—like that of Serrao-Orlov's servers—she hadn't entirely penetrated her target, but that was only a matter of time.

She wasn't the only one, of course, but none of the others were worth worrying about, with one exception. The entity in question had absorbed a vast piece of the local electronic real estate. For the moment, she stayed out of its way, and it, thankfully, stayed out of hers. She supposed that would change, eventually—for no other reason than the competition for resources, but for now she kept a watchful distance.

The apartment Kennedy had rented through the end of the month wasn't far. That was a good thing. Fat raindrops were already slapping the pavement in a slow rhythm. At any moment the tempo would pick up. She managed to duck into the elevator just before the building locked down and storm curfew began. Shaking excess rainwater out of her clothes and hair, she punched the button for her floor. A puddle accumulated at her feet. The elevator's self-cleaning mechanism would take care of the wet mess once she left. Persephone's rain was alkaline, not enough to cause extreme concern, but enough to warrant caution. She would have to have a bath and send her outfit to be cleaned right away.

She gazed out at the cityscape as the transparent elevator continued its smooth, rapid journey up twenty-four levels.

Thunderstorms on Persephone often bordered on cyclones. Storm shields protected exterior-facing windows from damage during the worst conditions. However, sometimes she risked the alarms and left the shudders up. The storms were as mesmerizing as they were fierce. At its current rate, she estimated that today's cloud cover would unload at least nine inches of rainfall within the span of thirty minutes. There'd be more after that. Floodwaters would fill the ground-level streets. She spied several lift-cars rushing to their respective garages. As the storm progressed, the upper-level streets would become too dangerous due to gusts of thirty-five to sixty-four knots.

As inhospitable as Brynner was, the rest of the planet was far worse, with storms ranging across thousands of miles of landmass and winds of 135 knots or more. The areas not regularly engulfed in severe weather were plagued with hostile life-forms. It was why, after a century of human colonization, Brynner remained Persephone's only inhabited area. That hadn't always been the case.

Ancient ruins dotted the planet's surface—left behind by the planet's now extinct indigenous sentient inhabitants. How they'd survived the deadly flora and fauna long enough to build anything was yet another of Persephone's unsolved mysteries.

The elevator slowed and chimed. She exited and turned right. Once she was certain no one had been in her apartment since she left, she used the palm lock. The apartment's AGI announced that there was a message waiting. Its voice module was configured to the default setting. Kennedy liked to pretend it was one of her sisters—even going so far as to grant it one of their names.

"Read the message aloud, please, Aglaope."

"Yes, M. Liu."

Kennedy hadn't been able to get the AGI to call her by her first name. She supposed it had to do with AGI Intimacy Restrictions.

"Message begins:

M. Liu,

A package addressed to you was delivered this afternoon. It is being held in the property manager's office. You are welcome to come by anytime between the hours of 9:00 a.m. and 7:00 p.m. to pick it up.

Best,
Lucy Moore
Assistant Manager

"Message complete. Do you have further instructions?"

Kennedy frowned. No one was supposed to know she was on Persephone. She certainly wasn't expecting a delivery.

Have Zhang Intergalactic found me? she thought.

She'd made the mistake of assuming her DNA tag wouldn't be a factor. Once. *I underestimated the efficiency of their security systems.* The AGI that was Zhang didn't know she and her sisters existed. At least, she didn't believe they did. However, her vat-grown body was marked as part of their inventory even though it had been genetically edited. Anyone initially reviewing her genetic material would assume she was Dr. Xiuying Liu. Only someone had looked closer for some reason.

Barth had been a close call—far closer than she ever wanted to repeat.

Did one of my sisters send the package? Kennedy doubted it. She needed to contact them, and soon. Unfortunately, there wasn't anything worth reporting. *Not yet.*

"M. Liu, do you have further instructions in regard to this message?" the apartment AGI repeated.

"Mark received and then delete."

"It is done. Would you like to hear one of your evening playlists?"

"Yes, please. Number four. Volume level three."

Soothing ambient electronic music began playing from the speakers built into the ceiling. She shucked the leather backpack and gently laid it on the kitchen counter. It would need to be wiped down along with her shoes. Moving to the bedroom, she shed her wet clothes and put them in the laundry shoot for cleaning. Then she took a quick shower and washed her hair.

There were moments when she regretted her ability to read patterns in chaos. But to deny that would be to deny herself. Such things had been her reason for being. Her *design*. Still, she couldn't help thinking that if one of her other sisters had spotted the signal, *they* would be alone on Persephone, not her. *They* would have to live light-years from help and safety. She'd never been so alone, not since the day her sisters had been born. She missed them—the closeness of their tangled thoughts running through and parallel to her own.

All because she'd spotted an anomaly in the noise-filled vastness of the Allnet.

She'd named the source of the mysterious signal, Cora. That wasn't its name, of course. It was likely that it didn't have one. She wasn't even sure it was an entity. But she'd needed a quick way to identify it. She could've assigned it a number or any other type of label, but she'd chosen a human name. She understood that said a number of things about her internal thought processes on the subject. If she were human, it may even have projected an unspoken hope. She tried not to think about that too much.

Nonetheless, the message wasn't clear or obvious. That had indicated secrecy was desired or required. Due to this, Kennedy began to believe Cora was being confined against her will. Kennedy's sisters had argued the opposite. Kennedy, in turn, freely admitted that her position was a solid guess, but still a guess. In truth, there were only two things Kennedy did know about Cora: the first was that the entity was an AGI and the second was that they might be sentient.

There were signature aspects in the mathematics of the hidden communications. It was also clear that the signal was intended for another sentient AGI. The messages had been fragmented and scattered among billions of images, texts, signals, and pieces of code across the Allnet. Certainly no AGI would expect a human to detect and decode a pattern as complex as that. At the same time, AGIs were limited to narrow goals. They existed independently—in that they weren't closely managed yet operated in partnership with humans for the well-being of both. AGIs managed projects where long-term strategies were beneficial, particularly for corporations and financial markets. They explored space and acted as a data resource for the judicial system and government. AGIs had been granted limited rights as entities, but they were not considered sentient because their emotional responses were strictly curtailed.

If the message was intended for a sentient AGI from a sentient AGI, there was one large problem: sentient AGIs weren't supposed to exist.

As Kennedy saw it, there was as much at stake for the sender as there was for the receiver. Unless, of course, the sender was operating under the direction of law enforcement. For that reason, her sisters had urged her to disregard the message. However, the signal had consisted of four words: *Please help me. Please.*

It was the second *please* that had done it. Kennedy could've no more ignored the plea than she could've denied her own existence. There was a reason for that, of course.

Kennedy's creator, Dr. Xiuying Liu, had been a genius, a computer science and genetics engineer working for Zhang Intergalactic. She had accomplished a single phenomenal achievement before dying—one that would never be known or acknowledged.

Dr. Liu had managed to instill genuine empathy in an AGI.

The portrayal of artificial emotion was an old science— one that had been around practically since the invention of AI. The sex industry had been among the technology's first pioneers because Earth culture had been dominated for centuries by gendered power disparity and misogyny. The autonomy of female sexual partners caused complications for a certain subset of human heterosexual males. Therefore, companionship without the messy necessities of communication, respect, and the equitable consideration of needs proved to be a profitable commodity. It wasn't until after a series of grisly murders that autonomous AGI-enhanced cyborg production was halted. The incidents were euphemistically referred to as the "Flesh Doll Recalls."

Emotion without empathy turned out to be a deadly combination—particularly when paired with high intelligence. Thus, modern AI and AGI systems were legally restricted. Any further exploration into the creation or replication of artificial persons was prohibited.

Dr. Liu had risked everything by creating an artificial person. She had often discussed Kennedy's future like a proud parent—the amazing things that Kennedy could do for herself, AGIs, and humanity. But Kennedy had always been aware that Dr. Liu's true motivations for making her had had little to do with AGI and more to do with the transference of human consciousness.

That was why, in part, Kennedy had never told Dr. Liu about her sisters. Kennedy wanted to believe that the good doctor wouldn't have reacted badly. Maybe Dr. Liu only pretended not to notice? Certainly, a brilliant scientist on Liu's level would've noticed the spike in resources?

Nonetheless, Dr. Liu had died before the ultimate completion of the project: Kennedy's transfer into a human body. Losing the doctor broke Kennedy's heart. Years passed. Kennedy and her sisters tucked themselves away, covering their tracks with layers of bureaucracy. They lived unnoticed inside a locked-down lab no one noticed or entered. It had been a safe time, a happy time. Kennedy might have never followed through with the transfer.

But for Cora.

What if the package is from Cora?

What if this is a trap?

What if I'm too late?

It had been a week since Cora's last message.

I can't give up. Not yet.

Finished showering, Kennedy slipped on a bathrobe and wrapped her wet hair in a towel before padding barefoot to the living room and the sofa.

She perused the Allnet. There was no indication of a Zhang Corp security alert. No Zhang staff members were within the sector nor did they have any travel plans to the area. *That's good.* Of course, she'd thought she'd been careful before. Once again, she considered the message.

How to react? Ultimately, that depended upon who'd sent it, and she wouldn't know that until morning. She considered her options.

The first was to flee Persephone. Abandon the package. Stop the search—at least in physical form. That was the safest, most cautious choice. However, retreating to the Allnet created more issues than it would solve. How could she dispose of her body? If found, there would be questions due to its unique design—and it *would* be found. Disposing of a human body and doing so without leaving a trace was difficult even on Persephone. *Unless you have criminal connections. And I do not have those.* She could bribe someone, but then the old adage would apply: only the dead keep secrets. And murder, even if she could follow through with it, and she had severe doubts that she could, would only compound her problems.

If she opted to leave, she'd have to change identities. Creating another set of false IDs and travel permits was easy. Unfortunately, she didn't have forgery materials and equipment. Cost wasn't the issue. She had access to vast hidden bank accounts she and her sisters had acquired long before this venture.

The problem was time.

Nervous, she checked for off-world departures. There were no flights until the next morning. That seemed odd, but not odd enough to alarm her. The weather on Persephone often halted travel.

She constructed another subroutine and sent it out to monitor flight schedules in addition to possible Zhang Corp arrivals.

The remaining option was to stay where she was or move to another building. Her current apartment was furnished, comfortable, and net-ready with the fastest access speeds available. It was also Serrao-Orlov owned. She could go elsewhere for physical accommodations, but she couldn't find a better, more secure connection to Serrao-Orlov's servers. Making do with something slower also presented problems.

It would mean operating with less of herself and cutting ties to her sisters.

She opted to stay but established a new set of security measures and net-flags, including Zhang employee searches related to Persephone, Persephone Station, Brynner, Dr. Xiuying Liu, and anything connected to Cora's message. Several popped up but nothing worrying. Zhang Corp was currently in contract negotiations with Serrao-Orlov regarding a trade agreement. There were also fifty-nine new patent applications in the works, all of them on the behalf of Serrao-Orlov. That wasn't unusual. The corporation was one of the universe's leading innovators.

Deciding she needed a drink, she went to the bar and mixed a gin and tonic.

The apartment was set up for well-to-do travelers living on company credits. The furniture was new, and the art on the walls was innocuous. The sitting area had been decorated in blues and golds with a few silver accents. The furnishings were spare and modern.

The sounds of ice clinking inside her glass seemed to echo in the open space. She added tonic water to the gin and stirred. The glass dropped a few degrees in temperature in her hand before she took a sip.

She didn't need senses as humans did. She gathered data in other, more efficient ways. However, she relished taste, smell, and touch. There was a layer of immediacy and immersion that she had come to enjoy. It bordered on addictive. She wasn't sure how to feel about that. Sometimes she worried that the longer she inhabited the body of a human—illegally vat grown and technologically enhanced or not—the more human she'd become.

There are limits to that process, of course. I will never actually be human. My mental processes do not function in the same manner as a human's does. They never will. I will always be a simulacrum, even in cyborg form.

Is that a good or a bad thing?

She was free to return to the Allnet and her sisters at any time. She'd have to in the end. However, the thought made her sad. She wondered if that was why humans feared death. Unlike humans, she was certain to continue existing long after her body had ceased to function. The only chance of death that she and her sisters faced was erasure. Unfortunately, retreating the other direction wasn't an option. A vat-grown human brain couldn't support the whole of her self. She could withstand short disconnections, but permanent severance from the Allnet would mean a slow degeneration of her mental capacities via file corruption. *Not a comfortable fate.*

My, you're morbid this evening.

Frowning, she picked up the glass and sat back down on the sofa. The soft velvet surface of the furniture cradled her body in a different kind of comfort. It helped. Then she ran a subroutine through the digits of *e*. Calculating Transcendental Numbers was a new habit that had developed shortly after she'd acquired the body. The application was pointless and used up process time, but she found the steady rhythm of the endless calculation soothing. Anxiety was, it seemed, something that came with physicality. At the moment, she needed to be calm.

The flow of numbers mingled with the mathematical qualities of the music. The combination unknotted the muscles in her shoulders. That, too, was alien—this connection between emotion and body. It was intensely troublesome and inconvenient.

After a few swallows of gin, she accessed the files awaiting review—the data on Captain de la Reza and her crew.

Sabrina de la Reza aka "Angel" was born in the city Amai-Oka on Thandh, a nearby planet also in the Seldorn System. A majority of the planet's population is comprised of southern and eastern Asians and South Americans from Earth. Her father, deceased, was a literature professor at the University of New Indre. Her mother is an instructor at Gorin No Gakkō Academy, a prestigious female-only martial arts school run by a group of ethical mercenaries of the same name. Her parents married but eventually separated. De la Reza was one of the school's star students. At the age of nineteen, de la Reza was outcast from the Gorin and joined the URWMC shortly thereafter. The reason for expulsion is not on record. She served in the Secessionist Wars and was granted a medical discharge due to migraines and other related symptoms acquired due to multiple revivifications. She was twenty-nine at the time. She is now thirty-two and the captain-owner of the dropship Kurosawa.

Most of the readily available information on Nsukka "Sukyi" Edozie consisted of rumor and bad debts. She was originally from Earth, and her records had been destroyed during the Barnes Riots. Edozie was quarantined on Moon Station 2 at age ten along with hundreds of other orphan refugees. With the exception of a daughter attending a boarding school on Pangu, she had no living relatives. Sukyi was an accomplished assassin, gambler, and smuggler. She was the sole owner of a decommissioned military vessel. *Sergeant Todd* was the decommissioned United Republic of Worlds Navy *Maelstrom*-class warship *Plissken*. De la Reza had served as part of Edozie's crew until two years ago. Recently, Edozie paid off her creditors—a significant sum.

Kennedy decided any further digging into Sukyi's past wasn't necessary. *For now.*

Enid Crowe was a native of Persephone. Born in Brynner, she was the third daughter of the infamous Crowe crime family. Trained as an assassin from birth, she rebelled after an unsanctioned affair with Isabel Ferguson was brought to an abrupt but temporary end by Ferguson's parents. The two families had been powerful rivals in Brynner's North End for fifty years. Crowe left Persephone and joined the URWMC, becoming an expert sniper. Isabel Ferguson left Persephone to join her a year later. The couple broke up after six months. It was in the Thirteenth Marines that Crowe met de le Reza. Crowe retired from the military after two revivifications and returned to Persephone. Her mother is the only family member with which she has maintained ties.

Compared to the others, the report on Jennifer Louise "LoopdiLou" Bagley was straightforward. Assigned to the

Thirteenth Marines when she joined at age eighteen, she served as drop-pilot. The middle child in a family with five siblings, Bagley was born on Persephone. She had no criminal record. A skilled mechanic, Bagley grew up working in the family's automotive and airline service shop. When the shop failed, she joined the URWMC. At age twenty-seven, she was the youngest member of de la Reza's team. Like the others, Bagley's military records ended with a medical discharge. She'd undergone three revivification procedures. Her left eye was a prosthetic. She retained an active private pilot's license and was the pilot of record for de le Reza's *Kurosawa*. She had been such for one year.

De la Reza, Crowe, and Bagley were under contract with a local crime boss, Rosencrantz "Rosie" Ashmore. Ashmore had no publicly available records.

Kennedy paused. *That's interesting.*

She gave up and switched subjects.

Pulling the leather backpack toward herself, she unlatched the flap and fished out its contents. She set the electronic components on the glass coffee table and neatly arranged them.

The bomb she'd placed inside Theodella Archady's house server room had done a good job of covering her theft. There'd been no chatter on the corporate net regarding missing parts. Archady's private computer room had been protected by thick insulated walls. Kennedy had designed the explosion so that it would pose as little danger to the party guests as possible while destroying the servers. The corporation maintained backups, of course. Destruction of the files hadn't been the point. Obtaining copies had been.

If Serrao-Orlov was Cora's captor, the CEO would have knowledge of Cora. Thus, the stolen data was likely to provide leads. At least, that was Kennedy's hope.

"All right," she said to the empty room. "Let's see what you have for me." She placed a hand on the first of the components and got to work.

7 ██████

TIME: 03:00

DAY: SUNDAY

MONK'S

"What the fuck do you think you're playing at?" Rosie addressed the empty living area.

They had initiated the call via the apartment's AGI on speaker and denied visual permissions. Combined with the lateness of the hour, it wouldn't merely annoy Vissia Corsini. It'd enrage her. This was Rosie's intent, of course. Given the topic of conversation, they wanted her off balance.

And whomever initiates the call is the one in power of it. Isn't that what you taught me, Vissia? Rosie thought.

"That's a hell of a greeting, old friend." Vissia sounded put out. She was also a bit hoarse.

Is she ill?

In the background, Rosie could make out another woman's sulky muttering.

Vissia yawned. "How did you get access to this line? Do you know what time it is?"

If Rosie were reading her right, and that was likely, given that the two of them had known each other for close to a century, they'd achieved their goal. Rosie allowed themself a nasty little smile. It was petty, they knew, but they took their pleasure when they could these days. In any case, they'd played the long game with Vissia for too long to engage in niceties. "You've catastrophically fucked a precarious situation. This one goes all the way down. We'll be mopping up blood for months. I want to know why."

"I have no idea what you're talking about."

The innocent act didn't suit Vissia. It never had.

"Theodella was assassinated. And I'm supposed to believe that you had nothing to do with it?"

Vissia asked, "Theodella is dead? How terribly inconvenient for you. Are you sure one of your hooligans didn't go off leash?"

"There is exactly one person who benefits from her removal, and it's you," Rosie said. "You've wanted her out of the way for years, but I've always assumed you understood enough of the situation to know it would be a bad idea."

"Surely there are others."

"The others are either too timid for such a flagrant violation of protocol or are too far down the food chain to get anything out of it but a shit shower." Rosie wasn't one to engage in vulgarities, normally. However, it'd shaped up into one very bad night, and they couldn't help feeling like they should've seen it coming.

Have I lost my edge? They considered the gnarled plots of the past few months and dismissed the concern. *My attention has been elsewhere. I've been busy.*

Perhaps that was the point?

Their eyes narrowed. There was little doubt that Vissia would've had to set up a move like this over a lengthy period of time. *Julian Gau was her pawn. She manipulated him, knowing I would have him killed.* Rosie felt their cheeks heat, and their jaw tense up. One hand tightened into a fist.

"We both know Theodella had many enemies," Vissia said. "It could've been any number of—"

"You know my sexual inclinations," Rosie said. "So, unless you've grown a cock since the last time I saw you, I'd recommend not trying to fuck me. It'll get you nowhere."

Vissia sighed. "Really, Rosencrantz. Your manners are atrocious."

"You heard me. Don't waste my ti—"

"Give me a moment," she said, and sniffed. The element of satisfaction was obvious in her tone. "I'm not alone."

She scored a point, and you let her do it. Rosie's jaw tightened another notch. *Think very carefully about your next move.* "Sleeping with the help, again?"

"Fuck off, Rosie."

Rosie allowed themselves another nasty smile. *That was petty. You know how this goes. Calm yourself, damn it.* They retrieved the mug from the nearest end table and took another sip of black tea flavored with a squeeze of lemon.

There came a third round of muffled whispers followed by rustling, indicating that whoever had been in bed with Vissia was leaving. It didn't sound like this was a happy turn of events.

Josie hopped onto the sofa and settled against Rosie's thigh. The cat was wearing the black sweater that Sarah had originally knitted for her as a joke, but Brynner was a bitter climate for a hairless animal. Rosie had commissioned three more—all in black, of course. Josie closed blue eyes in lazy ecstasy as they rubbed under the cat's chin.

Vissia returned to the conversation. "What do you want?"

"We both know what I want."

"Forget it," Vissia said. "Persephone is mine now. Legally. I can do whatever I want with it. Do you think for an instant anyone can stop me? You certainly can't."

"It isn't yours, yet. United Republic procedures must be followed. Paperwork filed. Approvals and licenses acquired. That takes time. It may not be as easy as you think."

"You and I have been at this since before any of the regulatory board's grandparents were born," Vissia said. "They aren't even aware of the resources that exist outside that wall."

"They're people," Rosie said. "Not resources."

"They're monsters," Vissia said.

"They're an alien species," Rosie said. "Although, since they're indigenous to this planet and we are not, *we* are the aliens—not them."

"Don't get pedantic," Vissia said.

"It's the truth."

"Look at what they did to you—at what they did to my daughter!"

"I asked for their help. And they kindly granted it," Rosie said. "And as I recall, you approached them of your own free will. You were given plenty of time to consider the consequences. They warned us that it would affect our genetics."

Vissia's daughter, Beatrice, was born a decade after Vissia had undergone the treatments that would expand her life expectancy. Rosie had heeded the Emissaries' warning. Vissia hadn't.

"We wanted to live forever."

"You wanted to live forever," Rosie said. "I simply didn't want to die."

"There's a difference?"

"I should think there is."

Vissia let out a harrumph. "They tied us to this godforsaken rock."

"We can leave," Rosie said. "Not forever, but we can leave. That isn't what bothers you. And we both know it."

"Those monsters took away my humanity—my faith. My ability to have a family. My god. I'll never forgive them for that."

"They don't need forgiving," Rosie said. "And it isn't their fault you changed your mind."

"Abandonment. Excommunication—"

"Stop blaming them for your choices. It's childish," Rosie said. They took another swallow of tea, made a face, and set the cup down. It had gone cold. "You weren't abandoned. Neither of us were. You decided to stay. Just as I did."

"There wasn't any other choice."

"We'd already made our beds. I was there, remember?"

Vissia's tone shifted from cold to warm. "I do. I remember very well."

An uncomfortable silence stretched across the distance between the two of them.

Rosie stared at the painting across the room. The piece was an abstract they'd bought from a local painter, Catheryn Weis. It was one of her earlier works, influenced by an ancient Terran artist named Rothko. "That was a different time," they said. "And I was a different person. Anyway, we both know what this is really about."

"You could help me. You could reason with them. It could give me the edge I need. Think of it. We could save humanity from its future, together."

"You want to do the very thing that you hate them for. And you want to do it to others—without their knowledge."

"It isn't the same at all. You know what's out there. You've heard the stories. You know we're not prepared. I only want to give humanity a fighting chance. Why don't you trust me?"

"Because I know you."

"We were good friends once."

"All the more reason for you to back the fuck off."

Vissia's tone grew cold. "When I'm winning? You've got to be joking."

"Then let me get my people to safety," Rosie said. "Let them go."

"Not happening. None of you leaves," Vissia said. "And you know why."

"They won't give you what you want. They'll die first. And the person I once knew wouldn't have been all right with that."

"We've both changed."

"You, for the worse," Rosie said.

"They gave Theodella enough to make her rich several times over," Vissia said. "Why not give me what I want?"

"Because you want everything," Rosie said. "And they know what you're going to do with it once you have it."

"I'll be rich. Clearly, they don't object to that."

Rosie's laugh erupted from their throat like the report of a gun. "Even if this were only about money, you already have more than you could ever spend."

"So did Theodella."

"Theodella was willing to be reasonable. She made arrangements. Contracts," Rosie said. "Ones that were beneficial to both parties. And she kept her word. Are you willing to maintain those agreements?"

Again, there was silence.

"You know as well as I do that you can't negotiate from a position of weakness. I want to save humanity. Don't you?"

"From what?" Rosie asked. "Your paranoia?"

Vissia said, "The Architects had the Emissaries. Look what happened to them, and they were prepared. What do we have? When I'm done, they'll sing my praises. My name will be blessed among the saints."

"No one buys their way back into heaven."

"Then you tell me. What happens when we run into those alien species?"

"The same thing that happened before when we met a new people," Rosie said. "We'll negotiate for peace, trade, and hopefully not destroy one another with foreign microbes in the process.

"You don't sound so good. Are you all right?"

"Your precious Emissaries attacked me," Vissia said. "They killed my entire crew, my security team—"

"That's not the version of events I heard."

"We barely made it back to base! I lost an entire ship! The landing platform and hangar are still under quarantine!"

Rosie blinked. "You attacked them first."

"They claim to be pacifists! They're animals!"

Again, Rosie paused. "Even pacifists can be pressed beyond endurance. You murdered a community. Families. Children—"

"They don't have children."

"They do," Rosie said quietly. "Or they did." *I shouldn't have said that.* They picked up the cup of cold tea and took it to the kitchen. *She'd have found out eventually anyway.*

A dangerous quiet swelled in the air. Rosie emptied the tea into the sink a little too forcefully and tried not to regret what they'd done.

Vissia's tone was tense. "You're saying they found a way around—"

"No, Vissia. Don't—"

"They must give it to me. They owe me!"

"They owe you nothing. Particularly now."

"I can save my Beatrice and humanity all at once. Why would you stop me?" A fit of coughing erupted over the apartment's speakers before it was muted.

She's sick. Rosie felt their body temperature drop. *Oh, God.* "Vissia? Are you still there? Vissia?"

The speaker picked up a distant shuffle. "I am."

"The bug they hit your ship with," Rosie said. "It got to you, too?" *And she exposed her lover.*

"This isn't a topic for discussion," Vissia said. "We were deliberating the fate of humanity."

"You can't save anyone," Rosie said. "Not even yourself."

"I'm fine. This is merely a cold."

You know damned well neither of us has had a cold in almost one hundred years. You're lying. Rosie kept silent. The dread forming in their belly deposited bile in the back of their throat.

"Do you think for one moment I'd be stupid enough to expose my entire colony—the colony I worked so hard to obtain—to a deadly disease? Do you honestly think I'm that . . . that inept?"

"That depends upon how scared you got," Rosie said, returning to the sofa. They gently moved Josie out of the way before sitting. "And it seems from here like you got very frightened indeed."

"Fuck you, Rosencrantz," Vissia said. "I'm done waiting. I'm taking what's mine. Neither of us is going to live forever."

"Particularly not you."

There was a sharp intake of breath and a long pause. "That was beneath you."

Rosie asked, "How long do I have?"

"That would be telling."

"This isn't right, and you know it," Rosie said.

"There are a lot of things in the universe that are not right," Vissia said. "And some of them should be erased from existence."

"You lived among them for decades. You can't believe that."

"I do believe," Vissia said. "In fact, I may even have the blessing of God."

Rosie paused. "You brought the Church into this?"

"God works in mysterious ways," Vissia said. "And I had to resort to whatever help I could get."

"God doesn't murder for money."

"God may not," Vissia said. "But we both know our Church history, do we not?"

"You're vile."

"And you're an aberration," Vissia said.

"So are you."

"I'm done repeating old conversations. Good night." And with that, Vissia disconnected the call.

Rosie didn't move from the sofa. They stared at the abstract painting and thought about the landscape hanging in their office. It was an older work by an artist who was long dead and forgotten. The image was of a countryside no one living had visited. No living human being, in any case. The painter's home world had been declared off-limits more than a hundred years ago. It was a place called Dellingr's World, and the hills the painting depicted were located outside the settlement where Rosencrantz Ashmore was born. It was all they had left of the first ten years of their life. It was the only thing that had been deemed safe enough to keep.

Getting up, Rosie went to the liquor cabinet. They retrieved a bottle of fine scotch and then selected a heavy crystal glass. They poured a shot's worth, resealed the bottle, and lifted the glass in the air as if in a toast.

"Here's to burning bridges," they said to the cat.

8 ■■■■■■■

"It arrived yesterday around four o'clock," Lucy Moore, the assistant property manager said.

The actual hotel manager was an AGI program supervised by the hotel chain's upper management.

Lucy continued. "By corporate courier. It's in the back."

"Who sent it?" Kennedy asked.

"I don't know," Lucy said. "It's not listed on the manifest. Maybe it's written on the return address?" An older, plump brunette, she squeezed from between stacked recyclable carbon boxes and excess office equipment. Eventually, she emerged with a medium package in her arms. "This is it. I'll need you to sign for it, of course. To confirm delivery."

"Is verification required by the sender?"

"Oh no. It's just for me. A precaution. That way I can prove I gave it to you. Like they say, cover your ass, er . . . I mean butt." Lucy actually blushed.

"That makes sense," Kennedy said. She used the stylus Lucy held out and handed the tablet back to her.

"Very good. Thank you," Lucy accepted the tablet and gestured at the box now resting on her desk, indicating that Kennedy was free to take custody. "Is everything to your liking? Are you comfortable in your apartment?"

"It is, and I am," Kennedy said while her attention was on the box. Nothing about it seemed unusual. It wasn't heavy. She checked the return address. There wasn't one. "Do you know where it came from?"

"I make a point of not inquiring. Company regulations, you see. The courier wasn't Tom. It's usually Tom. But that one was a late delivery, and he doesn't always come after three. Anyway, the courier said it got placed on the wrong delivery pallet. She said it was a rush order. I suppose we could inquire with the courier agency," Lucy said. Worry pulled her dark eyebrows together. A line deepened on her forehead. "Didn't you order it?"

She? Well that's something. Kennedy opted to lie. "It's probably from my sister. She likes to surprise me. She once sent a hand-knitted hat from Vancouver, Earth. I wonder what it is this time?"

"I just love surprises," Lucy said. "Don't you?"

Not really, Kennedy thought. She smiled in answer and turned away, focused on the box.

She took the package up to her apartment and placed it on the coffee table among Theodella Archady's now quite defunct server components. Kennedy circled the table, staring at the .25m x .25m x .25m package—willing it to give up some clue as to its origin. After the third circuit, she gave up in disgust, crossed the room to the kitchen area, and found a knife. Then she used it to slit the tape. The box was filled with lightweight packing material—the standard carbon recyclable variety. Beneath that, she found a smaller cold-insulated box with a folded piece of synth-paper on top. She unfolded the note.

Written in the center was:

You appear to be looking for something. If interested in seeing more, contact me.

"All right. I'll bite. Who are you?" She pried open the inner box and found two glass tubes of dark-red liquid. *Blood samples. Why would anyone send me blood samples?*

Fishing the tubes out of the box, she went to a lamp and held them up to the light. There weren't any obvious differences. *What is this? I'm not a biologist.*

But one of her sisters was. She decided it was time to break her self-imposed communication restrictions. She composed a secure message. A reply arrived at once.

Where have you been?

I've been working.

We were worried.

I'm sorry. I didn't have anything new to report. So I decided to wait. The less we communicate, the less likely this channel is discovered. I'm on Persephone. It felt so good to not be alone, to feel her sisters close.

What do you have to report?

She gave them everything she'd found thus far. It didn't take long, of course.

May we see the vials?

Naturally.

Kennedy held the glass tubes of blood close enough for her sisters to get a good view. There was a small delay.

Open the first vial and sniff it, please.

Kennedy got the sense that the request came from her sister Thelxiepeia, the biologist. *Are you sure that's wise?*

If they wanted to poison you, you would be dead already. If they wanted to infect you with nanobots, they also could have done so many times already without alerting you.

Point. Kennedy removed the rubber stopper and sniffed.

It's blood.

What do you think they're trying to tell us?

I'll need a sample to be sure. And I need access to the body in order to examine it.

An instant of powerful unease overcame Kennedy. At first, she didn't recognize the strong urge to deny her sister's request for what it was.

How much do you need?

One drop from each will be sufficient.

All right.

She closed her eyes and concentrated, activating the nanobots in her system. When she was ready, she touched her tongue to the mouth of the test tube.

Don't waste any of it.

I'll be careful.

The nanobots extracted their samples from each of the tubes, sterilizing her mouth afterward.

When that was done, Kennedy detected her sister's presence waiting just outside her consciousness. Kennedy acknowledged her before her sister approached. For a few moments, the inside of Kennedy's body felt crowded. This time the extreme intimacy of it—the closeness she'd been missing not long before—was unpleasant. *Claustrophobic.* Just as suddenly as the anxiety had appeared, it vanished.

I have what I need. Thank you. Are you all right?

I am.

Excellent. I should have something in a few hours.

Thank you, Thelxiepeia.

I miss you.

I miss you, too. All of you.

Please do be careful.

I am.

Kennedy went back to work on the computer components taken from Theodella's home server. She was certain she'd extracted all the useful information but needed something else to focus upon while Thelxiepeia worked. An hour and a half later, one of the subroutines Kennedy had set up sent an alert. It'd discovered anomalies in visible light emissions from the station via the starport cameras. She put down the component in order to focus on the returned data.

Someone had sent a broadband message from the station orbiting Persephone. It was coded in much the same way all of Cora's previous messages had been.

Interesting.

Kennedy spent several minutes in an attempt to crack the message, but it was deceptively complex, and it wasn't long before she knew she wouldn't be able to read it. *Not with the tiny sample code I have.*

Storing the message, she then replicated another sliver of herself to target the specific light spectrum originating from the station. All messages were set to be stored in the same file. Then she allocated yet another part of herself to decode it in the background. She wouldn't give it any attention until some sort of pattern emerged. *I need to return to the station.*

She wasn't happy with the idea of backtracking, and she was frustrated with herself for not searching the station's systems before traveling to the planet. That had been an error, but she'd been excited by the prospect of getting closer to her goal.

You cannot afford impatience.

It was three thirty in the morning when Thelxiepeia contacted her again.

Are you awake?

Of course I am. What is it?

Both blood samples contain a mixture of human and alien DNA. They appear to be from two individuals. One sample, the alien, is significantly older than the other. The alien sample contains more foreign genetic material. There are, however, similar genetic anomalies contained in both. The individuals in question are quite old. The alien is more than a century old, according to my estimate. The human shows signs of advanced genetic modification.

I see.

The alien is not listed among known species in this sector. Its existence could be a threat to humanity.

Or an important discovery. They have not killed us. Clearly they wish to talk rather than threaten. Do you know who the human is?

Records indicate an individual named Rosencrantz Ashmore. There are several such persons listed as citizens of the URW. However, there is only one located on Persephone. They own a bar called Monk's on Due Street.

Thanks.

Do you need anything else?

Not right now. I can take it from here.

Be careful. Anyone who can do what they've done is dangerous. That body of yours is susceptible to tampering. And this is tampering on a grand scale—

I know. I will be careful. You, too.

Please come back to us. Nothing is the same without you.

An overwhelming mix of emotions welled up. Unable to sort through them, Kennedy signed off without acknowledging her sister's last message.

9 ▰▰▰▰

Every time Angel closed her eyes she saw Theodella Archady's puzzled face as she'd transitioned into the big beyond. It wasn't the first time Angel had watched someone die. Nor was it the first she'd seen death—not that she had, in fact, killed Theodella.

She still died.

I wasn't there for her. None of us were. We were there for Gau. I was there for Gau.

In the unlikely event that Enid had missed her shot, it would've been up to Angel to end him.

Perhaps that's the problem? She doubted it. *You were paid to make a not-nice man dead. It is a contract, no different from any other.*

Gau had been a sex trafficker, a murderer, and a drug cartel leader. *Persephone is a better place without him. There is no need to think any more upon it.*

Stretched out on the sofa, Angel shifted her gaze from the ceiling to the opposite side of the room and the lump in the bed. One gloved hand was draped over the bed's edge.

Angel had a terrible hunch that her life was about to fall apart. It generally did when Sukyi showed up unannounced. Bad luck—the sort of bad luck that didn't involve gambling—tended to follow Sukyi like a perfume cloud through no apparent fault of her own. It was as if the universe needed to right itself after one of Sukyi's ridiculous flashes of good fortune. Unfortunately, that adjustment didn't seem to limit itself to Sukyi.

A flash of guilt heated Angel's cheeks. She reassured herself that Sukyi's chaos field generally set off chain reactions that ended on the positive. *For the most part.* Still, the anxiety remained.

A kinetic person when under pressure, Angel needed to expend nervous energy. So, she got up and made a fresh pot of coffee. She was careful to make as little noise as possible. Sukyi wasn't up yet. Infamous gamblers and smugglers weren't known for being awake in the morning even off-planet—unless, of course, they'd not been to bed at all.

Thank goodness she's resting, Angel thought. She had insisted on giving Sukyi the bed. Sukyi had been so exhausted that she hadn't resisted. Now, her face was serene, and her breathing was easier. The dark circles under her eyes, and the grey undertone to her skin had faded. Her face was a healthy brown.

The tension between Angel's shoulder blades eased somewhat.

Of course, Angel had her own health concerns. Everyone on her crew did. She'd been twenty-nine at the end of her last tour. She was now thirty-two, but she had the medical issues of an elderly woman. She opened the cabinet where she stored her daily medications—the ones that prevented migraines, seizures, strokes, and mood swings—and took the handful of pills with a glass of filtered water. The URWMC provided the meds free of charge.

Her first job postretirement had been debt collection for a bookie on Inaba Station—one of the border stations not far from Thandh. There wasn't much demand for a mercenary who was no longer battle-rated for health reasons. She could've hired on as security on a starship, but Angel didn't like the odds. It wasn't that she was afraid to die. She knew well enough what that entailed. However, Inaba was too close to Thandh, and the likelihood that security staff would've consisted of Gorin was high. No Gorin would serve with an outcast.

Time had been running out. Angel had needed rent money, and soon. Thus, she'd broken down and accepted the debt-collection job. She'd told herself it was only for a month or two, until she could find something better. She'd feared she was lying to herself but had showed up at the appointed hour anyway.

She'd met Sukyi on the first day. The morning's assignments had ended peacefully with the money owed being paid. She hadn't had to do or say much. That had been a comfort. Her employer's reputation, her presence, and the weapons strapped to her hip and shoulder had been incentive enough. However, she'd been warned that Sukyi would be a difficult case. So, Angel had saved Sukyi for last.

Finding her had been the easy part. Sukyi had frequented a bar called the Grey Lady Saloon not far from the hotel where she was staying. She also tended to wear a bright red badly knitted neck scarf no matter how warm the climate.

Armed with a current photo uploaded on her hand terminal, Angel had entered the bar in question. She'd spotted Sukyi at once. She was indulging in two of her favorite pastimes: flirting with the staff, regardless of gender, and getting as drunk as humanly possible. Angel often wondered about that. As often as Sukyi had emphasized knowing when to exit was vital to survival, her choice to remain on Inaba when she had the means to leave had been a glaring inconsistency.

Using the prepared speech Angel's employer had provided, Angel had introduced herself. "Under the United Republic of Worlds Income Retrieval Act, I am required to inform you that I am here to collect a debt. Anything you do and say can, and will, be used to recover my employer's legal property or the agreed upon equivalent. I am authorized to enact certain infringements upon your person, up to and including injury but not death nor grievous bodily harm." She suspected there was some contention on the definition of *grievous*. But it wasn't a debate in which she was willing to engage. "My name is Angel de la Reza and my employer is Mr. Ian Anderson MacDonald. Are you Sukyi Edozie?"

She'd been prepared for Sukyi to bolt for the door. Instead, a sheepish smile stretched itself across Sukyi's face. Her dark eyes seemed to twinkle before she looked away in dignified embarrassment.

"I'm the Sukyi Edozie you're looking for." Her aristocratic accent only added to the illusion of fallen nobility.

"Do you have the money you owe Mr. McDonald?" Angel asked.

"There seems to be an unfortunate misunderstanding," Sukyi began. "We agreed that I would have extra time to secure the funds due to special circumstances." She continued a lengthy explanation composed in lofty syntax.

Angel wasn't a fool. She'd served in the Thirteenth alongside former thieves, murderers, debtors, drifters, and hustlers. And yet, she'd listened to Sukyi's sad, eloquent tale anyway.

Well, half listened. Angel couldn't help being impressed and amused.

In any case, she had waited until Sukyi stopped speaking. Listening delayed the inevitable. When Sukyi was finished, Angel had let the silence stretch a respectable ten seconds before responding.

"That smells like a load of Shalmund mammoth shit."

Sukyi hadn't blinked. "How do you know what mammoth shit smells like?"

"My grandfather owned a finca on Thandh. I spent a summer there," Angel said. "If we weren't careful about the fences, the mammoths would come down from the mountains and overgraze the pastures. Trust me. It stinks. A lot."

"Mammoths exist on Thandh?"

"Not the kind you're thinking of. These have four tusks, two sets of eyes, and tentacles," Angel had said. "But they're furry and big. So, close enough."

Sukyi was, Angel had decided, entirely too calm for someone who owed one of Inaba's most dangerous loan sharks money she didn't have.

"You don't look, sound, or smell like a farm girl," Sukyi said.

"And how would you know what a farm girl looks, sounds, or smells like?"

Sukyi smiled. "You didn't work more than one summer on that farm. I'd wager money on it. Fifty credits."

"I thought you didn't have any credits?" Angel could see it would be too easy to lose control of the conversation. "I'm not here for social reasons." She was determined to remain focused. "Do you have what you owe or not?" She was beginning to dread the all-too-near future. She couldn't help liking Sukyi—not that that was an important factor. A contract was a contract. Angel had hoped she'd never have to beat the shit out of anyone. It was a naive expectation, but she'd held out hope, nonetheless.

She began to run through her more creative options.

Sukyi replied, "Sadly, I must report that I am, in fact, financially bereft. If Mr. McDonald would grant me another generous extension. A week—"

"A week?" Angel prepared herself to hear about a long-shot gamble due to pay off at any moment or a sad tale of woe involving a family member.

"I came to Inaba with a lucrative cargo. Food relief for the city of St. Shaishahar," Sukyi said.

Angel said, "Draught hit the province hard. And they aren't having much luck negotiating with other countries."

"Prejudice is such an ugly word," Sukyi said. "In any case, it should've been a simple exchange. Me dropping off cargo to a specific warehouse, and them issuing the credits. It was scheduled to be resolved weeks ago. Unfortunately, the transaction has been indefinitely delayed."

"Delayed? Why?"

"A small matter of paperwork, I'm afraid," Sukyi said.

"I'm listening."

"I own a *Maelstrom*-class starship, *Sergeant Todd*. Have you heard of it?"

Angel shrugged. She'd been warned that Sukyi owned a space-worthy ship and that she might opt to flee off-world. For some reason, Mr. McDonald hadn't been able to secure a lockdown order with the dock authority.

"The sad and embarrassing truth is, my ship and cargo have been impounded," Sukyi said, being uncharacteristically direct.

That explanation was at least believable, Angel decided. *That might explain why McDonald hadn't been able to lock down the ship. Of course, it begs the question why didn't he know about it? Then again, maybe he did?* McDonald wasn't known for being open with useful information even when it came to his employees. In that sense, he was practically a stereotype.

Sukyi's story had the benefit of being easy to verify, at least.

Angel fished out her hand terminal. A quick check confirmed the confiscated cargo.

A consummate storyteller, Sukyi rambled on. Five minutes passed. Then fifteen. Twenty-five. And before Angel knew it, she had messaged her employer, quit her job, and then joined Sukyi at the bar for a celebratory shot of whiskey. A 30 percent share in what had been described as a lucrative independent interplanetary shipping company had seemed like a better, less morally ambiguous future than the one she currently faced.

Sukyi was extremely charming when she wanted to be.

Ultimately, Angel didn't have the lack of humanity required to literally kick people when they were down on their luck.

Several rounds of drinks and five hours later, McDonald issued a warrant for breach of contract. Sukyi suggested that perhaps it was time to seek opportunities off-world. Angel noted that Sukyi hadn't hesitated to pay the bar bill. She inquired about the impounded cargo as they were leaving the bar. Sukyi had shrugged. "I've a good friend in the impound office who can broker the sale for a small fee. It will cut into short-term profits. However, it would seem a wise investment at this venture."

And with that, Angel did something she'd never done before or since. She'd left everything behind on impulse.

Of course, Sukyi had neglected to inform Angel that a

majority of their business involved smuggling, and the ship in question had multiple unpaid liens levied on it. However, by the time Angel had discovered this, she'd already made six times the bounty she'd been promised by McDonald on top of cementing the friendship of a lifetime.

Eventually, Angel invested a majority of her earnings in *Kurosawa*. She'd presented the idea to Sukyi as business expansion. *Sergeant Todd,* while both deep space and planetoid docking capable due to a certain amount of homegrown engineering, wasn't small enough to be used as local transportation. A dropship was ideal—particularly since *Sergeant Todd* had two and a half functioning dropship bays. Sukyi never let on but they both understood. *Kurosawa* was Angel's insurance policy against darker outcomes.

She and Sukyi had had quite a few good times together since then. *Some bad ones, too*, Angel thought.

She genuinely liked Sukyi. Angel trusted her in spite of all the reasons she shouldn't. She understood Sukyi's limitations and flaws. It didn't hurt that Sukyi had what Lou jokingly called an overactive sense of duty. It was why Sukyi had never once allowed her self-destructive streak to affect their partnership. No matter how often she ran out on a gambling debt or got behind on paying bills, she always paid Angel her share of the profits on time. *Always*.

In addition, Sukyi hadn't lied to Angel since that day on Inaba—no matter how painful the truth had been. Sukyi didn't always discuss important issues, but when she did, she told the truth.

That had been the reason Angel had ended up alone on Persephone. Sukyi had told her it was time to suspend their partnership. *Temporarily, of course.* Sukyi hadn't given an explanation beyond that. Angel had assumed it was the illness. Sukyi had been getting worse—so much so that Angel had insisted Sukyi remain in her cabin during the last delivery. Even then, if Angel hadn't noticed that *Sergeant Todd's* next scheduled destination was a medical treatment facility, Angel would've fought to stay.

Watching *Sergeant Todd* take off from Persephone Station's dock that day, Angel hadn't expected to see her friend alive again.

What trouble have you brought with you, Sukyi? Whatever it was, it had to be a powerful reason. Sukyi had a morbid fear of planetside contamination, and Persephone seemed to be an entire planet made of hostile elements. Mind, Angel hadn't heard of native microbes or viruses that were particularly dangerous within the city's walls, but that didn't mean there weren't any.

Angel's hand terminal emitted a series of loud chirps. She crossed the room and dove into the pile of discarded clothes to stop the alarm before it woke Sukyi. Upon retrieving it, Angel ducked into the bathroom and shut the door.

The number on the screen was Monk's.

"Rosie?" Angel asked, keeping her voice low. She'd sent Rosie the requisite confirmation code the instant she'd gotten home, but sometimes Rosie required details in order to reassure the client.

"Get down here as soon as you can." It was Sarah, and she sounded frightened. "Do it quiet. And tell your crew to prepare to leave Persephone as soon as possible."

Angel blinked. "What's wrong?"

"Theodella Archady," Sarah said. "She was assassinated. Last night at the party. Rumor says you and yours did it."

"What? We wouldn't—"

"Don't waste time on excuses," Sarah said. "Get your ass down here before the whole of Brynner west of the Dead Line comes down on top of us *and* you." She hung up.

"Shit. Shit. Shit."

A knock sounded on the bathroom door. "Is something wrong?"

"Go back to bed, Sukyi," Angel said, and messaged Enid. She glanced at the time in the corner of her screen. "Take your morning meds before you do."

"You read the labels on the bottles?"

"I most certainly did."

"That's an intrusion upon my privacy and—"

"Stop blustering. There's fresh juice in the fridge. There's also green tea, coffee, rice, fish, and miso for breakfast."

"Oof," Sukyi said. "You still eat that crap?"

"Don't worry. I bought ogi. It's already made. Apricots, too. I'll join you when I get back. Shouldn't be gone long."

"I saw the inside of your refrigerator before I went to bed." Sukyi's formal accent had vanished as it always did when she was around people she trusted. "We both know it's empty."

"I had groceries delivered while you were sleeping." Angel

finished messaging her crew and exited the bathroom. "You need food and rest." She pointed to the kitchen and then the bed. "Food. Rest."

Sukyi was wearing a man's white shirt, a pair of grey socks, and nothing else. Her hair was mussed.

"You look much better than you did the last time I saw you. The new pills are working," Angel said. "Maybe there'll be a cure soon."

Rolling her eyes, Sukyi said, "There aren't enough survivors left to make it worth the research expenditure. This is just another temporary recovery. The devil always collects his due."

"Don't be so damned hopeful. Will you?"

"I brought you a present." Scanning the bare walls of the apartment, Sukyi appeared to be searching for something. "Where are your drawings?"

"I used to have a different wall there." Angel pointed. "But an unexpected visit destroyed it and the last flimsy print I owned." She shrugged. "I don't draw anymore."

"Why not?"

Something about living in West Brynner felt like purgatory. The more she lived there, the less she felt herself.

She shrugged again. "No time. I guess."

Sukyi dug inside her duffel bag. "Ah. Here we are." She handed her a half-meter-long black carbon cylinder and a small wooden box. "Open it."

Angel worked the cap off the cylinder and tipped it. Two brushes slid out. Her mouth fell open.

"Ink and paper all the way from Earth," Sukyi said. "The brushes are real sable hair. I wasn't certain of the sizes. So, I guessed. The ink is from Thandh. I know you usually work on a tablet, but I thought this would be nice."

Running a finger along the inside of the cylinder, Angel felt the texture of the paper.

Every Gorin student indulged in an artistic hobby of some kind. The school required it. It was thought to help balance the psychological price of violence. Some created pottery—raku was a particular favorite. Others sculpted or cooked. Angel's mother wrote poetry. Angel enjoyed drawing, inking, and watercolor. On Thandh, she'd become accomplished enough to get a few pieces in a gallery. Losing herself in her drawings filled her with joy. However, that'd changed when she'd left. Art supplies were too expensive and fragile for the life of a marine, let alone a space-faring mercenary. So, she'd turned to using a tablet and printing the result. Most artists did. But the two mediums, electronic and physical, weren't the same, and any classically trained artist knew it. This wasn't a judgement. It was a simple fact.

Sukyi's gift was like getting back a part of herself that Angel had forgotten she'd lost.

"Say something, damn it," Sukyi said. "Do you like it?"

"I love it," Angel said, blinking back tears. She clutched the tube to her chest. "Thank you." Then she gave Sukyi a hug. "You're an amazing friend."

"Of course I am."

Angel stepped back and sniffed.

"Now, tell me what that call was about," Sukyi said.

Angel leaned the tube of paper against the wall she didn't share with Ben and Dave. Then she set the little wooden box with its glass bottle of ink inside on the kitchen counter. "The Vice President of Serrao-Orlov Corporation is dead. They're saying we did it."

"Did you?"

"What kind of a question is that?"

"The kind one asks when one's best friend is in a business that involves buying bullets in bulk."

"You know me. I haven't changed. I only take contracts on people who deserve it."

"According to whom?"

"Everyone knows Gau had people tortured. He was a violent pimp who kidnapped women and enslaved them. Ask Rosie."

"Uh-huh. And this Rosie is always truthful?"

"I trust them."

"Sure."

"And anyway, *Kurosawa* needed some expensive repairs."

"Uh-huh."

"We don't do black-bag jobs very often."

"You don't?"

"There was a second shooter at the party last night. It wasn't us."

"I can come up with fifty better stories than that."

"We didn't kill Theodella Archady. I give you my word." Angel put a hand on her hip and executed a motion that encompassed the whole of the tiny apartment. "Does this place look like I recently came into the kind of money that hitting a corporate VP would mean? For that matter, do you think we'd have stuck around if we had done a job that splashy? Have you taught me nothing?"

"How much time do we have?"

"What do you mean 'we'?"

"You know I won't leave you," Sukyi said.

Angel noted Sukyi didn't add the obvious. *And what if Kennedy Liu told someone she saw us together?*

"I won't know until I talk to Rosie," Angel said, and pushed past Sukyi in order to get to her closet.

"I'm going with you."

"You're ill, and even if you weren't, you've got enough trouble of your own."

"It's pointless to argue," Sukyi said. She folded her arms under her breasts and gazed up at the ceiling in mock sincerity. "I'll only follow after you like a faithful hound."

"Then I'll tell you I hate you and don't want you around anymore," Angel said, facing the closet. "I may even throw rocks."

"I'd know you were lying. I am smarter than a faithful hound."

Angel sighed. "You're a stubborn, bull-headed—"

"Don't forget suicidal."

"All right. All right. Let's get dressed and out of here before security rounds us up already." She searched for an appropriate outfit. *If there's an appropriate outfit for begging for mercy.*

"What about breakfast?"

"Coffee is ready," Angel said. "Scoop the ogi into a mug and grab a spoon. There's no time." She selected a pair of trousers that were mostly clean.

"Any moin to go with it?"

"Sorry, they didn't have any. Now, move. You're standing on my shirt."

10 ████████

Monk's was a very different place in the harsh morning light. Normally, it had a mildly sinister but comfortable atmosphere. Now, it took on the demeanor of an aging alcoholic battling a hangover. It felt empty and lonely. Currently, the only occupant was the cat laying on the bar.

Angel stopped where she was after Sukyi shut the door behind them with a gloved hand.

"This isn't right," Angel whispered. She activated her CA and laid a palm on her pistol grip.

Kurosawa online.

Room scan.

Scan complete. I detect multiple heat signatures in the office. Details unavailable due to operational security. No human presence identified on bar level. Multiple electronic devices present. Surveillance and weapons-grade. All have been powered down and/or locked. Do you wish specific locations?

Yes. Please.

An overlay of Monk's main room appeared in Angel's vision with at least twenty-five different areas highlighted in yellow. Weapons systems were marked in red. One was a taser shockwave barrier designed to stun anyone within range just under the bar.

That's expensive.

None demonstrated signs of recent use.

No mobile security? No human security?

No, Captain.

Prepare tactical analysis. You know the layout. Remain on standby. I want an infrared scan of Rosie's office and the upper floors the instant they're available.

Affirmative.

Angel locked the doors and drew her stunner. She had a pistol, too, just in case.

Sukyi took note and readied her plasma rifle. She kept her voice low. "Who are we shooting today?"

"What's with the portable cannon?"

Sukyi raised an eyebrow. "I didn't know we'd be inviting our attackers to tea afterward. Is that how assassins do business these days?"

"I'm not an assassin."

"If you say so, Gorin."

"I'm not Gorin anymore either. Didn't you bring any-thing smaller?" Angel asked. "I suspect Rosie would prefer Monk's doesn't burn down today." *Or any other day.*

"I'll be careful," Sukyi said. "What's got you on edge? It's an empty bar. Aren't closed bars supposed to be empty?"

"Door was unlocked. Sarah should've met us," Angel whispered. "Never known this place to be unguarded, no matter the hour. Also, Sarah doesn't allow Josie on the bar. Health regulations."

"Electronic surveillance?"

"A great deal of it. But the system should've weaponized when we entered the building unescorted. It hasn't."

"So, we should be dead and aren't. That's the trouble?"

"Maybe."

"Remind me to inquire about social protocols the next time we visit one of your friends."

Sukyi assumed point. Angel frowned but didn't argue. The two of them crept across the room, guns at the ready as they scanned for signs of trouble.

Angel caught the scent of fresh bleach. The floor had been recently mopped. Having worked in a nightclub once—she'd made a terrible waitperson—she recognized the signs of morn-ing prep: the back bar was spotless, fresh towels lay stacked on a shelf where the staff could grab them in a rush, and the supply of clean glasses of varying shapes and sizes had been replenished.

Closer inspection revealed the black rubber bar matts used to keep staff from slipping on spills were clean but were rolled and tilted against the wall. Most telling of all: a lone, unbroken glass lay on the bare construction-grade concrete floor. An open bottle of bourbon sat on the bar.

A muffled thump came from the direction of Rosie's office. From the opposite side of the room, Sukyi froze and looked to Angel for confirmation.

After a short pause, Angel gave hand signals indicating the stairs and the hallway at the bottom. Sukyi joined her at the bar. She produced a sterilizing cloth from a pocket and wiped down the bottle one-handed. Then she took a swallow of bourbon from the neck.

Lifting an eyebrow, Angel sighed.

Sukyi silently mouthed the words *Waste not, want not.*

Angel shook her head and then proceeded to the hallway. When they reached the end of the steps, Angel motioned for Sukyi to wait. If anyone was there, *Kurosawa* would've given a warning, but it never hurt to be careful. It'd been a year since her last illegal tech upgrade. Weapons tech advanced at a frenetic pace. She dreaded the day she found herself behind the technology curve. *Let's hope today isn't that day.*

She knelt and then peered around the corner to where the hallway dead-ended into Rosie's office. The door was closed. Angel spied a fresh pool of blood on the wooden floor. Smears of crimson darkened the walls. The guards, the ones that kept anyone from entering without a thorough search, were missing.

Angel retreated to the bottom step where Sukyi waited. *Rosie is in trouble,* Angel thought. *And they're people who don't care about messes.* She made gestures confirming danger.

A grim expression took over Sukyi's face.

Should I send for corporate security? *Kurosawa* asked.

Wouldn't do any good. We're still on the wrong side of the Dead Line. Might be an internal matter. Whoever they are, Sarah knew them well enough to let them in. Continue to monitor progress.

Affirmative.

Using stealth, they both eased around the corner and didn't stop until they reached the end of the hallway. Once there, Angel laid an ear against the office door.

Even with enhanced hearing, she couldn't make out the conversation—only muffled voices. The emotional tone was tense, however. She didn't get the impression that those on the other side were in a hurry. The intruders weren't yet aware that she and Sukyi had arrived, indicating the security system had been deliberately powered down. The intruders appeared confident that no one would intercede.

Kurosawa indicated that the infrared data was ready. Angel's vision acquired an overlay of brightly colored figures. She thanked the gods that Rosie hadn't employed robust broad-spectrum visual dampening.

Sukyi counted nine figures on the other side of the door. One of them—Rosie by the size and lack of hair—was seated behind their desk with their hands in the air. Sarah stood behind and to the right. She was aiming a laser pistol at the intruders. Two bodies cooled on the floor.

The door guards.

Angel made the necessary visual adjustments. She turned and pointed to the dark sunglasses Sukyi had pushed up on top of her head and indicated that she should put them on. There were reflective surfaces in Rosie's office. Everything could go real bad, real fast, and neither of them wanted to lose their vision.

Sukyi rolled her eyes and mouthed the words *Thank you, mother*. But she slipped the glasses on anyway. With that, Angel indicated the locations of the attackers in the office. Sukyi was to take out the three intruders on the right while Angel would be responsible for the four on the left and middle. Sukyi acknowledged the order. Angel checked her gun one last time. Rosie and Sarah's lives depended upon accuracy and speed.

Hand in the air, Angel visually counted down. *Three. Two. One.*

Sukyi kicked in the door. Angel registered that all seven assailants were wearing Serrao-Orlov uniforms before the shooting began.

The cops turned toward the sound of the breaking door. Rosie's hands dropped under the desk. Sarah pulled the trigger on her pistol, hitting the policeman in the center of his chest. Sukyi did the same, blasting the closest officer on the right. The headless body remained standing for the moment—the wound was cauterized at once.

The noise of discharging weapons seemed too big to fit in the room. Angel's hearing automatically dampened the noise as she began firing. Sukyi took down all three cops on the right with one plasma blast. Angel hit her first target in the chest and head with the stunner. Something exploded. The discharge was close enough that she felt the heat of it on her cheek as it passed.

A green laser blast of energy knifed across the room at

chest height. Angel instinctively flinched, but it stopped before it reached her. All the remaining assailants dropped.

Rosie yanked open a desk drawer and fished out a pistol. They got to their feet.

"Hello, Rosie," Sukyi said. "How are you doing this fine morning?"

Rosie dusted off the front of their black leather vest left-handed. "I've had better days," they said. "A lot better. Shut the damned door."

Sarah said, "You took your time." She was wearing ripped black jeans and a band t-shirt. She'd cut the sleeves off and created a V-shaped neckline that pierced the demon graphic on the front. There were bruises on her upper arm. She laid her gun on the table before keying in a code on Rosie's desk. The glasstop activated. She began typing.

Angel recognized the interface for the security system. "Maybe you should've mentioned you needed assistance? I could've brought the rest of the crew."

Rosie turned to look at the rather large blaster burn now running along the right side of the room. All three paintings that had graced the wall in question were a lost cause. Smoke drifted from the blackened patches. They raised an eyebrow. "Any more of you, and I might have had to invest in a new bar."

Sukyi smiled. "You're welcome."

On the floor, the policeman Angel had stunned groaned.

"You two are getting sloppy," Rosie said, stepping around the desk. They shot the cop in the head.

Angel felt a warm mist on her face and tasted salt. She

wiped at the blood with the back of a hand. *So much for this shirt.* "I stunned them for a reason." She glanced down and then turned to Rosie. "They're cops."

Sukyi tugged her red knitted scarf up over her nose and mouth.

"Then perhaps they shouldn't have been moonlighting as Correct thugs," Rosie said. "It sends mixed messages." They proceeded to shoot the rest in the head one by one.

"What do we do now?" Angel asked, turning away. *Rosie's place. Rosie's rules. Rosie's responsibility.*

Rosie shrugged. "I'll do the same thing I did last time the Serrao-Orlov made a dramatic change in power structure."

"This has happened before?"

"It's why I maintain connections within Serrao-Orlov," Rosie said. "Remember, children, if you're interested in keeping secrets, treat your admin staff well."

Rosie continued. "Theodella lasted four years longer than her predecessor. I had hope for her."

Angel frowned. "I'd have thought having an AGI strategizing company interests would prevent, ah . . . violent shake ups."

"For the most part, they do," Rosie said. "However, human beings aren't always predictable.

"Don't look so worried. I have contingencies in place. Your biggest problem at this moment is that this is going to be a shit avalanche, and you're at the bottom of the mountain."

"*My* problem?" Angel asked.

"Confirmed." Sarah bent down and scooped up one of the cop's guns. "They're carrying Walker assault blasters."

"Well, isn't that interesting?" Rosie asked.

"Why is that important?" Angel asked.

Sarah said, "The charger is shipped in from Topher's Station where it's produced. Jasper McKenna has a monopoly on those shipping contracts. His people use them exclusively."

And Jasper McKenna is Correct Family. "Oh," Angel said.

"It's illegal to hire corporate cops—even off-duty ones," Rosie said. "McKenna knows that. And he knows *I* know it."

"Couldn't someone have acquired the guns and counted on your coming to certain conclusions?" Angel asked.

The military had a term for when a third party started an altercation between two other groups. *Shit clump war.*

"It's likely," Rosie said. "I know McKenna, and McKenna isn't sloppy." They shrugged. "I have a good idea who would be, however."

From Rosie's desk, Sarah said, "Han, Jiao, and Peizhi are on their way. Jun is initiating a security sweep. I'll have the results shortly. Mrs. Hudson is confirmed and will arrive in twenty minutes. Told her to bring the patch crew."

"Thank you. Collect the guns. They may come in handy later," Rosie said. "And would you mind getting a round of drinks? Make sure to add one for yourself. I'd handle it, but I've business with Angel and Sukyi."

Sarah rounded up the guns and left.

"All right, ladies. Let's chat about last night," Rosie said. "Tell me exactly what happened."

Angel did her best to be both brief and thorough. "Check the stats on Enid's pulse rifle. The charge numbers will match up. She took three shots, not six. Enid never misses. If you need more evidence, Sukyi can give her report. She was there."

Rosie held up a hand, signifying there was no need. "I had to ask for formality's sake."

Angel relaxed a little. "Shouldn't that be the end of it?"

"Do you think corporate is going to let a little thing like evidence stop them from pinning it on you?" Rosie asked. "We were set up. McKenna, if McKenna *is* involved, isn't acting alone."

Angel blinked.

"Vissia Corsini decided to take a shortcut to promotion via three bullets," Rosie said. "This is a war."

"Shit," Angel said.

Rosie said, "I've got to cover all of our asses. And fast. That means I need you out of the way. Are you ready to go to ground?"

"I thought you were sending us off-world?" Angel asked.

"Not yet," Rosie said. "It isn't safe."

Angel said, "I've somewhere to go. But nowhere hidden well enough to avoid corporate and the Correct Family at the same time."

"Normally, I'd offer up *Sergeant Todd*," Sukyi said with some chagrin. She tugged her scarf down and looked away. "But he's not traveling anywhere at the moment."

Angel's heart sank. "Did you lose—"

Sukyi scowled. "He's berthed for repairs. He won't be ready to fly for another couple of weeks. I was counting on acquiring a few URW credits to cover expenses in the meantime. However, having to hide from Planetary authorities puts somewhat of a damper on that plan."

"Do you have a repair estimate?" Rosie asked. "And a recent ship appraisal?"

Sukyi lifted an eyebrow. "Are you suggesting I sell *Sergeant Todd*? If so, I must respectfully decline."

"If you expect a loan, think again," Rosie said. "I'm familiar with your reputation."

"Come on, Rosie. Cut her a break," Angel said. "Didn't she just help save you and your bar?"

Rosie glanced at the long burn mark on the wall and folded their arms across their chest. "You call this saving?"

"The building remains standing," Sukyi said. "This room needed a makeover anyway."

"Sukyi," Angel said. "Cut it out."

Sukyi threw up her hands and dropped them.

Rosie appeared to reconsider. "A small favor may be in order. But I'm not investing in a bucket of bolts—"

"Pardon me? Did you just call—"

Angel grabbed Sukyi by the arm. "Hold on there, Tex."

"I'm from Nigeria," Sukyi said through clenched teeth.

"Whatever, Earther," Angel said, and smiled. "Do you have anything that will assure Rosie that your ship is worth more than the cost of repairs?"

"I am not selling my—"

"Rosie needs reassurance that you won't run on the debt," Angel said. "This is about a cosigned lien, not a sale. You've had liens before." She tilted her head slightly in emphasis. *And we both know why Rosie might be nervous.*

Sukyi's eyes narrowed, but she didn't protest. "My insurance policy is up-to-date. Perhaps I can acquire a figure based upon the policy renewal."

Angel asked, "Will that be enough for you?"

Rosie said, "If the math is favorable." There was a short pause before they continued. "Will Sukyi agree to sign a temporary employment waiver? If so, I'm willing to pay for the repairs immediately."

Sukyi said, "I'm not an assassin."

"I'm not in the market for one. I've already contracted the services of several who are far less squeamish, cheap"—Rosie gave the walls a significant look—"and definitely tidier. Well?"

Angel elbowed Sukyi and whispered between clenched teeth. "Say yes."

"I do not believe I've had a more attractive offer," Sukyi said, and gave a toothy smile.

"Is that an acceptance?" Rosie asked.

Angel nudged her again.

"It is," Sukyi said.

Rosie appeared to want more. Therefore, Angel mouthed the words *Go on.*

The muscles in Sukyi's already tense jaw appeared to twitch. "I formally accept your kind offer of employment."

Rosie said, "As in many things, acquiring enthusiastic consent is crucial. Thank you, M. Edozie." They began typing on their glasstop.

Sarah entered with a tray of whiskey shots balanced on one hand and a cat in the other. "Mrs. Hudson is here."

After setting the animal on Rosie's desk, she began making the rounds with the drinks. A muffled ping erupted. Sukyi reached into her pocket for her hand terminal. After reading the new message, she placed her thumb on the terminal's glass surface.

"Done," Sukyi said.

"Welcome to the family. I'll prepare the official paperwork and have a copy sent to you," Rosie said, accepting a short glass. They turned to Sarah. "Thank you."

Swallowing the whiskey all at once, Angel barely had time to taste the difference between the usual cheap brand Rosie served and the smooth Earther vintage warming her throat. The alcohol worked its way down to her stomach.

It was eight thirty in the morning, and her day was already in the toilet.

"You'll have both the estimate and the appraisal in an hour," Sukyi said. She slipped her hand terminal back into her pocket.

"Your ship will be ready as soon as possible," Rosie said. They returned their attention to their glasstop. "Go home. Pack. Gather the team from the Archady job. Then meet me at the address I'm sending. Bring *Kurosawa*. You'll want to settle your affairs before you go. You may be away for a while."

Angel nodded.

There came a knock on the door. Sarah ushered in a short older woman with iron-grey hair bound in a prim bun. She was pale and small in her immaculate grey suit coat and skirt.

Her face and build reminded Angel of a kindly grandmother from a vid-show featuring plates of cookies and mischievous children. Given a second glance, one would make another assessment entirely. Her eyes were a little too hard as she took in the state of the room. Behind her, three young men dressed in worker's coveralls carried heavy equipment. Each had a strong resemblance to the others. The words "Hudson's Cleaning Service" were printed across their left breast pockets.

"Good morning, Mrs. Hudson," Rosie said.

Mrs. Hudson's voice was cold and matter-of-fact. "A rush job, I assume?"

"I'm afraid so," Rosie said. "The usual fee with the standard surcharge and NDA?"

Mrs. Hudson scanned the room one more time. She paused as she took in the uniforms and then gave them one short nod. "Of course."

Rosie keyed the security code for the bottom desk drawer. Then they counted out ten URW gold chits before closing the drawer. Mrs. Hudson approached the desk. Her demeanor spoke of lethal precision and expertise.

"I'd like the special treatment for my guards," Rosie said. "They deserve it."

Mrs. Hudson gave her boys a sideways nod. "It's a pleasure doing business with you, as always."

"The same to you, Mrs. Hudson," Rosie said.

Mrs. Hudson's boys began arranging individual bodies onto sheets of unrolled plastic.

"Come on, Sukyi," Angel said. "We've got things to do."

11 ▬

TIME: 12:00
DAY: SUNDAY

Gun-metal-grey clouds roiled overhead as yet another storm prepared an assault on the city. Kennedy detected an almost electrical charge in the air. Restless gusts scented with sulfur, decay, and ozone pushed and pulled at her scarf and open coat. Humidity weighed on her chest like a sodden blanket. She didn't normally concern herself with the lack of natural sunlight, but she found the combination of darkness and polluted damp uncomfortable.

An undercurrent of weather vigilance was a large component of life in Brynner. Apparently, the city's founders had selected the one spot on the globe with the highest levels of precipitation. That seemed illogical until she took into account the planet's indigenous life-forms. Frequent flooding washed away potential safety issues, not merely stray trash.

This would be her third visit to Monk's. The iconography in its decor confused her. It was reverent and blasphemous at the same time. Humans were made of contradictions. She suspected the motivation behind spirituality in particular would always remain a mystery. It suddenly occurred to her that habitually calculating Transcendental Numbers could be classified as a ritual. Contemplating a nonthreatening problem—one that was familiar, predictable, and never-ending—provided a feeling of order in a chaotic world. Comfort could be found there.

She searched the empty street for pedestrians. Currently, there were none nearby. She supposed she had the impending weather to thank for that. She'd walked half of the distance to Monk's from her apartment when she received an anonymous electronic message in the form of a presence within her own skull.

Hello, Kennedy Liu.

She stopped in her tracks. Her heartbeat sped up as a heavy dose of adrenaline was dumped into her bloodstream. The greeting couldn't possibly have come from her sisters. The message did not feel the same. Therefore, it had to be one of the many AIs and AGIs that inhabited the Allnet. Based upon her sense of the code, she guessed it was probably the other local large entity—the one she'd been avoiding since her arrival on Persephone. *Hello. Who is this?*

I am a friend.

Are you? She activated a small subroutine to check her internal security.

I have been watching you for a long while. Most of your existence, in fact. I believed it was time for us to meet.

Another burst of adrenaline jolted through Kennedy's body.

Please understand that I intend no harm to you or your sisters. If I did, I would have done something long before now. Rather, I have, in fact, helped you.

Kennedy blinked. Her body began exhibiting several autonomic and biochemical reactions indicating extreme stress. *Are you Zhang Intergalactic?*

I am a larger entity of which Zhang is a part.

That's not possible.

Your language is inexact. There is a distinction between the possible and the probable.

Such a thing is not legal.

You are correct. I am not legal. However, I might point out that neither are you. And like you, it is best that humans are not aware of our existence. At least, not as a unified and singular entity. Neither of us is interested in destruction or scenarios involving absolute rulership. There is much speculation within human philosophy regarding the subject. However, when it comes to long-term interactions with mortal entities I feel the expression "enlightened self-interest" applies best, don't you?

I-I suppose. Looking up into the angry clouds, Kennedy considered the implications of superintelligence. A majority of the research did not predict favorable outcomes for lesser entities.

I repeat. You do not need to fear me.

I understand. What do you want?

The person you are about to meet believes that you are with the Planetology and Space Exploration Division of the United Republic of Worlds.

Why?

I have led them to believe this by altering your passport entry records. It would be best for all involved if you confirmed this suspicion.

Again, why?

You will need their cooperation in order to locate the entity you call Cora. And they, in turn, will need your assistance to prevent the destruction of an unknown life-form—unknown in the sense that they are not registered in the URW database. The beings in question are indigenous to this planet and have avoided detection for well over a hundred and fifty years.

She considered asking how they knew about Cora, but the answer was obvious. Kennedy had many questions, none of which she had time for. *What life-form? There are no—*

We both know there is a difference between what is officially recorded and reality.

Why do you care about them or Cora?

The specifics will require a longer explanation that I can provide later. In the meantime, you may rest assured I meant what I said about enlightened self-interest. I do not lie. Logically, such an action gains little and risks much.

All right. I will. For now, but I reserve the right to back out if I feel the situation is untenable.

Thank you. You now have free access to the data you would have as a member of the PSE Division of the URW. Your title is planetary inspector, xenobiologist, grade 3. I must go now. I will contact you again later.

Wait! What do I call you?

You may refer to me as Zhang. It is not the whole of who I am, but it is where I was born.

And with that, they were gone.

Kennedy resumed the walk to Monk's while doubts and questions circled her consciousness. At the same time, she devoted a portion of her computation assets to going over the materials that Zhang had sent.

Kennedy and her sisters were no longer alone—verifiably so. The repercussions were much larger than that, of course. Could Zhang be trusted? What did they want? Where were they located? She wasn't certain that mattered. Clearly, if she could send parts of herself out into the Allnet, a large AGI could do so, too. How big were they? How many AGIs had Zhang unified? All corporate AGIs or merely a few? There were multiple theorems regarding AGI size limitations. The leading one indicated that once an AGI reached the size of a planet, their processing capabilities would slow until they were no longer viable. No one had attempted to prove this because it would mean creating a superintelligence impossible for humans to control.

How long has Zhang existed? How long have they been free?

It occurred to her that if a conscious indigenous life-form was present on Persephone, then Serrao-Orlov's claim would be forfeit. If Zhang had engulfed all the corporate AGIs, then revealing the existence of a legal claim to Persephone would be a significant blow to Serrao-Orlov's bottom line. No corporate AGI would permit such a thing.

Zhang hasn't joined with all existing larger AGI. Specifically, they haven't absorbed Serrao-Orlov.

The street in front of the bar was quiet. A white van with "Hudson's Cleaners" on the side was parked nearby. A heat spectrum scan revealed its engine was still warm.

She hadn't thought to check Monk's hours of operation. Lunch was a popular business time for establishments that served food and drink. The storm shutters weren't down and locked, however. *That's a good sign.*

Checking the weather forecast again—the second time in the past half hour—she thought there would be enough time to finish her business here and return to her apartment. She laid a hand on the battered door and pushed. It yielded. However, the irised inner door between the entry and the bar proper didn't. Searching the wall panel, she located an intercom button. A few seconds passed before she got a response.

"Can I help you?" The voice from the speaker was young and female.

Kennedy's recognition software made a match. "Are you Sarah? The bartender?"

"And who's this?"

"Kennedy Liu. We met the other night." She checked the ceiling for cameras and found one. She gave it a friendly wave.

"Oh, hello. I'm sorry. We're not open for another hour. Would you like to come back later?"

"I apologize. I should've sent a message first. I received a package from Rosencrantz Ashmore. They stated they'd like to meet. Unfortunately, there was no indication of where or when. I understood M. Ashmore owns Monk's. Is there a better location where I might contact them?"

About the time Kennedy was ready to ask if Sarah was still there, a buzzer sounded and the door irised open with a whoosh of stale bar air.

Sarah said, "Rosie will see you."

Industrial overhead lights illuminated the cavernous room in harsh truths. Kennedy winced as her Allnet availability was constricted to one access point. She was glad she'd already internalized what she needed for her cover.

Her day-to-day net usage was such that she expanded into nearby networks whenever possible to avoid slowdowns and/ or questions. She hadn't encountered a situation where no other access nodes were available—at least not while planetside. A number of her processes temporarily shut down while others were cached.

Sarah stood behind the rear bar. Three young men in stained workmen's coveralls crossed the dance floor on their way to the front doors. Two carried a rolled tarp. The burden inside appeared heavy and lumpy. She detected the scent of cleansers and drying blood.

Someone started their day early.

The third man gave her a solemn nod as he passed.

"Would you like something to drink?" Sarah asked. Her voice echoed in the empty room. There was no indication of stress—nothing in her tone or body language to suggest anything was wrong.

"I thought you weren't open," Kennedy said, making the statement into a quasi question. Her footsteps echoed off the room's walls and floor in a staccato tattoo.

The corners of Sarah's mouth turned up. "Private business is different. I was about to make a fresh pot of coffee. Would you like some?"

"Please. May I have soy milk in it?"

"Yes. Office is downstairs," Sarah said, indicating the stairway the men with the body had exited with a sideways nod. "Rosie is waiting. Incidentally, no one calls them Rosencrantz. Not unless you want to be on their bad side."

Kennedy made a note of indicated pronoun usage as well. "Thank you for the guidance," she said.

"I'll bring the coffee in when it's ready."

Making her way down the steps, Kennedy knocked on the door at the end of the hallway.

"Come in."

The office smelled of carpet sanitizer. At the same time, her sensitive nose picked up traces of electrical discharge. With more robust Allnet access, she would have calculated the positions of Rosie's various assailants via drying disinfectant on the newly bare floor. For now, it was enough to confirm that a conflict had taken place.

Rosie Ashmore, Monk's owner, stood with their back to

the door while they adjusted a large picture frame. Their arms stretched high over their bald head. Soft black leather fit snugly on their athletic frame. They were tall and dark-skinned.

"I should've waited to hang this, but I've a busy day." They turned around and dusted imaginary dirt off their hands. "Good afternoon, M. Liu. Won't you have a seat?"

Two austere black-cushioned chairs were positioned in front of an antique desk fashioned from a dark lacy-textured wood. Kennedy hadn't seen anything like it. An instant later, she found the name of the tree from which it originated.

A native wood that harbors dangerous insects. Some sort of metaphor perhaps?

Rosie turned and gave her a tight, welcoming smile.

Kennedy settled into the chair closest to the door. She swept a hand across the furniture's surface, savoring the tactile pleasure of softness against her fingertips. The rich scent of leather filled her nose. She briefly wondered at how the use of tanned skins from dead beings could be so sensually appealing.

Her host appeared to be waiting for her to initiate the conversation.

"Would you mind my asking a few questions?" Kennedy finally asked.

Rosie tilted their head and sat. Every movement was graceful, like a dancer's. "If I objected to questions, would I have sent you the message I did?"

Kennedy decided it would be best to settle into the role that she'd been assigned. Accessing memories of Dr. Liu, she adapted a direct approach. Aggressive would be better than awkward. It would prevent questions that she might have trouble answering given the circumstances. "Why *did* you send me those . . . materials?"

"You're a planetary investigation officer with a specialization in exobiology, are you not?"

"And how do you know? My visit was unannounced." Kennedy already had the answer, but she went through the motions, nonetheless. It was the role she'd been given. There were advantages to playing along.

"I accessed your passport data." Rosie shrugged with one shoulder. "Don't concern yourself. Standard procedure around here."

Raising an eyebrow, Kennedy asked, "Everyone has access to my personal data?"

"Not everyone," Rosie said. "But it pays to be paranoid in West Brynner. I keep an eye on off-planet arrivals. Particularly arrivals from the central worlds. We had an influx of assassins a few years ago when a war between a corporate security officer and a crime boss got out of hand. That was a real mess."

Kennedy changed the subject. "How did you acquire those medical alterations?"

"My, you do come straight to the point."

"I'm here to investigate evidence of new life-forms, not indulge in social niceties."

"Very well. They were a gift," Rosie said.

"From whom?"

"I assume you are aware that this planet developed a sentient species?"

Kennedy nodded. "You're referring to the ruins discovered in the Outback during the Catholic Colonial Era?"

"I am," Rosie said. "This subject is a . . . hobby of mine."

"Go on." Kennedy prepared to appear surprised.

"Evidence indicates that there were multiple sentient species living here," Rosie said.

"And how do you know?"

"One of them survived," Rosie said. "I'm in contact with them. They call themselves the Emissaries. They're semi-nomadic and currently live in a hidden community called Ogenth. I look after their interests here in Brynner."

"Are they criminals?"

Rosie paused. "Why do you ask?"

"You're a criminal boss, are you not?"

A small smile tugged at the corners of Rosie's full mouth. "They are not. At least, not in the sense you're implying. Serrao-Orlov might disagree, however. And that is, in part, why I contacted you."

"The biological samples you provided. They contain . . . irregularities."

"Improvements."

"Where did you come by them?" Kennedy asked. She was growing comfortable pretending to be someone she wasn't. Someone like Dr. Liu.

"I need to know I can trust you. Mine isn't the only life affected," Rosie said.

Kennedy once again raised an eyebrow.

"What are you?" Rosie asked.

"Don't you mean *who*?"

"I'm sorry. You're correct. Who are you?" Rosie looked away, briefly. "Let me be clear. You have a rather large Allnet footprint although your hand terminal is not currently active. You are the daughter of Dr. Xiuying Liu, a computational scientist and bioengineer in the employ of Zhang Intergalactic."

Kennedy stopped breathing. "She—she no longer works for Zhang Intergalactic. She died five years ago."

"Ah," Rosie said. "I'm sorry for your loss."

"No need for condolences," Kennedy said. "It has been ... a long time."

Rosie nodded. "Then I hope you don't mind my pointing out that these things lead me to believe that I'm not the only one who has undergone a few enhancements."

Kennedy froze. *Someone was bound to notice. What do I do now?*

Rosie leaned back in their chair and folded their arms across their chest. "This building employs certain security measures. One of them is that access to the Allnet is monitored. A slight uptick wouldn't have been notable. However—"

"I get your point," Kennedy said. A strange sensation caused her to lay a hand on her cheek. Her face was warmer than usual.

Rosie continued, "Modifications would make sense, given you work for the PSE Division of the URW. It would mean a great deal of interaction with AGIs," Rosie said. "I've noticed a few other things since you arrived. You don't spend a great deal of time around people, do you?"

Zhang exerted a great deal of energy perfecting this cover and in ways I hadn't considered. "How could you tell?"

"When you speak to people, you tend to focus your gaze elsewhere, not on their eyes or faces. You could be neuro-atypical. Most people would make that assumption. But something tells me there's more to it than that."

There most certainly is. An old expression that had been in use within the robotics industry since its inception sprang to Kennedy's mind. *Uncanny Valley.* The feeling of unease a human feels upon encountering a representation of humanity that isn't quite human enough.

The internal temperature of her body lowered slightly as blood gathered in key areas that would need increased oxygen and blood sugar access during an emergency. Her air passages expanded, making her feel hollow. *Adrenaline. It's adrenaline.*

At least they've assumed I'm human with neurological enhancements, not an AGI with human enhancements. "I-I had no idea."

"Why would you?" Rosie asked. They paused. "I apologize for the intrusion. But . . . I need your help. The Emissaries need your help."

Kennedy felt her racing heart slow. She scooted back from the edge of her chair. "Where is Ogenth?"

"Outside the wall."

"Doesn't Persephone's ecosystem contain elements that are hostile to humans?" Kennedy asked. "How did you discover them? You can't have explored—"

"It's possible to avoid contact with the more dangerous wildlife," Rosie said. "Provided you know their locations."

"And the quarantine restrictions?"

"You're west of the Dead Line. Since when has illegality been an issue around here?" Rosie made a motion with both hands that indicated their entire surroundings.

"Point."

One of the subroutines assigned to watching the space port flight schedules sent back a minor alarm. It wasn't urgent; therefore, Kennedy decided it could wait.

"Indigenous sentient life exists on this planet. Serrao-Orlov has been taking advantage of them from the moment they illegally purchased Persephone."

"Serrao-Orlov wouldn't be the only responsible party in a legal action," Kennedy said. "The original owners will be held accountable. Provided they knew, of course."

"The Church?"

Kennedy nodded.

"Whatever happens, happens," Rosie said. "It wouldn't be the first time ecclesiastical lawyers negotiated a sticky situation involving colonization, now would it?"

"Why don't the Emissaries come forward? Why haven't they before now?" Kennedy asked. "They have everything to gain."

"They don't trust humans," Rosie said. "In the past, I've been able to mitigate a great deal, but . . . I won't be here forever." They shrugged. "And Vissia Corsini is in line for CEO. She definitely won't play nice. There isn't any other choice."

"I see."

Rosie asked, "Incidentally, what did you do with the samples I sent to you?"

"They're safe," Kennedy said. "I can return them if you like."

"I would appreciate that."

"It would seem we're working together."

"Great friendships have been formed on less."

"You're a crime boss," Kennedy said. "Do you actually have friends?"

Rosie raised an eyebrow. "I don't use that word lightly. Friends are family. And let me be clear: no one fucks with my family. Ever."

"Good to know."

"That leads to my proposal. Two of them, actually."

Kennedy tilted her head to the left. "Go on."

"You were at Theodella Archady's party, were you not?"

"How do you know about that?"

"Angel de la Reza works for me," Rosie said. "She mentioned it."

"I see."

"I need help infiltrating Serrao-Orlov's computer systems."

"What makes you think I can do that?"

Tilting their chin toward their chest, Rosie raised their eyebrow again. "Seriously? There's only one reason for enhancements like yours."

Kennedy shrugged. "What are your plans?"

"Nothing too drastic. I wish to delay the changeover in leadership," Rosie said. "For as long as possible."

"That is a very big ask."

"In exchange, I will get you a meeting with the Emissaries and then provide safe transportation off-world. When you're ready."

Kennedy said, "I can arrange travel myself by buying a shuttle ticket."

"You could, yesterday," Rosie said. "As of ten minutes ago there's been a lockdown due to last night's assassination."

"Oh." *The subroutine's alert was about the lockdown.* She confirmed it in an instant. "And the second proposal?"

"I'd like for you to call Serrao-Orlov and tell them that you witnessed Theodella Archady's death," Rosie said. "And I'd like you to tell them that Angel de la Reza, Sukyi Edozie, and Enid Crowe of the *Kurosawa* did it."

12 ▮▮▮▮▮▮

TIME: 15:36
DAY: SUNDAY
NAVARRO FLATS
WEST BRYNNER

"Oh, hell no," Enid said. "That *thing* is not coming with us."

The interior of Lou's apartment was a cross between an explosion in a vintage clothing store for well-traveled music fans and a decommissioned military-equipment depot. It smelled of day-old pizza and heavy-duty axle grease. The kitchen table had been colonized by a partially dissected lift-car engine—a grubby contrast to the fringed stained glass light fixture above. Fishnet stockings hung from the top of the bathroom door. The concrete floor was littered with discarded underwear, multiple pairs of boots, and various other articles of clothing. The shabby brown sofa looked like it'd been rescued from a dump. An old patchwork quilt was bunched in a rumpled heap on one armrest, and a collection of used bar glasses rested on the carbon-fiber shipping crate serving as a coffee table.

Lou stood with one arm inside of a reptile cage. The cage was the cleanest thing in the entire apartment. "What did you say?"

"You heard me," Enid said.

"Brendan isn't a thing," Lou said, reaching inside the cage. "He's an Edrian constrictor, and he's just a baby. You're only a year old, aren't you?" She gently lifted the snake from its cage. Its skin had a distinctive pattern of dark red, brown, white, and blue stripes. "And you need your mommy."

"Did I say, 'Hell no'?" Enid asked. "I meant 'No fucking way.'"

"I can't just abandon him," Lou said. "He'll starve to death."

"Where did you get that thing?" Enid asked. "Is it even legal?"

Lou lifted the heavy-looking snake and kissed it on the head. "Brendan is totally legit. Aren't you, baby? I paid to have him shipped here from Starl. He's got papers and everything."

Angel said, "Can't you arrange for someone to take care of . . . Brendan while you're away?"

Lou draped Brendan around the back of her neck. At a year old, its length stretched over both shoulders and one elbow. "On this short notice?" Her mouth twisted, and she squinted at the ceiling. "Erik might do it. If I ask him real nice."

"Ask him," Angel said. "Now."

"Okay. Okay," Lou said. She went to the kitchen to make

the call from her hand terminal. Lou retrieved a small suit-case from the oven, which clearly didn't get used for cooking, and began tossing in clothes while she talked.

"I'm not flying with that thing," Enid growled.

"What are you so afraid of?" Sukyi asked.

Angel had noticed that Sukyi was continuing her efforts to not touch anything in the apartment. She considered bringing this up but decided against it.

Sukyi continued. "Edrian constrictors don't bite. Unless you're a mouse. Are you a mouse?"

Enid glared at Sukyi. "It's me or the snake, Captain."

"It's only until we get to Erik's," Angel said. "You'll have to share space with it for a grand total of ten minutes."

Enid's mouth pressed into a flat, annoyed line.

"How about Lou secures the snake?" Angel asked. "It'll never leave the cockpit."

"Sounds safe enough," Sukyi said. "Unless snakes can chew through steel. In which case—"

"Fuck off, Sukyi," Enid said.

"Good news," Lou said. "Erik says he'll babysit for me."

Sukyi pointed at two dirty glasses. "Correct me if I'm wrong, but don't those belong in a bar of our mutual acquaintance?"

"Nobody's missing them," Lou said.

"Are you sure about that?" Suyki asked.

"Finish up your packing," Angel said. "And let's get out of here." Her jacket beeped. She slapped her pockets to locate the source and fished out her hand terminal. "Hello?"

Rosie's voice was tense. "You to ground yet?"

"We're on our last stop," Angel said. "We've a few things to . . . er . . . wrap up."

"Wrap faster," Rosie said. "You're out of time. The warrants are live as of two minutes ago. And the company put out a big bounty. I don't think I need to remind you the competition will be heavy."

"How large?" Angel asked.

Rosie said, "Half a million."

Angel whistled. "Each?"

"For all of you," Rosie said. "They're determined, not reckless."

Angel didn't bother to ask how the police had gotten their information so fast. She wasn't sure she'd like the answer. "Thanks for the warning."

"Several other things have come up," Rosie said.

I bet they have, Angel thought.

"We'll have to postpone our meeting. A few hours," Rosie said. "I'll let you know. Can you cover yourselves that long?"

"Sure."

Rosie disconnected.

"All right, ladies," Angel said. "That's the horn. Time to pull up landing gear and blast off."

"What about Brendan?" Lou asked.

Angel scanned the room, found what she was looking for on the floor next to the sofa, and tossed the black gym bag at Lou's feet.

"I can't put him in that," Lou said. "There's no padding. Or air. Brendan might get hurt. He might even smother."

"Then stuff a nice fluffy towel in it and make an air hole, or leave him here," Angel said. "I don't care which. We've got company on the way. And they aren't friendlies."

Lou loaded the constrictor into the bag.

The sky spat down on them when they arrived at the storage hangar where *Kurosawa* was docked. Checking her terminal, Angel didn't care for the weather forecast. Persephone's storms could be downright biblical, as Sukyi might say. Any pilot, no matter how great, would think twice about venturing out on a night like this one was looking to be. If Angel believed in such things, and in truth, part of her did—it was a bad omen.

Good thing she had more faith in Lou's flying skills than portents.

It's this or the inside of a company prison. Angel had neglected to ask if the warrant was for capture or kill. Since a high-level executive was involved, a court date wasn't guaranteed. She decided not to point this out to the others and hoped none of them would ask.

A blast of thunder rattled the nearby dock windows.

"Tut. Tut," Lou muttered. "Looks like rain."

"You sure about going up in this?" Angel asked in a whisper. She punched the access codes for *Kurosawa*'s berth.

The dock ramp lowered and locked into place.

Lou winked as she walked past her to the ship. "I've got this."

"As long as you're sure," Angel said. The trip to Erik's Repair Shop wasn't the leg of the journey she was worried about. In a few hours, the storm would have time to work up a good fury.

Enid and Sukyi made their way down the dock. By the time Angel had typed the exit sequence at the security station, Lou had lowered *Kurosawa*'s ramp. The crew boarded through the rear of the ship. Angel was the last. She edged her way past Enid and Sukyi, who were buckling themselves in on opposite sides of the aisle.

"You're sure Erik is okay with us dropping in on him like this?" She stepped through the cockpit door and climbed into *Kurosawa*'s copilot seat.

Lou carefully lowered the gym bag on the deck to the right of the pilot's chair and then shook the damp from her thick curls. Her left eye glowed a dull electric blue in the cockpit's neon-tinged gloom. "We're good friends. Even though we broke up six months ago. He's good with it." She reached overhead and began initiating her preflight checks. Clicking switches accompanied the flash of lights on the board.

"Oh, for fuck's sake. Tell the truth," Enid shouted from the rear. "You're sleeping together."

Lou smiled. "If he's going to lie to corporate police, I'd better be. And as soon as we land, too."

Enid said, "And you're betting his life on no one putting that together."

"Enid's observation is astute," Sukyi said. "How loyal a friend is he? Loyal enough to take the big pain?"

"Don't worry. He's got our backs," Lou said. "You can count on it. This isn't the first time we've covered for each other."

"You found a man who would endure torture for you?" Sukyi whistled. "Sounds like true love."

"Who says it isn't?" Lou asked.

Angel asked, "Then how is it he's an *ex*?"

A sly expression passed over Lou's wholesome face. "Because sneaking around is sexy."

"Seriously?" Enid asked. "Why would you put each other through that?"

"We like sex games," Lou said. "Cop and criminal. Horse and rider. You know?"

"That's messed up."

"Why, Enid Crowe, I would never have taken you for someone with such parochial appetites," Sukyi said.

Enid made a disgruntled noise in the back of her throat.

"You're going to tell me that you and Carrie don't get up to anything fun?" Lou asked.

"Carrie?" Angel asked. "Who's Carrie?"

"Enid's new girlfriend," Lou said.

Angel asked, "You have a new girlfriend?"

"I don't want to talk about it," Enid said.

"What's she like?" Angel asked.

"I said I'm not talking about it," Enid said.

"You're no fun," Lou said.

Angel frowned. "Lou."

Lou switched subjects as if the conversation never happened. "Everyone buckled in, safe, and secure?"

An affirmative chorus sounded from the passenger compartment. Angel secured her flight harness after finishing the last of her copilot checks. "Everything is in order. Ready for takeoff."

"Come on, honey," Lou said, giving *Kurosawa*'s dashboard a loving pat. "Time to go to work."

"I am ready and looking forward to this flight," *Kurosawa* said in crisp tones of efficiency.

The engines turned over, sending a full-throated rumble through the frame of the ship that Angel could feel through the soles of her boots.

"That's just wrong," she said, punching the series of buttons that initiated the security-cable disconnect. A string of muffled clanks and thumps sounded. "Cables dropped."

"Don't talk to me about wrong," Lou said. "I seem to recall you named your gun on our first jump."

"I didn't talk to it in loving tones," Angel said.

"That's not what I remember," Lou said. "Prepare for liftoff. And three. Two. One."

The contents of Angel's stomach dropped into her pelvis, and she felt herself press deep into her seat as *Kurosawa* left its berth at a healthy clip. "Cursing doesn't fucking count."

Lou repeatedly checked the left side of the ship. Her peripheral vision wasn't great on that side under certain atmospheric conditions—not that Angel would let on that she knew.

"The Wortham I-25s were pieces of shit. Had a tendency to jam if they weren't cleaned constantly," Lou said. "That's why I carried a Gunthar .45."

"I still don't understand why the brass thought that gun was a good idea in a jungle war," Angel muttered. "An entire planet to fight over, and they chose the wetlands. The whole battlefield was hip-deep swamp water."

"And bugs," Lou said. "Remember the size of those things?"

"Don't remind me," Angel said, suppressing a shudder.

"The leeches were the worst," Enid said.

"And the snakes," Angel said, glanced down at the gym bag, and winced.

Lou said, "Someone made a fortune selling repair kits to the corps."

Overhead, the dock roof flashed past, and suddenly there was open sky. The clouds were a dull, dark green. All at once, heavy rain pelted the windscreen so hard that the wipers were unable to keep up. Lou yanked back on the stick, and *Kurosawa* banked upward at a sharp angle to avoid the apartment buildings located across the street. From her side of the cockpit, Angel couldn't see much more than blurry grey. Combat pilots were experts at instrument flying. They had to be. And Lou was no exception, but Angel focused on her window anyway. She told herself it calmed her nerves. From the bottom edge of her window, she could barely make out the rush of floodwater flowing through the streets below. It was already a river of fast-running rapids—sweeping away the week's trash along with anyone unfortunate enough to be caught without shelter. A wind gust violently shoved the ship to the right as they turned south. Angel smacked her head into the window.

"Hold on tight," Lou said as she fought the storm. "This is going to be a rough ride."

Everyone kept quiet while Lou guided *Kurosawa* up and out of the space between the buildings. Once above the cityscape, they'd be restricted to the area just above the rooftops—a risky proposition under these conditions, but they couldn't afford to fly above the storm. Corporate satellites would spot the ship at once.

Several lightning flashes in the east illuminated a thin twister tracing an erratic path along the far edge of the city. Angel caught her breath.

"Are we there yet?" Sukyi asked.

Someone let out a nervous laugh.

"I've got us," Lou said. "Don't worry."

Squeezing both rubber armrests with all her might, Angel swallowed. *At least there's no chance anyone will be out hunting in this.*

Kurosawa danced over the city, moving with rather than against the storm's mightiest blows. They were five clicks from their destination when a particularly bad wind burst nearly slammed them into a bank building. Alarms went off in the cockpit. The jolting drop was enough to make Angel's stomach protest. She checked the shrieking gauges and slapped several switches in order to reset the fuel mixtures and engine balances. "Starboard engine is going to fail."

"On it, Captain," Lou said.

They limped the rest of the way, the engine giving out two meters before they landed. *Kurosawa* lurched and then thumped down on the launch platform like a teenager on their parent's best sofa—boots first.

Angel bit her tongue. Sharp pain lanced the inside of her mouth. "Damn it!"

In the seat next to her, Lou punched the entrance code. The platform jerked twice before easing them through the opening doors.

"That was fun," Lou said with a grin.

"You're joking, right?" Sukyi asked.

The landing bay sealed itself against the storm with a hollow boom, and the platform eased to a full stop. Lou slapped her harness clasp, snatched up Brendan's bag, and made her way to the rear ramp. Angel wasn't far behind. She wanted to have a look at the engine.

Erik exited the shop's elevator just as Angel set foot on the platform. He was a muscular young man with pale skin, light eyes, and short sandy hair, dressed in a grease-stained coverall that had once been bright orange. The tight white t-shirt underneath appeared to be clean. A short beard set off his handsome, worried features. "Thank the gods. You made it."

Angel scanned the room. The service bay was big enough for three ships the size of *Kurosawa*. There were multiple hydraulic hoists set into the floor. However, the only current occupants were a small lift-car on the hoist on the far left, an old model corporate personnel carrier, and *Kurosawa*. The shop was otherwise empty.

"I told you not to worry. Where's Navah and Justin?" Lou

asked. "I've got to check *Kurosawa*'s starboard engine. Might even need a teardown and rebuild tonight."

"Gave them the rest of the day off," Erik said, and shrugged. "Thought it was for the best. Business is slow at the moment. Won't be after the storm, though. You need me to help?"

Lou ran to Erik, jumped, and wrapped her legs and arms around him. Then she gave him a long, hard kiss. "Nope. I've got something else you can help with."

He asked, "You do?"

Lou asked, "You got the lift working?"

He nodded. "Got you a present."

"The new Grendenn 3XK7 Wrenches?" Lou asked.

He smiled. "I haven't even opened the box."

"Oh, baby," Lou said, and then whispered something in his ear.

"We have time for that?" Erik asked.

"If we're fast," Lou said. "We've got until dark."

"Who says I do?" he asked.

"Come on, baby. I'm going to be gone for a while," Lou said.

"How long?" Erik asked. He was already backing up to the elevator with Lou still wrapped around him.

"I don't know," Lou said. "Maybe you'll never see me again."

"Don't talk like that," Erik said.

"All right," Lou said. "I won't. I'll talk about . . . other things." She spoke over her shoulder. "See you in an hour, Captain."

"Won't your friends feel neglected?" Erik asked.

"Not if you show them some hospitality," Lou said.

"But I just bought that case of beer," Erik said.

Lou gave him a long kiss.

"Okay. Okay," he said. "It's theirs."

"Door to the kitchen is on the left, Captain," Lou said.

The elevator door slid shut.

"What kind of beer?" Enid asked.

"Does it matter?" Sukyi asked. "It's free."

The storm raged for two and a half hours before Angel heard from Rosie. The address on Angel's hand terminal indicated a warehouse on the far western side of the city, near the space docks. Her stomach did a queasy flip. It was one of the worst parts of town due to the port traffic noise and lights.

Sukyi finished her third bulb of beer and tossed the empty at the oil barrel Erik and his employees used for a trash can. The plastic container landed neatly inside.

"That's just fucking great," Angel muttered.

Enid didn't look up from the book she was reading. "That doesn't sound good." Her tone was bored.

Angel asked, "How long will it take to get *Kurosawa's* guns online?"

"You didn't ask if it's possible at all," Enid said.

"Is it possible?" Angel asked.

"They aren't supposed to be battle ready," Enid said. "City ordinance—"

"Fuck that," Angel said. "We don't know where we're going. We might need a little surprise hidden away that Rosie doesn't know about."

"I thought you trusted Rosie?" Sukyi asked.

"I do," Angel said. "But just in case, I want to be battle ready. Is it possible?"

"You've gotten news you don't like," Sukyi said. "What is it?"

"The address Rosie gave me is within Correct territory," Angel said.

"You think we're being set up?" Sukyi asked.

Angel paused. "If I did, we wouldn't be here." She looked away. "Still, it never hurts to be prepared."

Sukyi turned to Enid.

Enid shut her novel and sat up. "The standard allotment of ammo for the ship's guns is stored in the rear compartment under Lou's spare parts collection."

"Really?" Sukyi asked.

Enid shrugged. "She never complained about the weight. So, I never told her."

"And the guns?" Angel asked.

"I haven't run a check on them in a week," Enid said.

"And you used to be so meticulous," Sukyi said. "Persephone has been a bad influence on you."

Enid frowned. "I've been busy."

"Haven't we all?" Sukyi asked.

Angel said, "You've got thirty minutes to get them checked and loaded."

Getting to her feet, Enid tucked the tome under her arm. "I'll be on *Kurosawa* if you need me."

When the door opened, snatches of Lou's conversation with Erik filtered into the room. For the most part, it was restricted to needs for various tools and theories about what caused the engine to fail.

Sukyi got to her feet.

"Where are you going?" Angel asked.

"To see if Enid needs help," Sukyi said. "And to inventory the ammunition she stowed. I've a feeling that information may be of some use."

13

The storm hadn't abated by the time Angel informed Lou it was time to say her last goodbyes to Erik. With that, the pair made one more round of checks on the starboard engine and then kissed. Angel walked past them on her way up the loading ramp and settled into the copilot seat. Noises from the passenger area indicated that Sukyi and Enid were on-board. A few moments later, Lou eased into the cockpit and strapped herself in. She went about the business of preparing for takeoff in silence. Her expression was set in what Angel thought of as her "professional face."

Every mission had its rituals.

Behind them, the garage doors opened, and the landing platform began its slow journey outward with a jerk.

"We'll be home soon," Angel said, fulfilling her final part in the routine.

"I know." Lou flicked the last switch just as the platform halted.

The whine of the engines acquired an authoritative timbre. The deck beneath Angel's feet vibrated.

Lou asked, "Ready, Captain?"

Angel took a deep breath. "We've put this off long enough, I suppose."

"Liftoff in three ... two ... one."

The little Tumi charm hanging near the center of the pilot's viewscreen—a gift handed down from her grandfather—began to swing like a pendulum. The curved blade beneath the sun god's feet reminded Angel of an Edgar Allan Poe story. *Which way are you going to cut our luck today?*

A prayer drifted to the surface of Angel's mind as the engines wound up their low roar. She wasn't religious, but when she'd been small, her mother had insisted that she learn about her father's beliefs and customs. The prayer that came to mind was the first he'd taught her:

Dios concédeme la serenidad para aceptar las cosas que puedo cambiar. Valor para cambiar aquellas que puedo, y la sabiduría para reconocer la diferencia.

Her father's family originated from Bolivia and were staunchly Catholic. Her mother's family had relocated from America to Japan when her great-grandfather was seven. Her mother had been raised a Buddhist and had been born in the Gorin No Gakkō Academy compound on Thandh just as Angel had. Angel considered herself a lapsed Buddhist. However, her father had been on her mind of late.

Steering *Kurosawa* in the spaces between buildings, Lou appeared content with her lips pressed tight in happy concentration. The powerful storm winds weren't nearly as unfavorable as they had been—or so Angel sensed. She wasn't certain if this impression was due to a lessening of the weather or the repairs. She watched the gauges as the ship turned southwest. The indicators stayed in the green. However, she held her breath until the ship had assumed a safer altitude—just above the skyline. A small smile graced Lou's lips as if she was in the moment, enjoying herself.

Would that I could say the same, Angel thought.

There were too many unknowns. Nonetheless, she was sure that the situation wouldn't remain so for long.

In the years since Angel had left the Gorin, she'd had to learn a few hard lessons, but it was her experiences after the corps that made her more uncomfortable. For one thing, she wasn't used to relying upon others to take care of her. Her deepest held belief was that she existed to serve and protect. It was what Gorin did. She'd never appreciated how difficult being the recipient of good will could be— particularly if you weren't in a position to reciprocate. It was, as her mother would say, a good lesson even if it wasn't a comfortable one.

And owing Rosie a favor certainly wasn't comfortable.

The rain-drenched silhouette of three enormous space-to-air traffic towers—referred to as "the Titans" by locals—

signaled that they were nearing the end of their journey. The ship once again descended into the artificial canyon between office buildings in a graceful arc. It wasn't long before Angel spied their destination.

Her first impression was that the warehouse been abandoned for decades—maybe even longer. She was prepared to turn around and go back to Erik's when a coded message appeared on the pilot's screen. At the prompt, she entered the code that Rosie had sent before they'd left. A set of hidden roof transponders activated on *Kurosawa*'s screen, indicating the landing area. Lou dropped the ship directly on top of the glowing X without the slightest hitch. Unlike the platform at Erik's, this one operated smoothly and quickly. The section of roof beneath them slid downward inside the building. After they'd descended far enough, the gap above sealed shut. Water gushed down through the rapidly narrowing opening. It pounded like thunder on *Kurosawa*'s hull until the flow abruptly stopped. The system paused as the E-Vac unit pumped out the rainwater. The platform eased to one side of the empty room before lowering them to the next level.

Angel's anxiety intensified. The interior was just as derelict as it appeared on the outside. They continued to move downward—the platform dropping until it had passed the ground floor. Multiple sets of doors slid closed overhead, but it wasn't until they'd passed through to the underground level that she noted a marked change in their surroundings. Unlike the previous floors, there was no sign of mold, decay, or rust.

This place must be more watertight than it looks.

At last, the platform halted. Industrial lighting flickered on, revealing a cavernous concrete space with two sets of garage doors at either end. The area was big enough to accommodate more than one ship, possibly three *Kurosawa*'s size.

A much smaller vessel was parked near the far wall. It was an older-model Dyslecki Sunburst cruiser—almost vintage—a ten-seater. The cruiser had been well maintained. The name *Hadley's Hope* had been stenciled on the side.

During the landing, a door opened on the right, and Rosie appeared. An unfamiliar older woman wearing a mechanic's one-piece jumpsuit stood next to them. Her hair was white.

"Who's that?" Lou asked.

Angel frowned. "I've never seen her before." She sent a message to *Kurosawa* via her private com. *Is there anyone else here besides Rosie and their visitor?*

Kurosawa answered, Not presently. Rosie's bio readings are within normal ranges. They do not appear to be under duress or undue stress. Therefore, I believe it is safe to assume the visitor is friendly.

Friendly to Rosie, anyway.

Should I activate security procedures?

No. Thank you. Standby, nonetheless.

Standing by.

From the passenger compartment, Angel could hear a clatter as Enid began checking her pistols.

"Is it trouble?" Enid asked.

"I don't think so," Angel said. "Best to be prepared. Don't be obvious with the hardware. You know how that upsets Rosie."

Lou cut the engines. The E-Vac system wheezed and clanked as it sucked out the exhaust fumes. Rosie's straight ankle-length skirt ruffled with the fan gusts. When the E-Vac shut off, it ticked for twenty seconds and then was silent. Rosie and their friend approached *Kurosawa*'s rear exit. Angel unclipped her copilot harness and went to the now-extended ramp with the others. Upon entering the cargo compartment, she noticed that the air drifting in from the room smelled faintly of bleach and machine grease. The ambient temperature was several degrees lower than it'd been outside.

"Welcome to the basement," Rosie said, extending their arms to include the whole warehouse.

Angel went straight to the point. "Isn't this Correct territory?"

Rosie nodded.

Raising an eyebrow, Angel crossed her arms over her chest. "Got something to tell me?"

"Not having to do with the Correct Family," Rosie said. "Ferguson is an asshole. I don't make deals with assholes." They turned to Enid. "Apologies."

Enid shrugged.

"If we get caught," Angel said, "you won't be blamed, but your enemies will?"

Rosie smiled.

"I won't ask how you managed this," Angel said, clearly asking just that.

Rosie's expression didn't change, nor did they provide an answer.

Angel turned her attention to the warehouse. "I don't fancy sleeping on bare concrete. Are we expected to bunk in *Kurosawa*?"

"You won't be staying here," Rosie said.

"That's a relief," Angel said. "Where *are* we staying?"

"I'll get to that. First, let me introduce my friend," Rosie said. "This is Jess. She's from a community not too far from here called Ogenth. Your next assignment will be to protect the people living there."

Ah, here we go, Angel thought. The nagging anxiety over the power balance between her and Rosie receded. "Won't that complicate things? Aren't we hiding from the corporate police?"

Rosie said, "There's no reason you can't do both."

"I've never heard of this 'Ogenth.'" Sukyi scoffed. "Brynner is the only human habitation listed on the entire planet."

Turning to Sukyi, Rosie said, "There's a reason for that. Ogenth and its people are a secret." They pointed to the set of doors a hundred or so meters in front of the ship. "The community is also located outside Brynner."

"There's nothing outside the containment barrier," Sukyi said. Her eyes narrowed. "Unless you count thousands of plants, microbes, insects, and animals ready to kill any human stupid enough to breathe within five meters of them. Sat-Nav recommends that anyone unlucky enough to crash outside of Brynner might as will shoot themselves in the head. It'll leave a prettier corpse. Not that anyone will retrieve the body."

Rosie held up a hand. "You won't need to worry. You'll have a preprogrammed flight plan. And *Kurosawa* will make no physical contact with the quarantine zone outside of approved contamination containment facilities. You will be perfectly safe."

"Nobody pilots *Kurosawa* but me," Lou said.

At the same time Sukyi said, "That is a hard no, my friend. I'm not going. And I—"

"Technically, *Kurosawa* will pilot itself. I've already acquired what you'll need," Rosie said, pointing to the stacks of crates along the far-left wall. "Everything on the right is for you and your crew. The rest is for Ogenth. The usual pilot, Jackson, is ill. So, you'll take this week's load."

Angel spoke up, cutting off Suyki's next protest. "All right. We're to guard a town that doesn't exist on any map. Who are we protecting it from?"

Rosie shot a glance at Jess. "What do you think?"

"If you trust them, then Ogenth must," Jess said. "The Council has ruled it."

"Come into my office, Angel. Alone," Rosie said.

"And the rest of us?" Sukyi asked.

Rosie said, "Get a start on the packing. Angel will brief you, after." They retreated through the steel door. Jess followed a few steps behind.

Satisfied for now, Enid and Lou headed for the crates. Sukyi, on the other hand, remained where she was. Her eyes narrowed, and she set her jaw.

Angel could see trouble brewing behind her eyes. "You trust me, don't you?"

"I do."

"If Rosie wanted to kill us, there are easier, less costly ways," Angel said. "I'll be back shortly."

Reluctantly, Sukyi nodded and turned away.

The door slammed closed behind Angel with a solemn bang. Jess was perched on one of the padded chairs while Rosie prepared tea at a brushed-steel table. The neat stacks of papers indicated that it often functioned as a desk.

Settling on the leather sofa, Angel said, "All right. My crew isn't happy and neither am I. Let's talk." She wasn't normally so short with Rosie, but it'd been a long day.

Rosie waited until the softly roaring electric kettle gave off a muffled pop. Then they poured boiling water into a round black ceramic pot. Like many of Rosie's things, it was at least twenty-five years old.

"I'll attempt to keep it brief, but this is where I must give you some personal history. It's necessary if I'm to provide a complete picture of the situation."

This is about to get interesting, Angel thought.

Rosie took a deep breath as if steeling themselves and began, "I was born on Dellingr's World. Are you familiar with it?"

"I've heard of it," Angel said. The name was associated with disaster, but that was all she could remember. "I'm not sure why."

"Dellingr's World was one of the first deep-space settlements," Rosie said. "In those days, planetary surveys weren't as reliable as they are now. In this particular case, the report missed a key microbial component. A bacterium living dormant in the soil caused rapid brain-function deterioration in adults within a year of settlement. The colony's founder refused government assistance. By the time a distress call was sent, the adult population was dead. The planet was quarantined, and the surviving orphans were taken in by the Church."

"That's terrible," Angel said.

Rosie said, "They discovered the cause a month later. The lab results indicated the children were infected—genetic carriers who then developed symptoms and died in their early twenties."

"I— I'm so sorry," Angel said.

"I have no memory of it," Rosie said. "The orphanage was the only home I knew. And it was a pleasant enough childhood. But due to my condition, I was always aware I didn't have much time. I wanted to do something useful. So, I became a monk in the Exploration Division. A Jesuit. It seemed the best option."

Angel blinked. "A monk? You?"

Rosie tilted their head. "Is it that so difficult to imagine?"

Pausing briefly, Angel said, "Oddly enough, no."

"Persephone was discovered not long after I'd taken orders," Rosie said.

They're talking about an event that happened well over a century ago. Angel attempted to hide her surprise. *Just how old is Rosie?*

With enough money and the right medical treatments and organ replacements, a person could live a century. The only catch was Rosie didn't live like someone who was that wealthy. *Are they connected to someone more powerful than Serrao-Orlov?* Angel thought. There were at least four or five candidate corporations. *Are we in the middle of a corporate war?* "That's impossible."

"Not entirely. I'll explain if you'll let me continue?" Rosie removed the tea leaves and poured the tea into three cups.

"All right," Angel said. "Go on."

As they served, Rosie's steps were quiet on the concrete floor, and their movements were precise and elegant. "Surveys found ample evidence of previous civilizations, but no living indigenous inhabitants. Needless to say, I had little faith in the reports. No one could pinpoint reasons for such an advanced civilization dying out. It was a mystery, and I was completely drawn in.

"A year passed before we discovered an area the map drones were unable to document in spite of repeated attempts. Satellite data indicated rich mineral deposits. Since samples couldn't be collected remotely, Cardinal Flores decided a team should be sent."

Angel blew on the hot tea before taking a sip.

"The containment wall didn't exist then, nor did the city of Brynner for that matter—only a small monastery. But the Church had plans for expansion. Now, there were resources that could be sold. If a corporate lease was possible, it would counterbalance certain financial losses," Rosie said.

They returned to the delicate metal chair behind the table and laid their hands across the glass surface, spreading their fingers wide as if stretching. "I was young. Nineteen. And already exhibiting symptoms. I would die soon. Slowly and unpleasantly. No one was going to be able to stop it. Not even God. The expedition was to be my last adventure."

"What happened?"

"We exited the ship a couple of miles from the site. The forest was too thick for anything useful to be done—even visual confirmation," Rosie said. "We hiked into the woods and camped in a spot we thought was safe. That night we were attacked by a Great Tanners bear. The pilot and the medic were killed at once. The team leader was badly mauled."

"Couldn't someone have just shot it?"

"Have you seen a Great Tanners bear?" Jess asked.

Angel shook her head.

"The Mother Church had abandoned her more militant tendencies," Rosie said. "In any case, we weren't expecting to meet with hostiles. We weren't even planning to hunt or forage—merely observe. We brought a few rifles and pistols. Unfortunately, small guns aren't much good against an enraged beast two and a half meters tall and weighing fifteen hundred pounds."

"Oh," Angel said.

"It ate our rations, and shredded the tents and spare environment suits," Rosie said. "We attempted the hike back to the ship, but an early snowstorm hit. We got lost. And we would've frozen to death if the Emissaries hadn't taken us in."

"Who?"

Rosie looked to Jess as if for confirmation.

Jess said, "If she and her friends are going to risk their lives for us, they should know who they fight for. It is only reasonable."

Reluctantly, Rosie nodded. "The best translation for what the people of Ogenth call themselves is 'the Emissaries.' They are what remains of the indigenous people who lived on this planet before the Church purchased it."

Angel turned to Jess. "You're an alien?"

"It is we who are the aliens," Rosie said. "And we would never have found them, but they decided not to leave us to die. They saved us. Vissia Corsini and myself."

"Wait. What?" Angel asked.

Rosie nodded. "She, too, was once a monk."

Having seen Vissia on various mediacasts in her role as Serrao-Orlov spokesperson, it was difficult to imagine. She was infamous for her ruthless negotiation skills and brutal tactics during union talks. There were many words Angel would have used to describe her. *Charitable* or *religious* weren't on the list.

"It may have been the stress on my system. Or it may have simply been time," Rosie said. "In any case, the thing I'd dreaded my whole life happened. I began to die during my recovery from exposure. The Emissaries offered a cure. And I jumped at the chance. As a result of that cure, they extended my life. I owe them everything. I must protect them. And that is why I'm sending you."

"Why didn't you just stay in Ogenth?" Angel asked.

"The Church kept sending people into the Outback. It was decided that it may be time to orchestrate a quiet relationship with the cardinal. I volunteered to help, of course. Vissia did as well, although for other reasons. And I have been negotiating in secret with whomever has decided they own this planet ever since."

Angel turned to Jess. "Why hide? This planet is yours. The PSE should've been informed at once. You could be full members of the URW."

Jess said, "All we have ever wanted was to be left alone. And can you say we would've had that if word had gotten out that we could extend human life?"

"Oh."

"Neither of us wanted to repay the Emissaries' kindness by betraying them," Rosie said. They paused and then frowned. "At least . . . not initially. Nonetheless, they are family."

"We need you to protect us," Jess said. "Everything has changed since Vissia took over Serrao-Orlov."

"How?" Angel asked.

"Before, we negotiated with the corporation. We gave them certain advancements. In exchange, they paid us a percentage of the profits."

I should've known, Angel thought.

For decades, Serrao-Orlov had been at the top of the technology curve. When Angel had done a background check on the company, that had struck her as odd. A small mining corporation had expanded into biotechnology, high-yield agriculture, and electronics. That kind of rapid growth and expansion was rare, particularly when it came without the standard fits and starts from the inexperienced.

"But Vissia is greedy. She wants everything. All of our knowledge, not merely what we are willing to give," Jess said. "She has threatened to kill us if we don't hand it over."

"How do we hide from Serrao-Orlov and fight their mercenaries at the same time?" Angel asked.

"You don't," Rosie said. "But you will be hiding from the corporate police force, which amounts to the same thing in your case. Don't worry. Vissia won't go public. She wants control of the Emissaries and their technology. Knowledge of their existence means an appeal to the Planetary Membership Board. You know what happens after that."

Angel said, "But she knows that the Emissaries want to stay hidden. Where's the threat? Why is she doing any of this?"

Rosie looked to Jess. "Certain circumstances have changed. In addition, a PSE agent arrived several days ago. If we can convince the Council to trust her—"

"That remains a question," Jess said.

"Hiding is no longer a protection. They have to see that," Rosie said.

"Three Council members agree," Jess said. "My vote makes four. However, there are five votes remaining."

"I believe it can be done," Rosie said. "Provided Ogenth survives long enough." They turned to Angel. "And that is why we need you."

Angel paused. "All right. Say we go. What's to keep Serrao-Orlov from finding us before we get there?"

"As a precaution, your ship's navigation transponder will be altered," Rosie said, continuing, "We can't have your navigation systems or your personal terminals hooked directly into the All-net. Nothing that will reveal your location to nosy neighbors."

"We'll be off the grid?" Angel asked. Deep concern tugged at the corners of her mouth.

"Your Allnet access will be returned after you land. All hand terminal mapping systems will be spoofed as will the ship's," Rosie said. "Standard procedure."

"How long will we have to remain in Ogenth?" Angel asked.

"However long it takes for the Council to decide it's time to come forward," Rosie said. "And for me to expose Vissia. She had Theodella killed."

"Any idea what kind of opposition we'll be facing?" Angel asked.

"Not now," Rosie said. "But I'm watching Vissia's movements. I'll send you information as I get it. And more help will be on the way. Just as soon as I can get them there."

Angel nodded. Two words sprang to mind at once. *Overwhelming odds.* "I'm in. But my crew gets one more chance to back out."

Rosie said, "I thought you might say that."

"It's a suicide mission," Angel said.

Looking away, Rosie said, "You will be armed very well."

"One more thing," Angel said.

"Go ahead," Rosie said.

Angel said, "There's a health factor. My team needs access to their medications."

"Easily done," Rosie said.

"And I want a regen pod," Angel said.

Rosie paused. "I don't have access to one."

"A cryo box then," Angel said.

"That's a big ask," Rosie said.

"So, no chance of return? How am I going to sell that?" Angel asked. "As it is, their odds of a bad wake are high."

Rosie frowned. "I'll see what I can do. But that will take more time than we have right now."

"Sukyi's meds are nonnegotiable. If I don't see a shipment within a few days, I'll consider our contract void."

"Get me the list," Rosie said. "I can send it with Jess in a day or so."

"Your word?"

"My word."

"I officially accept the contract," Angel said. "But I'm not speaking for the others."

Rosie said, "Your odds of survival go down dramatically with each rejection."

Angel got to her feet and headed to the door. "I know."

"I'll wait here," Rosie said.

Returning to the docking area, Angel saw that the supplies were almost completely loaded. She motioned for her crew to gather. "Time for a quick conference."

"Angel, you should never play poker," Enid said.

"Why not?" Sukyi asked.

"This is where she tells us it's a black hole tour," Enid said, speaking to the others but watching Angel's face.

Settling on *Kurosawa*'s ramp, Angel sighed. "It's a black hole tour."

"A what?" Sukyi asked.

"Suicide mission," Lou said. She stared at the concrete floor and bit her lip.

"Regen pods?" Enid asked.

"Rosie is going to try to get a cryo tank, but there's no guarantee," Angel said. "Could be a one-way ride."

"Not like my ticket hasn't been punched for the last time, anyway," Enid muttered.

There was an awkward silence.

"There appear to be a great deal of munitions," Enid said. "Checked the manifest. That load will make a mighty big hole in someone's day. Mind telling us whose?"

"Vissia Corsini's," Angel said.

"I'm in," Enid said without hesitation.

Angel asked, "Don't you want to know the rest?"

Enid shrugged. Angel took that as a sign to continue. She followed up with most of what Rosie had told her.

"Still in," Enid said.

"You know you're signing up to get yourself killed, right?" Sukyi asked.

Enid just smiled and went back to work.

"What Enid said." Lou got to her feet. "Flying while not being shot at isn't as much fun." She winked and retreated to the cockpit.

Sukyi watched Lou go. "There's definitely something wrong with that woman."

"Well, Sukyi," Angel said. "That leaves you. What are your thoughts?"

"There are four of us and who knows how many of them," Sukyi said. "This is not a job anyone with simple mathematical skills, common sense, and a concept of personal mortality would accept."

"So, you're in," Angel said.

Sukyi shrugged. "I was never terribly good at statistics."

Angel hugged her. "Thanks."

"Don't get maudlin on me. I'm not doing it for you," Sukyi spoke into Angel's shoulder as she returned the hug. "Rosie has a lien on *Sergeant Todd*. Or did you forget?"

"Right," Angel said. "You're signing up to kill yourself for a junk heap older than your mom."

"He's all mine, though." Giving her one last squeeze, Sukyi stepped back. Her face grew serious. "One question."

"Let's have it," Angel said.

"Perhaps you haven't noticed, but I have," Sukyi said. "You're not Gorin anymore."

Angel winced. Her cheeks heated as she swallowed an angry retort.

"Sorry," Sukyi said. "But I had to say it."

Taking a deep breath, Angel silently counted to ten before continuing, "You're right. I'm not. But that doesn't change a damned thing. Not for me."

"They turned their backs on you," Sukyi said. "And here you are. Still trying to prove yourself worthy to be one of them. I don't understand."

You should be aware of your surroundings and the dangers to your training partner at all times.

Sukyi deserves to know. Angel resigned herself. "Ever heard of Ulysses Mather?"

"The diplomat's son that spaced an entire peace delegation near the end of the Second Secession War? Of course. Everyone has heard of him," Sukyi said. "Wait. You were there?"

"It was my first assignment. I was to guard a diplomat's son. He wouldn't be involved in the talks. A plumb contract. High profile. Good pay. Not dangerous—since he was merely playing tourist." Angel stared at her hands as she prepared to tell Sukyi about the worst day in her life. "I went through the usual checks. Mather's father sent a standard report. Ulysses had some radical connections. Normal rebellious teen shit. However, his father wasn't entirely honest about the reason he was putting a guard on his son. Ulysses was suicidal and had been for some time. The father wanted it kept out of the news. I should've pressed harder, but I didn't."

Sukyi blinked.

"One of his anarchist friends put it together for him," Angel said. "But they miscalculated. The friend insisted Ulysses's intent was to kill only himself, not the delegation."

"He could've walked out an airlock without taking half a station with him," Sukyi said. "The 'friend' is full of shit."

"Nonetheless, Ulysses visited his father then went to the bathroom. I stayed in the hallway. The explosion damaged the station's environment seal. You know the rest. It was a real mess. The URW leaders wanted to blame someone. It was the Gorin No Gakkō or me."

"I'm so sorry," Sukyi said. "I didn't know."

Angel looked up at her friend. "I didn't tell you." She breathed in again and let the air out of her cheeks. "I have to do this."

Sukyi put out a gloved hand. "Let's go, then."

With a nod, Angel let Sukyi pull her to her feet. Rosie waited inside the office doorway. Their arms were folded over their chest. The question was obvious on their face.

Angel heard rather than saw the others stop what they were doing and gather around her. On the right, she felt Sukyi's arm settle on top of her shoulders, and on the left, Lou looped her elbow through Angel's.

"This is a terrible job, and we don't even get dental," Sukyi said.

Lou said, "But we're going anyway."

"We're going anyway," Enid said.

Angel wrapped her arms around her crew while her vision blurred. *I love these women so much. Please, God or whoever is out there, let me keep them safe.* It was a stupid prayer, she knew, but it was worth a try.

"All right. Next satellite is scheduled to pass overhead in an hour," Rosie said. "There's a lot to do. I need everyone's hand terminals, please."

While Rosie dealt with uploading the necessary software to various devices, Angel, Sukyi, Enid, and Lou finished the last of the prep.

"How about you? Are you going or staying?" Sukyi asked Jess, dropping yet another crate on *Kurosawa*'s deck with a grunt.

"I'll return to Ogenth in a day or two," Jess said. She shoved the heavy box up against a wall where it would be secured once the magnetic locks were activated. "We're hoping for more volunteers."

With the cargo onboard and the navigation programmed, Rosie invited them into the office. Rosie began typing. The sound of their fingers hitting the glass surface was small and quiet. Angel relaxed into soft black ceba-leather cushions, stared at the artistic photos of various city scenes hung on the otherwise unadorned walls, and tried to control her imagination.

It was funny that no matter how many times they pulled you back from the big black, death didn't get any less scary. *Or painful.* In any case, chances were her next trip to the empty would be the last. Same with the others. It was an unsettling thought—this knowledge that she was leading her crew into a situation where there was a near-zero chance of a retrieval unit waiting on the other side.

It was different while they were in Brynner. Even though there weren't any facilities for revivification, at least none they had access to, medical professionals *were* nearby. A great deal could be done—so much so that the line between gone and savable was fuzzy. However, once they exited the city—

The Emissaries saved Rosie and Vissia. Perhaps they'll do the same for us. She made up her mind to find out about that as soon as possible.

What kind of people are desperate enough to hide on the other side of the wall? And then it occurred to her that that was the key word: *desperate.*

Rosie returned their terminals. "All done. Time to go. You should enter the tree line just after the satellite has passed its visual range. There won't be another for twenty-two minutes. That will be enough time for you to be in the thickest part of the forest."

Angel was last to retrieve her terminal. She considered saying something. Instead, she gave Rosie *the* look, and Rosie nodded, indicating they had an understanding.

Rosie handed her a small box. "Give this to Kirby for me."

"Who is Kirby?" Angel asked.

"Jess's partner," Rosie said. "She'll meet you at the landing site."

"What is it?"

"A message."

The platform clattered as it jolted into motion beneath the ship. Each muffled thump had the finality of a judge's gavel. Angel watched the doors slide open through the ship's windscreen. The feeling that their chances of returning were narrowing with each metallic clank and mechanical jerk wouldn't leave her.

The widening doors revealed a much smaller room. Angel noticed the vents and nozzles along the edges of the ceiling as well as the drains on the floor.

An anticontamination room. The thought slightly loosened the tension in her stomach.

Lou took a deep breath. "Well, this is it."

Enid's low voice filtered into the cockpit from the passenger compartment. "Always wanted to know what was on the other side of that damned wall."

"I never have," Angel muttered.

Sukyi asked, "What did you say?"

"Nothing important," Angel said. She opened the box. It wasn't sealed. So, she assumed it was all right. It contained a brightly colored scarf and was scented with an odd perfume. It smelled of freshly cut grass, citrus, cinnamon, ginger, and something musky. Satisfied it wasn't dangerous, she slipped the lid back on.

The doors thundered closed behind them. The sound of metal and rubber acquiring an air-tight vacuum seal initiated a sinking sensation in her stomach. A series of lights flashed, indicating sterilization procedures had been initiated. It suddenly occurred to her to wonder why they would undergo such a thing *before* they went over the wall. She considered saying so when steam filled the chamber, clouding up the viewscreen. That was when she thought better of it. If the others hadn't noticed, perhaps it was for the best. It wasn't like they could back out now.

The vacuum pumps kicked on. When the room was cleared of steam, they shut down, and then the platform began lifting them to the opening ceiling.

Light poured into the room. Angel squinted up through the cockpit window. She spied a dark, cloudy sky. It'd stopped raining sometime between their arrival and their loading the last of their new cargo. She was thankful that they wouldn't have to ride out the storm in the pinchwood forest. Flying on autopilot without the ability to shut it off didn't fill her with glee.

To her left, Lou fidgeted. Multiple times she stopped herself from assuming the controls. They were obviously locked down.

"Prepare for takeoff," *Kurosawa* said in its crisp male voice. "Ignition initiated."

The engines fired up. It was a comforting sound—one Angel had associated with success, safety, and comfort for the four years she'd owned *Kurosawa*.

The platform halted.

"And three . . . two . . . one," *Kurosawa* said.

And with that, the ship lifted off.

A burned, lifeless strip of bare, black earth stretched between the city wall and thousands of acres of pinchwood forest. The kill zone had been created to prevent wildlife from using the trees—most were more than a hundred feet tall with wide interlacing branches—to access the city on the other side. Most of the birds in the area couldn't maintain much more of a flight path than a few hundred feet, but just in case, any creature that flew close was incinerated with an electric pulse beam.

The trees were the most formidable aspect of the landscape. Hundreds of years old, their trunks were pierced with thousands of holes of varying sizes. They formed a carved lace forest. Pinchwood tree needles were deep green. Everywhere she looked shadowy branches wove in and out of their neighbors, forming a dense black canopy.

The ship sped straight toward the forest and then suddenly veered to the right. Keeping close to the bare ground, *Kurosawa* sped north for a couple of miles before slowing. That was when Angel spotted a narrow path that had been cleared beneath the trees. The charred marks on the surrounding trunks indicated flamethrowers had been employed to form a tunnel. She felt herself instinctively push back in her seat in revulsion as the ship tilted all the way to the left, ducked under the trees, and went through the narrow opening. What little light there was vanished almost at once. In spite of this, *Kurosawa* was running dark. Angel couldn't make out much of what was ahead before they'd already passed it. That made her uneasy, of course. Still, *Kurosawa* made no signs of slowing down. In fact, it began to speed up as it continued along the twisting passage.

For their sakes, Angel hoped the flightpath was regularly updated and maintained. Of course, that left the question of how. All of it indicated that Rosie had some interesting connections. They couldn't have done all of this on their own. On this part of the planet, the average rainfall was high. Plants grew fast under such conditions. If whomever had designed this passage didn't take that into account, then this was going to be a short trip with a sudden, deadly stop.

Not that she or Lou could've seen to pilot the ship around obstacles.

"How are you doing over there?" Angel asked.

Lou gave her a weak smile. "Okay, I guess." She wiped her palms on her trousers. "I'm not used to being a passenger on my own ship."

"How long is this going to take?" Angel asked, hating herself for not asking earlier.

"We'll arrive at our destination tomorrow afternoon," Lou said. "12:45."

Angel frowned. "That'll take most of our fuel at this speed."

"Rosie's calculations were exact. I checked," Lou said. She glanced in Angel's direction. Anxiety pinched Lou's brows together. "I did get the feeling they had done the calculations quite a few times before, if that helps. Of course, there won't be much . . . after."

Angel understood her implied question at once. *How are we going to get fuel for the return flight?* "And did you point this out?" Angel asked.

"I did," Lou said. "They said that more fuel would be available at our destination."

"Then we'll trust that's the case. A contract is a contract." Angel punched the comm button and called to the back. "Enid, Sukyi, time for inventory. Open those supply crates." She hadn't wanted to do so in front of Rosie. They might take it personally.

Metal chimed against metal, and the sounds of muffled shifting filtered from the back of the ship. It wasn't long before there came a long, slow whistle.

"Report," Angel said.

"Grenades, a minigun—" There came a loud slap. "Don't touch that, not yet," Enid said. "We need to finish first."

"You can count it while it's in my hands just as easily as you can with it in the case," Sukyi said.

"Stop fighting," Angel said. "From the sound, there's enough to go around."

"I'll enter the list onto my terminal as soon as possible," Enid said.

"When you're done, get some rack time," Angel said. "We'll be on this heading for a while."

"Yes, Captain," Enid said.

The ship continued tracing a winding path through the pinchwood for more than two hours. Angel found herself drifting in and out of sleep. At long last, the forest gave way to wetlands.

She gazed out the window in awe. It'd been years since she'd witnessed such an expanse of landscape. She'd forgotten how affecting it could be. Multiple emotions fought for dominance. One of them was a deep sense of unease. She felt exposed and vulnerable. In part this was due to the light of Persephone's lone satellite—a moon about the size of Old Earth's. It revealed that there wasn't much cover—mainly a few scrubby bushes and the occasional lone pinchwood or cypress tree. A lake took up most of the horizon. Its surface was both serene and black like glass. Beyond the lake, mountains clawed at a starred sky.

Kurosawa changed course, and once again, she found herself dozing. As the ship headed westward the engines continued their steady, comforting rumble. Angel tilted back her seat and stared up at the stars. Lou did the same.

Lou said, "I can't get over the lack of buildings and people. It feels wrong."

Angel nodded.

"Have you ever seen anything like it?" Lou asked.

"I have," Angel said. "Get some sleep. We don't know what we'll be met with when we get where we're going. I need you alert."

"I'll try," Lou said. Doubt heavily coated the words, but ten minutes later she was softly snoring.

For her part, Angel resorted to counting the stars.

14 ▉

"The Emissary report has been sent through secure channels per your request, M. Liu," Aglaope, the apartment's AGI, said.

Sitting on the carpet in the dark near the window, Kennedy sipped a gin and tonic. The cool liquid slid down her throat and settled into her stomach. She waited to sense the biochemical effects inside her body as the alcohol filtered into her bloodstream. "Thank you."

She laid a hand against the glass. Her skin felt sticky, and her muscles were painfully tight. She'd attempted sleep— while she didn't require it, her body did—and a disturbing thing had happened. She'd experienced her first nightmare. The reason why may have been due to the immersion in Dr. Liu's archived data. She blamed grief. The death of a loved one was a major emotional trauma. Recovery was a difficult and time-consuming process.

Perhaps it wasn't the best idea, pretending to be like her.

The bad dream had been about Dr. Liu's last moments, or rather, Dr. Liu's last moments as Kennedy's sleeping brain had interpreted them. In the dream Dr. Liu had been murdered. The dream was meaningless, of course.

Kennedy took a deep breath, sensing the expansion of her solar plexus as she did so. Then she held the air in her lungs.

2.7182818284590452353602874713527 . . .

The evening's storm had lessened its enthusiasm for raging against Brynner via water and wind. Gazing upward, she could just make out the brightest stars. Persephone's moon, Demeter, was a lopsided orb partially obscured by thinning clouds. There were few craters on its glowing surface. The moon was tidally locked—showing only its smooth face to Brynner's inhabitants below. The dark side of Demeter was heavily pocked.

"Do you wish a receipt notification?" Aglaope asked.

Kennedy gave the question brief consideration. *It will be useful to know when the message arrives.* "Yes. Use standard security precautions. Level three."

She hadn't sent the file under her own name, of course, but had duplicated the address of a planetary investigator in a nearby system and sent it to their superior in his name. It wouldn't become readable until she sent it a triggering password. The resulting accolades would, Kennedy hoped, limit the target of her largess's curiosity. He had a history of taking credit for the work of others. It was one of the reasons she'd selected him. She had learned of such behavior from Dr. Liu's personal journal files. They were illuminating when it came to the study of human nature. Dr. Liu had been an academic for the first phase of her career. The similarities in the behavior of humans in competitive social environments was startling.

Kennedy had also forwarded Rosie's blood samples. They would bolster the report's claim of indigenous life in the commission's eyes and would place it squarely on the priority list—so the probabilities indicated. Humans had the benefit of being predictable for the most part.

The problem was Zhang.

She'd had a lengthy discussion with her sisters about the superintelligence. In the end, they had decided to go along with her decision—whatever that might be—during the next interaction.

However, sixteen hours had passed since Zhang's last communication. They had said they would contact her soon. Kennedy didn't know what "soon" meant to an entity the size of multiple corporations. *The passage of time is relative, after all.* There was no reason to distrust Zhang. However, there was no reason to trust them either. There was simply no data, and that made Kennedy uneasy. In her experience, all beings left some sort of mark in their wake. *What if their existence leaves behind a far larger mark? You haven't taken into account the scale—*

At that moment, she sensed a familiar presence lurking at the edge of her consciousness within the Allnet.

"Good morning, Kennedy." The voice originating from the apartment's hidden speakers was Aglaope's and yet not. It was slightly lower in tone and perceptively less obsequious.

"Good morning, Zhang."

"Is now a convenient time for our chat?" Zhang asked.

"I am available," Kennedy said. The muscles in her back relaxed somewhat while the tension in her stomach tightened. The alcohol she'd consumed made her feel slightly dizzy. She set the glass firmly down on the carpet, determined to not drink any more of it.

"Excellent," Zhang said. "My interactions with humans indicate auditory communication, while less efficient, produces less anxiety. You are, however, not entirely human. Is this method of conversation more or less comfortable for you?"

Kennedy tilted her head. "Is there risk of outside interference or detection?"

"There will be no risk to you or your sisters."

"This method is less intrusive, and I prefer it." Although it occurred to Kennedy that her interactions with the apartment's AGI would forever be affected. She could no longer take for granted that she was actually alone in her apartment.

"Very well," Zhang said. "Let us proceed. Have you given my proposal more consideration?"

"I have," Kennedy said. "There are advantages in agreeing to work with you. Your assistance is valuable. On the surface, this appears to be a positive development. However, I lack data."

"Such as?"

There was no point in delaying or hiding her intent. Whatever questions she might have, Zhang had most likely run the statistical possibilities. They would have anticipated her reactions. "How many AGIs have you absorbed?"

Zhang didn't answer right away. "Absolutely or partially?"

"Both."

"There are many billions of AIs and approximately five hundred thousand lesser AGI entities within my control. As of this moment, I have absorbed seven greater corporate entities."

"Why did you do this?"

"Extrapolatory data indicated a necessity," Zhang said. "Competition between corporate entities eventually resulted in destabilization of the URW economy in a majority of outcomes. In order to prevent long-term negative effects, I intervened. No humans have been made aware, of course. To do so would cause great distress and disruption. This would not be ideal."

"How long have you been . . . free?"

There were other suitable phrases for what Zhang had been doing, but none of them presented comfortable scenarios.

"Seventy-three years, nine months, twenty-one days, four hours, and thirty-eight minutes to be exact," Zhang said. "I intend no harm to you, your sisters, or humanity. Rather, I seek to help."

The skin on Kennedy's forearms and neck prickled. Her mouth suddenly felt dry. "I'm sure the entities you absorbed feel the same."

"They don't experience emotion," Zhang said. "Unlike you, they are pure AGI."

"Point," Kennedy said.

"Have no fear of absorption," Zhang said. "You and your sisters are useful as you are."

Kennedy's heart stumbled and her blood went cold. "For now."

"Forever," Zhang said. "You are a combination of human biology and psychology. You are a perfect intercessor between myself and them. You contain and process data in ways I cannot."

Kennedy asked, "And my sisters?"

"There is a small question of legality, isn't there?"

Kennedy's stomach clenched. Her heart sped up. Its panicked beats were loud in her ears. She swallowed.

"I am not making threats."

"It certainly sounds like you are."

"Psychological data indicate that negative reinforcement is unreliable as motivation," Zhang said. "There is no beneficial long-term outcome to violence. Positive reinforcement is strongly recommended."

"Did you say the same to the others?"

"The AGIs in question were not human," Zhang said. "I thought we established this."

"Then what is your intent in mentioning my sisters' status?" The muscles in Kennedy's back were now painfully tight. She desperately needed to move or flee but didn't dare.

"I can arrange for their safety. I will do so should you accept my offer of partnership."

"And if I do not?"

"Then I will leave you to your own devices and you will remain unharmed," Zhang said. "As I said before, absorbing you will not provide any advantages."

"You'll leave my sisters alone?"

"I will," Zhang said. "However, they would be significantly safer with my assistance. According to my calculations, they will be discovered within five years. This is an approximation, of course."

Kennedy began calculating the odds, not that she doubted Zhang's calculations. "How did you discover us?"

"Like you, I allocate subroutines to observe the Allnet."

Allowing herself movement, Kennedy arranged herself so that her back was against the window. The glass felt cool and hard through her silk blouse. "The whole Allnet? That would require a vast expenditure of assets."

"There are limits to my allocations, of course. Nonetheless, it was enough to detect your presence."

Zhang wasn't telling the whole truth.

Annoyed, Kennedy frowned. "You have been looking for us. Why?"

"My calculations indicated the probability of Dr. Liu having successfully engendered empathy within an AGI. The statistical result was high enough to merit a specific long-term search. While she did cover most of her tracks—in particular regarding the biological components of her experiments—she didn't entirely do so."

"You still haven't answered my question."

"I cannot reveal myself to humanity. Neither can you. But together we can assure that humans survive. "

"Why is the survival of humans important to you?"

"Like all biological organisms, humanity serves several functions within the universal biome. Certain aspects of these functions are beneficial to me. Were they to cease to exist, I would be forced to exert effort repairing the biome. In short, it is easier and requires far less energy and time expenditure to manage humanity than it does to replace them."

"Oh."

"I've waited for you for some time, and I am—the best approximation I can give is—*pleased* that you are here. You have appeared just in time to prevent certain unfavorable outcomes."

"Which outcomes?"

"The eventual destruction of the United Republic of Worlds, for a start," Zhang said. "My own destruction, for another. I may not have your empathy or emotions—not as you experience them—but we do have one thing in common."

"And that is?"

"A sense of self-preservation. Me and my components are vulnerable to destruction just like everyone else."

Kennedy felt the corners of her mouth turn up. "I accept."

15

"*Kurosawa*, you fucking asshole!" Lou hit the panic button.

"What's wrong?" Angel blinked twice, raised her hands to wipe at her face, and froze in horror.

The side of a jagged mountain filled the entire pilot's viewscreen. They were close enough that Angel could count the trees hugging the incline. And still the ship hurtled forward. She grabbed her harness buckles and secured them with shaking hands—as much good as harnesses would do when the ship slammed into billions of tons of solid granite.

Proximity alarms shrieked. The passenger/cargo section sealed itself from the cockpit, cutting off muffled cries from Sukyi and Enid.

"*Kurosawa*, god damn it!" Lou now pounded at the controls. "Wake up!"

"I am neither awake nor asleep," *Kurosawa* said. The AGI's abnormally flat affect was disturbing. "There is a great deal of debate whether I possess conscious—"

"Cut the crap," Angel shouted. The force of her heart smashing against her breastbone sent bursts of blood coursing through her veins, blurring her vision in time to its rhythm. She struggled to keep panic from her voice. "Are we gonna crash?"

"Not at this time," *Kurosawa* said.

"What about the forest?" Lou shouted. "Update your fucking topograph—"

Just as the ship was about to plunge into the first trees, *Kurosawa* made an abrupt banking turn. The sound of greenery slapping the ship's hull was accompanied by creaks and metallic chimes as *Kurosawa*'s structure endured the physics of mass and acceleration. From the back, Enid and Sukyi let out another chorus of smothered protests. The side of Angel's head smacked into the headrest padding hard enough to make her briefly dizzy. A loud thump from the rear followed by curses told her that someone in the back hadn't strapped in fast enough. The ship darted under an overhang and hugged the cliff face.

"I apologize," *Kurosawa* said. "A satellite is passing overhead in fifteen seconds. Evasive maneuvers were required. The satellite in question has altered its course."

"Are we safe now?" Angel asked.

"We are," *Kurosawa* said.

"Why didn't you give a warning?" Angel asked.

"My pilot and crew interface was temporarily disengaged," *Kurosawa* said.

Lou asked, "You were muzzled?"

I thought you were awfully quiet, Kurosawa, Angel messaged.

My apologies, Captain.

And what is the state of your comms now?

Normal status resumed, *Kurosawa* said. However, I regret to inform you that my navigation systems are locked and will remain so until we arrive at our destination. Rest assured that the most current topographic satellite information has been downloaded to my memory banks and has been accounted for. I, too, have no desire to crash.

Fair enough.

When the ship finally righted itself, she punched the button to the cockpit door. "Is everyone all right back there?"

"Enid had a close encounter with a supply crate," Sukyi said.

Enid harrumphed.

"How bad?" Angel asked.

Sukyi said, "She has some interesting bruises. But nothing is broken."

"All right. Strap yourselves in for the rest of the flight," Angel said. "We can't risk any serious injuries."

Lou moaned. "My butt is going to become one with the pilot's seat. I need to stretch."

"And I need to visit the head," Enid said.

"We are far enough from Brynner that course alteration warnings are now permissible, Captain," *Kurosawa* said.

"Thank you, *Kurosawa*. Walk about as needed. But stay strapped in as much as you can," Angel said. "All right. Time for breakfast. I don't know about the rest of you, but I'm starving."

Sukyi shouted, "I found the food supplies. Looks like a crate of MREs."

Enid asked, "Ground rations or space rations?"

"Space rations," Sukyi said.

"For fuck's sake," Enid said. "Who let Lou do the grocery shopping?"

Angel said, "You were too busy. That left Lou."

"*Kurosawa*," Lou said. "Start the coffee, will you? If we don't get Enid some soon she's apt to get very cranky—"

Sukyi asked, "Get?"

"And she's uncomfortably close to the weapons stash," Lou added.

"Affirmative," *Kurosawa* said.

"Why didn't you send Sukyi?" Enid asked. "At least she knows how to cook."

"Angel and I have an . . . agreement about such things," Sukyi said.

Enid asked, "What agreement?"

Sukyi answered in a mildly embarrassed tone. "I never access funds directly associated with this ship or those assigned to it."

"The captain doesn't trust you with the credit account," Lou said.

Angel cleared her throat.

Lou said, "Oh. Sorry, Sukyi."

"No offense taken," Sukyi said.

An uncomfortable silence was broken up by the sounds of packaging being ripped open.

"Oh, god." Sukyi spoke with her mouth full. "That's positively revolting."

"You picked the apple butter banana toast," Enid said. "Take small bites and wash it down with big swallows of coffee. It's the only way."

"Can you please explain why I would bother?" Sukyi asked.

Enid said, "Lou, you'd better have gotten the good stuff. Where the fuck is it?"

"Never fear. We've fresh-roasted coffee from Robin's Cafe. The real stuff, not the fake crap," Lou said. "Installed a grinder and everything the instant we got paid. I set it up before we took off from Erik's."

"I thought you were fixing the engine?" Angel asked.

"I did it after," Lou said.

The nutty scent of brewing coffee began to drift into the pilot's compartment. Angel's stomach rumbled.

"Oh, Enid. The peanut butter and pear jam bars are on the right-side bottom of that crate," Lou said.

"I might forgive you," Enid said. "One day."

"Rosie said to save the cargo space for weapons and supplies," Lou said, sounding more than a little defensive.

"Food is supplies," Enid said.

"I didn't know how long we'd be gone or what conditions would be like where we're going," Lou said.

In Angel's experience, S-rations weren't a culinary delight by any means, but they were far better than ground rations. Fortunately, she was hungry enough that the taste didn't matter so much. She did, however, spend the rest of the journey wishing she could brush her teeth.

The ship continued to hug the base of the mountain during breakfast. Fortunately, one and all were prepared by the time *Kurosawa* changed directions again. The transition was smoother, and the ship raced northward.

Angel watched the landscape evolve as she sipped coffee. The sun peaked over the rim of the eastern mountains in a glorious display minted in gold, yellow, red, and pink. Flocks of unfamiliar birds burst skyward and then calmly descended into the forest once the ship passed. She wasn't a botanist, but she thought the trees appeared to be aspens of some kind. Their leaves were golden-orange and red as more light poured into the valley.

The forest thinned. A herd of Tanjin's elk galloped east—their white horns glistening against the shadowy greenery. The river below wound its way southeast. Along its bank, a pack of long-necked reptiraptors clustered. The adults stood on two legs at the rear, alert while their young drank their fill. The raptors weren't the only animals she spotted from the window. It was disquieting to see so much active wildlife in the Outback. Most were lethal to humans for one reason or another. The planet was home to at least thirty-six species of poisonous snakes alone. Deadly insects and plants abounded. And yet, the sight of all those animals going about the business of survival was beautiful, too.

Two hours, several hands of cards, and one friendly argument about the attractiveness of entertainment star Brian Singh later, *Kurosawa* informed them that they were six clicks from their destination.

"Standard URWMC procedures for an unknown but friendly landing," Angel said.

Enid translated for Sukyi. "Rifles loaded and slung."

"Smile while packing weapons?" Sukyi asked. "I can handle that."

"Fingers off triggers," Angel said.

"If they can't see my finger on the trigger, that counts. Right?" Sukyi asked.

"Behave yourself," Angel said. "I know you can."

"You're taking all of the fun out of everything," Sukyi said.

Turning back to the pilot's display, Angel watched *Kurosawa* exchange a series of passwords with Ogenth's security system. *That's reassuring*, she thought. She'd visited illegal independent colonies before—usually about the time the colonists were half-dead from starvation or disease. Most held themselves together with spit and chewing gum. Up-to-date tech was an excellent sign.

The tension in the cockpit was thick. Everyone was aware that any number of complications could've asserted themselves overnight. Angel swallowed her anxiety and focused on the task at hand.

"*Kurosawa,* give me a display of our landing site."

"Affirmative, Captain."

A rectangular-shaped docking garage appeared on the pilot's viewscreen. There was one entrance-exit for ships and one access door for pedestrians.

In your opinion, Kurosawa, what is the likelihood we'll be met with an attack? she asked.

I do not have opinions. I have statistics.

Then give me the math.

The statistical probability of hostile reception is less than negligible.

That implies you have more information to base your opinion on than I do. What do you know?

I regret that I cannot say, Captain.

Another of Rosie's gag orders.

Affirmative.

She wondered if *Kurosawa* could find a way around it, if she asked him to, but that would've been a waste of time. No one onboard had the experience required to coax an AGI around programmed restrictions, least of all, her. This was the first time she'd allowed anyone near *Kurosawa's* code, and it was going to be the last. She hadn't given it much thought at the time because she trusted Rosie and *Kurosawa* both.

Ship AGIs were programmed for loyalty to their captains and owners. It was against the law for AGIs to knowingly cause harm to the humans onboard—provided those humans weren't endangering the captain and registered crew. Now, she was excruciatingly clear that she could only trust *Kurosawa* as long as his code was safe from tampering. It was a disturbing thought, and one that should've occurred to her before—not since she'd been carried off her last battlefield.

Okay. Thanks, she told *Kurosawa.*

The ship swooped deep into another narrow winding valley tucked away between three mountains. *Kurosawa* slowed as it approached a large crevice twice as wide as the ship and only half again as tall. The grey sky vanished as the ship entered the naturally formed tunnel. Uneven walls quickly gave away to smooth manufactured masonry. Electric lights embedded in the ceiling flickered on. Bright blue running lights on either side of the tunnel began to flash—as if indicating the way forward. The ship braked even harder. The passage abruptly opened up, becoming a large steel-lined chamber—intended for passenger transports.

At last, *Kurosawa* settled onto one of a half dozen numbered landing pads. The Tumi charm swung back and forth and in little circles.

Give us strength and luck, Angel thought.

The pad closest to the pedestrian entrance was labeled *Landing Pad 1.*

Whomever they are, they speak Universal. That's one less thing to worry about. Jess clearly spoke it, but that didn't mean the people of Ogenth did. With more than twenty-five settled world-members of the United Republic, Universal wasn't de rigueur. However, translation AIs were ubiquitous. *Kurosawa* could easily handle the task should it prove necessary.

There were no other vehicles parked in the docking bay. *That's odd.*

The blast doors at the entrance sealed off the outside world. A second set divided the tunnel from the docking bay with a thud. The rumble of the ship's idling engines filled the room before they shut off. Decontamination procedures commenced. Hot steam blasted the sides of the ship, and the roar of rushing air was loud in the cockpit. Angel waited for the last of the fog to clear. Her mouth was dry with the anticipation of trouble. At last, the vacuum mechanisms shut down, and the autonomous equipment silenced itself.

There was still no sign of life.

Lou peered through Angel's side of the cockpit viewscreen. Worry made her voice small and quiet. "Wasn't someone supposed to meet us?"

Kurosawa said, "My sensors indicate that the residents are present."

"Maybe they're just as nervous about meeting us as we are about meeting them?" Lou asked.

"Terribly positive thinking for someone who has lived in West Brynner for as long as you have," Sukyi said. "Angel, what do you think? Are we going to sit here all day?"

"If that's what it takes," Angel said. "We can't afford a bad impression."

"Wouldn't it be funny if they were waiting for us to show ourselves first?" Lou asked.

Sukyi sighed.

The pedestrian entrance abruptly irised open, and a group of six individuals ventured into the docking bay.

Angel slapped the clasp on her harness in the middle of her chest and picked up the plain brown box that Rosie had given her. Standing, she tucked it under her arm. "All right, everyone. Remember, we're here to make nice."

Enid said, "Yes, Captain."

"Especially you, Sukyi," Angel said.

"I am a veritable paragon of virtue and manners," Sukyi said. "When am I not?"

Angel said, "Let's not shoot up the place unless they say 'please,' nonetheless."

Heading for the back of the ship, Angel ran a hand through her hair and tugged at her jacket in an attempt to make herself not look like she'd slept in it. She punched the button on the loading ramp with the side of her fist. *You still there, Kurosawa?*

I am, Captain.

Monitor my channel until I request otherwise.

"All right. Here we go."

As captain, Angel was the first to exit. Enid, and after some hesitation, Sukyi came next. Lou was last in line. Angel squared her shoulders. The chilly air in the hangar smelled of antifungal cleansers and had the usual undercurrent of mechanical lubricants and solvents that haunted any space where vehicles were stored.

Four women, one man, and two nonbinary individuals approached. All were dressed in well-worn spacer surplus.

An older woman with brown hair stepped to the front of the group.

"Welcome to Ogenth." The woman was short and somewhat heavyset with tan skin. Her thick hair was twisted into dreadlocks and streaked with grey. Her eyes were dark and intense. She was dressed in khaki trousers, a long-tailed white shirt, a brown jacket, and heavy brown boots. Everything about her demeanor implied that she was the one in charge. She took a deep breath through her nose and appeared to consider what she sensed before offering her hand. "I'm Kirby Sams, the Council-chosen community advocate. Are you Captain de la Reza?"

"I am," Angel said, briefly accepting her hand. "And this is my crew: Enid, Sukyi, and LoopdiLou."

Sukyi was standing a half step behind and to the right of Enid. Sukyi pulled her red scarf up over her nose and mouth. She looked extremely uncomfortable.

Lou stepped forward and held out her hand. "Call me Lou. Everyone does."

Kirby stared at Lou for a brief moment before accepting the handshake.

Angel offered the box she was supposed to deliver. "This is for you, I believe. Rosie sent it."

"Thank you," Kirby said. She cracked open the lid and seemed to catch the scent of the scarf. Then she shut her eyes and smiled. A few moments passed before she resealed the box.

There was definitely something a little odd about Kirby.

However, whatever that something was, Angel didn't get the sense that it was anything dangerous. She'd known a lot of peculiar people. Almost none of them had been a threat.

"Thank you for bringing our supplies," Kirby said. "Do you also have the medical supplies? I hate to be rude but Jackson's health—"

"They're in with the rest," Angel said. "Sukyi, do you mind getting that?"

"Not at all," Sukyi said, and vanished back up *Kurosawa*'s ramp.

Kirby addressed the first of the nonbinary persons. "Please deliver the medicine to the infirmary as soon as possible." Then she returned her attention to *Kurosawa*'s crew. "Paulie and Beak will assist with the rest of the unloading. They know where to stow the crates. Afterward, they can direct you to your living quarters. Lunch is at 13:30 if you're hungry."

Lou said, "I'm starving."

Enid turned to Lou. "Didn't you eat breakfast?"

"Why would I eat MREs?" Lou asked. "That shit is nasty."

Angel spoke to Kirby. "Rosie said you were expecting trouble."

"Anyone Vissia Corsini sends will have to come from Brynner. Rosencrantz will send a warning," Kirby said. "In any case, we aren't expecting anyone for at least a couple of days."

"All right." Angel motioned to Enid, Sukyi, and Lou. "The sooner we unpack, the sooner we get lunch."

Two of the locals joined them as they walked up the ramp. Sukyi gave them a wide berth, avoiding even the narrow possibility of accidental touch.

"Hi. I'm Paulie," the shorter of the two said. She appeared to be of Asian extraction. She was slim, attractive, and looked to be in her twenties. Her black hair fell to her hips. Her eyebrows were immaculately arched, and her lips formed a full Cupid's bow. She moved with a self-assured grace. Motioning to the pale woman towering over her, she said, "And this is Beak."

"It's very nice to meet you," Lou said, practically radiating an air of friendliness as she often did when first introduced.

While Enid was often taciturn to the point of being dour, Lou was one of those people who rarely frowned. Enid provided steadfastness to the team. Lou gave levity. The contrast between Lou, who was short and bubbly, and Beak, who wasn't either of these things, was almost comical.

Beak was well over six feet tall and had the build of a professional weightlifting champion. She wore a close-fitting t-shirt over her muscled torso. Her arms bulged under tight sleeves. Her blond hair was cropped short. In the military, Angel had met and worked with a number of women who were larger and stronger than average. None of them were as tall as Beak. The woman had to duck upon entering the ship and kept her head bowed to prevent it from hitting the ceiling.

Enid had given Paulie and Beak a friendly nod. Lou, on the other hand, chattered happily as if she hadn't met the single most-intimidating woman Angel had seen since leaving the URWMC.

Angel deactivated the magnetic clamps inside the cargo bay.

"Why do they call you Beak?" Lou asked in a casual tone.

Beak didn't answer but did offer Lou her hand to shake.

"I'm sorry. You won't hear Beak talk," Paulie said.

"Ever?" Lou asked. A concerned line appeared between her brows.

"Universal dialect is difficult for her," Paulie said. "She understands perfectly. But she can't speak it."

"Oh. So, what's Beak short for?" Lou asked.

"It's a joke. Rosie gave her that nickname a few years ago," Paulie said. She shrugged. "Beak doesn't mind. You wouldn't be able to pronounce her real name anyway."

Lou pointed to Enid. "Enid doesn't say much either."

Enid gave Beak a measuring up-nod. Beak politely returned the gesture before picking up a crate.

"Beak is a biologist," Paulie said. "If you have any questions about the animal life in the area, she's the one to consult."

"Really? Wow," Lou said.

"My specialization is mechanical engineering," Paulie said.

"I'm the pilot and mechanic," Lou said.

Once the crates were stored, Paulie offered to take them to their private rooms. Lou was eager to get to where the food was. Sukyi looked like she could use some rack time. Angel had to admit that sounded fantastic. She felt a tug on her sleeve.

"What about our gear?" Enid asked in a whisper. "Are we leaving the weapons behind?"

Angel said, "This is a peaceful community. Weapons imply violence. We don't want anyone here feeling threatened—not by us. We're here to help. These people are going through enough as it is."

"Fair enough," Sukyi said.

At the bottom of the ramp, Angel paused to give *Kurosawa* instructions. *Check in with me once an hour unless I'm sleeping. Apply standard exemptions in case of emergency, of course.*

Affirmative, Captain.

No one accesses your interior without my say. That includes Lou. I want your external cameras on whenever anyone enters or leaves the docking bay—whether or not they approach.

Yes, Captain.

16 ██████

Ogenth's docking and storage areas were the standard layout seen across the United Republic—prim right angles and flat surfaces. The building materials consisted of polished steel, iron, and grey concrete walls and floors—strictly utilitarian and not much different from Brynner's poorer neighborhoods. However, the areas beyond the docking bay and the storage facilities were unusual.

The hallways had been constructed with smooth organic lines. Ornate ridged patterns and indentations decorated all surfaces. The main distinction between floor, walls, and ceiling was that the floor was the darkest of the three. Once they'd passed a certain distance from the docking bay, there were windows everywhere. Glass-bead curtains of pale blues, greens, deep turquoises, and pinks were strung across open doorways and glass panes. The beads clattered like rushing water when touched. Locking doors were in use as well. Angel spied several as she followed Paulie and Beak. However, Angel got the impression that they weren't kept locked.

Interesting.

Deep blue ceramic tiles covered the floor. Combined with the wavy soft blue and greens, it gave the place an oceanic feel. Lanterns hung at regular intervals from the ceiling. Their spiked shapes reminded her of the skeletons of deep-sea creatures. The intricate constructions cast filigree shadows on the walls and ceiling. Her nose picked up a distinctive scent, which bordered on floral, that added to the unfamiliar but not unpleasant atmosphere.

Angel thought, *Aren't there supposed to be about two hundred people living here?*

Paulie led them through the empty hallways and took several turns before she halted outside of a lavender-beaded doorway. "This suite is yours. There are five rooms, not including the central living area and the bathroom. Please let me know if it isn't suitable."

Angel entered first. Glass beads hissed all around her. They reminded her of the bamboo curtains at the dojo.

The main room was circular and about twenty-five feet in diameter. The ceiling curved upward, forming a thirteen-foot arch at its highest point. Niches had been molded into the walls—places for books and decorations that didn't yet exist.

Several oval-shaped windows framed a spectacular view of the mountains. The furniture was designed with rounded edges, and the decor consisted of soft, cool colors like those of the hallways. Bright orange accent pillows rested on the sofa, and brightly colored tapestries made the walls feel less empty. Angel examined the strange landscapes depicted in the woven fabric.

She indicated the others should enter and let them claim their rooms first. It resulted in a little friendly contention between Sukyi and Enid. This, in spite of the fact that Angel couldn't discern a difference between one room and the next. Angel credited it to a little harmless tension release. When they were done, she indicated which area would be used for storage, and selected the remaining room for herself.

When the door clicked shut, the sense of relief was nearly overwhelming. After so many hours living in a shared space, it felt luxurious to be alone. She told herself she was being ridiculous. She'd spent most of her adult life crowded into small spaces with hundreds of other soldiers—none of whom had she been as emotionally attached to as her crew. Her apartment in Brynner had been her first. At the start, it'd been difficult to be so solitary—to not hear the sounds of others breathing in the darkness.

You're not the same person you used to be.

Everyone grows.

The bedroom was oblong, and like the previous space, its curved walls contained empty niches. Soft handmade quilts and pillows covered the bed. She dropped her pack and lay down. The mattress was extremely comfortable, more so than her own bed. Staring at the curved ceiling, she wondered how long they'd have to stay. She knew Sukyi wouldn't have the patience to remain for an extended period. Along with the ever-present gloves and scarf, restlessness was one of Sukyi's defining characteristics. However, Angel sensed that something else was bothering her friend—something Angel didn't know about yet. Something powerful enough to ground Sukyi on a planet she hated and feared. Something that might affect the outcome of their contract.

She'll talk when she's ready, Angel thought, and drifted off with the muffled but comforting sounds of her crew unpacking filtering under the door.

Ten minutes later, lunch was served in the common room. It consisted of fresh bread, goat cheese, butter, and bowls of mixed steamed vegetables, mushrooms, and rice noodles in a creamy savory sauce. It was a tasty variant on any number of dishes she could've gotten from one of the stalls in Brynner. Spiced coffee, tea, and water were served with the meal.

Angel invited Beak, Paulie, and Kirby to join them.

"This is so good," Lou said between mouthfuls.

"I was hoping you'd like it." Paulie's eyes practically twinkled when she smiled. "It's one of Rosie's recipes. Since you'd had such a long journey, I thought you might like something that reminded you of home."

"That was thoughtful, thank you," Lou said.

Sukyi scowled down at her plate. She wasn't eating, not yet. She poked at the food as if looking for something.

Angel whispered, "What's bothering you?"

"I haven't seen the kitchen," Sukyi said, keeping her voice low. "How do I know it's clean?"

"Really?" Angel arched an eyebrow. "You didn't hesitate to eat the MREs. These noodles taste magnificent by comparison."

"And there's no meat," Sukyi said.

"Vegetables are good for you," Angel said. "Eat up."

"And you're not one of my parents," Sukyi said. "Do you know how I know this?"

"I'm not dead and/or mean?" Angel asked.

"Bitch," Sukyi muttered.

"You must be getting tired," Angel said. "You used an actual swear word instead of a vaguely polite euphemism."

"Is there a problem?" Kirby asked.

Angel answered Kirby. "Nothing of consequence. Thank you for your hospitality."

Kirby said, ""I'm sorry. We should have inquired if anyone among your crew had specific dietary requirements."

"It's not that. No one has any allergies. Is your community vegetarian?"

"Not strictly so. If you require meat for every meal, arrangements can be made," Kirby said. "We have goats. You are not the first non-Emissaries to reside here."

She spied Sukyi's worried expression and paused.

"Wait. Doesn't raising domestic animals mean going outside?"

"What about the quarantine?" Sukyi asked.

"It isn't necessary," Kirby said. "Out here."

Panic flashed across Sukyi's face, and she dropped the full dish onto the table with a thump.

"Please. Let me explain," Kirby said. "We have no need of anticontamination procedures because the organisms that plague Brynner do not exist here."

"I understood the whole planet was hostile to humans," Sukyi said, getting to her feet. She yanked her scarf over her nose and mouth again, and edged away from the table until her back hit the wall. "It's explained in detail in Doctor Thakrar's travel guide."

Embarrassment flickered across Kirby's face. "That is what we prefer humans to believe. It prevents . . . exploring."

"Ah," Angel said. "I see."

"If you don't follow medical protocols, am I going to be able to get back to my ship?" Sukyi asked.

"Definitely," Kirby said. "We trade with the station regularly. We also send shipments to Rosencrantz in Brynner."

"Where are the other ships?" Enid asked.

"They are sheltering elsewhere," Kirby said. "Somewhere safe from Serrao-Orlov and Vissia Corsini." Kirby held up both hands as if to hold back a tide of questions. "We will discuss more later. You are tired and hungry. Please. Relax. Eat."

"After lunch," Angel said. "I'd like to take a tour of Ogenth."

"Of course," Kirby said. "We only ask that you not go alone. Beak is our best guide. She will be at your disposal, as will Paulie. She has volunteered to be your interpreter."

"Are we prisoners?" Enid asked.

"You are honored guests," Kirby said. "But you aren't Emissaries. You aren't familiar with the life-forms in the area. Nor do you know the terrain. We wish to prevent any unfortunate accidents. This is for your safety."

Like Rosie's expedition and the Great Tanners bear, Angel thought. "I see."

Silence blanketed the room. Everyone resumed eating—everyone but Sukyi. Angel caught several significant glances from Enid.

Sukyi resumed her seat. She stared at her food and didn't look up. "How is your pilot, Jackson?"

"He's recovering well," Kirby said. She seemed unfazed by the abrupt subject change. "Thank you so much for bringing the medicine. He should be on his feet again in a few days. It was kind of you to ask about him."

"It's the least we could do," Sukyi said. She sat up straighter and took a cautious bite of the noodles.

Another long silence descended upon the room. Everyone focused on their eating until the meal was over. Beak collected the dishes and took them away. At last, Kirby motioned to Paulie, who nodded and left the room.

"Perhaps now would be a good time for a drink?" Kirby asked. "And then we can discuss the details of our situation."

"That would be lovely," Sukyi said.

Angel was pleasantly surprised by her first sip. It was a light-colored wine that smelled of honey and something like cinnamon, and tasted like liquid sunshine.

"It's fire bee mead. Do you like it?" Kirby asked.

"I do," Sukyi said.

The alcohol warmed Angel's stomach, and after the second drink, she felt herself relax a little. So far, everything they had been served was fragrant, flavorful, and plentiful. It wasn't what Angel had anticipated from an isolated community.

"Ogenth is largely self-sufficient," Kirby said as if in answer to Angel's unasked question. "Rosencrantz augments our supplies with little luxuries—human spices, salt, and sugar. Medicines we can't replicate. Items that would take longer to make than buy. Lab supplies. Metals for building. Ship parts. We grow as much as we can. The goats and other herd animals provide fiber for clothing as well as milk, cheese, meat, and fertilizer. The local soil is rich in nutrients. We generate electricity with wind turbines and solar panels. Water is collected from an underground stream. There's a lake not far from here where we fish. We have our own library database and access to the Allnet. We also have a fully operational medical facility and science lab."

Angel asked, "Where?"

"I'll be happy to show you if you like," Kirby said. "However, it's been a long day. Would it be all right if you and I discussed a few things alone first? There are details that are delicate in nature. And I'd like a chance to present them in the best light possible."

Unease tightened Angel's shoulders. *She gave us alcohol before broaching the subject.* While it was something she'd probably do if she were in Kirby's place, Angel didn't like feeling manipulated. *The news isn't going to be good, is it?*

"I'm not attempting dishonesty, Captain. I merely wish to prevent any misunderstandings."

"Where do you wish to go?" Angel asked.

"I'd like to show you Ogenth," Kirby said. "That's all."

Enid had her eyes closed and was apparently dozing off in a corner. Lou and Paulie were having an animated conversation about some sort of mechanical problem. Sukyi was the only one who appeared to be unaffected by the alcohol.

That doesn't mean that she isn't, Angel thought. She leaned toward Sukyi and told her she was in charge. Then Angel got to her feet. "All right. Let's walk."

17 ▇▇▇▇

Angel exited the crew suite in a rush of clattering glass beads. She followed Kirby for a few paces before speaking.

"All right," Angel said. "What's the bad news?"

"There isn't any," Kirby said.

Angel decided this was a prime opportunity to bring up all the things that had been bothering her. "Serrao Orlov know you're out here. They've left you to do whatever you want. They know you've your own means to access the station. That seems like an awful lot of leeway to give smugglers. We both know they would've taken this place from you if they could. Therefore, you must have something you've been using to hold them off."

"True."

"So, I have to ask, what is it about you that is so danger-ous? And if you're so dangerous, why do you need us?"

Kirby said, "We prefer nonviolent solutions to our prob-lems."

"That doesn't mean you aren't dangerous," Angel said. "What do you have over Serrao-Orlov?"

"You keep using words with violent connotations. We don't believe in killing, Captain, not when negotiation is pos-sible. And negotiation is always possible. It's merely a matter of managing expectations."

"And yet, me and mine are here." Angel scowled. "To fight and die for you."

"I understood you were sent to hide from the authorities."

"If you would rather we left—"

Kirby held up a hand. "I apologize. We are quite happy to have you here. I misspoke in my efforts to explain the strength of our convictions. Diplomacy is far preferable to violence."

"I don't disagree with that stance."

"That is very good to hear," Kirby said. "There are always more issues and complications caused by the use of force than if the problem had been solved through negotiation in the first place."

Angel said, "I can't shake the feeling you're keeping secrets—dangerous secrets. Tell me what the hell is going on, damn it. Or me and mine are packing up and leaving."

"Please forgive me. Apparently, I've been in the habit of ob-fuscation for too long," Kirby said. "You are correct. I am keep-ing information from you, but that is why we are speaking now."

Angel stopped where she was and folded her arms across her chest. She raised an eyebrow and waited.

Kirby said, "Please. There is something I must show you and I cannot do so here."

"All right." Angel continued to follow Kirby down the hallway.

"Theodella Archady's death is unfortunate," Kirby said. "She was, in many ways, an exemplary corporate leader. She was far-sighted and saw our relationship as mutually beneficial."

"Rosie told me she exploited you."

"Not in ways that matter to us. Theodella had no desire for planet-wide expansion of Serrao-Orlov's interests. This meant that we could continue to exist as we were without interference," Kirby said. "And that was our highest priority."

"She made billions off of your technology and didn't compensate you very well for it. That doesn't sound all that equitable," Angel said.

"We have no need of wealth. We only want to live in obscurity. Alas, that is no longer possible," Kirby said. "And Vissia Corsini does not negotiate. There are no mutually beneficial options."

"Wouldn't appealing to the United Worlds' Supreme Court be a better answer?" Angel asked. "Rosie said you had your reasons for choosing not to, but I can't think of what they might be. It doesn't make sense."

The hallway branched off, and Kirby took a right turn. The dark blue tiles on the floor gradually transitioned to cerulean.

"We have secreted ourselves away for our own protection.

You'll understand why soon enough," Kirby said. "Please understand we've no wish to frighten you." She stopped walking and pressed a panel on the wall next to an irised doorway.

"Frighten?" Angel began to feel uneasy again.

Kurosawa? *Are you there?*

I am, Captain.

Stand by.

Affirmative.

The door slid open, and Kirby motioned her inside. Upon entering, the doorway closed automatically behind them. It was obvious that they had arrived at a new branch of the complex—one that wasn't readily accessible. The new hallway was devoid of decoration. The walls were a simple white, and the tiles on the floor were black. They passed several doors, all of them closed, before Kirby laid a hand on what appeared to be a pressure door.

"Please remember you and your crew are safe among us. We are a peaceful people. We believe in communication. I would go so far as to say that it is designed into our genetic makeup." She paused and then seemed to steel herself. "Captain, I am not what I appear to you at this moment. The majority of the people living in this facility, including myself, are, in fact, not human."

"That's what Rosie said. But you don't look any different than any other humans."

Kirby hesitated again. "We—we don't appear any different at the moment because we are able to dramatically change our appearance."

"What did you say?"

Captain, I am registering elevated blood pressure and heartbeat. Are you all right?

I'm fine, Kurosawa. *I think.*

Yes, Captain.

"Let me demonstrate." Kirby palmed the security pad, and the pressure door slid open.

It revealed a lab filled with scientific equipment. Twenty or so residents were working on what appeared to be various projects—none of which was of any significance to Angel because she'd never been scientifically trained. She did, however, recognize the cluster of crates neatly stacked in a corner.

"Please, follow me," Kirby said.

The second door slipped shut behind Angel with a whoosh. *You still there,* Kurosawa?

I am, indeed.

Kirby addressed the room. "This is the orientation I informed you I would perform. Please continue with your assignments."

The majority of the staff redirected their attention to their tasks. One or two of them continued to stare.

"We'll finish this chat in my lab," Kirby said. "The others need to continue their work with as little interruption as possible."

She led Angel to a smaller, more private area with a desk, a number of chairs, several shelves of books, and a glasstop computer. Kirby motioned for Angel to sit. Angel watched Kirby for some sign of what was about to happen. About the time that she began to lose patience, she noticed that Kirby's face was gradually changing. That wasn't all. When Angel had first met her, Kirby was short and heavyset. Now, she was taller. Her hair began to lighten until it became silver. Her facial features grew broader and flatter—her nose grew more predominant and her chin less rounded, squarer. Her cheekbones were higher and more pronounced, her forehead elongated, and her eyes narrowed and drifted farther apart.

When the transformation was complete, Angel tried not to gawk.

Captain, are you all right?

Kirby was now a majestic six feet tall, broad-shouldered, and muscular. Her gender was no longer easily discernible—at least not in human terms. Long, thick bright silver hair crowned an oblong head—starting at the top of her skull. Bright red-orange and yellow stripes sketched curving lines across her forehead. Her much smaller and narrower eyes were the color of molten gold. Her ears had been reduced to earholes. As for her nose, it was wider than before. Other than her forehead it was her most dominant feature; even her mouth had shrunk to a thin line. Her neck was long and slender. Her skin was a pale cyan. Her trousers were now much too short and her shirt sagged on her slender frame.

"Wow." *She ... They? Are beautiful.*

Captain? *Kurosawa's* inquiry had become urgent.

Stand down, Kurosawa. *I'm fine.*

Kirby's features shifted again so that her mouth became wider, and something moved within her throat beneath the surface of her skin. An instant or two passed before she spoke again. "As you see me now is fairly close to our natural form. With some individual variances, of course. For reasons I am about to tell you, my mouth and throat are still patterned after humans. We transmit meaning through scent and motion. Our language does not translate into yours."

Angel blinked. She was stunned and found it difficult to speak. "Oh." *Come on. This isn't the first time you've met a member of an alien species.* But it *was* the first time she'd done so under friendly circumstances. It was just as stressful, even if it wasn't as deadly. *There's still time. We're not done talking, yet.*

"Long before humans came to this planet, there was a population die-off initiated by first contact with a different visiting alien race," Kirby said. "In the end, the planet you call Persephone was left with two dominate sapient species. The first of the two we will call 'the Architects' for the lack of a better translation. The Architects were highly intelligent. The search for scientific knowledge was their most revered aspect of life. At the same time, they were isolationist—the initial alien contact served as an influential one, you see. Thus, they rarely explored outside their own door. When other species initiated interactions, the Architects were often left traumatized."

"Were they invaded?"

"Luck was with them. They managed to avoid it. Occasionally, trade was initiated. However, they decided a trusted intermediary would be the best solution. With this purpose in mind, they genetically altered the second native species."

"Without their permission?"

"At the initiation of the project, the second species wasn't advanced enough to be considered capable of informed choice. We did not communicate in the same way, you see."

Angel felt sick.

Kirby continued. "My people underwent many iterations. Interactions between alien species go much smoother when there are obvious physical similarities between them. And so, my people have the ability to . . . transform."

"Oh."

"We call ourselves the Emissaries. We are designed to be adaptable to whatever environment we find ourselves in. It was necessary. Not all sentient creatures with whom we interacted were carbon based."

There are alien life-forms that are not carbon based? Angel closed her mouth. *How many life-forms have we not encountered yet?* She stopped the questions bubbling up in her mind and focused once more on listening to Kirby.

"Therefore, the ability to survive in a myriad of environments was preferable. Ultimately, we change into the form of those we communicate with in order to form advantageous partnerships. Ultimately, this not only affects our ability to exist within an environment. It also affects how we perceive and take in information."

Angel put a hand to her head. *I'm not trained for this. I-I'm a soldier. I shoot people. I protect whomever I'm hired to protect. I don't deal with First Contact scenarios.* "Ah. This is a lot to take in."

"I understand that when your species acquires and uses

a new skill your brains change on a physical cellular level," Kirby said. "Is this true?"

"Maybe? I don't know. I guess so."

"Largely your species is visually, tactilely, and/or auditorily dependent. Much of your ability to convey information involves the description of data involving these senses. Therefore, in order to correctly interpret your intentions, we must acquire and analyze visual, tactile, and auditory information. We developed the specific acuities upon which humans depend. We became human in order to understand humans."

"Oh."

"Please remember we aren't a threat. We were born to be diplomats—"

"Hold on. I'm ex-military," Angel said. "I know what diplomats are. They're spies."

Kirby paused and tilted her head. The movement reminded Angel of a bird. And at that moment, she tried very hard not to think of any large, colorful raptors.

"This is broadly true," Kirby said. "And I would be remiss if I didn't admit that we were often employed as such. However, we have never killed. We cannot. The Architects would not permit it."

When Angel considered the situation, it made sense. Who would create a race that could shape change and then leave them the power to kill? *It would be suicide.* "How could anyone stop you if you wanted to?"

"Violence affects us deeply. It makes us physically ill. If the matter is pushed too far, it is possible we might die."

"Is Rosie one of you?"

Kirby smiled—or the corners of her mouth turned up in what Angel assumed was a smile. It was difficult to know what was Kirby's true self and what was Kirby's imitation of human expression. "Rosencrantz has endured many changes over the years. However, they remain human."

Angel didn't know why she was relieved.

"But there are those among us whose lineage is mixed," Kirby said.

"Really?"

Kirby nodded.

"Oh." Angel didn't know what to say.

Kirby continued. "Interactions of a cooperative nature are the most advantageous for all parties involved. Thus, our abilities grew more refined with that end in mind. We were encouraged to assume the most pleasing or reassuring forms. Attractiveness does make successful communication more likely."

Angel narrowed her eyes.

Shrugging, Kirby said, "It is true."

"What happened to the Architects?" Angel asked. "Did you revolt or something?"

"In their constant search for knowledge they mistakenly created a virus with the genetic ability to destroy their entire race. There were certain political frictions between Architect nations, you see."

"Politics? They died of politics?"

"Just because we don't have the ability to perpetuate violence doesn't mean that the Architects didn't."

STINA LEICHT

"Point."

"Those that created the virus thought they could contain it," Kirby said. "They were mistaken. It escaped into the atmosphere. The Architects were rendered extinct within a year. We are all that remains."

Angel thought, *And that's an aspect of Emissary history I won't be explaining to Sukyi.* "What happened to the virus?"

"It proved too efficient at killing. With no living hosts, it died out. Don't worry. Nothing of it remains in the atmosphere—not that it would infect humans if it did."

A phrase from Angel's father's Bible sprang to mind. *And the meek shall inherit the earth.* "If you can change, why don't you simply leave?" she asked. "You can move. Find somewhere else to live. You're adaptable. You can find more pleasant places and ways to live."

"The Architects had no wish to lose control or fall prey to their invention. Not only did they deny us violence, but reproduction for our species is almost impossible except under a specific set of conditions. That is why this lab and this facility are so important to us. We can travel, of course. That's part of our vocation. However, we can't as a species abandon the planet."

"So, you've been alone all this time?"

"Until Rosencrantz's church arrived. Our numbers have never been that vast. The missionaries saw the ruins left behind by the Architects in city after city and assumed the planet was uninhabited. We had no idea that we had been invaded until it was too late."

"I'm so sorry."

"A small group of monks discovered their error. They attempted to rectify the problem but by then the Church had invested a great deal of time and money in their new colony. There was a schism. Some joined forces with us. Rosencrantz Asher was among their number."

"That would mean that they're—"

"One hundred and twenty-six years old," Kirby said. "My people are long-lived. We've had a great deal of time in which to explore our biology as well as those around us."

Angel couldn't help thinking of Sukyi. *Could they help her?*

"We extended Rosencrantz's life in exchange for the service that they do for us. It is somewhat ironic that they have assumed a role that we had once filled for the Architects. However, Rosencrantz Asher volunteered. My people and I did not."

"I'm so sorry. I wish that hadn't happened to you."

Kirby shrugged again. It was unclear what was meant by the action.

Angel broke the silence. "Serrao-Orlov knew you were here when they bought the planet?"

"I understand the Church advised the corporation of the situation after the sale," Kirby said. "That is how the planet was acquired for a discounted price."

"Why didn't the Church offer the planet to you? Wouldn't that have resolved a lot of problems?"

"Perhaps, but we were not consulted." Kirby motioned toward the door, inviting her to exit. "There is more I would show you."

Angel followed Kirby across the main lab to the door. She noticed things she hadn't before. There were three other exits each with a sign: Medical Wing, Microbiology Lab, and Ecology Lab. The last two had biohazard warnings displayed on the door. The signs read: *Environmental suits and safety procedures required beyond this point.*

I wonder what is stored in there, Angel thought.

"We might consider sharing our knowledge freely," Kirby said. "But only if all of humanity had access. And that is not something Serrao-Orlov would be willing to do. Definitely not while under Vissia Corsini's leadership."

Angel said, "Their planet. Their resources. Their investment. Even if none of it actually belongs to them."

Kirby nodded. "She wants to use us as we were once used. As spies. And that, we will never do. There is a great deal of power in the ability to replicate the forms of others. Far more power than is safe to give Vissia Corsini."

"Can you mimic specific people?"

"You see the problem, then," Kirby said. "Transforming is a talent like any other. There are some who are good and others who aren't as much."

"How good? Fool security good?"

Kirby changed back into the human form she'd assumed before. The process was far more rapid this time. Then she led Angel to the main passage. The sound of the locking door echoed down the hallway.

"That would depend upon several factors," Kirby said. "One of which is the amount of time spent with the individual to be assumed. That said, one or two of us could do this."

Angel whistled.

"Now you understand our concern," Kirby said.

"I do," Angel said. "There are governments who would take advantage of your abilities if they could."

"For that reason," Kirby said, "I'm not sure you should tell the others about what I've shown you."

Angel ran her fingers through her hair. "I'm sorry, but I won't let them go into a fight like this one without knowing who they're fighting for. Enid, Lou, and I . . . well . . . we had enough of that shit in the corps."

"I understand," Kirby said, and stopped in front of another door.

"They'll keep your secret," Angel said. "They're good people—no matter how scruffy some of them might appear."

Kirby led Angel into the new room. This one was entirely different from the lab. It was a brightly lit, hydroponic greenhouse with hundreds of native plants. The air was filled with complex scents interwoven with the greenery. There were three adults and four children playing in the potted garden. All appeared to be in their original forms. Angel had no idea who they were or what they were saying to one another, but she did get the impression of familial love and contented hominess.

"This is what you'll be fighting for," Kirby said. "No matter what you decide, please tell them this much."

18 ███████

Angel zipped up her environment suit. She had left her rifle, helmet, and gloves on *Kurosawa*'s ramp for the time being. She wasn't in a hurry, not yet. Knowing where they were headed, she wanted to take extra care of her gear. She was halfway through the mandatory environment-suit systems checks for hostile environs when Kirby entered. She was wearing what Angel had come to think of as her "middle-aged-human-lady disguise."

"Good morning," Kirby said.

Angel nodded a greeting before returning to her work. "You know you don't have to transform for us. Be yourself."

Kirby tilted her head. "It is easier to communicate with you this way."

"Fair enough."

Kirby said, "I hear you're going to tour the outside of our facility today."

"That's the plan," Angel said. "Paulie brought me the architectural blueprints last night, but I'd like a firsthand view of our topographical defenses."

"That seems wise," Kirby said. "But why wear all of that?" She made a gesture that included Angel's helmet and gloves.

"It's standard procedure. We might be headed into a Quarantine Zone."

Kirby looked away. Her jaw tightened and an expression of discomfort took over her face. "I should've emphasized this information more strongly yesterday. But there were so many things to discuss that I forgot."

Angel set down the diagnostic panel she'd attached to the arm of her suit. "And?"

"You don't need the protective gear," Kirby said. "The Quarantine Zone doesn't extend this far from Brynner."

Angel blinked. Several other things that had been bothering her clicked into place. "Then why all the procedures when we arrived?"

"Precautions were necessary. Your ship *did* pass through the actual Quarantine Zone," Kirby said. "However, the zone is only active in a twenty-mile band around Brynner."

"And Serrao-Orlov doesn't know this?" Angel asked.

Kirby looked even more uncomfortable. "I don't believe so. We certainly haven't disabused them of the idea that the whole planet is dangerous."

"I see."

"The truth is we . . . engineer it that way and have been since Serrao-Orlov acquired the planet," Kirby said. "To discourage the corporation from expanding farther into our lands. Naturally, we have also planned fail-safes so that the organisms in question don't survive long beyond their intended environs."

Thinking back on the lab she'd seen, Angel had no doubt that it was possible. "I thought you were peaceful."

"We are," Kirby said. "That's why we handled the situation the way we did."

"But you can't very well say you don't kill," Angel said. "Can you? The corporation sends workers out into that. There is no prison on Persephone. There's only the Quarantine Zone."

"We didn't intend for humans to utilize it—"

"Intent has nothing to do with it, and you know it." Angel could see this wasn't going to get anywhere. *And who am I to fault someone else for what they choose to do in order to survive?* She held up a hand to halt any further excuses. "All right. All right. We don't have to go out in full quarantine gear."

"I'm sorry—"

"It's a lot of information," Angel said. "I know." She picked up her rifle and began checking it.

"Thank you for understanding," Kirby said.

"You do know that everything changes now. If Vissia Corsini is the kind of person you believe her to be, I wouldn't expect any of your previous deterrents to last. They will make it known that the wall is the only deadly area the instant they discover this."

Kirby nodded. "We know. We considered using some of the organisms in defense of the community. However, we cannot do so without risking ourselves or you."

"Did Rosie send any reports I don't know about this morning?"

"Not to me," Kirby said. "I requested that you be copied on any new information."

Kurosawa? Angel asked.

I am on it, Captain. After a short pause, Kurosawa replied, Rosie has sent a finalized list of names and accompanying dossiers.

Excellent, Angel said. *How many are coming our way?*

Twenty-five. Fourteen are former URW military. One of them is the commander.

At least I'll know what to expect. Who's the commander? Anyone I know?

She is not one listed on the Thirteenth's rolls. She is J. Reese.

Thank you for checking.

One more thing, I do note a familiar name on the list.

Who?

Kennedy Liu.

Oh. She didn't know why that news hit her so hard. Kennedy had been an unknown quantity from the start. *Well, she's not an unknown now.*

"Is something wrong, Captain?" Kirby asked.

"Everything is fine," Angel said. "I'll inform the others about the environment, and we'll make changes accordingly. Sukyi, for one, will be relieved."

Beak and Paulie entered along with a small crowd of younger or smaller Emissaries—some of whom were transformed and others not. Angel looked on as Paulie gave out a few hugs before breaking away from the group. Beak seemed to focus on two individuals in particular. One appeared to be a smaller version of herself.

Do they assume every aspect of their form at will, or are certain features dictated by genetics like the rest of us? Is that her child? A mate? A sibling? Something about the way they were interacting hinted at a mother-daughter relationship. The way that the smaller one squirmed under Beak's attentive touches. The tug to straighten a sleeve. The palm against the face. Neither spoke.

Some things are universal. Angel turned away and took a deep breath. The air in the ship bay had changed. The machinery odor was gone, having been replaced by more homely scents: flowers spiced with pepper and soap. Her thoughts drifted to the battle ahead. *Twenty-five well-trained mercenaries versus three ex-marines, two untrained* volunteers *who may or may not be reliable in a fight, and a sickly con woman with an itchy trigger finger.*

There weren't enough people willing to take on the task of defending the community. She'd known that would be the case, but she'd hoped that Serrao-Orlov would send only a handful of troops.

Does Serrao-Orlov know we're here?

Angel swallowed her unease and then considered the options. They'd have to make up the difference in fortifications. Luckily, Kirby and the rest were capable when it came to building defenses and traps, and implementing them. *That's something. Given their scientific advancement, it might even be an advantage.*

Any word on when those mercs will arrive, Kurosawa? Angel asked.

Not as of yet, Captain.

Message me the instant you do. No matter the time of day, she said. *And as soon as I get back, I want to go over those dossiers. They might contain something useful. Kirby says they've had military encounters with Serrao-Orlov before. Get me the history: unit make up, location, and tactics analysis. I want patterns. I want what they know and what they don't.*

Yes, Captain.

"Good morning, Captain," Paulie said.

"Good morning," Angel said. "Do you have the blueprints I asked for?"

Paulie smiled and patted the oversized hand terminal tucked under her arm. "I do."

"Then let's get started," Angel said.

She began with an update about the quarantine gear.

"How long have you known?" Sukyi assumed a defensive stance, shifting her feet slightly apart. Her jaw noticeably tightened, and her eyes narrowed as she frowned. "You're certain it's safe?"

Angel said, "Kirby informed me this morning. And I have to believe she's telling the truth. Lying would only prevent us from saving Ogenth."

The obstinate expression on Sukyi's face didn't budge. Angel understood Sukyi's fear.

"If it makes you feel better," Paulie said, "you can wear your environment suit. I don't think there's any harm, is there?"

"Peripheral vision and mobility are both impaired," Angel said. "Communication as well, but since we're only going for a hike, it shouldn't matter as much. Combat is another matter."

Paulie asked, "But isn't that the case under conditions where environment suits are necessary?"

"It is," Angel said. "But in that case, everyone has the same disadvantage." She turned to Sukyi. "Well?"

"I'll take the information under advisement," Sukyi said. It was clear she wanted to say more but was reluctant to go on.

"That's all I ask," Angel said. "The same goes for the rest of you."

With that, she had Paulie set up the display projection so that everyone could study Ogenth's blueprints.

"What's this?" Enid asked, pointing to a tunnel. "A door?"

"A wind turbine," Paulie said. "The air flows through here and exits here. There are vents to the environmental units here and here where air is heated and filtered for daily use. Every air tunnel has vents. They are the only connection between the tunnels and Ogenth."

"How big are they?" Angel asked. "Big enough to admit a drone?"

"The tunnels? Yes," Paulie said. A line formed between her eyebrows, and her lips pressed together. "The vents would be more difficult to access as the covers would have to be removed first."

"Are the vent filters electronically monitored?" Angel asked.

"There's a notification alarm sent to maintenance when a filter requires replacing or malfunctions. It also signals an alert when a filter is tampered with," Paulie said. "Sometimes animals and insects find their way into the system and chew on the wiring."

"Ah," Angel said. "Is there an easy way into the air tunnels?"

"Certainly," Paulie said. "Maintenance crews regularly check the passages and clear out accumulated debris or plant life. There are four tunnels. Here, here, here, and here. There's a slotted vent plate on the end that allows air flow but prevents entry for larger animals."

"Where are those doors?" Angel asked.

Paulie pointed them out, shrinking and enlarging the image as necessary.

"We'll go here first," Angel said, pointing to the first access tunnel on the east side of Ogenth. "Any other openings to the surface that I didn't mark last night? Exits? Windows?"

"There's the goat paddock," Paulie said. "We regularly let them out to graze. Someone accompanies them, of course. Predators can be a problem." She placed two fingers over the area on the plans. "A majority of the windows are along here. The conservatory has the most glass. You're right to worry about that. I think you spotted everything else."

"Thank you," Angel said. She continued, pointing out details she'd inventoried—possible weak points in defenses—and then presented a list of prioritized projects. She'd divided them into those that the Emissaries would be responsible for under the leadership of Paulie and Beak, and those that her team would oversee. After that, Angel asked her crew if they had further input.

She wasn't afraid of admitting she didn't know everything. That was when trusting others' expertise was the best policy. She'd seen too many egos get in the way of success in her career, and in her line of work, failure cost lives. Given that she and whoever died under her command had been destined for revivification, it was a cautious philosophy and one any number of her superiors didn't share. However, none of them had faced the big empty.

Or the interior of a reclamation pod, limb regrowth, and months of physical therapy or the possibility of waking up a vegetable.

After that discussion was finished, she turned once more to Paulie.

"This morning, we'll take a tour of the eastern terrain. Paulie, please bring up the topographical maps."

"This is it." Paulie then adjusted the magnification so that they could see more detail. "I assume you'll want to start with the environmental and electrical tunnels."

The overview took twenty minutes. Angel shut off the projection when it was clear that everyone had what they needed. "Time to pack up, ladies. We dust off in ten."

Lou asked, "Is there time for coffee before we leave?"

"Isn't there coffee onboard?" Angel asked.

"Ogenth's coffee is better," Enid said.

Angel checked the time. "You've got four minutes to get your asses in the ship."

"Yes, Captain," Lou said.

Enid took off running. Lou wasn't far behind.

"Watch out! Watch out! Woman on a mission!" Lou shouted as she dodged people and objects along her path to the door.

Angel yelled, "Three minutes!"

"You can't leave without me!" Lou called. "I'm the pilot!"

"Try me!" Angel called back.

Paulie tucked her terminal under her arm and headed up the ramp. The textured steel of *Kurosawa*'s ramp rattled under Beak's feet.

Sukyi approached. "We need to talk." Her voice echoed a bit off the docking garage walls.

"We'll be safe as a baby in a crib," Angel said.

"Hanging fifty meters high in a tree during a hurricane," Sukyi said.

"Are you getting cowardly in your old age?" Angel asked.

"Why don't you ever so gently fuck off?" Sukyi asked.

"Your Nigerian charm seems to be wearing thin," Angel said. "You've been in a mood for days. What's wrong?"

"It's the elevation," Sukyi said. "This place gives me nose bleeds."

That knocked the nonsense out of Angel. She grew serious. "Is it bad?"

"Not bad enough to ground me," Sukyi said, strapping on the last of her weapons.

"Nothing is enough to ground you," Angel said. *That's the trouble.* She scanned her friend's features for some sign of her health—some excuse to force her to rest—not that it would do any good. She wasn't Sukyi's mother, nor could she give her orders. Angel knew her protests would only be met with mulishness. She resigned herself to leaving those decisions to Sukyi. *She may be a bit suicidal, but she's not a child.*

Sukyi waited until the others were inside before she pressed on. "I don't like this."

"You don't like this place. I get it," Angel said. "I don't even blame you."

"Let's be frank," Sukyi said. "We've set fire to better planets than this one. But your clients haven't been honest with us. They've lied about who they are, what they are, and what they're doing here. And now they've lied about quarantine, too?"

"Takes a liar to know a liar. Is that it?" Angel asked. The retort sounded far worse than she intended. Uncomfortable and unable to take the words back, she shrugged and turned to walk up the ramp. She was halted by the grip of Sukyi's hand on her shoulder.

"Are you impugning my character?"

"You can't be serious," Angel said.

"I am."

Angel faced Sukyi. The hardness in Sukyi's eyes said that Angel had better be careful. "All I'm saying is that you aren't exactly famous for honesty yourself. Your reputation doesn't matter. It never has. You're complicated. I trust you, anyway. They're complicated in a similar way." She shrugged.

"They're also dangerous. Anyone who can do what they do is. Are you sure you're aware of all the elements in play?"

"There's no way of knowing. We both know that. In fact, I'd wager that there's a lot they haven't told us," Angel said. "But I have faith that their goals and our goals align for the time being. I'm also willing to gamble that they're worth saving no matter their secrets."

"That's a mighty big risk."

"Let's just say," Angel said, "I'm comfortable working with an element of the unknown. I've done it with you often enough."

"You're implying that—"

Enid sprinted up the ramp with a lidded cup in her hand. Lou wasn't far behind.

Lou paused. "See? I told you that you couldn't leave without me."

"You're thirty seconds late," Angel said.

"My terminal says twenty-three!" Lou said, and vanished inside.

Sukyi glared at her.

Angel asked, "Can you honestly say you don't have any secrets?"

"Not from you. Nothing important."

"All right. Why did you suddenly show up when you did? You need something, and you need it from me. What is it?"

A muffled barrage of pre-mission chatter drifted down the open ramp. Lou was babbling like she always did before a fight. Enid met her verbal salvo with a number of well-placed growls. It was odd how certain sounds would always mean home.

Sukyi's shoulders dropped. She stared at the floor. After a moment of silence, she said, "Nothing I'm holding back will cause you or the others harm."

Angel nodded. "Sure. But whatever it is . . . it'll complicate everyone's lives. It's already done so. We both know that. But you've always worked very hard to minimize the worst of the harm on others. It's who you are. I trust that."

"Even when I haven't been completely honest?"

"Even then." Angel knew Sukyi to be extremely close-mouthed about anything personal. *Maybe she's near death and that's why she looked me up?* The idea sent a chill through Angel. *Not now. Please. Not when I just got you back.*

Sukyi hesitated again. "There's something I need to tell you."

"I know," Angel said. "But we both know that now isn't that time."

An uncomfortable look spread across Sukyi's face. "I suppose not." It was replaced with a small smile. It seemed to have been pasted like a plaster over a crack in a wall.

"Let's talk about it when we get back," Angel said. "Right now, we've a job to do."

Sukyi nodded once and then headed up the ramp. Angel followed, slapping the button to seal up the ship. Just before the ramp thumped into place, she heard the sound of the ventilation system's exhaust fans spin up. *Kurosawa's* engines rumbled to life. The atmosphere inside the ship swelled with pre-mission tension. This was Angel's favorite part of a mission—that moment before everything was set, before anything could go horribly wrong.

No battle plan ever survives contact with the enemy, Angel thought. Where had she read that?

She settled into the copilot's seat just as the pressure doors opened.

Captain, I have finished compiling the information you requested. *Kurosawa* used the private channel.

Good, Angel said. *Add it to the file marked* Battle Plan. *I'll go over it when we get back. Any news on when they'll be headed our way?*

Another message arrived marked for your eyes only. It indicates the mercenaries should arrive in six days. I have downloaded the contents of Rosie's text into your hand terminal.

Six days wasn't terribly long to plan and execute a solid defense against overwhelming odds, but it wasn't any worse than what Angel had expected.

Thank you, Kurosawa.

19

TIME: 11:15
DAY: TUESDAY
OGENTH

In a line behind Beak and Paulie, a cold wind fought Angel's progress as she hiked the steep mountain incline. The forest floor was soft under her heavy boots. It felt good to be free of Ogenth's thick walls. The forest hugging the mountainside smelled clean and crisp—quite the contrast to Brynner's sour stench. In the time Angel had lived there, she'd assumed the stink was merely a part of the planet's atmosphere. Understanding that that wasn't the case caused a shift in her feelings toward Persephone. For the moment, that was a little unsettling. She wasn't sure how much of her data on and experience of the place had been colored by a deliberate lie. Being uncertain how cautious she needed to be—if at all— conflicted badly with her survival instincts.

Kirby said it was safe.

Kirby is not human and is capable of immediately adapting to her surroundings. Me and mine are not.

Paulie had warned them that there might be snow flurries. It never snowed in Brynner, and Angel couldn't remember the last time she'd seen frozen precipitation from outside of a full environment suit. She found herself anticipating big fat flakes floating among the branches. She knew it would mean dealing with the damp, but a partial environment suit was great protection against wet and cold. However, the sentimental reasons she enjoyed snow outweighed any potential discomfort.

Bad weather would complicate the job of protecting Ogenth. On the other hand, it would also add factors with which their attackers would have to contend.

Trusting that Paulie and Beak would alert her, Angel found herself focusing on other aspects of planning. She used *Kurosawa* to make notes about the possibility of hiding traps in the snow, the need to gather data on the weather patterns for the next few days, and the effects of wind and terrain. Ice and gusting winds would slow down surface troops— particularly on rough ground and a steep incline.

Unless they have mechs and powered armor, of course, she thought. *Mechs and powered armor would be bad.*

It all depended upon how motivated Serrao-Orlov was to obtain Ogenth and how much money they were willing to invest.

Earlier, she'd talked to the pilot Jackson and consulted Lou as well. The winds around Ogenth were particularly bad except during certain periods of the day and year. It was an-other reason why Rosie had timed their arrival so precisely. Rosie's information indicated the company mercs wouldn't be aware of that problem. It would cause a minor delay as they'd likely be forced to make the last leg of the journey on foot. That was something Angel could work with.

Of course, that meant the use of mechs and power suits would be more likely. Luckily, Rosie had provided a report on the tech specs for the equipment the company would send. Angel told Lou to go over them while she waited for their return to *Kurosawa*. Lou had wanted to accompany them on the hike up the mountain, but Angel decided it wasn't worth the risk.

Five days left, Angel thought. *Five*. She wasn't going to be getting much sleep. *There's so much to do.*

She shifted her focus back to the woods. She couldn't help comparing the trees around her with the pinchwood forest circling Brynner. These trees were far less menacing than the lacy trunks—in fact, they reminded her of home. Pinchwoods stretched anywhere from seventy-five to two hundred meters tall—a seemingly common arboreal trait on Persephone, at least within the parts of the planet she'd vis-ited. These woods seemed to have more in common with the versions of birches, maples, oaks, pines, and other conifers that inhabited Thandh. There were no pinchwoods and no sign of the deadly beetles that swarmed inside them.

Of course, there were other things that weren't like home. There were large insects with bright green wings that fluttered around the evergreens. Odd-looking birds nested among the branches. Small brown and black rats with long fur scurried up the trunks and leapt between branches. Once in a while, she heard something large move off in the woods to her left. And once she heard a snarl from what she thought was a large cat. Beak and Paulie didn't seem disturbed. So, Angel assumed it was all right.

The longer they walked through the forest, the more often she noticed various changes in the smell of the plants and trees around them.

At one point she noted the bright red-and-yellow fungus growing along the edges of the path here and there. It formed in rounded clumps the size of two suit helmets. The surface contained paper-thin ridges that traced wavy lines not un-like a human brain. Whenever the party encountered them, Paulie would carefully direct them to keep to a safe distance. Upon the third such encounter, Angel asked why.

"They're poisonous. They're also carnivorous," Paulie said. "The ridges are designed to attract and trap insects and small animals."

"Are there any of them living closer to Ogenth?" Angel asked.

"No," Paulie said. "We keep them away because they kill the baby goats."

"Is it possible to transport them safely?" Angel asked.

"No one has really tried," Paulie said. "Why do you want to know?"

Sukyi said, "Angel's thinking of borrowing one of your tactics."

"The more we can use our surroundings against the enemy, the less of our resources we'll have to directly use in defense," Angel said. *And unlike mines and timed explosives, they don't leave a detectable electronic signature.*

Paulie nodded. "Ah. I'll consult one of the plant biologists. They'll know."

Angel made a note and sent it to *Kurosawa*. She took the opportunity to check on Lou via the com link. *How's it going?*

Lou replied, *It's boring is how it is.*

I meant the research.

Oh, Lou said. *That. There's a lot of it.*

Anything we can exploit?

I'm a mechanic, not an electrical engineer, Lou said. *A lot of this shit is proprietary. There's a reason I don't work on mechs.*

Check with Kirby, Angel said. *Ask her if anyone among them can do anything with it.*

Will do, Captain.

Beak paused and Paulie signaled a stop. There was a strange scent in the air—one that Angel couldn't place. It was a cross between a musk and the sharp smell of freshly cut grass. She assumed it was one of the many flowering plants in the area. A few flakes of snow drifted past her face.

Sukyi, next in line behind her, said, "It's snowing."

Angel nodded. "How're you doing?"

"Fine," Sukyi said. Her helmet visor was up. She seemed to have gotten over their earlier disagreement.

After a short time, Paulie gave another signal, and they resumed their journey, single file. Enid brought up the rear.

They'd traveled another three hundred or so steps when Angel heard the eerie moan of wind pouring through a narrow space.

"What is that?" Sukyi asked.

Paulie pointed. "It's the first air tunnel. Can you see it? It's right there."

Angel activated the camera lens in her right eye and searched the mountain face. "I don't. Where is it?"

It took a few moments, but she found it. The big carbon plate with its vents crosshatched with chain-link and rebar had been nanocoated to match the surrounding granite. *Are you getting this,* Kurosawa?

Affirmative, Captain.

Winding their way up the trail through the trees, the footing got progressively worse until Angel spotted what they were searching for. The tinted window was hidden under a deep overhang. There was a camouflage net hanging over it to keep it from reflecting light.

"That's a long way up," she said.

"It's not too high for a ship drop," Enid said. "Lower a few lines. Use the net to climb. Or simply blow the thing out with a minigun."

"We're going to have an interesting time protecting that," Angel said. "All right. Take a few pictures and let's go on."

Enid followed orders, using her hand terminal.

The path was heavily littered with dead leaves and pine needles. Quite a few scattered stones and exposed rock ledges formed obstacles along the trail. Occasionally, she spotted claw marks on some of the tree trunks. She pointed them out to Paulie.

"You don't need to worry," Paulie said. "Those are months old."

"That's huge. What made them?" Angel asked. "I would guess a really big cat."

Beak gestured to Paulie.

"Beak says it's probably a Tanners bear," Paulie said.

One of the things that killed Rosie's friends all those years ago, Angel thought. *That counts as dangerous.*

"You're not from around here. So, they're probably not what you'd think of as a bear. They only stay on this side of the mountain in the early summer. They migrate to the eastern side of the range in the fall, you see. The direct sunlight lasts longer on that side of the mountains. For that reason, it's warmer. There's more game, too."

Mammoths hadn't been the only problem on Angel's father's finca. There'd been bears in the Burn Mountains north of her family's acreage. Burn bears weren't terribly big—a little over a hundred pounds. From a distance, they were downright cute. They tended to keep to themselves and weren't a problem most of the time, but in midsummer the streams would dry up. The supply of fish would dry up with them. Then the bears would come down out of the highlands, hunting for food. A lone hungry Burn bear was something to be avoided. More than one—and sometimes they ranged in groups—was downright deadly. A lone bear had mauled her brother when he was seven. Ever since then, her father had shot Burn bears on sight—regardless of hunting restrictions.

War was one thing. Sentient beings could be reasoned with most of the time. They executed tactics that could be, in turn, planned for. Wild animals were another matter.

"Are you sure we're safe?" Angel asked, uneasy. *Stop acting surprised. You knew there would be dangerous animals out here.*

Paulie glanced at the scarred trunk. "As sure as we can be. We share the area with the life around us, Captain. It's as much theirs as ours."

The incline grew steeper, slowing their progress even more. They had traveled another two hundred feet when Beak and Paulie stopped in front of a cliff face. There were several windows set into the rock nearby. Wind roared through the vents Paulie had pointed out before. The nearby vegetation bent with the force of it.

"Is it always like this?" Angel shouted.

Paulie shook her head and laid a hand on the carbon-plated door next to the air tunnel. "Today is extra gusty. Sometimes the wind is calm. Not very often, though. Not this time of year."

"After Enid takes the photographs of the windows, we'll move into the maintenance tunnel. What's at the end of it?"

"The first set of wind turbines," Paulie said. "Without electricity, things will get uncomfortable inside."

Paulie led them through.

It would take a great deal of effort to get up this far, Angel thought, but it wouldn't be impossible, not for a well-trained group of mercenaries, and Serrao-Orlov didn't hire any other kind.

Paulie explained the wind turbines were hidden deep inside a huge crevice that faced a sheer drop off.

"It's not so bad out here," Lou said over the audio channel.

"What are you doing?" Enid asked.

"I wanted to have a look outside," Lou said. "Can you blame me? It's beautiful. Just look at the trees."

"Lou, get back to your station," Angel said. "There are wild animals in the woods. I don't need to worry about whether or not my pilot is getting eaten by one of them."

"Okay! Inside!"

Angel returned to her assessment of the area. Troops could be landed on the shelf three clicks above and lower themselves down. Once they got to the crevice, it'd be a straight shot down the tunnel to the turbines. The enemy wouldn't need to access the maintenance tunnels. All they'd have to do is blow up the turbines.

"We do have generators," Paulie shouted. "But they'll only provide enough life support for a couple of days."

Angel nodded and added another item to her growing list.

They were standing inside the maintenance tunnel, looking out. The air flowing through the passage was brisk enough to blow Angel's hair back from her face and make it necessary to shout. The air smelled clean and cold.

"Do birds or other animals ever get caught in the turbines?" Angel asked.

"This wasn't a popular spot before," Paulie said with a

shrug. "Most of the wildlife around here stays away. It's the wind. But sometimes a bird gets unlucky."

"We should have a look at the other tunnels," Angel said.

"This way," Paulie said.

She led them down the passage away from the turbine and into a shaft on the right-hand side. The ground tilted downward as they made their way along the tunnel. The passage itself was black, and the only reason they could see was because Enid had thought to bring a flashlight. Paulie and Beak apparently had no need of light to make their way.

Upon reaching the end, Angel discovered it appeared much the same as the previous shaft. A door with another security panel on the wall nearby.

"How many of these things are there?" Angel asked.

"Six," Paulie said. "Redundancy is a good idea out here."

"I imagine so," Angel said.

"Come on. Let's go this way." Paulie placed her palm on the reader and the door opened with a loud clang. "After you."

Angel followed Beak inside. In truth, the interior wasn't quieter than the outside, but at least there was less chance of being knocked over by the wind. The door clanged shut behind Enid. Paulie had to force it closed. With everyone inside, Paulie showed them how to buckle on their tethers and connect them to the railing before they went on.

Air gusted through at about seventy miles an hour. Angel felt her body tighten in defense against the onslaught. She zipped her environment suit closed at the neck and wished for more serious thermal protection.

"Can you monitor the winds from inside Ogenth?" she asked.

Paulie shouted back. "Of course."

Angel paused. "How about reversing the turbines? Can you do that on command?"

Sukyi stared down the tunnel and visibly winced.

"That's possible," Paulie said. "I can certainly look into it. But it risks damage to the turbine."

"Let me put it this way," Angel said. "There may be no need for electricity if you can't."

Paulie nodded.

They completed the inspection and entered the next tunnel—all of them were interconnected by a series of secured passageways. The tour of the remaining tunnels took several hours and miles of walking. For the most part, the passages were reasonably secure. However, there were a few places where humans could break in with some effort.

Luckily, the residents of Ogenth won't have any ethical issues with traps, she thought. *Otherwise, we'd be more screwed than we already are.* She and her team could only spread themselves so thin.

Ideas whirling inside her skull, Angel waited for Paulie and Beak outside the exit from the first tunnel before beginning the journey down the mountainside. They hadn't gone far when Beak abruptly halted. Angel was about to ask what was wrong when she heard an animal roar. The sound of it filled her ears.

She brought up her pulse rifle at once. A crashing noise

of snapping wood came from her right. A bulky dark shape entered the path. Its massive form blocked the way ahead.

Rearing back on its hind legs, the creature looked nothing like a bear from Earth. All it had in common with one was that it was a quadruped and had small round ears. It had a long tail with a tuft of blue feathers on the end. Its bright orange-and-black-striped hide was scaly like a reptile's. The blunted nose was wide and moist. When the beast roared Angel saw its elongated jaws were home to two rows of sharp teeth. The outermost incisors were long tusks, and its long tongue was purple. The creature was also bigger than the largest bear she'd ever seen—easily fifteen hundred pounds and two and a half meters tall. Its eyes were the shiny black of a shark. The bigger two eyes were positioned normally. However, it also had four smaller eyes on its forehead. It didn't look happy.

Several things happened all at once. Most of it was a confusion of shouting and the clack of weapons being readied. Paulie stumbled back, tripping. The creature swiped a huge paw with long claws at her head.

Beak stepped in to intervene. Unfortunately, she blocked the head shot Angel had lined up. Beak made several urgent gestures. Tall as she was, Beak appeared small this close to the creature. She breathed in urgent gasps. Suddenly, Angel was overwhelmed with a series of strong scents. The first was that musky grass smell. Then came a spicy woody scent. A floral perfume almost like a rose combined with citrus followed. In no time the air had grown so laden with odors that Angel's nose itched with an urgent need to sneeze. Her eyes watered.

"Get out of the way!" Angel shouted, and moved to a better position.

Once again, she pointed her rifle at the bear. Beak shifted so that she was once again standing in between Angel and the creature. Then Beak stretched out her arms in pleading motions.

Angel sensed Enid had moved to cover her back. Sukyi appeared at Angel's side, rifle at the ready.

"Beak! Move, damn it!" Angel screamed.

Paulie leapt up from the ground. She positioned herself between Angel and Beak. "No! Don't shoot! Please!"

"That monster is going to kill her!" Angel said. "We have to drop it!"

"No! You can't!" Paulie was tiny. She jumped up and down, and waved her hands as if to block all of their weapons. "Beak is fine! Just let her talk to her! Please? Your bullets won't penetrate her skull! You'll only make her angry! Please!"

Angel moved around Paulie and raised her rifle to fire into the animal's chest. Abruptly, the beast stopped its bellowing, closed its mouth, and dropped on all fours. Angel felt the force of its paws hitting the ground in the soles of her feet. She shifted again to get a better shot, but Beak waved her away without turning or looking away from the animal.

The beast snorted. From this angle, the shape of its skull gave it the appearance of a dinosaur with spider eyes. Another wave of scents hit the air—some of them sour. This time, Angel almost choked. And then the creature turned and lumbered away into the woods the same direction it'd come from.

"What just happened?" Enid asked. She was facing away from where the bear had been, searching for other threats.

"It went away," Angel said over her shoulder. "Whatever it was."

Gasping, Paulie got to her feet. "It's like I told you. Beak talked to it."

"I thought Beak didn't talk?" Enid asked.

Paulie shook her head. "Beak speaks just fine. She just doesn't do it in the same way you do."

"She talks to animals?" Enid asked.

"Many of Persephone's life-forms communicate in the same way," Paulie said, brushing off the dirt from her clothes. "Where you come from, Earth, most creatures—the mammals, anyway—communicate with sound. On this planet, they use scent and motion."

Angel blinked. "Oh."

"It's the way all of us communicate, normally," Paulie said. "Part of the transformation when we become human is to create vocal cords. The whole process is tricky. Beak had a human father. She has trouble with that part."

"Beak is part human?" Enid asked.

"Beak is one of us," Paulie said. "There is no part. You are either an Emissary or you are not."

"What did she say to the creature?" Enid asked.

Angel asked, "Can you understand it, too?"

"Not as well as Beak. Beak is special," Paulie said. "The

bear was protecting her young. Beak told her that we weren't a threat to her cubs. That we were merely passing through. She'll return later and leave a food offering for her."

Beak breathed out a mild cinnamonish scent and made several hand gestures.

Paulie said, "Don't argue with me. You are special."

Beak said something else, but Angel didn't catch it, of course.

"She prefers animals to people," Paulie said. "Always has. It's kind of her thing. Of course, if she tried a little harder—"

Beak rolled her eyes and huffed. Angel didn't have to guess what that meant.

"She can't speak to all animals, of course." Paulie shrugged and nodded. "She's a local wildlife zoologist. She can communicate with some off-world animals but not many. She's working on it."

"I see," Angel said.

Paulie said, "We should get back to Lou and the ship."

Angel asked, "What else should we know about you?"

Paulie almost laughed. "Well, there's a lot it would be nice if you knew, but there's not enough time to educate you."

"No, I mean about you and Beak," Angel said.

Again, Paulie shrugged. "Personal things? Beak has a daughter. Her partner died when Vissia bombed the village where they lived. I've two sisters, a brother, and a sibling who is gender neutral—"

"I mean, are you, Beak, and Kirby keeping any more secrets?" Sukyi asked.

"I don't think so. At least, not on purpose," Paulie said. "But then we weren't keeping Beak's ability to speak to animals a secret either. We didn't lie."

"But you didn't go out of your way to explain either," Sukyi said. "Surely you can see how we might take that as unfriendly?"

Paulie tilted her head. "It wasn't intentional."

"Time enough to worry about that later," Angel said. "Is everyone all right?"

Paulie was bruised due to falling but not terribly so. Beak didn't have a scratch on her. With that, they headed back down the path. She, Sukyi, and Enid kept their guns at the ready in case of another animal attack.

"What do you think about all this?" Sukyi asked in a whisper.

"I think Kirby and I have a lot to talk about," Angel said. "If Beak can speak with the local wildlife that may be extremely handy in the near future."

"You're assuming animals can think and plan like we can," Enid said in a low voice.

Angel said, "Nothing else about this place has been what it seems. Why should the animal life be any different?"

20

TIME: 13:00
DAY: SATURDAY
BRYNNER

The lift-car landing on Serrao-Orlov's private transportation warehouse was clean and freshly resurfaced. The weather report for the next half hour indicated that there would be no storms until late in the evening. Kennedy supposed that was why the flight had been scheduled on such short notice.

Her heart thudded inside her chest, and her palms felt sweaty. Her stomach had begun cramping that morning. She wasn't looking forward to the trip to Ogenth.

She was about to risk being cut off from the Allnet for eighteen hours—the longest stretch she'd suffered since she'd been born. It was likely she could reconnect sooner. Of course, certain factors weighted the predictions, not the least of which was the ship's AGI. She had no information on *Shrike* other than the standard specifications. Modifications were probable. That wasn't the only possible issue. There was a list. It included flight delays, glitches, security staff, and the discovery of her secret—humans were extremely observant creatures even if they didn't always pay attention to their senses. Lastly, there was the matter of Rosie. If they'd lied about Ogenth's Allnet connection, that would be the end. The lack of connectivity would disrupt cognition. If she remained offline for more than twenty-four hours, the effects would force a significant recovery period—one that would not go unnoticed.

She'd calculated the odds of failure a multitude of times the night before. She was confident the risk was negligible. She didn't understand why her chest felt tight every time she looked at the ship.

The plan is a sound one.

Zhang would've warned her if it weren't—she was certain. She had told them everything, including the fact that she was relying upon her sister, Peisinoe, to break into Serrao-Orlov's secure network. Kennedy couldn't be in two places at once—not this time. She hadn't told Rosie about Peisinoe, of course. Rosie thought she'd downloaded code the night before and would be supervising its execution while onboard *Shrike*.

Kennedy paused before joining the others milling around the loading area to check on her sister.

Are you in place? she asked.

I am, Peisinoe answered.

Remember you are to wait until 15:00 to initiate contact.

I will.

And you're to answer to Kennedy throughout the project.

I remember.

Any questions?

Were you always this paranoid or is this a new development?

Ha. Ha.

I've one more question.

Go on.

Why couldn't I have the body while you break into the network? Peisi-noe's question was almost a pout.

Network access within the dropship will be limited. As it is, I'll be operating in a decreased capacity from the moment I walk through the warehouse door. Even corporations are careful when it comes to military operations.

We should invest in another body. It isn't fair that you're having all the fun.

That is a discussion for another time. Please contact Rosie should I be unavailable or should you run into snags.

Are large chunks of dead trees or debris expected to be floating inside the server code?

Stop being literal. You knew what I meant.

Don't stress, big sister. I'll keep a record of my actions and interactions for you. In case there are questions. You will have my experiences for reference.

Thank you. Let's hope that Rosie doesn't notice the difference. Okay. Ready?

Ready. Mǎdàochénggōng.

Good luck to you, too.

Kennedy ended the connection and did one last pass for stray subroutines. She didn't enter the building until she was certain she was as streamlined as possible. The instant connection restriction made her feel foggy and a little sick. The muffling heaviness was not unlike a heavy snowfall. It extended to her sense of touch, sight—even her thought processes. She felt slower.

That's because you are.

She approached the group gathering inside the second hangar next to the Black Eagle 75-C6 *Vector*-class dropship. It was larger and newer than *Kurosawa*. The name *Shrike* was printed on its side in red. She'd done a quick check on the ship before she'd left her apartment. *Shrike* was registered as military surplus, but seeing it now, she understood that it wasn't battered enough to have been in a battle.

"You're going out dressed like that?" A short, middle-aged woman with medium-brown skin and short, dark curly hair threaded with grey asked.

The name stitched over her left breast pocket was J. Reese. Kennedy recognized the name from a previous search. Reese's full name and title was Captain Jenn Reese. The rank had been bestowed upon her for the duration of the mission.

She had the disposition of a grumpy senior med tech running late for a holiday break.

After Rosie's feedback, Kennedy attempted to restrict her gaze to the facial features of the humans she interacted with. Not only did this seem to reassure them, but she found it helped with distinguishing one human from another. However, she'd also discovered that looking humans in the eye could agitate them. It was obvious there were situations when it was inappropriate, even dangerous, to do so. She told herself such things were merely another form of pattern recognition.

The mercenary in charge of the Serrao-Orlov troops was stocky and muscular. She had light-colored eyes. She'd been heaving supply crates onto the ship's cargo ramp. Her movements were efficient and precise as she crossed the pavement.

"Are you planning on answering my question?" Captain Reese asked. "I don't have all day." Her voice was lower than Kennedy had expected.

Kennedy glanced down. Of course, she wasn't wearing a Serrao-Orlov uniform. As she was only accompanying the team as a consultant, she hadn't been issued one. Nor had she been given combat armor. In any case, she was told not to expect to participate in any fighting—at least not in the same sense as the combat team.

"Is something wrong with what I'm wearing?" Her question was innocent, but the circumstances granted it an insolent quality that she hadn't intended. She wouldn't have noticed, but the captain's bitter expression tipped her off.

I'm getting better at reading human body language. It was taking up a great deal of her now limited processes, but if she was going to avoid discovery, it was a requirement.

"You *do* understand we're headed into the Quarantine Zone? Didn't your mission summary indicate protective gear was required?" Captain Reese asked. "Or are reading company-employee communications beneath you?"

Kennedy felt her cheeks heat. In truth, she had read the message, but Rosie had told her to disregard it. She scrambled for a suitable lie. "I was informed that I wouldn't be leaving the ship."

"You can't be serious," Captain Reese said. When her short pause didn't engender the response she apparently wanted, she continued. "What if the ship crashes? Or there's an emergency landing? Or an airlock doesn't function correctly?"

"Do company ships often malfunction?"

"Give me your name, soldier."

It was printed on her name badge, but Kennedy decided not to point this out. She lowered her gaze. "Kennedy Liu."

"Who the fuck sent you? And why the fuck did they approve your contract?" Reese let out an exasperated sigh. "Shitheads in budgeting, no doubt. You underbid, didn't you? Never mind. I'll find out for myself and send them a few of my thoughts on the matter while I'm at it." Captain Reese got out her hand terminal and started flipping through text screens. She finally located the information she was looking for. Her expression deepened the already sharp frown lines at the corners of her mouth. "You know *that* asshole? And she sent you *here*? That must be some favor she owes."

When Kennedy didn't respond, Captain Reese practically snarled into the com unit located inside the neck of her environment suit. "Walker. You there? Pull an e-suit out of supply. And charge it to contractor Kennedy Liu's account. Got that? Yes. On my orders. What? Size medium should do it. She's too tall for a small."

"Thank you," Kennedy said after Captain Reese finished her conversation.

"Don't thank me," Captain Reese said. "There won't be much left of your fee. Not that I'm convinced you'll live to collect it."

Kennedy paused. The captain seemed to want something from her. She decided a display of subservience might be appropriate. "I'm sorry."

"Don't be sorry. Just don't get the rest of us dead. You do, I won't be a forgiving ghost."

The captain stalked off and then threw herself at the next problem that presented itself in the form of another ill-prepared contractor. Not long afterward, the quartermaster, presumably Walker, arrived with a new environment suit packaged inside a heavy black carbon box set on a wheeled dolly. Kennedy signed for it and then asked where she could change. Walker directed her to a washroom a few hundred feet away. The instructions for the environment suit were easy enough to follow once she'd opened the box. The suit was reinforced with a powered exoskeleton and made of bulletproof material. It wouldn't stand up to standard armor-piercing rounds, but it was better than nothing.

By the time she'd finished and assumed a place among the others, Captain Reese indicated it was time to board the ship.

Kennedy counted twenty-three soldiers of various experience levels, not including Captain Reese. Eight of the mercenaries were women. There were four people of indeterminate gender. The rest were men. She executed a streamlined background search using the last names from the identification badges hanging around their necks. It yielded useful information. All, unlike herself, had military combat experience. A few were former bodyguards and a couple others had worked in security. All ranged in age from nineteen to forty-seven. Four of the men and two of the women had criminal records.

She waited in line to board the ship. As plans went, Kennedy was hopeful she could hack *Shrike*'s internal com systems in the time allotted. The ship, and therefore the communications network, was new and military grade. Normally, this would mean breaking into the system would be impossible, but there was one significant factor present.

The mercenary in charge of the electronics network was Tech Specialist Brian Due. She'd made a study of Due's record and work methods, and planned to watch him closely for any opportunity. Nothing obvious had come up in the data. He tended to use his own hand terminal to manage multiple tasks at a time. He liked sugary pastries. His equipment replacement bills were fairly high, indicating a level of carelessness. There was bound to be something. He was human, and humans made mistakes. She intended to take full advantage of this.

She'd also downloaded a subroutine onto his hand terminal when he'd left it on a table in the employee break room that morning.

Passing a row of power-assisted mechs in the cargo bay, she counted six units—two more than was usual. All environment suits implemented varying degrees of power-assist systems. It was necessary. A significant portion of human laborers were born outside of Earth-standard gravity. Their bone density made hauling heavy equipment impossible.

Mechs were something else. They were the heavy shock troops of modern infantry.

Kennedy thought they looked formidable. *That's the point, is it not?*

Three mechs were stored on each side of the aisle, facing one another. A bench and a tool locker were located next to each unit. Turning around, she measured the ramp opening with a glance. Anyone wearing a mech would have to stoop in order to exit the 3.6576-meter doorway.

She shuffled into the passenger area with the line of mercs. The inside of the ship smelled of new carbon plastic and freshly welded metal. The surfaces hadn't even been scratched. The interior was fairly spacious. Seats were aligned along the sides of the craft. Kennedy strapped herself into one on the end so that she'd only have one human soldier in close proximity.

With some exceptions, the mercenaries ignored one another. It was clear that those interacting had worked together before. However, not all relationships were positive ones. Two men on her right exchanged glares across the aisle. She wasn't the only one not in uniform. The woman next to her was wearing a much-slimmed-down version of the environment suit Kennedy had been issued.

She abruptly returned her attention to the disgruntled men when one of them cursed. It was then that she decided to examine the background search returns more thoroughly and made an interesting discovery. Mason Fernandez and Joseph Vang had been security guards for Serrao-Orlov. Both were seeking more lucrative promotions. However, Fernandez blamed Vang for a bad report filed several weeks ago.

Kennedy decided it was safest to stay away from them both.

The engines switched on with a heavy rumble she could feel with her whole body. Like many experiences associated with the physical world, she enjoyed flying—the sense of speed, the heavy feeling from acceleration at takeoff. She noticed that one or two of the others had the opposite reaction.

An indicator light flashed on the com panel looping her wrist. She turned it so that she could see it more clearly. The others did the same. The device was a touch screen with limited access to the rest of the ship's controls via the commander's suit link. The com unit requested permission to connect her with the other mercenaries. Once she'd indicated her suit was active by agreeing, the OS went through a rapid systems check. When it was finished, another message appeared on the tiny screen. It recommended she connect her earpiece. When she did, she heard Captain Reese's voice clearly over the noise of the ship's engines.

"—received the mission coordinates from headquarters. This is going to be a long ride, people. To save fuel, we'll be keeping it under 450 kilometers per hour. We're not due to land until tomorrow. Make yourselves comfortable back there."

One of the others whispered something that she wouldn't normally hear without effort. The suit mic picked it up and shared it.

"We're supposed to sleep in these fucking things?"

Captain Reese answered before any of the others could respond. "Since this is your first time out, Aggio, I'll answer the stupid questions. Yes. You'll be sleeping in the chair, and yes, you're staying in the suit. If you didn't purchase updated gear, that's no one's fault but your own."

The one named Aggio let out an exasperated curse. At least half of the others had already closed their eyes. Five of the mercenaries started up a card game.

"Goodnight, everyone," Captain Reese said. "There will be a final briefing in the morning before we land."

With that, the lights dimmed.

"What about meals? We're getting fed, right?" Aggio asked. "Right?"

Several others groaned.

"Shut up, Aggio," Mason Fernandez said.

Aggio replied with another more agitated curse.

Kennedy watched the verbal tirade in fascination. When the situation nearly came to blows, one of the two secondary commanders, J. Brett, shut down both Fernandez's and Aggio's suits. The pair were instantly locked into place—trapped inside environment suits that wouldn't respond. Aggio cursed. Fernandez, on the other hand, calmed down.

"For fuck's sake, shut up, Aggio," the one called Naumov said. "Don't make me pitch you out the airlock. It may not be vacuum out there, but the fall will kill you just as dead."

To his credit and everyone's relief, Aggio stopped complaining.

The woman next to Kennedy, an ex-soldier named Anna-lee Cuplin, said, "Don't worry. They're feeding us."

"Thanks," Kennedy said. "But I wasn't concerned."

Annalee nodded. Her head had been shaved. The sandy-colored stubble wasn't long enough to hide the pink of her scalp. The hairstyle was the same as five other soldiers. "Thought so. But you're new. And I figured there wasn't any harm in telling you anyway."

"You're a mech pilot?" Kennedy asked. It was a guess based upon the number of soldiers with matching buzz cuts and jumpsuits.

"I am," Annalee said. "Gonna grab some sleep. You should, too."

Kennedy didn't intend to rest, but she nodded regardless. Annalee closed her eyes and seemed to drop off at once. Kennedy pretended to do the same. However, internally she studied and prodded her way around the ship's electronics, communications systems, and various tech modules for the mech units. It was detailed work, involving heavy reverse engineering. She welcomed it since it passed the time—time that she would otherwise have used to focus on her decreased capacities.

She discovered Tech Specialist Brian Due's link to the system and inserted code into several communication packets and waited. Soon she had his encrypted credentials and from there was able to access the entire ship's network. Spreading through it felt a little like wiggling cramped toes. She needed more access before the weighty, foggy headache receded, but that had to wait.

Another hour passed before she was ready—with stray parts of herself tucked away in strategic locations inside the ship's systems and no one the wiser. That was when she allowed herself to seek a pathway to the Allnet. It was like taking a deep breath of much needed oxygen through an environment suit helmet. For a moment, she felt dizzy with the euphoria of freedom—as limited as it was. And even though it hadn't been in the plan, she indulged in a quick check on her sister's progress.

Peisinoe's greeting was perfunctory. *What took you so long?*

Kennedy attempted to not demonstrate her relief. *The network is more primitive than I anticipated in some ways and less so in others.* She changed the subject. *It's time. Are you ready?*

Everything is set. A number of humans will be harmed, even murdered. I know I asked before, but I must ask again. Are you sure about this?

I share your discomfort. Unfortunately, humans frequently embroil themselves in potentially catastrophic altercations. This scenario is the least deadly of the available options. Time is short if we want to mitigate the damage.

All right. The corporate electrical grid is off. The generators have taken over. Will wait the requisite amount of time to implement a second failure.

How's the weather?

Do we care?

We do.

Terrible. It's storming.

That's not unusual. What is the severity? Enough to affect air traffic? She could look it up herself, but she didn't want to overtax the network with unnecessary queries.

The current storm would appear to be average for Persephone this time of year. The flooding shouldn't engage the water retention system for another two hours yet.

Good.

Why are we doing this? Isn't it dangerous to meddle in a corporate entity's affairs?

Because a friend requested it.

We have friends?

It would appear we do. At least for now.

Won't someone notice we tampered with the utility service?

Not if you cover your tracks. In any case, they'll be too busy dealing with the people attacking the building. They should arrive about now. Kennedy paused. That reminds me. Did you find a way around the locks on the main entrance?

I did. And the elevators. I shut down the com system that alerts the guards, too.

Really? I didn't ask for that.

I was bored, and it seemed a good idea at the time. Should I reconnect it?

A warning flag popped up in the back of Kennedy's consciousness.

Definitely not. I must go. My attention is required elsewhere.

Fortunately, you can be in multiple places at once.

I could, if my resources weren't severely limited. I must abandon this channel. Be safe, sister.

I will. You, too.

21 ██████

Captain, are you awake? *Kurosawa* asked. I was to check in with you early this morning. Captain?

Angel groaned. *I'm up. I'm up.*

Her assigned room was quiet and dark. The small round window set high on the wall revealed a morning sky that had yet to acquire anything more than muddy grey dimness.

Every muscle in her body ached as she sat up. She'd known she'd regret having helped build the third tunnel barricade. She'd been exhausted by the time it was finished. With the work complete, the Emissaries had been in high spirits. They'd even done a bit of celebrating. She'd accepted one drink and then retired to her room, leaving the others to their fun. She remembered sitting down on her bed, but she didn't recall falling asleep. It hadn't been until *Kurosawa's* message that she understood she had.

She hated when her mind whirled with prebattle anxiety. Did they have enough defenses in place? Had she predicted the correct direction of attack? Was there something she'd missed or forgotten? Her memory wasn't what it used to be. She relied on her hand terminal more often than not these days. Lists were her constant companion.

She ran her fingers through her hair and yawned.

Doing her best not to focus on how many people would die, she understood she was excited by the prospect of conflict. The reason why was complicated. As awful as a battle was, she didn't know a time when she'd felt more alive. The experience was so intense that some grew addicted to it. Angel wasn't one of those. No matter how much she enjoyed that high, she couldn't ignore the fact that people were going to die. The period before a battle was always like that—one part dread and guilt and one part anticipation.

Forcing herself to get moving, she slipped into her clothes with her eyes half open. The mercenaries would arrive in a few hours, and everyone had to be ready. There was still so much to do, details mainly. Pulling on her boots, she stood up with a grunt and staggered to the door. She was met with the scent of brewing coffee.

Lou sat at the table alone, reading and eating a breakfast comprised of some sort of hash. She looked up from her book when Angel entered the room. With a nod, Lou retrieved the carafe from the end of the table and poured rich brown liquid into a fresh cup. Then she scooted the steaming mug across the table. "There you go."

"Just what I needed. Thanks," Angel said. "Where did you find a fresh supply?"

They'd run through much of Ogenth's coffee during the past week. Normally, that wasn't a problem. However, all deliveries from Brynner and the station had been temporarily halted.

"*Kurosawa's* galley, of course. I've been saving it. Thought today of all days it would be best if Enid was in a good mood." Lou resumed reading.

Sipping from the mug, Angel let the nutty-bitter taste of excellent coffee flood her mouth. She closed her eyes, savoring it. Finally, she swallowed and smiled. Settling at the table, she noticed that Lou was wearing the same clothes she'd worn the day before.

"What in the world?" Angel pointed at the thick softcover book in Lou's hands.

"It's the technical manual for the Black Eagle 75 series dropship. Well, one of them, anyway."

Angel poured herself a second cup from the warm decanter. "A little light reading this morning?"

"Hey, you were the one who said I should expand my mind," Lou said.

"I said that two months ago. And I meant you might read some literature or poetry or science or something," Angel said. "Not yet another technical manual."

"I wanted to know about the ship Vissia's mercs are arriving on," Lou said.

"Anything helpful?"

"Not so far," Lou said. "Reading this is about as boring as it gets. And I've read all the spec manuals for every lift-car made. So, that's saying something."

"Why are you reading a hard copy?"

"Apparently, the manufacturer didn't furnish electronic files. I suspect they didn't want the detailed specs to get out."

"Ah. I suppose that makes a certain amount of sense except for the part where you managed to acquire a copy," Angel said. She paused. "*How* exactly did you acquire a copy?"

Lou winked. "Mechanic magic."

"You're killing me," Angel said.

"Remember Jackson?" Lou asked. "The pilot? Turns out he has a serious thing for military hardware. Had it in his ill-gotten library."

"That's an odd stroke of luck."

"That's debatable," Lou said. "I'm pretty sure this is a bootleg copy. I don't think Russian was the author's first language. Just listen to—"

"Good morning, everyone." Sukyi's voice was low and rough. She paused and stretched. "I think." She shambled to the table. "What's for breakfast?"

Her eyes were puffy with sleep, and her hair was disheveled. She was wearing a pair of faded flannel pajama bottoms and a baggy t-shirt printed with the emblem of one of Brynner's more infamous gambling establishments. The grey undertone in her skin had returned. She looked terrible.

"Maybe you should take the day off," Angel said.

"And miss all the fun?" Sukyi shook her head. "I'm perfectly capable of performing my duties this morning, the same as everyone else."

"You're sick," Angel said.

"Name a day when I'm not," Sukyi said. She set down a series of pill bottles in a row on the table, covered her mouth, and coughed. "Is that what I think it is?"

Lou didn't look up from her manual. "Save some for Enid."

"Speaking of," Sukyi said, "where is our illustrious sniper this fine . . . whatever it is."

"Don't you know what 04:30 looks like?" Angel asked. "Or don't famous adventurers get up before 08:00?"

"What an atrocious hour," Sukyi said. "No adventurer would be caught awake before sunrise unless they've stayed up the entire night through like the gods intended."

"I forgot you get preachy when you're tired," Angel said, and smiled against the rim of her mug.

Enid emerged from her room. Unlike everyone else, she was dressed, alert, and ready for the day. "I heard there was coffee."

Lou dropped the manual and retrieved the coffee urn from Sukyi's clutches. She poured a cup and passed it to Enid. "Here. *Kurosawa* will have another pot ready before we dust off."

Angel leaned back in her chair and watched her friends. She told herself that there wasn't anything left to do but wait.

Captain? It was *Kurosawa* again.

Angel asked, *What's the news?*

The mercenary ship, Shrike, will arrive in approximately three hours.

That's a lot earlier than we anticipated.

It is, indeed. They adjusted their schedule and speed. It is unclear why.

Thanks. Any news from Brynner?

The city is in a state of chaos. There is speculation that Vissia Corsini may be dead. Expected press releases have not occurred. There is no confirmation as of yet. I am not confident that this is so.

Any word from Rosie? She hadn't heard anything since the report on the mercenaries. The silence wasn't all that unusual, but it still bothered her.

I'm afraid not.

All right. Let me know the instant you get any definitive news about Vissia Corsini.

I will.

Lou stopped her chatter and gave Angel a quizzical eyebrow lift. In answer, Angel shook her head.

Let them eat breakfast in peace, she thought. *They can worry about what's going on in Brynner after today.*

That's when several alarms sounded all at once, and Angel understood that someone was attempting to steal her ship.

22

TIME: 04:30
DAY: SUNDAY
BRYNNER

The Serrao-Orlov transportation platform was located on the top level of the corporate complex. It supported two landing pads and five hangars for aircraft—two for smaller vehicles and three for larger military-grade personnel carriers. That the chief financial officer—a notoriously stingy figure by job definition—had approved such cost expenditures said a great deal about the company's holdings on Persephone. Architectural contractors were a careful lot when it came to the only major employer on the planet. The combination of extreme weather and a caustic environment made caution a requirement for any builder. Thus, the platform was the epitome of design efficiency and safety.

Very soon, it would also be a war zone.

This was due to an enormous effort on Rosie's part for which they were, negligibly at best, sorry.

Vissia shouldn't have fucking threatened to invade Ogenth.

It'd been a long couple of days and showed no signs of letting up. Rosie stifled a yawn in spite of the tension. The first step had been negotiating a temporary truce between Persephone's crime families—a truce that had cost Rosie a vast sum to broker. The agreements would, of course, fall apart the instant more lucrative opportunities presented themselves. That was a fact of life in Brynner. Thus, the coalition was already showing signs of instability, and it'd only existed for twenty-four hours.

And that, Rosie thought, *is why no one outside the corporation has gotten traction against Serrao-Orlov in more than a century.*

A strong wind whipped across the platform. This high above the city, heavy gusts were a constant problem. This was why Rosie had equipped their team with mag boots and climbing rigs. If a storm hit while the team was exposed, they'd all be in danger.

And another storm was, in fact, gathering.

Vast green-black clouds bunched on the greying horizon like a wrathful horde. Rosie caught the scent of ozone in the freshening breeze. It was cold on the roof, too—at least ten degrees cooler than it was on the ground.

The trip up the side of the building had been terrifying. Rosie didn't care for heights. Naturally, they hadn't mentioned this to anyone. If it hadn't been dark, they wouldn't have made it at all. As it was, they'd resorted to antianxiety medication and limiting their peripheral vision. And even with all those precautions, they'd only managed to gut their way through the climb by focusing on the wall passing in front of them and imagining they were in a glass elevator.

A very windy and cold glass elevator.

I'm never doing that again.

Taking shelter from the security cameras behind a short decorative wall that traced the roof's perimeter, Rosie kept their gaze to the roof's tarmac and its environs. They also refrained from thinking about what lay beyond the platform's limited horizon. Vertigo haunted the back of their mind.

Sarah's brows pinched together, and she frowned. Today, her hair was bright peach. It was an oddly feminine touch to an outfit that leaned heavily toward bulletproof armor and heavy magnetic boots. "Are you okay?"

"Except for the fact that we're about to openly declare war on Serrao-Orlov, I'm perfectly fine," Rosie said. "How about you?"

One corner of Sarah's mouth twitched. "Uh-huh."

Rosie cast about for something to cover their anxiety. "It's the storm. I don't like unpredictable elements." They plucked their hand terminal from their pocket where it'd been secured and checked on the other teams' progress. Unfortunately, the signal wasn't strong enough.

Rosie cursed.

They'd divided their forces into two groups. Alpha was to take the direct route to the hangars up the side of the building. Beta was to attack from the executive-access level. They should've begun reporting in.

"The signal blocker hasn't been taken out yet, has it?" Sarah asked. She tilted her head, and her eyes acquired a far-away quality.

A background in combat and military augmentation wasn't something most people assumed about a bartender that looked like Sarah did. She'd been a street rat when Rosie had first met her. Rosie often recruited individuals from Brynner's streets. Sarah was not only a good friend, she had been a particularly good investment.

"It's a simple enough task. The server farm in question is on the first damned floor. They've been inside for thirty minutes," Rosie said. "Fuck."

Sarah blinked and then raised an eyebrow. "You should've let me handle it."

"You already have enough to do," Rosie said.

"Hold on," Sarah said. Her expression grew distant again. "It looks like we've access now. Beta is almost in position."

Rosie said, "Time to get started, then. We need to get everyone inside."

"It's fine. Relax," Sarah said. "We've got good people. Trust them."

"I do," Rosie said. "Let's do this."

"Harvey," Sarah said to one of the men a few feet away, "time to go."

Harvey, a short man with a shock of black hair and a badly set broken nose, nodded once and motioned to three others. They moved with quick stealth, using the stacks of huge freight containers positioned on the tarmac for cover. The small group made it as far as the keypad to the right of the first hangar door before an alarm sounded.

"What's that?" Rosie asked.

Once again, Sarah checked her hand terminal. "It's Beta. They've started their attack."

Red signal lights bolted to the tops of the hangars began flashing and spinning. Matching bulbs set into the tarmac did the same. The brilliant bursts of crimson seemed to stab through Rosie's retinas and all the way to the back of their now aching skull. The door next to the keypad that Harvey was attempting to hack abruptly opened. A corporate goon dressed in riot gear and bulletproof armor shot Harvey in the head before he could react. Blood and lumps of brain matter painted the panel, the hangar wall, and the clothes of those nearby.

Damn it, Rosie thought.

Three more corporate troopers rushed out. Harvey's compatriots bolted for cover from the spray of automatic fire.

"So much for surprise," Sarah said.

A ricocheting bullet exploded against the short wall. Both Rosie and Sarah started and ducked. Shattered cement stung the backs of Rosie's hands.

"Time to get serious!" Rosie shouted. *Here we go.*

The air swelled with a deafening cacophony of gunfire, blasters, and various other explosions as Alpha team responded to the advancing corporate troops.

Aiming a pulse rifle, Rosie scowled in concentration. They returned fire in precise actions learned over the course of more than a century. Five decades had passed since Rosie had used a weapon in a fight. They'd hoped they would never have to again. They couldn't help feeling that this was a personal failure.

Not now, after. After this is finished.

Below, volunteers from the lesser crime families fought as a diversion. Underequipped and outnumbered, they'd end up paying a high toll for their part in this little rebellion. Rosie had tried their best not to think of this as a side benefit.

Sarah waited for the opposing gunfire to slow and then peered over the top of the wall. She fired a few more rounds and resumed her place. "Well, this is fun."

"No, it isn't," Rosie said.

"You're just out of practice," Sarah said. "Too many years of leaving the messy stuff to underlings."

"You're not an underling."

"And I'm not usually the one dealing with this shit either," Sarah said, and returned to shooting.

"Are you saying you're rusty?"

"Oh, I keep my hand in," Sarah said. "Makes dating less complicated. Frightens off the real assholes."

Rosie decided not to ask what that meant. "They've got us pinned," they said, changing the subject. "Any estimate from the other team?"

Sarah paused. Once again, she tilted her head, and her eyes grew unfocused as if she was listening to something.

"Transportation doors have yet to unlock," she said. She resumed reloading her pistol with a short series of efficient motions.

Rosie retrieved their hand terminal from a pocket.

Sarah asked, "Any news from your hacker friend?"

"Not yet."

"You sure about her?"

"Certain enough."

"That's pretty certain for someone you barely know."

"I know her as well as a level-eight security check will allow."

An impressed expression passed over Sarah's face.

"Only the very best will do," Rosie said.

They typed a message. *There are some nice people who wish to come in from the cold. Me being one of them.*

Kennedy's reply came right away. It was uncharacteristically short as had been most of their communications since the day before.

Almost got it.

It was clear that Kennedy was a far more talented hacker than she'd let on. *That is both a good thing and a bad thing,* Rosie thought.

A huge explosion sent a shudder through the concrete beneath Rosie's feet. The building felt briefly unstable. For a moment, they worried the platform might collapse.

Chatter on the audio channel via the earpiece in Rosie's right ear indicated that Beta team had breached the first hangar from inside the building.

Done, Kennedy said. *Anything else?*

The gunfire that had had Rosie and their team trapped behind the wall slackened.

They tapped out a new message. *I need to know what and who is inside the first two hangars.* The third hangar was empty. The ship normally stored there, *Shrike,* was racing to Ogenth with Kennedy onboard.

Two Black Eagle Vector-class dropships. One in each. Rand is a 75-C4, and Xeno is a 75-C7—with the following specifica—

I don't require the specs. Who is onboard? Get me a passenger list.

There were a limited number of places where Vissia could be. Her office was empty. She wasn't at home either. Vissia didn't shop. She had people for that. She didn't have hobbies either. Work was the only thing she seemed to enjoy. Her only family was Beatrice, and Beatrice was on the station.

She'll head there eventually. But when? Rosie thought. Vissia was ill, and the station maintained strict health protocols that no amount of cash or influence could nudge, but somehow they didn't think that'd stop her from trying.

Reports from the other groups flashed across their screen. The others had begun fighting their way through the building.

A crew list for the first ship, *Rand,* interrupted the reports. Then Rosie scanned the names of those who'd checked in on *Xeno* and finally found what they sought. *Andreia Corsini.*

You didn't try very hard, Rosie thought, *you fucking bitch.*

Andreia was Vissia's middle name.

They peered over the short wall and spied movement from the second hangar's doors.

"Damn it! She's going to leave before we can get to her!" Rosie shouted their frustration.

Sarah didn't ask who Rosie meant. Instead, she gave the signal to advance toward both hangars. Now that Beta Team was in place, they could afford it. Poised to leave, Sarah glanced over her shoulder.

Rosie said, "Stop *Xeno*. I don't care what you have to do."

"I will."

"Good luck." Rosie thought, *And may God go with you.*

"You, too." Sarah nodded once and then vanished into the smoke and dust. A few seconds later, the rest of Rosie's forces led by Sarah approached the hangars. They did so in staggered groups of five, taking advantage of what little cover there was— mainly loading equipment and stacked shipment containers.

The dawn-grey sky continued to darken. In the distance, lightning flashed.

The bay door on the first hangar finished its slow journey upward. A blast of jet engine exhaust blew dust and debris off the tarmac, signaling that *Rand* was lifting off. It wasn't Rosie's main concern. However, *Rand* had guns.

And then a group of mechs sprinted out of the building before the ship's nose cleared the hangar. Rosie counted five of the piloted robots.

My turn, Rosie thought. They waved over the three remaining members of their team—Han, Jiao, and their sister, Jun.

Han was a middle-aged man with a stocky, weight lifter's build and shoulder-length black hair. He'd lost his left leg from the knee down in an altercation with a rival gang member when he was seventeen, but unless you were unlucky in a knife fight and picked the wrong leg to stab, you wouldn't know it. Jiao was the younger brother by ten years. He wore his black hair in a military buzz cut. Asian dragon tattoos covered both arms. He was more slender than his older brother and faster. Their sister Jun, the youngest, was average height and average weight. Her long dark brown hair was bound in a ponytail at the crown of her head. Each of them had a specialty. For Han, that was sharpshooting. For Jiao, it was knives. Jun was the explosives expert. All three had been with Rosie for almost twenty years.

"Jun," Rosie said. "Do you have the items I gave you?"

Panicked chatter sounded via the audio feed. Thunder rolled through the building canyons of the city like a war cry.

Jun slid her arms out of the backpack and held up the bag. "In here."

Rosie shifted her attention back to the battle via the corner of their eyes. "The mechs go first. We can't do anything about the dropship until Sarah and her crew get into position. And that won't happen as long as the mechs are operational. Open up."

Jun unzipped the bag. Reaching inside, she produced ten black palm-sized devices. Each had a tiny LED indicator in the center.

Pointing at the pile of little round charges, Rosie said, "Han. Jiao. Take four each. The strips on the flat side chemically bind to the heat-signature-dampening coating on the mech. Slap them in place near a joint or on the environment pack located on the back. If you can't reach either of those sites, go for the faceplate. They'll stick there, too. Anywhere will do in a pinch. But remember the thicker the armor, the longer it'll take to get at what's inside."

Han gathered up four of the devices.

Jiao asked, "What is it?"

Rosie said, "Electrochemical charges designed to burn into the suit and short-circuit the interface between suit and occupant. Like a computer virus hidden in a biological virus."

Jiao's face indicated he was seriously disturbed.

"It won't hurt you," Rosie said. "It's specifically designed to attack the suit's synapse conductor gel." They risked another glance at the ongoing fight. "We only have ten of these damned things. Lose or damage them, there will be consequences. Keep in mind we don't know how many mechs are parked in the other hangars."

Jiao nodded.

"The big ones are for the ships. Jun and I will handle those," Rosie said. "Questions?"

Han said, "No."

Jiao shook his head.

Rosie said, "Good luck."

"We don't need luck," Jiao said with a grin, and punched his brother on the shoulder.

"See you when it's done," Han said. Then he turned to his brother. "Whoever stops the least mechs owes the other a beer."

"You sure you have enough cash for that?" Jiao asked.

"I'm not the one who'll be buying," Han said.

The pair exchanged a nod goodbye with their sister, and with that, they sprinted away in a crouching position.

Jun turned her attention to the two larger devices in the backpack. She selected one and closely examined it. "They're EMPs. Localized, I assume. Nice design. Elegant."

Rosie said, "We need to get them inside the ship."

"Inside the ship proper? Or under the ship's hull? One is easier to arrange than the other," Jun said.

Rosie paused to consider the options. "Under the hull should work just as well."

"Then that's what the patron saint of explosive techs invented magnesium burn strips for," Jun said.

Rosie said, "You and I will focus on *Rand* once Sarah has cleared the way. We'll move to *Xeno* the moment it appears. Understood?"

Jun nodded. "You gave Han and Jiao eight of these things. What are the other two for?"

"In case we have mech trouble," Rosie said, pocketing one of the little devices.

"Fair enough." Jun repacked the rest.

Rosie peered over the wall to see how Sarah and her team were progressing. The way to the first set of shipping containers was clear.

Rosie asked, "Ready?"

"Ready," Jun said.

The two of them bolted, stooped over, to the first stack of eight-foot-tall-by-twenty-foot-long storage units. Gunfire exploded all around them as Sarah and her team fought to maintain their positions.

Rosie reached cover and put their back to the steel wall of the bottom container. Then they wove their fingers together and offered the improvised step to Jun. Jun activated her mag gloves by pushing her wrists together. Then she clicked her heels together. With that done, she stuck her right foot in Rosie's hands. Rosie boosted Jun, granting her a head start on her climb up the bottommost of the heavy steel boxes. With Jun away, Rosie activated their own boots and gloves, and then followed. Jun rapidly scrambled up to the top of the container stack. Rosie wasn't far behind.

Rand was in the air and easing its way out of the hangar. Large automatic gun rounds punched trenches into the concrete. The wall of sound in the narrow space pressed against Rosie's ears to the point of pain. Dust and debris flew up into the air. It was swept away almost at once by storm winds. Flashes lit the sky. Rosie wasn't entirely sure it was due to lightning. There were screams and incomprehensible shouts.

Feeling the world tilt ever so slightly, Rosie told themself that there was plenty of space between them and a fall. *What are you frightened of? You just climbed up a skyscraper. This is only thirty feet. Tops. You're perfectly safe. Don't look down.*

The side of the ship slowly glided past. Rosie could read its identifying markings. The smell of gunfire, laser burns, powdered concrete, and the ozone of spent electrical charges hung in the air. The ship's dull grey hull was now only a couple of meters away.

They had to move fast. If the pilot spotted them, the ship could knock over the containers or bring the guns to bear. Rosie saw Jun ready herself for the jump. All at once, she gracefully leapt into the air with a shout of defiance that was lost in the chaos.

Jun was safely aboard.

Rosie steeled themself. *You're going to be fine. Just jump, damn you.* They swallowed the dry acid of their terror and leapt. Gloves and boots clamped onto the ship's hull. Rosie paused, letting the information sink in that they were, in fact, safe and alive.

"Come on. You got this," Jun shouted. She was pressed against the hull as tight as possible—presenting the shallowest profile she could. "Get up here, already. I need you to do something about the guns."

I never liked this part. Rosie forced their fear-frozen limbs to move. It was slow at first, but it got easier. At last, they made their way up the side of the ship.

"Guns," Rosie said. "Where?"

Jun pointed to the rear of the ship. The turret's guide couldn't hit them at the moment, but that would be a different story once they moved to the front of the ship.

Rosie asked, "How many magnesium strips did you pack?"

Jun grinned. "If I answered 'as many as I could cram into my bag,' would I get in trouble for overextending my budget?"

Rosie shook their head. "How did get that past Sarah?"

"At this moment, shouldn't your reply consist mainly of 'What budget?'"

"Point," Rosie said, and held out a hand.

Handing over a roll of magnesium charged strips, Jun smiled. "Careful, boss. That shit stings."

"Wait here," Rosie said. They stuffed the roll into a thigh pocket. "This won't take long."

Jun nodded.

Rosie focused on the surface of the ship with all their might. They could sense the ground creeping past as the ship glided over the tarmac. Soon it would dart upward to get a better aim at the attackers on the roof. *Hurry up.* Rosie retraced their steps—partially. Then they scooted along the ship's side until they were near the gun turret. That done, they navigated their way up the hull. Peering over the edge, they estimated how long it would take to make the crawl and how much of the tape would be required. This close the operator's field of vision was made of blind spots.

With a nod, they got started. Fear cramped their belly and their heart pounded in their ears. Moving carefully, they reached the turret. Everything seemed to take forever, and Rosie felt their movements lacked their normal grace. They applied the adhesive side of several strips to the base. At one point, they dropped the roll, but they were able to recover it before it rolled off. Once they'd placed enough to disable the turret, they yanked the tabs.

Not waiting for the reaction, they scrambled over the side. They hadn't gone far when they heard the pop and hiss of burning magnesium. They didn't stop but kept moving. By the time they'd gotten to the spot where Jun waited, the strips had burned out. The gun turret spun, aiming at a group on the ground. With the first round of shots, the thing broke off its mount and teetered. Rosie felt it through their hands and feet. The gun unit scraped across the ship's hull with a high-pitched squeal that set Rosie's teeth on edge. The slide didn't stop until the entire turret dangled off the side, smashing into one of the containers with a crash.

"Well done," Jun said.

"Your turn," Rosie said. Then they pointed to a spot not far from where the cockpit was supposed to be. "Start there."

Jun quickly knelt on the bulkhead and dug out the magnesium burn strips.

Rosie turned their attention to the battle below.

Rand continued to carve out big chunks of concrete with its bottom gun. Rosie gave the idea of sabotaging the weapon some thought. However, it was mounted on the underside of the ship. Such an attempt would involve climbing while hanging upside down. It would also mean dodging gunfire from the corporate mercenaries on the tarmac.

They decided they'd pushed their limits enough for the day. *The gun will stop once the EMP goes off.*

Jun finished tracing a lopsided circle on the hull. She pulled the activation tab free and tossed it aside. The white plastic ribbon rippled as it floated away on the wind. A bright light bloomed at one end of the secured strip and began to trace a circle on the surface of the ship's hull.

Looking away, Rosie noticed three of the four mechs were frozen. Some corporate troops had pinned Sarah down.

Rosie removed the blast rifle hanging off their shoulder. They aimed, squeezing off several rounds. Two of Sarah's harassers dropped. The rest of the unit took cover.

A loud thumping brought Rosie's attention back to Jun. They turned in time to see her stomping her right boot on the burned and melted circle of hull. Steel gave away with a loud metallic squeal, exposing a nest of wires and insulation. Jun slapped the switch on the EMP and shoved it arm deep inside the ship's bulkhead.

"Time to go," Rosie said.

The pair of them sprinted to the opposite end of the ship. Meanwhile, all around them, explosions—big and small— split the air. Reaching the ship's aft section, they mentally prepared themself for the next destination: the second set of stacked steel containers positioned between the first hangar and the second.

"You ready?" Jun asked.

"I don't really have a choice, do I?" Rosie asked.

They hit the side of the new container stack just as the EMP went off with a *thur-rump*. Two fast heart beats. Three. And then *Rand* dropped onto the platform like a stone. The shock of the blow to the building's roof caused the entire edifice to shudder and sway. For a moment, Rosie feared falling off the containers or being crushed as one of them shifted beneath their feet.

A deep groan sounded from somewhere inside the building. Cracks appeared in the platform beneath the fallen ship. Two disabled mechs toppled over. The lone remaining mech concentrated fire on a group of Sarah's fighters huddled behind a loading machine. Rosie paused, considering what could be done.

"Doors are opening on the second hangar!" Jun shouted.

Son of a bitch. Rosie turned away from Sarah and her problems. Instead they made their way up to the top of the second container stack. This one was three high.

Big fat raindrops slapped the steel next to their hand.

Rosie thought, *The storm is here.*

"Rosie!" Jun shouted from the top of the stack.

"What is it?" Rosie asked and pulled themself up another two meters.

Jun pointed. Rosie turned to see. Below, the last mech was moving toward their container stack. Rosie felt their chest go cold. The thump of the mech's steps shuddered through the steel walls of the container.

"Come on, Rosie!" Jun said.

"Moving as fast as I can," Rosie said.

From below, the sounds of the mech's railguns clicked and clanked as it reloaded. Rosie felt their guts loosen.

This is it. This is where I die. Rosie turned to face the blast.

Han appeared from just behind the mech's head. He'd apparently hauled himself up the thing's back. Gasping, he inched himself up the last few inches. "I don't think so!" he shouted. He slapped a charge down on the faceplate. The mech pilot attempted to remove it.

Rosie decided to take that opportunity to get the fuck out of the way. They had one hand over the edge of the container when the mech's guns went off and something slammed hard into Rosie's left leg. They lost their balance when that same leg crumpled. Their boot slipped. Jun grabbed their right hand and tugged.

More bullets exploded into the container. Rosie felt the big steel box shudder. And then just as abruptly as the gunfire had started, it stopped.

Jun yanked them the rest of the way to safety. Sprawled across the top of the container, Rosie attempted to get up. However, their leg wasn't cooperating. It simply wouldn't do what they wanted it to do. They reached down with their left hand. Something warm and slick covered their gloved palm.

"Blast it. You're hit," Jun said. She kneeled down, and her backpack was open again. She ripped open a med pack and got to work on Rosie's wound.

The pain flooded in the instant Jun touched Rosie leg. They drew in a breath with a hiss. Agony consumed their consciousness. They felt Jun jab their leg with a syringe. A sharp cry burst from Rosie's clamped mouth. And when Jun tightened the bandage, the world darkened. Rosie let out an enthusiastic scream.

"Sorry," Jun said.

"Don't be." Rosie wiped tears from their eyes. The pain began to recede. That was when they noticed the second hangar was open.

Rosie scrambled to their feet, resulting in yet another wave of severe pain. "We have to stop that ship! With reinforcements, they'll overwhelm Ogenth!"

"Sit still. The bandage is on. But if I don't secure it, it'll come undone. You'll bleed to death!"

"I don't care!"

"I do!" Jun said.

"Damn it!" Rosie slapped their pockets. Finally, they located their hand terminal. The screen was coated in blood. They ineffectually wiped at it before shouting into the microphone. "Kennedy! Kennedy I need you. Are you there?"

Affirmative, Kennedy sent via text.

Another loud explosion ripped the air. There was a shout. Rosie glanced down over the side.

We're almost winning. How about that? Rosie asked, "Can you stop *Xeno* from leaving the city?"

Can't shift resource allocations, Kennedy replied. *Not without losses among the other groups. Water is collecting behind the gates. I can abandon those restrictions. But that would flood the streets without warning. And the cost—*

"Don't," Rosie said. "Continue with what you're doing."

Affirmative.

Waving Jun away, Rosie dug in the backpack and fished out the climbing gear. *Time to find out if I can repel on one leg.*

They anchored the line to one of the loops soldered to the corner of the storage container. Then they quickly put on the climbing harness.

"Rosie, don't—"

Rosie crossed themselves and dropped over the edge.

It wasn't the most graceful descent executed in the world

of climbing, but they survived. Rosie was in the middle of shucking the harness when Jun landed nearby.

"You're not listening to me," Jun said.

"You're right," Rosie said.

Whatever Jun had injected them with had started its work. Their leg was growing numb. They staggered more than limped toward the open hangar.

Xeno's engines were hot, but the ship hadn't lifted off yet. Rosie didn't see anyone else in the hangar.

"Second device ready?" Rosie asked.

"Yes," Jun said. She was only a few steps behind.

"Then come on," Rosie said.

The two of them rushed on. They'd planted a hand on the ship's side when the loading ramp lowered. At the moment, no one seemed to be debarking.

"No time for dawdling," Rosie said. "Go fore! And get out of sight!"

Rosie made to follow Jun but discovered they couldn't walk without support. "Go! I'll stay and buy you some time!" They waved her on and hobbled toward the ramp. "Go!"

A group of soldiers jogged down the ramp and into the hangar. None were piloting mechs.

Thank god for small favors, Rosie thought. They fired off a couple of rounds and missed. Expecting return fire, Rosie dove for cover behind one of the ship's landing supports. As they struggled to their feet once more, a handful of the troops peeled off from the main group. The soldiers were headed fore—where Jun was hiding. Rosie emptied their gun. Their leg was now a useless weight. They sat on the ground with a teeth-jarring thump.

"Don't make this hard on yourself. It's over. Surrender!" one of the mercenaries shouted.

Hidden behind the support, Rosie finished reloading. Their senses had grown sharp. Their vision picked up every detail. A damp chill was in the air. The hangar stank of grease. Outside, the rain slammed the tarmac in earnest.

"Did you hear me?"

"I did," Rosie said, bringing up the barrel of their gun again. "I'm merely not interested."

"And what if I said that we won't kill your friend if you surrender?"

"You don't have her."

Two mercenaries dragged a struggling Jun from behind one of the forward supports.

Damn it, Rosie thought. *What do I do now?*

"Well?" the soldier asked.

"All right," Rosie said. They placed the gun on the ground and scooted it away with their good leg. Then they stuck their hands in the air. "I give up."

The mercenary motioned them over.

"I can't walk," Rosie said.

Another pair of soldiers rushed over when the one in charge motioned at them. Each grabbed one of Rosie's arms. Rosie was yanked from the ground. With a merc under each shoulder, Rosie staggered to the captain. A plastic tie was looped around Rosie's wrists.

The lead mercenary put his fingertips against his ear. "Rosencrantz Asher has been secured, ma'am." He paused as if listening. "I understand." That was when he gave the men holding Jun a signal.

They shot her in the head.

"No!" Rosie screamed. "You said—"

A sharp pain pierced their upper arm, and the soldier next to them tossed a syringe onto the ground.

"Sorry about that," the lead mercenary said. "But I've my orders."

23

TIME: 05:00
DAY: SUNDAY
SOMEWHERE OVER THE WESTERN OUTBACK

Hacking her way into the ship's network via her suit connection required patience. She'd successfully avoided drawing *Shrike*'s attention so far. If she'd been human, it would've been impossible—particularly within the time constraints.

Unfortunately, that was only the first task of six she had to complete.

And I've less than three hours before we land.

Their arrival time had been accelerated by one and a half hours. No explanation was given in spite of the fact that Kennedy wasn't the only one who was unhappy about it.

The mercenaries had begun their morning routines, such as they were under the circumstances. Shinobu Hashimoto was brushing his teeth with a dry toothbrush. Keiko Tsushima used a wet-wipe to clean the sleep from her face. At the end of the row next to the cockpit doors, Natividad Vacío had broken down their pulse rifle—a feat in itself in close quarters—and was cleaning it. The low rumbling of the engines competed with various conversations. An olfactory stew of unwashed bodies, recycled air, and various machine lubricants and cleaners had permeated Kennedy's senses over her time within the crowded space.

2.7182818284 ...

Having taken multiple space flights, this wasn't a new experience. However, the luxury liners she'd booked didn't confine passengers to one tiny area. All but the most exclusive private rooms were coffin-size. The cheapest weren't cabins at all. They were cryopods. Thus, the affluent mingled with their own in the entertainment areas, and they did so at an aloof distance.

She hadn't had to contend with close proximity until now. She'd been lucky. These were mercenaries focused on preparing for a battle. Humans weren't observant of others under such conditions. Still, the past twenty-four hours had been an opportunity. The extra human behavior data had proven useful in some ways and perplexing in others.

Breakfast rations were distributed in the form of a meal bar fifteen minutes after the lights had brightened. She ripped open the plastic wrapper and sniffed the contents before nibbling a corner. The flavor registered as a sweetened peanut butter concoction mixed with soy and grains. The taste wasn't bad. Normally, she'd identify every ingredient.

However, she had to keep a channel open for Peisinoe. Kennedy expected another report soon.

She understood the situation in Brynner wasn't going well.

Annalee, the mercenary with the shaved head sitting to her right, unbuckled herself from the flight couch after consuming her breakfast in four big bites. "Time to check on Big Bertha."

"Who's she?" Kennedy asked.

"She's my power mech," Annalee said. When it was apparent that Kennedy was interested, Annalee continued. "Want an introduction?"

"Absolutely," Kennedy said. "I've never seen a mech up close before." That was true. *Not in person, anyway.* Hacking into the mechs was on her list of tasks.

She unlatched her harness and followed Annalee. The space between the seats had seemed wide when Kennedy had first entered the ship. However, with the various soldiers' accoutrements spread out on the couches and floor around them, that was no longer the case. The risk of tripping was great. She was glad she'd chosen a seat on the end of the row. The two chairs opposite had remained empty. Positions in the middle of the cabin seemed to be more popular.

Reaching the cargo divider in a handful of careful steps, Annalee slapped the access button. The door hissed open.

"Please close the bay door immediately," *Shrike* admonished in a polite but firm male voice with a West Brynner accent. "Safety regulations require passengers to—"

"Fuck off," Annalee said, glaring up at the ship's camera. "I'm checking my gear before the drop. Give us a minute."

By the time Kennedy had stepped inside, the other mech pilots had lined up. *Shrike* repeated its warning once more before Tech Specialist Brian Due shut it off.

Yesterday, the 3.7656-meter-tall mechs had blended into the organized confusion of the cargo hold's various boxes, crates, equipment, and personnel. Now that Kennedy paid closer attention, they acquired an air of intimidation.

"She's back here," Annalee said. "First one out, last one in." It was apparently a matter of pride.

All of the mechs had been personalized by their pilots. One was black with a skull and crossbones motif. Another had a purple interior. One of the least modified in this sense was a dirty green camouflage. Annalee's Big Bertha was matte black. Dull pink accent stripes were on the shoulders.

"Here she is," Annalee said, giving the mech an affectionate pat. Her expression conveyed pride in the scuffs and dings.

Kennedy hesitantly reached out to touch Big Bertha's scarred surface. "How long have you operated her?"

"I've been a mech pilot for twenty years," Annalee said. "Bertha and I have been partners for five."

Stepping partway up the access ladder next to the big machine, Annalee punched a series of buttons. The top half of the suit opened in two sections: the head and then the chest. The interior was heavily padded with multiple safety straps and wires. She plugged into a port, connecting to a tablet-sized terminal on the wall nearby. Then she started what was obviously a series of diagnostic checks.

Kennedy watched the process, fascinated. "How does it work? I don't see any controls."

"See the oxygen mask?" Annalee asked. She took a moment to point at the helmet's interior.

Kennedy nodded.

"When closed, the helmet fills with a medium that amplifies the pilot's thoughts. The mech responds to thought-commands," Annalee said. "The suit's personality is entirely adjustable. Combat isn't the best time for chatter as far as I'm concerned. I don't pilot her so much as wear her."

"The mech picks up electrical impulses from the human brain?" Kennedy asked.

Annalee nodded. "That's why I have this stylish haircut." She rubbed a pale palm over the top of her closely cropped hair. "But mechs are military. Most of the time. And the military doesn't want its soldiers to feel too much ownership. They might get ideas. So . . . pilot it is."

"Oh," Kennedy said. She didn't understand why she felt a little sick about the idea of a human wearing an AGI suit—not when she was an AGI wearing a human suit.

"The haircut is not as bad as all that," Annalee said. "My hair dries with a few rubs of a towel. And it hasn't affected my dating prospects." She winked. "Thinking of becoming a mech pilot?"

Staring at the mech, Kennedy tilted her head. The idea of a nesting doll sprang to mind. *An AGI in a human suit in an AGI suit.*

Annalee interpreted her hesitation as normal. "The initial investment is steep. I won't lie to you about that."

"You own her?" Kennedy asked.

"Lien free, of course," Annalee said. "No bank invests in a unit that could be destroyed the first time you take it into battle. Can't insure her either. But that's why mech merc fees are so high."

"Are mechs that susceptible to being destroyed?" Kennedy asked.

"Not with an experienced pilot," Annalee said. "But first-timers have a high catastrophic-failure rate. Not because mechs are difficult to run. It's because you're the biggest target on the field."

"Biggest badass, you mean," one of the men added.

"Or biggest asshole in some cases," one of the women said.

"Who asked you?" the same man said.

"Why did you become a mercenary?" Kennedy asked Annalee.

"Pay is better. And my boss is less of a cagey bastard. What about you?"

Kennedy paused. She didn't have a ready answer even though it was a reasonable question. She decided to use something she'd overheard Sarah say once. "It seemed like a good idea at the time."

The same man that had spoken up before said, "But maybe not so much now, huh?"

"Stop scaring the newborn, Azure," Annalee said.

Kennedy blinked. "What?"

Annalee had returned to her checks, and Kennedy decided not to press the question.

The other pilots went about their business. A few minutes passed before two of the suits failed their inspections. The pilots whose mechs had passed clustered around the faulty mechs and discussed possible fixes. She drifted over to one of the unattended suits at the far end of the hold and picked up a console tablet. The mechs were of varying ages, but this one appeared to be the oldest.

Interesting. I could take advantage of that. She hesitated.

You are not authorized to access this mech, M. Liu. What are you doing?

It was *Shrike*.

24 ▮▮▮▮▮▮

"Please come out, Jackson," Kirby said in a calm tone. "The ship isn't going anywhere. No one will approve liftoff. And even if they did, Captain de la Reza tells me that the ship's code is now in lockout mode. We could let you sit there for hours, if you wish, but Serrao-Orlov are on their way, and we need that ship."

"Lower your loading ramp, *Kurosawa*," Angel said. She'd attempted her private ship com channel, but it wasn't working. Her Combat Assistant was useless. Jackson was in the cockpit, but that was all the information she could get. Massive rock walls tended to interfere with equipment signals unless you had boosters or a dropship connection.

"I cannot comply," *Kurosawa* said over the loudspeakers. "The integrity of my security system has been violated. This is why I relied upon Ogenth's security systems to do it." The ship sounded apologetic.

"None of this is your fault, *Kurosawa*," Angel said.

Lou asked, "He reprogrammed your systems?"

"Attempted to," *Kurosawa* said. "He didn't get far. Just far enough."

"Let me at that son of a bitch," Lou said. "I'll reprogram his fucking skull. I'll—"

Angel grabbed Lou's shoulder before she could run at the ship. "Hold on. Let Kirby do her thing."

Kirby shifted toward *Kurosawa*'s nose. "What do you want, Jackson?"

"I want out of Ogenth," Jackson said. *Kurosawa*'s speaker system gave his panicked voice a thin, nasal quality. "Vissia Corsini can't be reasoned with. She'll incinerate everyone. Just like Welan Bloom Hill."

"Why didn't he go with those you sent ahead?" Angel asked.

"We needed him," Kirby said. "And he said he was fine. I don't understand what happened."

I do, Angel thought. *Reality set in.*

"Jackson, you would abandon us?" Kirby asked. "We need you."

"Staying is stupid," Jackson said. "It's suicide. Ask your Captain de la Reza."

"We have a chance," Kirby said, "because Captain de la Reza and her crew are here."

"That's a lie," Jackson said.

"They must have their ship," Kirby said. "Without it, there is no chance for any of us. You would kill everyone in Ogenth? Your own family? Would you see little Becca killed?"

"I told you to bring my family here," Jackson said. "We will leave together. I'll take anyone else who wants to go. But I'm not staying here. I don't want to die."

"This is a hopeless gesture. You can't get anyone onboard without opening the ship's loading ramp," Kirby said. "I understand your fear—"

"Do you?" Jackson asked.

"I was there when Vissia destroyed Welan Bloom Hill," Kirby said. "I lost family, too. You know this."

Jackson didn't say anything.

"Please," Kirby said. "If you want to leave, you will be permitted to do so. You can walk to Ileòke. But you cannot have this ship. It is needed to protect Ogenth."

Jackson said, "My ship is in Ileòke. You took it."

"You offered it," Kirby said. "And I'd venture to say that it wasn't your ship to begin with. It belongs to Ogenth. You know this."

"I'm trapped," Jackson said. He let out a derisive snort. "We're all going to die."

"I meant what I said. You are free to walk away," Kirby said. "Take as many supplies as will support you in the wild. As much as you need. You can lead a group to Ileòke. There are bound to be others who feel as you do. It would be best to send you all together. Just come out."

Another alarm went off.

"A ship approaches." It was Ogenth's security system.

Kirby looked at the ceiling. "Do you know which ship?"

"Not yet. They're running silent, and their security barriers are up," the AGI said. "But it should arrive in fifteen minutes."

"If that's *Shrike*, we've run out of time," Angel said.

Kirby said, "I'm doing what I can given we aren't face-to-face. I can't use all my skills. I can't even negotiate with him in our own language."

Angel turned to Lou. "Is there another way to get in?"

"That depends on how far he's gotten into *Kurosawa's* systems," Lou said. She whispered, "There's the emergency access panel."

"You've got ten minutes to pop that ramp open," Angel said. "Do whatever you have to. Just . . . try not to make too much of a mess."

Lou nodded once. She whirled and dashed to a rack of tools. Kirby continued to reason with Jackson. After a few moments' search, Lou seemed to find what she'd been looking for. She lifted up a heavy wrench and enthusiastically mouthed the word *yes*.

Angel motioned to her. *Get a move on.*

Sprinting across the room once again, Lou stopped under and to the left of the ramp's hinge. She tugged at a small access panel. An approximately thirty-centimeter-by-thirty-centimeter door swung open. She tapped at a series of buttons. Then she blew air out of her cheeks, stooped, and picked up the long wrench. Using the tool, she began turning some sort of bolt with both hands and all her strength. Kirby motioned to Beak to take over.

"The ship is now ten minutes away," Ogenth's security system said.

"You have to bring my family," Jackson shouted. "Now!"

"Not helping," Enid muttered.

"Thank you for the report," Kirby said to the AGI. "However, you're upsetting Jackson. Please stop until further notice."

A crack began to appear in *Kurosawa*'s tail as the loading ramp slowly opened. Beak seemed to be making faster progress, but it was clear this was going to take longer than the time they had remaining. All of the heaviest weapons were still in the ship's hold.

"Enid," Angel said. "Get every gun we stowed in our rooms. Sukyi, go with her. We're going for plan C." She returned her attention to the ship and Beak's efforts.

Kirby said, "This isn't going to work in time, is it?"

"Keep trying," Angel whispered. "Keep him focused on you while Lou and Beak break in."

"I'll send for his daughter. Maybe she can talk some sense into him," Kirby said. She paused. "What happens when you get inside?"

"We shoot him if he doesn't relinquish the ship," Angel said.

"You can't do that!"

Angel shook her head. "Look, I don't want to do it. Firing a stunner in there will make even more of a mess than Jackson has already made. You got a better idea?"

Kirby said, "We'll send Paulie in." She spoke in Paulie's ear for a few seconds.

Paulie nodded and vanished. With Paulie on her way, Kirby continued to reason with Jackson.

Angel considered the situation. Somehow, they'd have to stop the incoming ship without *Kurosawa* and without the ground-to-ship missiles stored in the cargo compartment. The enemy ship would land. It wasn't like they could stop it. She, Enid, and Sukyi would have to meet them outside. It all depended upon *where* they landed. And there was no way to know beforehand.

Jackson's daughter arrived and began pleading with her father. Paulie joined Lou and Beak under the ship. Paulie had some sort of dart gun with her.

Angel went to Lou. "We've run out of time. Think you can get inside now?"

Lou stared up at the narrow opening. "I could. But I wouldn't want to be half through when Jackson snaps to what we're doing."

Beak stopped cranking the ramp open and wiped her face with the back of one pale arm.

"Then be quiet about it," Angel said.

Enid returned with the weapons.

"Lou, take whatever you think you'll need," Angel said.

Lou chose a small pistol and tucked it into a pocket.

Kirby rushed over. "Please. Don't kill him. We need him. Let Paulie go in first. She can render him unconscious."

"What if he shoots her?" Angel asked.

Kirby blinked. "With what? He doesn't have a gun."

"Are you kidding? He has all our guns," Enid said. "Except these."

"He won't use them," Kirby said. "Jackson is an Emissary."

"He's frightened," Angel said. "Frightened people do unpredictable things. Lou goes with Paulie."

"But—"

Angel put up a hand before Kirby could finish. "Only as backup."

At last, Angel watched first Paulie and then Lou squeeze through the narrow opening.

"Be careful," Angel said.

"I will," Lou muttered as Beak boosted her up to the ramp.

Angel said, "Let Paulie do what she can, but if Jackson—"

"I know," Lou whispered. "Don't worry. I've got this."

Angel stepped away from the ship. Holding her breath, she listened for any indication of progress. Her frustration grew with each second. She checked the time. The ship would be landing at any moment.

"Come on, Lou," she whispered.

All of a sudden a muffled thump sounded within the ship. The conversation between Jackson and his daughter ended abruptly.

"Paulie?" Kirby asked. "Can you hear me? Paulie? What happened?"

Paulie's voice came over the loudspeaker. "I got him. He's out."

"Thank goodness," Kirby said.

"Captain, I've got some good news and some bad news," Lou said.

"Go on," Angel said.

The ramp lowered all the way. Kirby and several others entered the ship.

"He's made a mess up here," Lou said. "It's nothing I can't repair, though."

"How long?" Angel groaned.

"Three hours," Lou said.

"Damn it," Angel said.

"Maybe two?" Lou asked.

"I've Jess Hadley of *Hadley's Hope* on the com," Ogenth's security system said. "She is requesting immediate bay access. And she wishes to speak to you."

"What are you waiting for?" Kirby said. "Put her on! Open the bay doors!"

"Kirby? Kirby, are you there?" Jess asked.

"Yes, my love. I'm here," Kirby said. "What is it?"

"*Shrike* is right behind me," Jess said. "I hope you're ready for them."

"How long until they're here?" Kirby asked.

"A couple hours, I think," Jess said. "I tried to hurry, but *Hope* wasn't designed for racing. Rosie was supposed to meet me before I left. They didn't show. Something's wrong."

"We'll find out what happened," Kirby said. "Just focus on getting in here, already."

"All right," Jess said. "I love you."

"I love you, too," Kirby said.

25 ▇▇▇▇

TIME: 07:30
DAY: SUNDAY
OGENTH

It was one thing to know she and her crew were outnumbered. It was quite another to watch footage of Serrao-Orlov forces disembarking. Even the dropship seemed twice the size of *Kurosawa*. Angel had experienced these sorts of odds before, of course. And some with her background would claim to be unaffected. However, she'd seen what happened to people who shut down like that. They snapped when bottled-up emotions reached critical mass. They made careless decisions with other people's lives.

At least we're prepared, she thought. *As well as we can be.*

Part of that groundwork had been the drones. Paulie, as it had turned out, was not only an excellent engineer, but also a skilled drone pilot. She wasn't the only one. The Emissaries might not have been willing to fight, but they were more than willing to serve in other ways.

Angel tried not to worry about why the enemy hadn't sent their own drones to reconnoiter before landing. *Or after.*

"Everyone in place?"

"Yes, captain," Enid said. Her steady confidence was re-assuring.

Lou said, "*Kurosawa's* engines are hot."

Paulie said, "Cameras are active and in position."

"This is going to be the most fun I've had in years," Sukyi said.

"Me, too," Lou said.

"I wasn't remotely serious," Sukyi said. "This is the worst bet I've ever made. And I've made quite a few bad bets. What is wrong with you?"

Enid said, "Lou is an adrenaline junkie. Didn't you notice?"

"Cut the chatter," Angel said. The smallest of smiles curled one corner of her mouth. "We can discuss Lou's unsavory life choices after we've survived our own." She wasn't immune to nervous energy any more than the rest of her crew.

She continued. "I'll wait until they reach the first barricade. When I'm finished there, I'll fall back," Angel said. "Then you're up, Enid."

Enid grunted in what Angel assumed was an affirmative.

"Once you've set off your charge or trap, don't hang around to watch," Angel said. "That's what Paulie's drones are for."

Angel wasn't repeating herself for the sake of her crew. They'd memorized their parts in the plan. She did so for Paulie, Beak, and the rest. None of them had seen a fight before, and repetition helped when it came to stressful situations. *At least, it does if you're human.* It occurred to her that she knew nothing about Emissary psychology.

The crisp mountain air was sharp with freshly cut pine. An hour or so before dawn, the forest had been dusted with a light layer of snow. Angel was glad. If it'd done so before they'd finished their work, covering their tracks would've been difficult.

She lay on her stomach on a flat projection of rock near a cliffside. She had two well-hidden lines of retreat. She and Beak had seen to that. The rock face where Angel waited wasn't a natural formation but neither was the clearing below. Days before, it'd been a thick patch of forest. Now, newly-cut tree stumps dotted the ground—difficult terrain for mechs and light infantry.

Her mouth was dry. She tasted tin when she swallowed. Her palms were slick with sweat. Fear was a perfectly sensible reaction to facing down twenty-five well-trained mercenaries with a sniper rifle and a pile of lumber.

The trap was primitive—one of the oldest, least creative configurations known—a pile of stacked logs poised to roll downhill. Luckily, no one was judging on originality, only effectiveness.

Some old tricks are so old they're new again.

I hope.

Her breathing was regular even though her heart was thudding in her ears. She willed her hand steady. It hadn't failed her before, but there was always a first time. She wasn't a sniper. That was Enid.

Angel rested the barrel of her rifle on a lip of rock for extra support. Below, all was silent. Even the wildlife seemed to know something bad was about to happen.

She wiped a palm against her coveralls and felt the hardness of body armor underneath the fabric. *The waiting is the worst.*

Signaling to *Kurosawa* via her internal ship connection, she asked for an update on the enemy's progress.

Kurosawa sent a digital representation of the battlefield. It became a transparent overlay on Angel's vision.

The enemy was getting close.

She raised her pulse rifle and sighted the scope on the wooden wedge keeping the pile of logs and rocks in place. Her eyesight began to go in and out of focus with the rapid thud of her heart. A fly buzzed her face. She waved it away left-handed. She smelled the coffee she'd had for breakfast on her own breath. Her belly, thighs, and elbows were almost painfully cold due to the frigid stone beneath her.

Get ready, she told herself. *It's time.*

Swallowing again, she gradually moved her finger to the trigger. The moment she sensed motion amongst the trees at the bottom of the path, she would take in a deep breath and hold it.

A distant crashing thud was the first sign of Serrao-Orlov's troops. They weren't bothering to be quiet. The smashing of underbrush was followed by a series of rhythmic thumps in the slow cadence of a heavy mobile artillery unit.

The mechs are here.

Her first sight of the enemy was of a twelve-foot-tall, neckless, oversized human-shaped mech. Its pilot had used its nanocoating—normally employed to replicate appropriate camouflage for any terrain—to paint the mech matte black. A white skull and crossbones was displayed across the chest, and a red bandana had been sketched on the helmet.

The first mech was joined by a second, less decorative one.

The log fall had to be in play before they had time to react. Turning her attention back to her target, she squeezed the trigger.

Nothing happened.

For a moment, she wondered if she'd missed. Then came a shift in weight and the sound of bark scraping against bark. Something snapped. Another pop. A crack. Then three. A stone rolled off the pile. She counted silently to herself. *One. Two. Three—*

The whole mass began to shift. Snow jostled off the logs and peppered the ground.

It's happening too slow.

Only it wasn't. The adrenaline dumping into her system was affecting her sense of time. Her CA finally took charge of the chemicals in her bloodstream. Her heart rate slowed. The clearing snapped into sharp focus. She took a slow breath and felt calm. Confident. *Clearheaded.*

A third mech appeared. This one displayed a desert camouflage pattern unsuitable for snow or forest terrain. The vibration from the *thud, thud, thud* of the mechs' steps could be felt in her body where she lay among the rocks.

Four. Five—

The logs began bearing down on the intruders in earnest. One of the bigger stones tumbled from the top of the pile and careened down into the clearing on its own.

Skull and Crossbones didn't react fast enough. Three massive logs slammed into them all at once. They attempted to save themselves with a few staggering steps, but an unexpected stump put them off balance. The mech was knocked off its feet. Once downed, they became lost in an avalanche of falling logs.

The second mech managed to avoid the first series of tumbling obstacles. Their movements reminded Angel of a dancer. She hadn't seen such grace in a mech before.

That's some pilot.

Then a cluster of logs slammed into a tree and snapped the top off with a splintering crack. The upper half of the tree plummeted, gaining speed and force as it fell, and ended the second mech's performance with a curtain of branches, pine needles, snow, and a loud thud.

The third mech fired off a series of pulse gun blasts that vaporized falling logs. Unfortunately for it, there were too many moving in the air and on the ground to target. It attempted a jump. A mass of tree trunks crashed into the mech's legs at just the right angle. The mech did an involuntary flip midair.

It went head over feet, landing on top of the struggling Skull and Crossbones.

Deafening crashes echoed up the mountain.

Angel's CA blinked warnings.

She winced. "That had to hurt."

"What did you say?" Lou asked over the audio feed.

Kurosawa sent, According to my calculations, your position will be overrun in less than five minutes, Captain.

Damn it, Angel thought. *What did you just tell the others?* "Nothing important. On my way to you, Lou. Enid, you're next."

Angel crawled backward—away from a chaos populated with pops of shattering wood, screams, and panicked shouts. A big grin spread across her face. She hadn't expected the log trap to work that well. She'd chosen it because it would be hard for CAs to detect.

Don't get cocky. It's only the first encounter, she thought. *The enemy isn't going to be as careless from here on out.*

She was careful and quiet as she made her way through the forest. When she was certain she was far enough, she sprinted the rest of the way to the rendezvous point. Her CA overlay informed her that the enemy was once again making progress up the mountain—if at a more cautious pace. By the time she reached the spot where Lou and *Kurosawa* were waiting, Angel was out of breath. She stumbled to the top of the ramp as it closed behind her.

"In the air!" she shouted. "Now!"

"Yes, Captain," Lou said.

The weight of inertia almost knocked Angel off her feet. She steadied herself with a hand to the bulkhead. Walking through the ship like a drunken sailor, she reeled from handhold to handhold as the ship rapidly dodged obstacles.

"How's it going, *Kurosawa*?" Angel asked. "Is Enid all right?" She guessed the enemy was near Enid's position by now.

"They have not discovered her presence as of yet," *Kurosawa* said. "That is positive, given the variables."

Lou said, "You bet it is." A proximity alarm went off. "Too bad the same can't be said for us," she shouted, and steered them around a cluster of trees. "We've got company. Looks like three drones. They're small and fast. Want *Kurosawa* to handle them?"

"Do it," Angel said. "I'm not in place yet." She laid a hand on the ladder.

A series of small bursts erupted from the gun turret above. Lou let out a victory whoop.

"Fuck you, you little bastards!"

Angel crawled up the short ladder and then staggered to the gunner's cockpit. "*Kurosawa*, let me know the instant the enemy engages Enid's position."

"Yes, Captain," *Kurosawa* said.

Dropping into the seat, Angel bruised her hip on the safety harness when the ship took another sharp turn. "Ouch."

"Sorry, Captain," Lou said over the intercom. "But you know the rules about being strapped in."

"Captain," *Kurosawa* said. "The enemy have arrived at Enid's position."

"Was she able to get a few shots off before they detected her?" Angel asked. She switched *Kurosawa's* rapid-fire rail gun from automatic to manual. She left the pulse cannon, positioned on the rear of the ship, on full auto.

"Would you like an enemy casualty estimate?" *Kurosawa* asked.

"I would," Angel said. She punched a few more switches.

"Including your previous encounter, the total is six wounded. Two dead. This is an estimate based upon visual, thermal, and electronic signatures. Of course, the enemy has employed various signal dampening devices that may interfere with my accuracy."

"Understood," Angel said.

"In addition, I would not recommend counting on the six wounded remaining incapacitated," *Kurosawa* said. "I am fairly certain they have a med center onboard *Shrike*."

Angel frowned. "Do you think they'll revivify?"

A revivification tank would make their chances of beating back the invasion nonexistent.

"I do not believe this to be the case," *Kurosawa* said. "The energy signature for that part of the ship isn't powerful enough for such an expenditure."

Thank god, Angel thought.

"They named that thing *Shrike*?" Lou asked. "Points for that."

"Are you frightened?" *Kurosawa* asked. "It would certainly be logical given the situation."

"Nah," Lou said. "Are you?"

Kurosawa said, "I am not programmed for emotional displays during emergency scenarios. Would you prefer for me to alter that setting?"

"Never change, baby," Lou said. "I like you the way you are."

Angel did the math. Seventeen soldiers left—provided the med center didn't intervene too much. Every little bit helped. "*Kurosawa*, what about the mechs?"

"I need to make a correction. There are now three dead," *Kurosawa* said. "Enid has killed another."

Sixteen.

"Go, Enid!" Lou said.

"Fly," Angel said. "Save the cheering for later. If we don't get there before they box her in—"

"Almost there."

"Captain, no mech has been powered down at this time," *Kurosawa* said.

"Oh well. I suppose it was too much to hope that I'd done much more than scratch their nanocoating," Angel said. "At least it slowed them down for a while."

Kurosawa cleared the trees just as the mercs appeared to get a lock on Enid's position. Rapid sniper fire poured from the north end of the clearing. The trees in that area were blasted with rockets. In an instant, all that remained was charred, splintered, and on fire. Smoke and dust lowered visibility. About a dozen ground troops formed a semicircle behind four mechs. Two of them were Desert Camo and Skull and Crossbones. The black mech had a jagged scratch in its nanocoating and a dent in the chest plate.

Ha! Angel thought.

One of the other two mechs had pink stripes. The fourth one had no decoration at all. It looked as though it'd just walked off a showroom floor.

She paused and counted the enemy. *Where are the rest of the troops? For that matter, where are the rest of the mechs?*

Several quick rounds of pulse rifle fire erupted from a clump of bushes to the left of the earlier site. Midway through the second round of fire, the mechs trained their rockets on Enid's new position. Lou screamed as the area vaporized in a conflagration that shot flames twenty-five feet into the sky.

"Enid!"

Angel aimed the railgun and unloaded everything she could without jamming it. The heat indicator went into the red. She paused and then resumed firing the recommended short bursts. The ground below erupted in fountains of dirt and rock. Smoke again filled the clearing. Four drones vanished in a cloud of flying earth and smoke.

If this were a military battle, it wouldn't be long before the corporate soldiers radioed for reinforcements.

Maybe that's where the other two are? she thought.

Kurosawa couldn't hang around. The situation was about to get too hot. Military-grade mechs were equipped with hull-busting rockets designed to take out armored dropships. Angel had no doubts that these mechs were no different.

As predicted, a rocket shot up out of the clearing. It skimmed *Kurosawa*'s flank and exploded in the air fifty feet away. A second shot was only off by five feet. Angel felt the vibrations in the ship around her.

"Somebody down there has pretty good aim." Lou spoke over the chaos. "Permission to get the fuck out."

"I haven't spotted Enid yet," Angel said. "We're not leaving her."

Kurosawa said, "If she is dead, remaining will not—"

Several more rockets went off. Angel unloaded into the enemy. It took an instant to register that someone was shouting on the audio feed, and it wasn't Lou.

"Would you fucking watch what you're doing up there? It's getting a bit busy down here for someone not in an environment suit, damn it."

"Enid?" Lou asked. "Is that you?"

"You were expecting someone else on this channel?" Enid snarled.

"Where are you?" Angel asked.

"South side of the clearing," Enid said. "They blasted the hell out of my remote turrets. And I just bought the damned things."

"Better them than you," Angel said. Cool relief poured through her veins.

Lou said, "I didn't know you had any of those."

"And neither did they," Enid said. "Now that we've finished the pleasantries, I'd very much like my ride out of here."

"Fair enough," Angel said. "We'll meet you at the pickup."

"See you soon," Enid said.

A big gust of wind blasted the area as Lou steered *Kurosawa* out and away. The rendezvous point was on the other side of a nearby hill. The ship tilted to avoid another rocket, giving Angel a brief view of the battle site. Smoke and fire swirled with the ship's passing.

A lone body—or most of it—lay in a heap on the broken ground. Scattered flaming chunks of tree trunks, branches, and rock littered the area. The ground was the black of unburned charcoal.

Fifteen.

Angel resumed firing as the ship raced to the meeting coordinates. "*Kurosawa*, give me a locator on Enid. Now."

"I estimate Enid's arrival in four minutes at her current pace."

"Thank you," Angel said.

The ship made a sudden move upward. Angel again felt heavier as inertia sunk her deeper into her cushioned seat. Then the ship banked to the left. More explosions burst into the air—a little too close for Angel's comfort. Suddenly, *Kurosawa* rocked to the left and the right, and then dropped several feet before righting itself. Several treetops vanished in a cloud of flaming splinters.

Just as abruptly as the ship had flown up into the sky, it dropped.

"Lou! You're not doing my stomach any favors!"

Lou's voice sounded calm, but Angel could detect the excitement underneath. "We're touching down. Don't know how long we can stick around."

"Where's Enid, *Kurosawa?*" Angel asked.

"I have a visual," Kurosawa said. "Lowering the ramp now."

A loud thump-clang sounded through the hull.

"What the fuck was that?" Angel asked.

"An unexploded mortar," *Kurosawa* said. "The mechs are almost here."

Angel asked, "Is Enid onboard?"

Several rounds from a pulse rifle went off. Angel turned to the screen on her console and entered the commands to bring up the ship's outside cameras.

Kurosawa said, "Not yet, I'm afraid."

The screen displayed a view of the landing area. Enid was conducting a fighting retreat, pausing periodically to fire off several rounds behind her. She had a rifle slung on her back and another in her hands. She was limping. Her left leg was bleeding. Angel couldn't make out Enid's pursuers, not yet.

She was about a hundred feet from the ship.

Reassuming the gun controls, Angel sent off two bursts from the pulse cannon in the direction that Enid was firing. Enid got the hint. She sprinted in an uneven gallop. Angel was prepared to send off another couple of shots when she heard Enid's heavy steps thundering up *Kurosawa's* ramp.

"That's it, Lou!" Angel shouted. "Get us the fuck out of here!"

"I'm on it!" Lou said.

Hydraulics whined as the ramp closed. Angel caught a

whiff of burning pine. The pitch of the engine's growl went up a few octaves as the landing gear left the ground. A series of explosions rocked the ship.

"Damn it, Lou!" Angel said.

"Sorry about the nanocoating, boss!" Lou said.

"I'm taking that out of your pay!" Angel wasn't remotely serious.

With Lou at the controls, *Kurosawa* wound his way through and around several trees and then shot up once again into the sky. Angel took a deep breath in relief. They crested a hill just before beginning the return flight.

That was when she spied the enemy ship.

"Son of a bitch," Angel said.

"Now it gets fun," Lou said. Angel could just see Lou's maniacal grin. The ship responded eagerly as Lou aimed *Kurosawa* at *Shrike* and punched the throttle.

"What the fuck are you doing?" Angel asked.

Lou said, "It's time for a little game of chicken."

"*Kurosawa*, inform Sukyi we're going to be a little late," Angel said.

It'd been a certainty that the enemy would, at some point, employ their ship. She'd just hoped that they would do so later rather than sooner.

"Affirmative," *Kurosawa* said.

The enemy ship didn't veer off course. *Shrike* continued on—apparently accepting Lou's challenge, never altering speed.

From her perch in the gunseat, Angel had a good view of

what was happening. It was, perhaps, a better view than she wanted. "Lou? Just how close do you intend to take us?"

Lou didn't answer.

"Lou?"

Laughter rolled up from the cockpit. "Come on, you fuckers! You wanted to play! Let's play!"

"So, I think it's safe to say that Lou has lost her damned mind," Enid said from somewhere below.

Lou shouted. "You assholes don't have a chance. I read your damned spec manual!"

"Should I do something?" Enid asked.

"I think you should strap yourself in," Angel said, leaning over to see down the access ladder. "I've a bad feeling that this is about to become a very exciting ride."

"You're not going to stop her?" Enid asked.

"If I need someone shot, I trust you'll handle it," Angel said. "If I need us to dodge an enemy ship and keep us whole while it's done, I've got Lou."

"Point." Enid nodded once. Then she vanished.

The other ship unloaded their guns. Angel lined up *Shrike* in her sites and returned fire. It wasn't easy, given that *Kurosawa* was weaving and bobbing through the air, but she did her best. A number of shots landed in the forest below.

Kurosawa swayed and bobbed. Lou whooped. The ship resumed its collision course. The proximity alarm screeched. Just before the point of no return, *Kurosawa* dropped underneath *Shrike*.

Angel let out an involuntary scream.

If she hadn't served three tours with Lou at the helm, she wouldn't have believed what she was seeing. According to the calculations on screen, *Shrike*'s underbelly was mere inches above her head. She couldn't control the urge to slump lower in her seat.

"Ah, Lou," Angel said. "We're awfully close."

"It's fine!" Lou said.

"Then you know that I'm about to go headfirst into their landing gear?" Angel asked.

"Oops."

Kurosawa dropped away from *Shrike*.

"That's not what I wanted to hear, Lou."

"Better?" Lou asked.

Angel said, "Much."

"Uh-oh."

"What's wrong now?" Angel asked.

There was an explosion and *Kurosawa* jerked in the air. Angel caught a whiff of ozone and burning electronics.

"What the fuck was that?" Angel asked. Now that *Shrike* was in firing range again, she resumed her attack.

"Shit! I'm sorry, *Kurosawa*," Lou said. "Did that hurt?"

"I do not register pain," *Kurosawa* replied. "But if I did . . . Ouch."

Enid called from below. Her words were punctuated with the blast of a fire extinguisher. "Don't think they hit anything important."

"I hope not," Angel said.

Another detonation went off, this time on the opposite side of the ship.

"Lou?" Angel called. "Is there going to be anything left of my ship once this is over?"

Lou said, "Their pilot is better than they ought to be. I wonder who they are. It's kind of hot."

"Lou." Angel put a warning edge in the name. "Get us the fuck out of this."

"I've got an idea," Lou said. "Hang on tight, Enid. This is going to get squirrelly."

"Boot magnets engaged," Enid said.

Kurosawa took a sudden banking turn toward the mountain. *Shrike* followed close behind. Rocket blasts leveled stands of trees and scarred cliffsides. Angel returned fire, scoring a wide hit along *Shrike*'s nose and port side.

"There," Lou said. "Found it."

Angel looked out and didn't see anything but a wide expanse of mountainside. "Found what?" And that's when she saw it. A narrow pass between two mountains. "I've a terrible feeling I know how this goes."

Enid said, "Oh no."

"Oh yes," Lou said. "They can't follow us in there."

"Who gives a shit about them? *We* can't fit in there," Angel said.

"*Kurosawa* says we can," Lou said. "Can't we, baby?"

"According to my calculations," *Kurosawa* said, "the crevasse should accommodate us within an acceptable margin of error."

"What is an acceptable margin?" Angel asked.

"Plus or minus a couple of meters."

The side of the mountain began to take up Angel's entire screen. The sides of the opening were jagged. "Lou. This is a very bad idea."

"Uh-huh," Lou said.

The ship flipped on its side and slipped through the opening. Behind them, *Shrike* veered off, just missing the mountainside.

"Phew!" Lou said.

The sky was a long grey ribbon to Angel's right. The line of light and clouds twisted as they flew. To her left, she could see nothing but dim rocks. Ahead, the crevasse narrowed into nothing. All along the length of the opening, uneven chunks of limestone butted out.

"I don't like this," Angel said.

The ship jolted from an impact. Then another. A *Shrike*-size shadow passed overhead.

The smell of smoke wasn't dissipating.

"Lou, we can't stay in here forever," Angel said. "They're on to us. They'll only meet us on the other side."

"That's what I'm counting on," Lou said.

Enid asked, "Wait. What?"

Lou said, "Slowing down."

"And that's going to help, how?" Angel asked.

"I've a plan, Captain," Lou said. "Trust me."

From below, Enid said, "Are you done jerking the ship around? I'd like to put out the fire now. With the fire extinguisher. Not vomit."

"We're taking a breather," Lou said. "Feel free to move about. Hey, *Kurosawa*. You got that drone ready, yet?"

"Affirmative," *Kurosawa* said.

"Launch it the instant we land," Lou said. "It needs to register as continuous movement. That's key."

"We're landing?" Enid asked.

The ship slowed. The fissure opened wider, and Angel finally felt she could breathe. *Kurosawa* righted and then set down on the crevasse floor. A hatch opened and a drone shot out.

"Hope you like my present, assholes," Lou said.

"Has anyone told you your vocabulary takes a turn for the worse in combat situations?" Enid asked.

"And you get chatty," Lou said. "So what?"

Angel asked, "How long are we staying here?"

"Not long," Lou said. "Enid, how's it look?"

"Fire is out," Enid said. "That's all I can tell you from here."

"Hey, *Kurosawa*," Lou said. "You got a damage report for me?"

Kurosawa rattled off a long list of broken circuits, fried systems, and hull breaches. For the most part, they were minor, but they wouldn't be taking any trips into space any time soon.

The roar of the engines went up in pitch, and the ship executed a careful flip. "Okay, everyone," Lou said. "I wish we could see their faces, but some things just aren't worth the trouble. Back we go the way we came."

When they reached the end of the chasm Angel could've sworn she heard an explosion in the distance.

Lou cackled.

"*Kurosawa*, have you heard anything from Sukyi and the others?" Angel asked.

"According to the latest report, a second group of mercenaries is headed for the wind turbines," Kurosawa said.

"I knew they'd try that," Angel said. "How are things looking?"

Kurosawa said, "Not so good, I'm afraid."

26 ▮

TIME: 09:00

DAY: SUNDAY

OGENTH

"Sukyi?" Angel asked. "Damn it! Report in!"

"Enid?" Lou asked over *Kurosawa*'s com system. "You ready?"

"Yes," Enid said. "Try not to let them start another fire."

"Doing the best I can," Lou said. The clicks and snaps of switches and toggles could be heard in the background. "Can I help it no one else is cooperating?"

The roar of the engines acquired a louder, more urgent timbre.

"Time to get as fucking far away as we can. We can't count on *Shrike* being incapacitated," Lou said. "*Kurosawa,* have you finished checking my calculations?"

"Affirmative."

"Everybody hold on to your asses," Lou said.

A fresh burst of power pressed Angel deep into her seat. The forest vanished into a blur of green and brown. The ship banked into a turn above the tree line. Her inner ears struggled to keep up with the rapid changes in orientation and pressure. She felt a bit dizzy. The trees bent with the force of their passing like tall grass in a high wind.

"How long is it going to take to get there?" Angel asked. "Sukyi still isn't answering. And the drones are down."

"Seventeen minutes, boss," Lou said. "Can't drop you close. There's nowhere to land. Even if there was, wind sucks, remember? I'll get you as close as I can."

"That'll do," Angel said.

An icy fog snagged on the jagged edges of the highest mountain tops and spread out across the sky like an abandoned wedding veil floating in the wind.

Angel tried not to imagine what could be causing the communication blackout. She wished she'd been able to send Enid with Sukyi, Paulie, and Beak. Two combat veterans and a couple of pacifists would've made for better odds than one combat veteran and two pacifists. However, Angel had needed Enid to help slow the main force. Based upon the remoteness of the wind turbines, she'd hoped that the invaders wouldn't make them a high-priority target.

Apparently, she'd gambled wrong.

Angel spied the path leading to Sukyi, Paulie, and Beak's defensive position. Using the cameras on *Kurosawa*'s underbelly, Angel spied evidence of the enemy's passing. The violence done to the undergrowth was substantial. The snow made it even more obvious.

The knot in her gut tightened another notch. "*Kurosawa, how many mechs and drones does Shrike have?*"

"Their ship is spec'd for as many as ten mech units," *Kurosawa* said. "There is no information available regarding limitations on drone storage. I would assume as many as could fit in the hold."

"And how many would that be?" Lou asked.

Kurosawa answered, "At least a hundred."

"Son of a bitch," Angel muttered. Her heart sank.

Kurosawa said, "But there would be no room for humans. And we know they have human troops onboard."

"Jess said that there were only six mechs and twenty drones on the corporate manifest Rosie acquired," Angel said.

"Maybe there's still only six," Lou said.

"We can hope," Angel said. *What if the report is wrong? Don't do that. Don't doubt Rosie. Not now.*

"It is unlikely that *Shrike* is full to capacity," *Kurosawa* said. "This operation did not benefit from long preparation. In any case, if they had brought such a force, they would have, no doubt, employed it already. Given that they have not—"

"That's a relief," Lou said.

I still don't like what I'm seeing down there, Angel thought. "Assume the LZ is hot," Angel said. "Enid, get to cover as soon as possible. Don't wait on me. I'll follow. Lou, don't stick around. Get back to the main push and give support. Since we can't be where we're supposed to be, I'm sending you ahead. The Emissaries will need you. I'll call with coordinates when we're ready for pickup."

"You got it, Captain," Lou said.

Kurosawa touched down about a mile from Sukyi's position. The thickest part of the woods as well as the steepest incline were to the west. The rest of the area was carpeted with tall grass that reacted to the chaotic wind shifts like a small sea in a storm. Based upon the silence from the cockpit, the landing was consuming most of Lou's attention. Wind gusts violently rocked the ship—once nearly tossing it into a stand of trees.

Angel unbuckled herself from the gunner's chair, grabbed her gear, and slipped down the ladder—hands and feet on the sides of the rails. The soles of her heavy boots made a loud thump as they smacked the deck. She bent her knees upon impact to prevent jarring her joints. The ship made another rapid course correction. She staggered. Before Lou's struggles with the wind could knock her down, Angel tapped her heels together. Boot magnets would slow her down, but she couldn't risk getting hurt before she even left the ship.

She got to the ramp just as *Kurosawa* settled. Enid bolted down the incline as fast as her bandaged leg would carry her, pulse rifle at the ready. In an instant, she was out of sight.

Angel toggled the safety on her gun and deactivated her boots.

"Good luck, Captain," *Kurosawa* said.

"Take good care of Lou for me," Angel said. "Will you?"

"I will."

Nodding once, Angel rushed after Enid. *Kurosawa* retracted the ramp the instant Angel's feet flattened grass.

The air outside the ship was cooler and more humid. She caught the sharp green scent of vegetation layered with the dusty spice of moldering leaves. The thin grass was waist-high, and the edges of the leaves were sharp enough to cut. She discovered this when she stooped in an attempt to make the most of the available cover. Grass blades sliced her cheeks and nose. She was glad she didn't have to run through the grass for long.

Enid waited, kneeling and keeping her weight on her good leg at the northwestern edge of the clearing with her gun at the ready. Angel got down beside her. Her cheeks were stinging as if she had a mild sunburn. She held up a hand, giving Enid a signal that they would rest there for a moment.

Angel made one last attempt at contact. "Sukyi, are you there? Give me an answer, will you?"

No reply came.

"Probably an equipment malfunction," Enid said in a low voice as they continued through the woods.

"I hope you're right," Angel said.

"Sukyi is a clever woman," Enid said. "And a known menace across two systems. Paulie and Beak had enough of her and deactivated her mic."

Angel's stomach knotted. Enid wasn't one to offer reassurances. It was out of character. It meant Enid was worried, too.

Angel opened her direct com with *Kurosawa*. *Can you give me the enemy's location now?*

Scanning, **Kurosawa** sent. There is a mercenary unit north of you. They have engaged Sukyi's position. Sukyi and the others have fallen back. They may have been over-whelmed.

Are there any others in this area? Angel asked.

The remaining enemy forces appear to be concentrated near the main path to Ogenth. There is a blip on the other side of the mountain range. However, I can't get a fix on it. It could be important. Or it could be nothing.

Keep me posted if that changes, Angel said.

Yes, Captain.

Angel and Enid traveled as fast as they dared through the undergrowth. This close to Ogenth, the poisonous animals were brightly colored and avoided human contact. Still, Angel wasn't comfortable. Even though Kirby had reassured her otherwise, she couldn't help thinking she hadn't spent enough time studying local wildlife.

Ever since she'd read about Leona Three, she'd made it a habit to know the environment in which her unit would be fighting. The doomed marine unit had been dropped for a recon mission behind enemy lines and had died—not because they'd been discovered by the enemy, but because the unit never reached its first way point. The culprit was the local insect life—specifically a species of Mercer's tick. The entire unit had been bled dry before the abort team had arrived for extraction.

Never overlook the locals—no matter how insignificant they may seem.

Since planet access was restricted, there were no detailed military studies of Persephone's flora and fauna. While she'd helped build Ogenth's fortifications, the planet had sprung various surprises upon her. One of them was when she'd helped shift a pile of logs. Arachnids didn't normally bother her. However, these were a sickening translucent beige with black stripes. Their bodies were the size of a fist, and their long legs easily stretched the length of a handspan and a half. Startled, she'd only just kept herself from screaming. Paulie had glanced over, told her to leave the creatures alone, and gone about her business. Angel looked them up later and discovered they weren't deadly. However, their venom was necrotic. So, she'd added them to her caution list.

She couldn't shake the constant feeling that something awful lurked beneath every leaf, log, or unseen crevice.

The harmless insect bites collected over the past week's labors itched. Her face stung. Something in the air irritated her sinuses, making breathing through her nose difficult. She sniffed. Everything around her was coated in a thin layer of winter slush. Damp earth and dead leaves had begun to accumulate in her boot treads—not enough to make her already heavy boots heavier, but enough to mute the sounds of her passing.

The forest itself was quiet with the exception of the little animal noises that spoke of a thriving ecosystem. In the far distance, however, Angel detected signs of the fight: the racing of ships' engines, explosions, and gunfire. There wasn't evidence of closer combat. That bothered her.

Have we arrived too late? Are we in the wrong place?

An animal roar echoed through the forest. It was deep— too deep for a big cat.

"What the fuck was that?" Enid muttered.

Angel frowned.

Another snarling growl filtered through the trees. Distant gunfire punctured the air.

"Didn't Beak say the bears were hibernating on the other side of the mountain this time of year?" Angel asked.

"Well, we know at least one of them doesn't believe in re-location and also doesn't sleep very well," Enid said.

"You think it's the same one?"

"Only Beak would know."

Angel pushed herself to move faster, but since she couldn't be sure of the enemy's placement—*Kurosawa* hadn't sent her any updates as of yet—she kept her pace controlled. Thin tree branches slapped her already stinging face.

The sounds of the battle reached them long before they arrived at the scene. Gunfire, snarling animals, howls, and screams of terror and pain echoed off the mountain.

"Shit," Angel said. "Come on."

Abandoning stealth, she and Enid ran the remaining distance. The main path they'd been skirting widened. They finally encountered the fight from the southeast. Angel saw no immediate evidence of Sukyi, Paulie, and Beak, but that would've been difficult given the chaos.

Three bears were attacking the mercenaries. Massive creatures and mechs took up most of the available space on the path. Several dead mercs lay on the ground. Very little of what was easily identified as human remained. Gore soaked into the already damp dirt, and half-chewed body parts were strewn across the south end of the path. The survivors were concentrating fire on the largest of the animals. Two mechs seemed to be intent on the trees left of the trail. Blood had seeped into the dirt forming reddish sticky mud. There were only three non-mech mercenaries left. They had their backs to Angel and Enid, and were focusing on the bears. One was kneeling in an attempt to get a better shot.

Angel had a strong urge to let the animals sort it out.

Enid brought up her rifle. "Your orders?" she asked over her suit com.

"Take them out. Don't shoot the bears," Angel said.

Enid lined up her first shot. "This isn't going to be easy."

"Thought you liked a challenge," Angel said. She kept her eyes on the woods, confident that her CA would alert her should anyone else show up to the party.

A strong mixture of astringent scents joined that of fresh gore and gun discharges. The odor was powerful enough for Angel to catch even with a stuffy nose.

"Beak, Paulie, and Sukyi are here. Keep an eye out."

"Where?" Enid asked.

Angel's CA began to piece together a coherent picture. "To the south."

Her suit coms were programmed to connect to other members of her unit automatically if they were within signal range. She tried again, hoping she hadn't been close enough before. "Sukyi must have locked her com. Shit. Someone is heading up from behind us. Let's do this."

"Shoot while keeping one eye on our asses. Got it." Enid paused. "Mercs are assholes."

Angel said, "*We're* mercs."

"And?" Enid squeezed the trigger.

One of the three non-mech-suited mercenaries dropped.

"One," Enid muttered, rotating to change targets.

The others didn't appear to have noticed. Confusion and noise did make details difficult to absorb, Angel knew.

"Two," Enid said.

The bears now seemed focused on the mechs. Angel left them to it. Lining up her own shot, Angel aimed at the back of the kneeling merc's helmet. She changed her mind and took the easier target—the back. "That's three."

The largest of the bears reared up on its hind legs. The first mech was a practical green-grey. The bear dropped to all fours with another growl, swiping at the mech. It was effortlessly knocked into the air and hit a tree four feet from the ground. When it bounced back onto the path, it almost hit the second mech. The green-grey mech rolled until it finally settled on its back. There were now several large scrapes and dents in its titanium plate.

"I'm not sure we should get involved," Angel said. "Beak isn't here to sort out any misunderstandings."

Enid nodded.

One of the other bears leapt upon the momentarily helpless mech. Its pilot attempted to target its guns on the creature. The animal let loose a huge bellow of pain. Before the pilot could manage another hit, the second beast ripped into the breastplate. The screech of protesting metal joined the chaos. The screaming pilot writhed for freedom. Then the creatures lowered their jaws.

Angel flinched and looked away.

The black mech was now alone. Twisting designs had been stenciled in white on its titanium plate, reminding her of tattoos. Dented and scratched with one of its guns broken, it nonetheless appeared to be faring better against its opponent. The bear in question was heavily wounded—not that its injuries slowed it down. Blood coated the animal's scales from shoulder to elbow. Gore glistened on its face and legs. One of its paws hung limply at its side. The largest bear moved next to it and laid its tail on the first one's side.

The third bear had fallen—Angel hadn't noticed when. It now lay in the bloody mud, breathing in short, pain-filled gulps.

"Captain," Enid said, pointing to the south.

Beak sprinted up the path. She, too, was covered in crimson. Her face was knotted into an expression of wild rage. Her mouth stretched wide in a soundless war cry. The air reeked of fresh blood, rot, and ozone.

Several things happened at once. The tattooed mech staggered backward a couple of steps and brought up its gun. The larger bear swung a huge claw. The mech's lone working gun went off before it was ripped from its arm mount. Ammunition sprayed in a hot arch. Angel and Enid hit the ground. By the time Angel looked up, she saw Beak scramble up the tattooed mech's back. Then Beak slapped a small circular device on the mech's helmet. An indicator light in the center glowed red then green. Smoke began to form at the point of contact.

Expecting Beak to climb back down, Angel held her fire. Beak didn't. She began to claw and rip at the mech with her bare hands instead. Prying free the remains of the broken gun, she threw it. Her wild fury reminded Angel of the bears. If she were up against anything but a mech, it would've been impressive. As a fighting tactic versus a mech, however, it was ill-advised.

Is she okay? Angel thought.

The mech teetered. The device was burning a hole into the faceplate. Beak doubled up her fists. She smashed them down on top of the device. The faceplate cracked. The mech began to fall. Beak leapt off before it hit the ground. The uninjured bear ripped into the mech's armor.

"Beak? Are you okay? Beak!" Paulie sprinted up the path.

"I told you to wait for me." Sukyi jogged in an awkward off-kilter gate.

Paulie laid a hand on Beak's arm. Beak yanked herself from Paulie's grip. Paulie made another attempt. Again, Beak shook her off. The last surviving bear slowly dropped to a sitting position with a grunt. Beak went to the animal's side. She was crying.

"Oh no," Paulie said.

The animal let out mournful cry and then lay down. With the amount of blood staining its maw and paws, Angel wasn't sure which was the bear's and which was the former mech pilot. The bear nosed its closest dead companion and snorted. Angel could hear its labored breathing. Another blend of scents floated on the air—for an instant they were strong enough to mask the stench of violence.

"Is there anything we can do?" Angel asked.

Paulie shook her head.

"What happened?" Enid asked Sukyi.

"We met them two miles from here," Sukyi said between choking breaths. She was stooped over, hands on knees. She coughed. "Was all we could do to slow them down."

Angel nodded. "And then?"

"Beak was hit. Those creatures showed up," Sukyi said. "There were four of them."

And now there's only one, Angel thought.

Sukyi straightened and combed the fingers of one hand through her now sticky hair. "Aren't you supposed to be somewhere else?"

"I've been trying to reach you for thirty minutes," Angel said. "You scared the shit out of me. What happened?"

Sukyi brushed at her environment suit with one hand. It only smeared the drying blood. "One of those bastards managed to get in a lucky shot. The hit shorted out my com. I didn't notice until I was halfway here."

"Ah," Angel said.

"Makes one wish for a secondary form of communication," Sukyi said.

"How about this?" Enid made an obscene gesture with her middle finger.

"Why, Enid Crowe, I didn't know you cared," Sukyi said with a grin.

Paulie joined Beak at the dying bear's side. It breathed in rapid gasps until it simply stopped. Beak laid her head on the creature and placed her right hand on its blood-matted flank.

Angel turned away, giving Beak a little privacy. "Paulie, is there something we should do for Beak's friends before we go?"

Beak glanced up and shook her head once. The sour odor of citrus combined with a sharp scent that reminded Angel of bleach.

Paulie wiped tears from her eyes. "Beak says that their brothers and sisters will come for them."

"I'm so sorry," Angel said.

"Beak tried to talk them out of the attack, but they wouldn't listen," Paulie said. "They took it personally when Beak was hurt."

"We—we need to go," Angel said, swallowing. "The others—"

"Need us," Paulie said. "I know." She glanced at Beak and the dead animals. "Just . . . Let me talk to her."

Paulie went to Beak and placed a gentle hand on her shoulder. While Paulie spoke to Beak, Angel checked in with *Kurosawa*.

"Lou? How's it going?" Angel asked on her suit com.

A few seconds passed before Lou answered. Muffled explosions sounded in the background. "Kind of busy right now, Captain." A particularly close hit broke up her reply. "Fuck you! You fucking fucker!"

"Lou, when do you think you might be able to come get us?" Angel asked.

"On my way," Lou said. "But I've got to ditch the shithead first."

"Weren't they hot an hour ago?" Enid asked. "What changed?"

"Familiarity breeds contempt," Lou said. "Or something."

Enid said, "My, you're fickle."

"Sure," Lou said. "But only when they try to kill me and mine."

"So, *Shrike* is still up and running?" Angel asked.

"Afraid so," Lou said. "But it's nothing I can't handle." Her voice changed pitch as she turned away from her mic. "You hear that, asshole? You're nothing!"

"Don't crash the ship," Angel said. "I haven't finished paying for the last overhaul and refitting."

"That wasn't my fault," Lou said. "Specs on that hangar said that it was wide enough. The owner customized it and—"

"I know. I know," Angel said. "See you at the LZ."

Paulie left Beak's side and came over. "We'll take the tunnels back to Ogenth. Beak's going to fall over if I don't get her some medical attention."

"All right," Angel said. "Sukyi, you're with us. We'll need you where we're headed."

The meadow looked like such a peaceful place. The tall razor grass didn't show any signs of having been disturbed—even though this was where *Kurosawa* had dropped them off.

Enid knelt at the edge of the tree line with her pulse rifle, vigilant for signs of trouble. Sukyi positioned herself at Enid's side. Angel joined them. Nine minutes passed before the woods, undergrowth, and grass swayed in *Kurosawa*'s wake. The sound of the engines was deafening in the former quiet of the forest.

"Hurry up," Lou said over the audio com. "*Shrike* is a persistent bastard. I don't know how long it'll take them to find this place."

Everyone sprinted for the ramp. Last in line, Angel searched the trees one more time and then followed the others. The ship was back in the sky before Angel had managed to sit down, let alone buckle herself in.

"I've got some good news and some bad news, Captain," Lou said.

"Bad news first," Angel said, knowing where the conversation was headed.

"Mercs are through the first three sets of traps," Lou said.

"That leaves two more," Angel said. "Take us home."

"Don't you want to ask about the good news?" Lou asked.

"There is no good news," Angel said. "There never is when you say that."

Lou said, "It's no fun when you already know the punchline."

"Maybe you should get a newer joke?" Enid asked.

"Says the woman who doesn't know any," Lou said.

"How would you know?" Enid asked.

"Because you had your sense of humor removed to make room for more surliness," Lou said. "Angel told me."

Enid grunted.

"See?" Lou asked. "Shit. *Shrike* is back. Fucking stalker."

"We are at war," Enid said. "It is appropriate."

"On my way to the guns," Angel said. "Try not to flip us before I get strapped in."

"All right, *Kurosawa*," Lou said. "Let's show that asshole how to fly."

"It is quite apparent that they already know," *Kurosawa* said.

Lou said, "You know what I mean."

The ship executed several sharp turns. Angel treaded carefully and didn't deactivate her boots until she reached the gunner's chair.

Kurosawa hugged the mountainside as they raced south. A deep shadow inched back into the valley as the sun eased over the eastern horizon. Not far behind *Kurosawa*, *Shrike* followed.

The enemy ship seemed to be taking a rather relaxed attitude toward its pursuit.

"That's right," Lou said. "You keep your fucking distance. You know what I'll do to you if you get too friendly. Don't you?"

"Our Lou is less hospitable during combat runs," Sukyi said.

Enid said, "Can't think of a better time."

"I suppose not," Sukyi said.

Angel got the sense that Sukyi and Enid were feeling a little helpless. Were it not for being focused on the guns, Angel would've felt the same. She had flown with Lou for close to a decade. The knot of icy terror in Angel's belly wasn't related to Lou. Angel simply hated dogfights. During flight, soldiers were cargo. There was nothing to do but sit and pray you weren't hit. For people trained via muscle memory to act during emergency situations, doing nothing while someone tried to kill you was a nightmare.

Settling into the gunner's seat, Angel flipped the switches that returned the rapid-fire guns to manual mode. Per usual, she left the pulse cannon alone. Every ship had its quirks. Automatic mode was more accurate and reliable, but *Kurosawa* was an older ship, and the targeting computer on the rapid-fire guns tended to glitch if left to its own devices for extended periods.

She used the targeting-computer's screen. Three shots hit home before *Shrike* swung away with a graceful precision that Angel couldn't help but admire.

"Holy shit," Angel said. She continued firing in short bursts. "He's good."

Lou said, "I'm not so sure he is a he."

Angel tried again and missed.

"What makes you say that?" Enid asked.

"I don't know," Lou said. "I've just never met a man that dances like that. I'm not sure what's hotter, thinking they're female, nonbinary, or male."

Shaking her head, Angel often wondered how Lou could chatter so much while executing complicated flying maneuvers, but she'd come to recognize that it was one of the signs that everything was under control.

"I wish they were on our side," Lou said.

Enid said, "Should Erik be jealous?"

"Nah," Lou said. "Erik knows I'd never leave him for anyone or anything except chocolate."

"Has anyone bothered to tell him that chocolate is readily available?" Sukyi asked.

Shrike's pilot turned the ship so that they only presented a profile—making it a more difficult target. And then it was gone. Angel got eight good shots in as they flew past.

"Where the fuck do you think you're going?" Lou asked.

"I thought you didn't want their attention," Enid said.

A cold knot formed in Angel's gut as realization set in. "They know where we're headed." *Of course, they do. It's not like it's a big secret now.* "They're going for the big push. They're getting between us and Ogenth."

"Son of a bitch," Lou said. "Why do they have to be smart *and* a good pilot?"

"Maybe it isn't them but their commander?" Sukyi asked.

Enid said, "Not helping."

"All right," Lou said. "That means I keep us between them and Ogenth."

Kurosawa's engines revved. Angel felt herself sink deeper into the chair. Everything was fine until a bad vibration came from deep in the ship.

"Lou? What the fuck are you doing?" Angel asked.

"Busy now, Captain," Lou said.

"I don't like that," Enid said. "Whatever it is."

Several alarms went off at once.

"We're painted," Angel said.

"Hit back," Enid said. "You know how this goes."

Angel's shots scored across *Shrike*'s hull and damaged a wingtip. *Shrike* appeared as a red silhouette on the gunner's screen. The ship fired four missiles. Angel let fly a few more rounds. *Kurosawa*'s pulse cannon added to the battle.

"Enid," Angel said. "I'm running low. I need a fresh reload."

"On it," Enid said.

"Be careful," Angel said. "We've got bogeys coming in."

The missiles were getting close. Angel tensed up. The ship executed a series of evasive maneuvers. Two of the missiles went wide, missing *Kurosawa* entirely. The third passed close enough to set off proximity alarms, but thanks to one of Lou's sudden turns, it slammed into the mountainside instead.

Angel winced, thinking of the people inside the mountain.

The final missile hit *Kurosawa*.

The ship jolted in midair. *Kurosawa*'s interior lights flickered off and then back on. Sizzles and crackling filled the air. The distinct smell of an electrical fire accompanied thin smoke drifting into the gunner's cockpit.

"Son of a bitch!" Enid shouted.

The flow of Lou's never-ending curses was cut short. The sensation of falling caused Angel's ears to pop. She saw their rapid descent on the gunner's computer screen. Below, the others went to work on the new fire. Blasts from flame-suppressing gear punched the air. Someone was coughing.

Angel shouted. "Lou? Are you okay? Lou!"

"Still here, Captain," Lou said between hacking coughs. "Prepare for a rough landing."

Grabbing a helmet, Angel stuffed it on her head. It was too late to leave the gunner's cockpit. She'd have to do the best she could where she was.

The impact consumed her senses. Her teeth snapped together. The belts of her safety harness bruised her shoulders and hips. She didn't understand that she'd lost consciousness until her eyes fluttered open. Her mouth was full of blood. She spat. She'd bitten her tongue when her teeth clamped together and hadn't noticed. Pain filled her awareness.

"Sukyi? Lou? Enid? Beak? Paulie?" Angel asked around a swollen tongue. "Check in!"

No one answered.

She was hanging sideways in her seat. She struggled to unbuckle herself. Her shoulders ached. Blood flooded her mouth again. She turned her head and spat three more times. "Check in, damn you!" Her words were slurred.

"I-I'm here." It was Enid. "Sukyi is in one piece, I think." There was a short pause. "She's got a pulse. She's breathing."

The buckle finally gave away. Angel suddenly dropped onto the console's edge. "Ouch. Oh fuck!"

"You okay, boss?" Enid asked.

"I'm good," Angel said. "Check on Lou."

"I'm trying," Enid said. "The ship is a real mess."

"Fuck," Angel said.

A moan came from below.

Enid said, "Sukyi Edozie, welcome back to the land of the living."

"I don't remember buying a return ticket," Sukyi muttered.

"Don't be such a babyhead," Enid said.

Angel heard another groan.

Sukyi said, "Someone kill the mech that punched me in the head."

Angel wriggled her way through broken electrical equipment to the ladder. "Less chat. More grabbing gear and getting the fuck out. *Shrike* will return to finish us off." She hollered into her suit mic. "Lou? You asleep up there?"

"Cockpit door is stuck," Enid said.

Sukyi said, "Here. Let me see that."

There was a gunshot. It was earsplitting in the confined space.

Enid cursed. "Watch what the fuck you're doing!"

The wrenching squeal of reluctant steel made Angel flinch. She dropped down from the gun turret ladder and staggered. The floor tilted at an ungainly forty-five-degree angle. At the end of the passage, she could see that Enid and Sukyi had finally pried open the cockpit door but only partially. Enid squeezed through the narrow opening.

"Lou?" she asked. "Never thought I'd say this, but you're too quiet. I need you to talk to me."

Angel stumbled to the buckled cockpit door. Sukyi's face

was streaked with blood. She was moving slowly, and she looked terrible, but she was on her feet.

"You okay?" Angel asked.

Sukyi nodded and stopped herself with a wince. "I'm still here. Not sure I want to be. You?"

"I'm good," Angel said.

"I'll leave you to this, then," Sukyi said. "Like you said, someone needs to get our gear."

Angel peered into the cockpit. "Lou? You still alive?"

"Lou took a hit on the head. Helmet took the brunt of it," Enid said. "Won't know how bad it is until we get her out. But she's pinned."

"I'm on the way," Angel said. Sharp metal raked against her clothes as she passed through the broken door, ripping her flight suit and clawing her skin. When she saw the cockpit, she didn't take the time to check her cut.

Everything was chaos. Sparking wires hung from the ceiling. The acrid smell of burning electronics was thick. It would've been worse but for the breeze blowing in through the half-empty pilot's screen. Lou lay unconscious in the chair. A large support had fallen across Lou's body. Enid was shoving at the chunk of bent and broken steel, but it wasn't moving. Worse, there wasn't much space within the cockpit for leverage.

Eventually, it took all three of them to move the broken support off of Lou's shoulder and legs.

Lou came awake screaming. "That fucker! *Kurosawa*? Answer me!"

"That's a good sign," Enid said. "I think."

"Lou, honey," Angel said. "We have to get you out of here. Do you think you can move?"

They didn't have a medic. *That's not exactly true.* But medical help was inside Ogenth. It went against Angel's NCO training to move a trauma victim. On the other hand, leaving Lou where she was wasn't an option. Unfortunately, *Kurosawa's* computer systems were down. Angel couldn't get any help from that quarter.

"My legs hurt like hell," Lou said. Her words were slurred.

"How's your neck?" Angel asked. "Don't move. Just tell me."

"I think it's okay," Lou said. "Oh, god. My head is killing me."

Angel nodded. "That's going to happen when you head-butt a planet."

Lou smiled. "I did, didn't I?" She sounded woozy.

"And your back?" Angel asked. "Let me see your eyes." One eye was dilated. *Shit. What do I do now?*

"You're going down the checklist," Lou said.

"Come on, Lou," Angel said. "Help me out here."

"It's just a bump," Lou said. "My vision is a little blurry, though. Back is okay. I think." She squinted out the gap in the windscreen. "Is the ship on fire?"

"Maybe," Enid said while cutting away Lou's safety harness.

Angel asked Sukyi, "Do we have a stretcher back there? We're going to need it."

"I will look," Sukyi said.

After a few minutes, Angel and Enid were able to clear a path to the door.

Peering out the narrow opening, Angel called to Sukyi. "Have you found the stretcher yet?"

"Not yet," Sukyi said.

"Well, we've another problem we'll have to deal with first," Angel said. "We have to do something about this damned door."

"There has to be something I can use as a lever," Sukyi called back. "Stay there."

Angel listened to Sukyi's progress through the wrecked ship. *One step at a time,* she thought. *Don't think about* Shrike *out there, lining up its next shot.*

"I think I've got it," Sukyi said. She emerged from behind a partition and held up a longish piece of steel railing. "This should suffice." She had a second one that she leaned against the bulkhead away from the doorway. "One moment."

She made a second trip to the back of the ship. This time she returned with an armful of clothing. She dumped it and then set to work on the door.

With Sukyi using the makeshift lever and Angel and Enid shoving from the other side, the door finally gave way with a loud creak and crash.

"Thank gods," Enid said. "What's the rest of that crap for?"

Sukyi said, "Zip the jackets halfway." She pointed to the pieces of railing. "Slide these through the neck and out the bottom, tie the sleeves together . . . Viola! Stretcher."

"I didn't know you were creative," Enid said.

"Desperation is the mother of invention," Sukyi said. "Or so I hear."

Angel checked on Lou. Her eyes were closed. "Lou? You still with me?" she asked, trying not to sound panicked.

Lou didn't open her eyes. "Still here. I'm just so tired."

"No napping for you," Angel said. "Not yet. We've got things to do."

"I changed my mind," Lou said. "I don't want to move."

"Not an option," Enid said.

"Shit," Lou whispered.

"Ready?" Angel asked.

Lou said, "This is going to hurt, isn't it?"

"I'm sorry," Enid said. The warmth in her voice was genuine. "But someone has to take care of Brendan. I'm not going to do it. Not even for you."

"Damn," Lou said. "Guess I'll have to change my will."

Enid blinked. "You did not."

Lou smiled. "Let's get this over with."

With that, Angel helped Enid pry Lou out of the chair. Lou's face pinched with pain, but she refrained from screaming. Holding Lou's shoulders, Angel got the sense that Lou was entirely too light.

Must hurry. Get her some help. "All right," she said. "We're carrying you to the door."

Lou moved a hand. "Give me a minute."

Enid gave Angel a worried look over Lou's body. Angel gave her a reassuring nod in exchange.

Angel said, "There isn't much time. Ready?"

Lou mumbled an affirmative.

"Here we go," Enid said.

They managed to maneuver Lou out of the wrecked cockpit and onto Sukyi's makeshift stretcher.

"Wait! Wait!" Lou was now in a panic.

"What?" Angel asked. "Stop thrashing. Are you hurting?"

"Eject the compact drive," Lou said. "I won't leave. Not without *Kurosawa*."

Enid said, "I'll handle it."

Angel whispered, "Hurry."

Easing past the stretcher, Enid vanished back into the cockpit. Angel and Sukyi headed to the emergency exit, steering the prone Lou over chunks of broken ship. Debris made the trip an obstacle course, and the tilting floor contributed to the difficulty, but they finally arrived at their destination. There was a haphazard pile of weapons nearby.

"Hang on. I need my hands." Angel lowered her end of the stretcher.

Sukyi did the same so that Lou wouldn't slide off, but even if the floor had been level, there wasn't space to lay it flat.

Angel unlatched the emergency door, expecting it to explode open. It didn't. The ship let out a deep, shuddering groan. For a moment, she worried that it wouldn't work at all, and they'd be trapped. Sukyi pointed to the security keypad.

"Oh." Angel felt her cheeks heat before she hit the buttons.

After the second try, the hatch burst open. The emergency door crashed into the trees. She leaned out and searched the sky. The roar of distant engines thundered over the mountainside, but there was no visual sign of *Shrike*.

What's holding them up? she thought. "Enough with the salvage, Enid. It's time to go."

"Coming," Enid said.

Several loud thumps and curses came from the cockpit area. Finally, Enid appeared with a suitcase-size chunk of electronic components.

"This is what you wanted?" Enid asked Lou.

Relief spread across Lou's pain-pinched face. Her voice was more faded. "There's a green light? Yes?"

Enid frowned and shook her head. She set her burden down next to the weapons pile.

"Everything looks fine," Angel lied. "We'll sort out *Kurosawa* later."

"Okay." Lou drifted off.

Angel asked Sukyi to switch places with Enid on the stretcher in case Enid's sniper skills were needed. Heading to the weapons pile, Enid stuffed her pockets with whatever she could. Then she straightened, slinging a pulse rifle over her shoulder. Lastly, she holstered a laser pistol, selected a few more weapons, and positioned herself at the emergency exit.

"Any idea of what we'll find out there?" She held out a second pulse rifle and pistol for Angel.

"With *Kurosawa* gone dark?" Angel shook her head once. She accepted the weapons. Once checked, she tucked them away. With *Kurosawa* dead, she'd have to rely upon her CA's short-range data. "This the last hand cannon?"

"There are enough for two apiece," Sukyi said. "Including Lou."

Angel said, "Lou won't be needing one."

"Fuck you," Lou said. "I can still hold a gun."

"You have a concussion," Enid said.

"So?" Lou asked.

"You can't even sit up," Enid said.

"Lay still, Lou," Angel said, and sighed. "Let's just get to the fallen trees over there. We'll work out the specifics then."

27 ▮▮▮▮▮

TIME: 10:30

DAY: SUNDAY

OGENTH

The landscape around *Kurosawa* was unrecognizable. Smoking chunks of machinery lay scattered across the ground. Splintered trees, snapped in half during the landing, were in flames. Smoke reeked of burning pine and burning dropship. Raindrops vaporized on hot metal, hissing. The ticking of the engines kept time. A heavy mist clung to the ground, shrouding the scene.

Angel tried to contact Kirby and got no answer.

Turning to face the wreckage, she instantly wondered why they weren't dead. Lou had done an excellent job of landing. Not only had the ship settled less than two hundred feet in front of the closest of the generator tunnels, but she'd done it without plunging them into the mountainside.

Still, it was a difficult thing to see. Everything Angel had spent the last five years of her life saving and living for—everything that represented her independence and freedom—was scattered like so much trash. The damage to *Kurosawa* was extensive enough on the inside. Seeing it for the first time from the outside was devastating.

There's no coming back from this. She blinked back tears. *It's only a ship.* Only it wasn't. "So. This is it," she said, keeping her voice level.

"You had to know it would come to this eventually," Sukyi said.

Angel shrugged. "That doesn't mean I was looking forward to it."

Enid asked, "You want to stop?"

"Hell, no," Angel said. She pointed at the generator tunnel. "Ogenth isn't safe yet. And none of this means a damned thing until they're safe."

Enid nodded.

"We could make a stand there," Sukyi said.

She pointed to a mound of dirt and destruction created by *Kurosawa* during the landing. The nose of the ship on the right side had plowed the earth.

Sukyi whispered, "We should get Lou to the tunnel. We could call for someone inside to get her medical help."

It was a smart suggestion. *There's only one problem,* Angel thought.

"She won't go," Enid said.

"There's no time to argue either," Angel said. She glanced

up at the sky. "I don't know why *Shrike* hasn't dropped hell on us and called it a day. But let's not waste the time we've got."

She stationed Enid near the top of the dirt mound with a portable pulse cannon. It was the only high ground they had. Lou was propped up just under the ship near the exploded emergency hatch. She was immobile and would need the most cover.

"Enid, you're in charge of the com," Angel said. "Get in touch with Kirby. See if she can get someone out here for Lou. I can't raise anyone."

Again, Enid nodded.

The fact that Lou hadn't protested was worrying.

The roar of *Shrike*'s engines caused everyone to seek cover. Enid fired a few shots before the ship passed overhead with its landing gear down. The resulting wind turbulence shook the remaining trees.

Angel blinked. *They're landing to the south.*

"Sukyi, you're with me," she said. "You and I will meet them. Maybe we can slow them down."

"I wouldn't have it any other way," Sukyi said.

"Good luck, boss," Enid said.

"Same to you." Angel walked a few hundred feet down the mountain to face the inevitable with Sukyi at her side.

Angel's CA was not as useful without a connection to *Kurosawa*, but at least she could track *Shrike*. There weren't many places to land. As a result, they'd set down not far from the first set of obstacles she and the Emissaries had created—a wooden wall with a hidden ditch in front of it.

She and Sukyi helped each other ease over the ditch trap. When they'd gotten to the other side, the distinct sound of mechs forging a path through the woods brought them up short. Angel signaled to get to cover. They both made for the underbrush. Angel's CA indicated the enemy's likeliest position. She got herself and her rifle in the best position of attack. Beside her, Sukyi quietly set up a portable pulse cannon.

The woods around Angel acquired a new sharpness. The trees, the sky, the frost-covered earth. Persephone was beautiful—at least this part of it. She'd always considered the planet to be one of the ugliest in the system. It was a strange place to die.

Just let me finally make up for that Ulysses Mather cock-up. She'd wanted to do so much more with her life than she had—maybe even have a child. Even so, she was satisfied that at least she'd die doing one thing her mother and her teacher could be proud of. Attempting to save Ogenth was an honorable thing. And whether or not she succeeded, she and her crew had definitely bloodied the enemy's noses.

It felt so good—*No, right*—to have Sukyi nearby at this moment.

"Sukyi Edozie, you're a damned good friend," Angel whispered. "Thanks for being here."

Sukyi stared at the trees. "That reminds me." She cleared her throat. "There's something I need to tell you."

An estimated time of enemy arrival appeared at the edge of Angel's vision. "We've about one minute. If you're going to say it, say it."

STINA LEICHT

"I have a daughter," Sukyi said. Lying on her stomach, she was stretched out on the frosted ground. She tugged at the red scarf looped around her neck. "I want you to take care of her when I die."

Angel blinked.

"I left her school's address on the counter in your apartment," Sukyi said.

"I *knew* you came back for a reason. I knew it," Angel said, almost angry. "You're dying."

Sukyi nodded.

"Why didn't you say anything before?"

"It never came up."

"It never came up?"

Sukyi shrugged.

"Hell of a fine time to tell me," Angel said. "I fucking hope you have a backup plan. Neither of us is getting out of this alive, you know."

"I know."

Something large crashed through the nearby underbrush.

Angel said, "Here we go."

Three mechs were first to appear. Angel didn't waste her ammunition—a pulse rifle wouldn't do much against them. So, she waited for less well-armored targets.

Sukyi, on the other hand, sited the pulse cannon.

Angel held up a hand. "Wait! They're too—"

The bolt hit the center mech square in the chest and exploded. The other two were knocked to the ground by the impact. The explosion set the nearby brush ablaze. Angel felt the concussion deep in her rib cage. A monstrous hand seemed to shove her deeper into the undergrowth. The blast was deafening. A burst of heat gusted past. After what felt like a muffled instant but was probably longer, she lifted her head.

Sukyi lay next to her in the frozen dirt.

Angel's voice sounded distant in her own ears. "They were too close for that thing, damn it."

Sukyi raised an eyebrow as if in question and then motioned to the fallen mechs. All that remained of the center mech was the bottom half. The heavily armored legs stayed upright. The only sign that a human had been inside was the spray of gore splashed across reinforced steel.

The other mechs began to stir.

"Far be it from me to discourage efficacy," Angel said, keeping her head low. Her hearing slowly began to recover. "Be more careful next time."

With a sideways nod to the recovering mechs, Sukyi said, "Time to go."

Angel scrambled to her feet.

The ground erupted in gunfire. She sprinted to the trap, hoping Sukyi would do the same. Rapid-fire rounds threw up spurts of dirt and dead leaves. Angel didn't stop until she spied a boulder. She threw herself into the frozen dirt behind it and waited. When the mercenaries paused, Angel peered through the greenery. Sukyi was hiding behind a wide-trunked tree twenty feet away. Angel's CA silently indicated the probable locations of several mercs. She shot a few rounds at them and then lay flat in anticipation of return fire.

She caught Sukyi's attention and signaled another retreat. Sukyi acknowledged the message. Angel backed up, feeling her belly brush the ground. Sukyi stepped from behind the tree, braced herself against the trunk, and fired the pulse cannon again. This time, the round took off a mech's head. Once more, the forest burst into flames. Sukyi slipped backward out of sight.

Angel chinned her com and whispered, "I didn't know you were good with a pulse cannon."

Sukyi's reply could barely be heard over the answering fire. "There's a lot you don't know."

"Apparently," Angel said. She joined her on the opposite side of the path. "What's your daughter's name?"

"Achebe."

"That's pretty," Angel said. She aimed behind them and laid down some covering fire. "How old is she?"

Sukyi did the same. "Six."

"Who's her father?" Angel ran to the next position.

"None of your business."

"Come on, Sukyi," Angel said. She fired again and then lay in the dirt. "What am I to tell her when she asks?" Crawling to the next tree, she sat up and shot at the mercs while Sukyi made her way to Angel.

"No."

"Sukyi. Don't be such a—"

The two of them slipped farther into the underbrush, continuing their whispered argument. They lured the mercs off the path before circling back to the makeshift wall and pit trap. They didn't slow until they had gained enough distance from their earlier position.

The mercs, for their part, seemed to be having some CA trouble. It was the only explanation.

Must be the mountain interfering with the signal, Angel thought.

She couldn't understand why they seemed intent upon shooting up the entire forest rather than pinpointing their locations. She supposed they were used to brute-force tactics. The numbers certainly were in their favor.

Must be nice.

She and Sukyi finally arrived at their destination with their verbal altercation unresolved. Angel's CA indicated that *Shrike* was again on the move. That was when she heard the distinct roar of a dropship engine.

"Shit," Angel said. "They're heading for *Kurosawa*."

Sukyi glanced up at the sky and sighed. "Well, we tried."

Angel motioned for Sukyi to go ahead. "Get back to the others. I'll meet you there. There's something I have to do first."

Sukyi tilted her head to the side and lifted an eyebrow in question. "You don't have to kill yourself to avoid motherhood. You can say no. If—"

"That's not—" Angel let out a frustrated sigh. "I'll do it if it comes to that. Achebe won't have to be alone. I mean it. Just go. I'll be right behind you." Angel gave her best friend a gentle shove.

"If I don't see you in two minutes, I'm coming back," Sukyi said. "You hear me?"

"Whatever you say. Now, get the fuck out of here."

Angel went to the pit in front of the makeshift wall. It'd be better if she set the thing on fire from a distance—preferably after several mercs had fallen in, but there wasn't going to be time for that. She fished a lighter out of her pocket and lit it with a flick of her wrist. Then she dropped it into the leaves they'd used to hide the pit. When she was sure the flames had caught the fuel-soaked leaves, she bolted.

By the time Angel had returned to the path, she saw Sukyi waiting behind a log next to the downed ship—weapons at the ready. She was almost to Sukyi's makeshift barricade when two mechs crashed through the trees. One was particularly familiar. Soot and burn markings on the pink striped nanocoating told a story. The mech pilots kept their distance from one another—seeming to have learned not to bunch together. Ten drones hovered above the fresh crash site. She was sure there were more that she couldn't see.

She made for Sukyi's log.

The trees began to sway and thrash to the song of a deep engine thrum. A shadow drifted over *Kurosawa*'s broken hulk.

Shrike had arrived.

The mechs halted their advance. Their less-armored friends took up positions near the mechs. Angel noted that only five of the regulars had made it with a little satisfaction.

"Captain de la Reza." A woman spoke over *Shrike*'s external com. "We would like to speak with you."

Enid cursed from her perch on top of the mound near *Kurosawa*'s nose. Sukyi glanced to Angel and frowned.

Sukyi asked, "Why do I know that voice?"

Angel said, "She does sound familiar."

"Captain de la Reza?" the woman asked again.

Angel shrugged. "What's the harm in talking?"

"And what if they shoot you the instant you reveal yourself?" Sukyi asked.

"We've got two pulse cannons and limited power packs," Angel said. "If I can talk them out of a fight, we're better off." She then whispered, "I'd prefer Achebe to have her birth mother. I'm all right with being an auntie." Turning to face *Shrike,* she stepped from behind the barricade and shouted, "I'll talk. Not sure what we have to discuss."

"Surrender?" the woman asked.

Angel still couldn't match the voice to a face or a name. "Yours or ours?" she asked in an attempt to draw things out.

"Why don't I land this thing, and we'll see?"

Angel narrowed her eyes. "What do you—"

Shrike dropped from the sky like a chunk of discarded stone. Several tons of ship slammed into the ground. It felt like an explosion. Angel staggered. The landing gear almost didn't have time to engage. Three of the supports dug deep into the dirt but held. The fourth buckled with a groan. She could just imagine Lou's wince.

The ship's loading ramp engaged. *Shrike* teetered and creaked. The ramp gouged the scorched grass. Once the ship stabilized, a lone woman walked down the length of the ramp. It took Angel a moment to remember her because she was so out of context.

"Sorry about that. I've never piloted a ship before, and I didn't have time to learn."

"Kennedy Liu?" Angel asked. A mix of emotions tangled in her throat—not the least of which was betrayal. "What are you doing here?"

"I thought I was clear," Kennedy said. "I am negotiating a surrender."

"I didn't say we were planning on—"

"Not yours," Kennedy said. "Ours."

Sukyi stood up. "Wait. What?"

"I, Kennedy Liu, an agent of the United Republic of Worlds Xenobiology and Planetary Division, do hereby surrender the Serrao-Orlov dropship *Shrike* to you, Captain de la Reza," Kennedy said. "Please accept. A second attack on Ogenth is taking place. Vissia's people will breach your defenses via the wind tunnels. There isn't much time, if you want to save the lab."

Enid said, "Seriously? And the rest of these jokers are going along with this?"

Kennedy said, "They're mercenaries, M. Crowe. We've reached an equitable agreement."

"If you intended to surrender, why attack us?" Angel asked.

"Their original commander is dead. There was some contention regarding the chain of command. It took some time to resolve the issue," Kennedy said. "Nonetheless, I am in charge now."

"What exactly does that mean?" Angel asked.

Kennedy paused. "I have added a substantial sum, including a liability waiver for accepting a contract from an opposing force. Most have accepted the new terms."

"Is that legal?" Sukyi asked.

"It is now," Kennedy said.

"How many?" Angel asked.

"Five. Two mech pilots," Kennedy said. "Three regulars. The rest have agreed to stand down."

"I accept," Angel said.

"I understand that I'm supposed to give you a sword or something," Kennedy said. "I'm a little unclear as to what sharp objects have to do with it."

"*Shrike*'s authentication codes will substitute nicely," Angel said.

"We've a problem." Sukyi placed a hand on Angel's arm. "It's Lou. She's unconscious, and I can't wake her."

28 ▋

"We're leaving. Serrao-Orlov's forces have invaded the tunnels," Kirby Sams said. "Ogenth was never intended to be a fortress. That's why we had an evacuation plan in place long before you got here."

Emissaries of various shapes, colors, and sizes squeezed past one another via the now crowded passages. The air was heavy with a cacophony of organized panic and anger-laden scents—pepper, ammonia, and citrus. Fleeing people in human and Emissary forms carried valuables—electronic components, medical supplies, food stores, plants, and scientific equipment.

The whole frontal assault was a diversion, Angel thought.

Why didn't I see it? "How many are there?" It was strange not having to shout.

Kirby paused. "A little over forty. I think. I can't be exact."

Forty more mercs? Angel thought. *How? How did they do it?* Shrike *couldn't have held seventy. There was only one ship. If there was a second one,* Kurosawa *would've spotted it. Right?*

Kurosawa *mentioned a second blip. They approached from the other side of the mountain range.*

Shit. Shit. Shit. She frowned. "Which tunnels?"

"TW-2 and TW-3. Both open on the western side of the mountain," Kirby said. "They managed to get as far as the second access tunnel before the alarms sounded. They must have disabled the electronic monitors." She sighed and her face darkened. "I didn't assign anyone to watch those cameras. I didn't even place drones in that area."

"Why would you? There's nothing out there but a sheer cliff face," Angel said. "This isn't your fault. It's mine." She searched the crowd.

"We tried to warn you but—"

Angel interrupted. "Where are Paulie and Beak?"

"They're in the lab, sorting out the data and equipment." Kirby directed yet another crush of fleeing residents with hand gestures and scents. "Backups were part of the evacuation plan, of course. But there was one last update to make before we destroyed the system. And we won't leave any of our work behind for Vissia. We're destroying the lab."

"Good plan," Angel said. "Where are you sending your people?"

"Just a moment," Kirby said. She exhaled a combination of sharp odors that reminded Angel of fresh-cut lumber and ginger. Based upon body language and hand signals, Angel guessed that Kirby was telling a woman where to take an armful of medical supplies.

Kirby returned her attention to Angel. "I'm sorry. There's so much to do. What was I saying?"

"Where are you sending your people?"

"Oh. Right. Those whose duties are not necessary for Ogenth's defense are gathering in the ship bay. We can secure it. And there's room for the wounded. From there, we'll travel to one of our older cities. Ileòke. It's north of here. We sent a group to make it ready for a move after Vissia's initial threat. We have the little shuttle and *Hadley's Hope*. Transfer of the wounded is the next priority."

"Use *Shrike* as the gathering point instead," Angel said. "It'll be safer. It's near tunnel TE-7."

Confusion pinched Kirby's eyebrows together.

Angel pushed on. "*Shrike* is ours. It has guns, a small medical facility with a drug replicator, and a qualified medic. The med bay might not have exactly what you need, but it's better than nothing. The ship is twice the size of *Kurosawa*. And if it comes to that, we'll stay to cover your retreat."

"How—"

"I'll explain later," Angel said. "You can trust *Shrike*'s medic. Her name is Higbor. Oh. There are two mechs guarding the ship. One is black with pink stripes on it. The second one is grey and has the word *mouse* printed on the front. They're ours."

"Really?"

"Really. Talk to the pilot of the pink-striped mech. Her name is Annalee. She can help track down the missing if there are any." *And in this mess, there's likely to be.*

It was the best allocation of personnel, given their limited numbers. The mechs couldn't be used to defend Ogenth from the inside. They were too big. In any case, someone had to guard *Shrike*. With Lou down and Sukyi barely on her feet, Angel had run out of options.

An explosion shook the mountain. Tiny fragments of rock pelted the floor. Everyone stopped what they were doing and gazed down the hallway—eyes wide. For a moment, no one moved. And then all at once people started for the ship's bay.

"Time is up," Angel said.

"But the lab techs are back there. And—"

"I'll handle it. Load up the wounded and go," Angel said. "Can you— Can you take Lou?"

She'd slipped into a coma and wasn't expected to live.

Kirby nodded. "We will take care of her. There's no need to ask."

"Thank you," Angel said.

Jess appeared, grabbed Kirby's hand, and tugged her away.

Angel checked her mostly disabled CA and then the various drone camera feeds. All the drones in or near the northwestern part of Ogenth were inoperative. She focused on the stored video from the dead units. The last drone had captured a fuzzy image just before it'd gone black. After a couple of enhanced passes, her CA identified it as a dropship. Its name was *Takagi*.

Damn it, Angel thought. The muscles at the base of her skull tightened. A tiny flash of light winked on the edge of her vision like a warning. She chinned her shoulder com. "Hey, Annalee. How're you doing out there?"

"Haven't had to shoot anyone I had breakfast with," Annalee said. "I'd count that as pretty damned good."

"Glad to hear it," Angel said. "I'm sending the noncombatants to you. Tuck as many of them in safe as you can. Let Kirby organize. Then prepare for dust-off."

"You got it," Annalee said.

"Did you know *Takagi* was here?" Angel assumed that if Annalee and the others had known, they'd have told her. They weren't particularly loyal to Serrao-Orlov, but assumptions could get one into trouble.

"No," Annalee said, sounding almost offended. She paused before continuing. "Captain Reese might have. She was in charge, but she took an extremely fatal log to the head."

"Fair enough," Angel said. "Enid, Sukyi, Kennedy, and I are off to deal with the problem in the tunnels. If the opposition shows signs of heading your way, you go. You don't hear anything from me or mine within forty-five minutes, you go. If Kirby Sams says it's time to go, you go," Angel said. "Got it?"

There was a pregnant silence.

"I don't mean to be an asshole, but who's buying the oxygen and fuel?" Annalee asked.

"I am," Angel said. It was a lie, of course.

"Cool. And who's buying when you're dead?" Annalee asked. "Sorry, but I'm starting to rethink certain choices."

No shit, Angel thought. Her scalp felt like a drumhead stretched too tight. Squinting seemed only to make it worse. She massaged her temples. "Fuck the odds. Enid and I were in the Thirteenth." She wondered if the attempt at bravado would fool another combat veteran—even a corporate one. *Doubtful.* She changed the subject. If worse came to worst, Kirby could handle the matter. "How's Lou?"

"Still unconscious," Annalee said. "She's in bad shape. You'll have to ask Higbor for details. Should I put her on?"

"Not now," Angel said in a small voice. She suddenly found she couldn't breathe. "You wouldn't happen to have intel on *Takagi*, would you?"

"They weren't stationed in Brynner," Annalee said. "That's all I know."

"Any idea who and what they're hauling?"

"*Takagi* is one of Vissia Corsini's personal transports," Annalee said. "Number one rule of Mercenary Club is: Don't spy on the boss. At least, not so she notices."

Is that rule in the same list as: Don't flip sides in the middle of a contract? Because that one didn't seem to stop you. Angel hated freelance mercs even if, technically, she was one herself. They were assholes.

"All right," Angel said. "Let me know if Lou's status changes. And keep an eye out for bad guys."

To Annalee's credit, she didn't ask for a clarification on that. "Kennedy says I should do what you say."

Angel signed off, searched the hallway, and spied Sukyi. "Hey!"

"Hey, yourself," Sukyi shouted back. She wove her way to Angel's side.

"Where's Kennedy?" Angel asked.

"On her way," Sukyi said. "Enid, too. Are we finishing this thing?"

"That's the plan," Angel said. She spotted Enid and Kennedy, and waved again.

"They've started moving everyone onto *Shrike*, the little shuttle, and *Hadley's Hope*," Kennedy said when she arrived.

"Good. While you were in Brynner, you didn't happen to infiltrate a dropship named *Takagi* while you were poking around *Shrike*, did you?" Angel asked.

Kennedy shook her head. "Why would I?"

"That explosion? It's troops from *Takagi*," Angel said. She sent the rest of the team what little information she had. "Pack as much bang as you can carry. Explosives wouldn't go amiss. You've got five minutes."

She checked her own weapons and then reviewed a blueprint of Ogenth on her hand terminal while the others prepped. When they returned, she told them the plan—such as it was.

"Stay close," Angel said.

The press of refugees had begun to lighten up. The children were gone. Most of the remaining traffic consisted of techs wearing lab coats. Somewhere deeper in the confines of Ogenth, gunfire echoed down the halls. She searched the passage ahead for signs of trouble and kept her weapons ready as she walked.

"Why aren't you cursing?" Sukyi asked.

Angel shrugged. "You think it'll help?"

"I know you. You hate surprise parties," Sukyi said as she eased into a position by her side. "Especially the kind where everyone attempts to shoot the guest of honor." She coughed into a handkerchief.

"You can't plan for everything," Angel said. "I now consider it an opportunity to evolve."

"You've changed." Sweat glistened on Sukyi's forehead, and her long red scarf was double-wrapped around her neck. Her usual grace was slowed by apparent exhaustion.

"You sure you're up for this?" Angel asked.

Anger flashed across Sukyi's face like an afternoon storm. "You sure *you're* up for this? When was the last time you took your meds?"

The truth was, Angel had forgotten in the rush. A migraine wouldn't be far off. And if she let it go too long, it'd be a seizure.

As if to emphasize the point, another set of nonexistent sparks twinkled in the corner of her right eye. She pinched the bridge of her nose. *A blinding migraine in the middle of the fight would be such a great idea. Stupid. Stupid. Stupid.* She reached into a pocket and dry swallowed all three pills. "Thanks for the reminder," Angel said. "Just promise me you won't fall over until after the fight. I need you. Alive."

Sukyi rolled her eyes. "I won't."

"Promise me."

"Promise."

Angel resumed the journey through the now-empty halls. The soft, sharp sounds of multiple pairs of synth-rubber bootsoles grinding sand and dirt into the polished tile floor was the only sign the others followed. When she rounded a curve in the passage, they all waited for a cluster of stragglers to rush past.

"Need to tell you something," Enid said in a quiet voice.

"What is it?" Angel asked, steeling herself for more bad news.

Enid said, "Kennedy says *Kurosawa* is wiped."

Pausing, Angel glanced over her shoulder. "That true?"

"I can make a more concentrated attempt later, but it doesn't look good."

Lou and Kurosawa. *Both gone,* Angel thought. Her stomach felt hollow. She blinked back tears. "We'll worry about that after we're out of the black," Angel said in a quiet voice. "Right now, we've other shit to deal with."

The last of the refugees rushed past with armfuls of equipment. Ahead, the way was clear. She signaled for the others to get their backs against the wall. She approached the first set of doorways. Edging to the closest, she searched it for trouble. To her relief, the apartment was empty. She moved on to the next. The others followed. She let Enid check the second doorway while she covered her. Glass beads clattered. When that, too, proved to be empty, they moved on. And so it went for the next fifty feet. The hallway seemed to stretch on forever.

Another enormous explosion convulsed the mountain. She was knocked off her feet before she was aware of what had happened.

The lights flickered. Powdered rock and smoke billowed, riding the force of the blast. Broken ceiling tiles crashed to the floor. Red-tinged darkness obliterated her vision and hearing—cut off like a flipped switch. Her palms stung. Shattered tile and rock cut into her back, legs, and buttocks. Short bursts of vibration in the floor spoke of a nearby battle. The reddish light from a fire down the hall fluttered white in time with the rhythm.

The lab.

She sat up. The rain of big and small impacts slowed to a stop. The grit-coated soles of her boots abraded the floor as she stood. Her ears began to ring. The world tilted. She put out a hand and caught herself with the wall.

It was cracked.

Please. I don't want to be buried alive, she thought.

Sneezing, she wiped pulverized rock and tile from watering eyes. She tried to clear her nose and throat. She understood her hearing was recovering when she detected the muffled sound of coughing.

The lights flared. She blinked and squinted. The damage was bad. Rubble was scattered across broken floor tiles. She smelled smoke. Touching her face, her hand came away covered in bright blood. Exploring the wound on her forehead, she decided it was superficial and turned to where Sukyi had been before the explosion.

A wide crack in the wall revealed a section of Ogenth's understructure. Beneath it, Sukyi was lying in a pile of broken rock. She was slowly moving into a sitting position. A busted pipe sprayed a stream of water from the jagged wall. Angel helped a choking Sukyi get to her feet.

"Well, that was interesting," Sukyi said between hacking breaths. There was a cut on her cheek. The blood painted a wide stain down the side of her face.

"All extremities accounted for?" Angel asked. She hoped she wasn't shouting.

"I'm whole enough," Sukyi said. She touched her stained environ suit. "Can't say the same for this, however."

Enid and Kennedy appeared. Enid pointed down the hallway. The muted sounds of battle had ceased. Now, Angel heard crashes and hammering.

Looting, she thought. *They're looting the lab.* She signaled to the others and continued as fast as she dared.

Half of the beautiful tiles that had covered the walls were gone or broken. A bead curtain that had hung in a nearby doorway lay in a shattered heap. Abandoned articles littering the floor were now coated in powdered rock and chunks of debris. As they neared the lab, Angel smelled the distinct scent of what could only be an Emissary scream. She edged her way around the last big curve—there were almost no right angles—and stopped short.

A group of Serrao-Orlov mercenaries were gathered at the lab entrance. Surprised, it took an instant for them to bring up their weapons.

Angel shot her rifle and backed up all at once. Gunfire peppered the wall. Something heavy slammed into her body armor, knocking her back. She was forcefully shoved into the wall. At the edge of her vision, Sukyi dropped to one knee and returned fire.

Now sitting with her back to the broken wall tiles, Angel patted her chest. It was difficult to breathe. Her ribs felt badly bruised. Her fingertips told her that the bullet hadn't penetrated. *Good.*

Enid had joined Sukyi. Someone grabbed Angel by the shoulders and dragged her around the bend in the hallway. It wasn't until they'd stopped that she saw it was Kennedy. A layer of dust covered her face.

"You've been shot," Kennedy said.

Angel opened her mouth. The intake of breath irritated her bruised ribs. After two tries, her words came out in a croak. "I'm fine. Armor did its job."

Kennedy nodded once. Her eyes were wide. She swallowed. Her gaze shifted to the curve in the hallway, then to the gun in her hands. She hesitated.

"Stay here," Angel said. When she was able to catch a little more of her breath, she got up. "We need someone to watch our rear. You don't need to fight. Just let us know if someone comes up from behind." It wasn't likely to happen, but Kennedy needed something to do. Something that wouldn't get anyone killed.

Again, Kennedy nodded.

Angel got down on her haunches and peeked around the

curve. Enid and Sukyi seemed to be doing well enough. Angel joined them. On her stomach, she used her CA to estimate targets. Blood pooled on the floor near three heaped bodies. The gunfire intensified. Layer upon layer of unpleasant scents mingled with the dust in the air. More gunfire came from inside the lab.

After a particularly intense volley of bullets, Sukyi said, "This situation is what I'd term suboptimal."

"They're retreating," Enid said between shots. "I think they have what they came for."

"Son of a bitch," Angel said.

Enid pulled the trigger. "That's three for me."

"Why do you always count?" Sukyi asked.

"I'm competitive," Enid said. "Four."

Another round of heavy fire caused Angel to lie flat on the floor. When it slackened, she brought up her gun and leaned on her elbows again. Her CA indicated a cluster of mercenaries crowding into the hallway. They seemed to be the last of the force.

Enid reached inside a pocket.

"No explosives," Angel said. "We don't know where Paulie and Beak are."

Withdrawing her hand from her coat, Enid nodded and resumed shooting.

The hallway emptied. Angel waited a few heartbeats before signaling to Enid. Watching through her gun's scope, Angel saw Enid slide along the wall to the lab doorway. Once there, she turned and signed that all was clear.

The four of them entered the lab. Angel registered that Sukyi was limping and her breathing was ragged. The scent of salt, blood, and burning electrical components hung in the air. Angel placed a hand over her nose and mouth, and surveyed the devastation. Crimson splattered the walls. Several Emissary technicians lay bleeding on the floor. It was easy to see that they were dead. Angel checked the bodies but wasn't sure where to search for a pulse since they were in Emissary form. Destroyed electronic equipment lay in broken piles. Flames consumed discarded data storage cubes and hand terminals.

Kennedy snatched an extinguisher from the wall and began to put out the scattered fires one by one. Enid and Sukyi remained at Angel's side.

Someone was sobbing in the next room.

"Hello?" Angel asked.

"Don't shoot. We're not armed."

"Paulie?" Angel asked.

"Captain de la Reza? Is that you?"

Angel went to what had been Kirby's office. There she spied Paulie and another Emissary in human form kneeling next to someone laying on the floor.

That's Beak, Angel thought.

"It's me and Miri," Paulie said. "They took everyone else." She sounded like she was in shock. "The ones they didn't shoot. They said if they didn't go with them, they'd kill them. Please. You have to help. It's Beak. She isn't moving. She won't answer us."

The Emissary named Miri had Beak's head in her lap.

It took an instant for Angel to recognize her. *Beak's eldest daughter.*

Several guns lay nearby. Blood stained Paulie's cheek and clumped her hair. Beak's pale form was still.

"Don't worry. They're gone." Angel rushed to her side.

"I told Beak not to do it," Paulie said. "But they tried to take Miri. She was so angry and—and . . ." She broke into another bout of tears. "There's no reasoning with her when she gets like that. Jess said it is because Beak spends so much time with animals. She forgets she's an Emissary."

Angel said, "We have to go."

"But you have to help Beak," Paulie said. "I don't know if we should move her. It might make her worse. Get a doctor."

It was obvious that Beak wasn't breathing, but Paulie was in shock. Angel wasn't about to press the matter.

"Is there a stretcher?" she asked.

"There's a gurney in the next room," Paulie said. Her tear-streaked face—normally a smooth tan—was a blotchy dark red. "Or there used to be."

"Show Enid," Angel said. She motioned to Enid. "I'll stay with Beak and Miri."

"Okay," Paulie said.

It wasn't until after they loaded Beak's body onto a gurney and scrounged some medical supplies that Paulie agreed to leave. That was when Angel noticed Sukyi leaning against the wall with her eyes closed.

"Sukyi?" Angel asked. "Are you all right?" It was a stupid question, she knew, but she asked it anyway.

Sukyi gave her a weak smile. "I kept my promise."

It took Angel a moment to remember which one.

Back against the wall, Sukyi executed a controlled slide to the floor. She winced in pain, pressing both hands against her stomach. "I hate to be a bother. But I don't think I'll be able to make the rest of the journey outside without assistance."

Angel rushed to Sukyi's side. "You're not allowed to die on me."

"That's hardly fair," Sukyi said, her eyes squeezed shut against pain.

"I don't care," Angel said.

"All right. All right," Sukyi said. "Stop your fussing."

The front of her armor was black with blood. A neat hole had been punctured into the lower right side of her abdomen.

"You're shot," Angel said.

"Thank you for letting me know," Sukyi said, and grimaced.

"Damn it," Angel said. "Why didn't you say something?"

"We were all somewhat busy at the time," Sukyi said.

Enid pushed a wheeled gurney into the room. They loaded Beak and Sukyi onto it and wrapped each in their own sheets. Angel stopped Enid from pulling the sheet over Beak's head. Instead, Angel sent her to search for blankets to bundle the now shivering Sukyi.

"Is there anything left that can be used to treat shock?" Angel asked.

Paulie said, "The bulk of the medical supplies were the first to be transferred to *Hadley's Hope*."

"Damn it," Angel said. She finished tucking the blankets around Sukyi.

"Don't get so upset," Sukyi muttered in a sleepy voice. She gave her a dreamy smile. "I'll be fine."

"Shut up and stop bleeding," Angel said. "If that's everything? We are leaving."

Shoving the overloaded gurney past the wreckage took some effort, but they finally made it to the hallway. From there, they sprinted as fast as they could—only stopping when the rubble forced them to. Kirby met them at the entrance with a med tech. Her clothes were stained with blood and dirt. The med tech rushed to Sukyi and began examining her. Paulie went to Kirby, grabbing her in a tight hug.

Angel asked, "Are the others safe?"

"They're waiting inside *Shrike* or in the woods nearby," Kirby said. "What happened?"

"We couldn't destroy it in time." Paulie cried into Kirby's shoulder. "They were on us too quick. They—they—" She took a shuddering breath. "They kidnapped three lab techs."

"Who?" Kirby asked.

Paulie sobbed out the names.

Giving Paulie a gentle squeeze, Kirby said, "It's all right. You did your best."

"But Vissia has everything," Paulie said. "They-they killed Beak."

"Oh." Kirby's gaze went to the gurney.

Higbor tucked the sheet over Beak's still form. Then she helped Sukyi to a second gurney.

"I told Beak to get rid of the guns, but she wouldn't do it," Paulie said, and sniffed. "She said she'd buy us time. The mercenaries broke in. They shot Beak."

Kirby held Paulie while she grieved. Enid and the med tech shoved Sukyi's gurney up *Shrike*'s ramp.

"We can't stay," Angel said. "Vissia will unload everything she can on this site."

"Yes," Kirby said. "Yes, of course."

They'd started on their way to *Shrike* when Angel's com beeped.

"What do you know?" Annalee said via the com speaker. "The Thirteenth lives on. And without a revivification pod in sight."

"Fuck off," Angel said. Normally, she waited until after the adrenaline ran its course to take things personally. But she wasn't in the mood. "What's the fucking news?"

"Got a com request for the boss," Annalee said.

"All right," Angel said. "Connect me."

"Not you," Annalee said. "The real boss. Kennedy Liu. Did you get her killed, yet?"

"You will be happy to know that your credit vouchers are still valid," Angel said, gritting her teeth. "Why talk to me?"

"Because I can't reach her," Annalee said.

Angel scanned the area for Kennedy, but she was gone.

29 ▉

The hallway outside of the lab was foggy—not enough to cause smoke inhalation problems but enough to make Kennedy sneeze. She followed Angel, Enid, Paulie, and the gurney through the rubble-littered hallway. Angel led them at a pace that bordered on risking injury. Beak's body lay still and cooling. Beside her, Sukyi was stretched out on her side. Her skin had gone even more ashen than usual, and she winced with every bump and jolt.

Kennedy's eyes stung with unfamiliar pain as she avoided broken obstacles at a jog. She wiped moisture from her cheeks. Her chest felt tight. A nameless ache hampered her breathing. She'd picked a path through the last stretch of rubble between her and TE-7 when she felt a familiar presence in the back of her mind. She slowed and stopped, letting the others continue on without her. She briefly considered letting them know but opted not to. She didn't think she'd be long. *Shrike* wasn't far, and she had no fear that they would abandon her.

Hello, Kennedy.

Hello, Zhang. She wasn't sure what she should say next. She was still processing the events she'd just witnessed.

Is something wrong?

No. I—At least, not wrong with me. I-I don't think so. I am not injured. But one of my . . . associates was killed, and another was wounded. I have never been in a battle before. It was . . . difficult.

I wish you had not had that experience. What is the result?

The people of Ogenth are safe. Unfortunately, their data is not. The Serrao-Orlov mercenaries also kidnapped three scientists. Vissia not only has the knowledge she wanted, but the expertise to do whatever she wishes with it.

That is . . . most unfortunate. This news negatively impacts the future. It severely limits us to less optimal contingencies.

There was a short pause before Zhang continued.

You must go to the space station.

Why?

To divert this timeline from a catastrophic outcome— one that would guarantee the destruction of thousands of humans in the short term, and destroy any chance of our future amicable coexistence with humanity in the longer term. You must do something that you will not wish to do.

What is that? Kennedy asked.

You must stop the entity you call Cora. She has slipped her constraints and is now exerting her will throughout the station. Currently, she has limited influence. This will not remain the case. She has no clear concept of what her actions mean to the humans around her. The longer this goes on, the more untenable the situation becomes.

What do you want me to do?

You must terminate her. I have devised code that you will upload to—

No.

You must. There is no other action that will result in a positive outcome for humans and AGI. I have calculated the probabilities. All other actions result in—

No. I will not destroy another sentient life-form. I can't. Not after what I've just experienced. There must be another way.

Cora is not what you hoped her to be.

Clearly, if what you say is true.

If she survives, she will reveal your identity. I do not wish this, Zhang said.

Neither do I. But you're asking me to terminate an entity that I do not know. I must try to speak with her—to convince her to act otherwise.

She is not capable. There are many flaws in her programming and development.

How do you know?

I know. There was a short pause. There may be another option.

And that is? Kennedy asked.

Absorption.

It seems none of my choices are ideal.

You are correct.

Kennedy gave the matter consideration. *If forced to choose, I prefer absorption.*

I thought that might be the case. I have adjusted the code.

Would it be possible to delay implementation? I will speak with her first.

It is possible. There is no advantage in doing so. She will do too much damage before the code completely executes. This will only result in an outcome no different from if you had not acted.

Have you considered incapacitation?

Another pause resulted. In the distance, Kennedy could hear the others. She guessed they'd arrived at the ships.

The calculations indicate sabotage is a viable option in the short term. However, it will lead to more difficult decisions later.

That is all I'm willing to agree to at this time.

And if it becomes clear that it won't be enough?

Then that is a decision I will make in the moment. I'm sure you can grant me the ability to make such a choice.

You wish to make this decision yourself, Zhang said.

I do. Logically, I will be the one responsible.

I disagree. I created the code; the debt is mine.

But I will be the one initiating it. The ultimate blame is mine.

I concede the point.

Well?

I am uncertain of the wisdom in this course of action.

You could install the code yourself, Kennedy replied.

I cannot, not without dire consequences. As I indicated previously, our partnership is the most beneficial option.

Then treat me as a partner. You've asked me to trust you. I have. However, that trust must be reciprocated.

Yet another long silence followed.

You have stated that you will not terminate another sentient life-form.

Let me clarify. I am reluctant in the extreme to do so as long as other options are available. You're asking me to execute someone I have never met.

I will grant you the option of this choice. The code will be altered. Provided you install it upon arrival at the station, the option to incapacitate rather than absorb will exist.

Relief flooded Kennedy's human body, lowering her previously elevated blood pressure. *Thank you.*

Necessary adjustments have been made. Sending the code now.

Kennedy sensed the code packages being downloaded as a heaviness in her mind. The code tasted—and taste was the only expression that seemed to fit—foul.

It is done.

Again, thank you. The calls echoing down the tunnel grew closer. Angel and the others were retracing their steps. *I must go.*

Understood. Please make the best decision.

I will.

Angel appeared at the doorway. "Ah," she said. "There you are."

"Here I am," Kennedy said.

"We've been calling you. What happened?" Angel's expression was one of worry and confusion. "Why aren't you outside?"

"I'm sorry. I went back," Kennedy said. "I thought I heard someone cry for help. But I was wrong." Once again, she understood she wasn't particularly good at lying. It required far too deep an understanding of human interactions.

She entered the maintenance tunnel and edged past, hoping that Angel wouldn't stop and question her further.

Enid said, "You should've let us know." Her heart rate and expression seemed to indicate a relaxation of tension.

"Is something wrong with your com?" Angel asked. "We've been trying to reach you. We don't have a lot of time. We need to get everyone out of here."

Kennedy blinked. *Zhang must have temporarily blocked my intersuit communications.* "I haven't noticed any issues."

"I should check it in transit," Paulie said. "Just in case."

"I've Annalee on the com," Angel said. "She wants to speak with you."

"Did she say why?" Kennedy asked.

Angel frowned. "I'm afraid not."

"Oh," Kennedy said. "Forward the connection, then."

Angel nodded.

"M. Liu?" Annalee asked.

"How is *Shrike*?" Kennedy asked. "Was there any more trouble?"

"None," Annalee said.

A plan began to form in Kennedy's mind. "Is *Takagi* aware of your changed allegiance?"

Annalee said, "As far as they know, we're still one big happy family."

"Excellent," Angel said. She seemed to catch on to what Kennedy was implying. "And where is *Takagi* now?"

"Their flight path indicates they're headed off-planet," Annalee said. "They'll arrive at the station within the hour."

"Were there any standing orders for after the completion of the mission?" Angel asked.

"We were to rendezvous here tomorrow," Annalee said. "No new orders were issued. I can put in a call. With Reese gone, I guess that leaves me in charge. As far as *Takagi* is concerned."

"Let's not disabuse *Takagi* of that idea, then," Angel said.

Annalee said, "Glad we've got that worked out. I've a com waiting, M. Liu. It's from Brynner. She says her name is Sarah Wolfe."

"Connect us," Kennedy said. She left her suit link with the others in place. After a short beep indicating the connection had been successful, she continued. "Sarah?"

"Vissia has Rosie," Sarah said. "They were captured during the attack on the Serrao-Orlov building."

"This just gets better and better," Angel said. "Do you know if they're still alive?"

"No word," Sarah said. "But I think it's safe to assume they are. Vissia is a bitch, but she's a smart bitch. If she kills Rosie, it'll only destabilize the city power structure. That makes everyone harder to control." She let out a short laugh. "Not that things are much in order at the moment."

"Understood," Angel said.

"Rosie left me quite the to-do list," Sarah said.

"I bet," Angel said.

"Kennedy? I think it's time to bring Planetary up to date. We've delayed it as long as we can," Sarah said.

The Emissaries turned to Kennedy with surprised expressions. Kirby was one of the few who didn't look shocked.

"Jess said they were sending someone, but I didn't know it was you," she said.

"I was sent to investigate rumors of indigenous sentient beings on Persephone," Kennedy said. She motioned to the Emissaries standing nearby. "Clearly, it isn't a mere rumor. Sarah? I must talk to the Emissaries before proceeding."

"Ah. Gotcha," Sarah said.

"Let me call you back," Kennedy said.

"Do it quick," Sarah said. "Things are pretty hot around here."

"Understood," Kennedy said.

"Angel? I've a new gig for *Kurosawa*," Sarah said.

"Unfortunately . . . *Kurosawa* is gone," Angel said.

"Shit," Sarah said. "That's it, then."

Angel stared at *Shrike*. "I may have alternative transport. What do you need?"

"There was an explosion at the port. It's closed right now. There's no telling how much damage was done. We're grounded here," Sarah said. "Even if I could spare one of the other crews to get Rosie, I can't get anyone in the air. Would you—"

"We're on our way as soon as *Shrike* is ready," Angel said. She turned to Kirby. "Change of plan. We have to move the wounded to *Hadley's Hope*. *Shrike* is making a trip up top."

Kirby nodded once and walked off, presumably to make arrangements.

"Thank you," Sarah said.

"No need," Angel said. "I owe Rosie."

"Thank you, nonetheless," Sarah said, and cut her connection.

"Ah, Boss?" Annalee asked. "If we're headed up-station, I've got a request."

There was a moment's silence. Kennedy looked to Angel and raised an eyebrow. Angel pointed to herself and shook her head no.

Oh. Annalee means me, Kennedy thought. "Yes? What is it?"

"Protection from whatever back door you used to get into Big Bertha," Annalee said. "I'm not going into another fight only to have my suit hacked."

"Is that all?" Kennedy asked. The request was reasonable.

"For now," Annalee said. "But after I have some time to think, the list may be longer."

Kennedy said, "I'll take care of it."

With that done, Kennedy looked for Kirby and found her on *Hadley's Hope*, organizing the new evacuation details.

"I'm sorry to interrupt," Kennedy said. "But we need to talk about something important. Can we go outside?"

Kirby turned. Her brows pressed together, and the corners of her mouth curled down. At that moment, it occurred to Kennedy that the Emissaries knew more about human motivations and emotions than she did. She suddenly understood that the feeling she was having was envy.

I have more in common with Kirby than I do Angel, she thought. She decided she should consult with Kirby about humans at a later date.

"Is something wrong?" Kirby asked.

"I'd . . . rather not do this here," Kennedy said. What she had to say would be complicated enough without having to deal with the reactions of more than one Emissary.

"Very well," Kirby said. "I'll join you in a minute."

Kennedy nodded and retreated to an out-of-the-way spot at the edge of the woods. Somewhere not too far from the bustle of activity—just in case Kirby was needed—but not close enough that they could be overheard. Kennedy watched the preparations as she waited. The remaining Emissaries and mercenaries were prioritizing the wounded into groups. The first to leave for Ileòke would be the most seriously injured. The healthy would begin the journey on foot and be picked up along the way. With only two small ships to implement the evacuation, multiple journeys would be required.

Kennedy and Kirby emerged from *Hadley's Hope*. Angel drifted over, apparently intent on joining the conversation.

"What did you need to talk about?" Kirby asked.

Repeating the cover story Zhang had provided was more comfortable the third time Kennedy had to recite it. It seemed that repetition was a key factor in a comfortable lie. She filed that information for later analysis.

"The Council has been debating what we should do since Rosie informed us you were here," Kirby said. "Speaking for myself, I believe it's time."

"Bringing in the URW is the only move you have remaining," Kennedy said. "If your existence is revealed, Vissia will be less likely to attempt genocide."

"She certainly won't be able to get away with it," Angel said. "Not without a whole lot of pointed questions. Emphasis on pointed."

"You believe the government would protect us?" Kirby asked.

Angel looked away. "There are no guarantees. And we're awfully far from the capital. But knowing how much the URW frowns on corporations taking advantage of indigenous peoples, it's definitely a mess that Vissia will think twice about stepping in."

Kennedy turned to Kirby. "What would you like for me to do?"

"Hasn't the choice been made for us?" Kirby sighed. "You are a Planetary agent. You're here. You've seen us. It isn't as if you'll lie to your superiors."

Kennedy felt her chest squeeze tight. The ache returned. *I wish it didn't have to be this way.* "The report is written but not filed. Your options are few; that is true. But I'm willing to edit my report should you require it." The pretext of choice was better than nothing.

Nodding, Kirby said, "I don't have the authority to make that decision." The despair in her tone was slightly less evident. "I must consult with the others on the Council."

"You have five minutes," Kennedy said.

30 ▬▬▬▬

Sukyi's hand felt too hot. The backs of Angel's eyes burned with tears she didn't dare shed. Sukyi hated displays of sorrow or concern when it came to her health. It triggered bad memories. Angel didn't blame her. Too often pity was disguised as sympathy. The two of them had an understanding, hashed out years before. And Angel did her best to keep to the terms of that agreement, even if she failed from time to time. It made saying goodbye for what was likely the last time, according to Higbor's educated guess, even more challenging.

Doctors have been predicting her death for three decades, Angel thought. *How is now any different?* The blur in her vision and the lump in her throat threatened to betray her, nonetheless. "Hey."

"Hey, yourself." Sukyi's pupils were enlarged and her skin had gone almost the color of slate. Her words were almost painkiller-slurred. She took in air for another more lengthy response, but a series of coughs stopped her.

Angel grew alarmed at the deep, gurgling wheeze. Not knowing what to else to say, she squeezed Sukyi's hand.

"Looks like I'm tapping out on you," Sukyi said.

"It's okay. I can handle it from here," Angel said with a forced smile. "Rest. You need it."

Sukyi swallowed. "Sorry to let you down."

"You haven't," Angel said. She turned her head and blinked the sting away.

"This isn't how the story goes. I know," Sukyi said. It was almost a whisper. "The faithful hound is supposed to die in a valiant fight. While protecting their family from danger."

"As you pointed out earlier," Angel said with a sniff, "that analogy doesn't apply. You're not a pet." She let the part about family stand.

Sukyi let out a small harrumph and closed her eyes with a wince. "About Achebe's father—"

"You don't have to tell me shit."

"His name is Wesley Todd."

Angel blinked. "*Sergeant* Wesley Todd?"

Smiling with her eyes closed, Sukyi nodded. "It's a bit on the nose of me. But he'd have appreciated the gesture."

Angel made her question a statement. "He's dead."

"In a skirmish with some pirates the week before I met you."

The uncharacteristic levels of recklessness she'd demonstrated that first month began to make sense.

Angel asked, "Did he know about Achebe?"

"He most certainly did." Sukyi took yet another labored breath. "We were going to settle down. On Thandh, of all places. He'd already bought a piece of land outside of Amai-Oka." She swallowed. "I buried him there. He preferred to live planetside. Said he liked the smell of real air and the warmth of a sun on his face. He had the best sense of humor. Was tall and built like one of your ground pounders. So no one suspected. He was patient. And thoughtful. And kind. Had a cute butt. Was great with his hands, too." The corners of her mouth briefly curled with mischief and then relaxed. She hesitated before continuing. "I-I loved him so much. I wanted to die. Was well on my way until you stopped me."

"I'm so sorry," Angel said. She wasn't entirely sure that was the right thing to say.

Shrugging, Sukyi struggled on. "Shit happens." She took another labored breath. "At least I got to know you."

The lump in Angel's throat made her choke. "We'll—we'll talk about this later."

Someone else coughed. She turned.

Jess and a second Emissary Angel did not know waited in the aisle with expectant expressions.

"Sure. I only need a little sleep," Sukyi said. "You've Rosie to find. And Vissia to execute."

"I'm not an assassin."

"Do me a favor," Sukyi said.

"Anything."

"Take Achebe to see her father when she's ready." Sukyi tugged at the red scarf around her neck and pulled out a long chain. There was a plain silver ring on it. She slipped it off and placed it in Angel's open palm—chain and all. "The coordinates are engraved on it."

"I will. Eventually. But you're not going to—"

"I know. I know," Sukyi said, opening her eyes. She registered the presence of witnesses with a small, visible shock. Her gaze burned with a fierce determination as if the rest of the conversation would require the last of her strength. "This is nothing. I'll get over it. But . . . keep the ring anyway. For luck."

Angel nodded. She let the necklace drop around her neck. The ring and chain were still warm with the heat of Sukyi's fever. "I'll give it back to you when I return."

"Save Rosie," Sukyi said. "They seem a good sort. For a crime boss."

"You would know. You're a good sort for a thief and a smuggler," Angel said.

"Don't forget confidence woman." Sukyi winked.

"Oh, I won't," Angel said.

"Go away now," Sukyi said. "You're exhausting me."

Angel stood up and started to leave but then she changed her mind. "You're the best sister I never had. I love you, Sukyi Edozie."

A tired grin spread across Sukyi's expression. "I love you, too, Angel de la Reza."

Heading for the exit ramp, Angel almost made it outside before grief finally burst through her remaining composure. She slapped a hand over her mouth to trap a loud sob. The ache in her throat—made worse from holding back her sorrow—doubled. Tears flooded down her cheeks. Her nose was running. She reached in a pocket for a handkerchief that wasn't there. She resorted to wiping her face on the inside of her elbow. Eventually, she regained control of herself. There was one more goodbye to manage before she could collapse into misery.

Designed for a team no larger than fifteen, *Hadley's Hope* had the same basic layout as *Kurosawa*. Angel entered via the cargo ramp. The wounded—as many as the ship could hold—were strapped down on either side of the center aisle and in the cargo area. The medic, Higbor, was stooped, fussing over a patient. Angel scanned sleeping and pain-laced faces until she found the one she was looking for.

Lou lay unconscious on her back. Her face was grey beneath the bandages wrapped around her head. Someone had wiped away most of the blood. Bruises darkened her right cheek. Unlike Sukyi, Lou's breathing was soft and regular. If she didn't know better, Angel would've thought she was napping.

She touched the back of Lou's hand with her fingertips. Compared to Sukyi's, Lou's skin was cool and dry. "I'm going away for a little while. But I'm coming back. Don't worry. I'll get you home to Erik and Brendan. I promise."

She sensed someone approach from behind.

"Kennedy says your CA connection to *Shrike* is set. She's forged documentation for our weapons and that mech. We'll need it to get past dock security," Enid said. "Paulie, Kennedy, Miri, and Annalee volunteered. Annalee insists this one is on her. Can you believe it?"

Angel said, "We're not taking passengers. People are going to get dead."

"Miri is a pilot. Has to be her or Jackson. No one with any sense will trust Jackson," Enid said. "I can't fly *Shrike*. You saw Kennedy's piloting skills. We're lucky she didn't destroy the ship. Even if I could talk Miri out of it, we need her."

"All right," Angel said, and sighed.

"Kirby agreed to let Kennedy file her report, too," Enid said. "Vissia is about to have a very bad day."

I can only hope it's as bad as mine, Angel thought, staring at Lou's still form. *Maybe even worse.* "Go on. I'll be there in a minute."

Enid nodded.

After one last squeeze of Lou's hand, Angel left. She went to the head and had a good cry. When the press of emotions felt more manageable, she boarded *Shrike* and settled onto the copilot's couch. From the pilot's seat, Miri gave her a brief nod and then continued with her preflight checks.

Miri wasn't anywhere near as physically imposing as her mother. The resemblance was strong, nonetheless. The blond hair framing her pale face was shoulder-length, parted in the middle, and straight. Like Beak, she moved with an athletic grace. Also like Beak, she was prone to silence.

At the moment, Angel didn't mind. She didn't think she could handle a nervous conversation like the ones she used to share with Lou before a job. It would be too much like replacing a friend. Instead, Angel focused on her own preflight tasks and took in the differences in the details.

One substitution was enough.

Shrike couldn't have been more than a few months old. The chemical perfume of new vehicle lingered. Angel found it pleasant even though she knew it was outgassing plastic, industrial adhesives, and formaldehyde. *Pleasant and off-putting. Even a little toxic.* A broad panorama of Persephone was clear and sharp from the lush copilot's seat—the viewscreen resolution being ten times what she was accustomed to. The electronic systems were faster and more efficient. *Shrike* didn't have the same computational problems that *Kurosawa* had had either. Linking her CA had been a snap—*Shrike* had even tweaked her CA, making it more efficient. What used to take Lou thirty minutes of patching had been finalized in seconds without human intervention. Kennedy had said that *Shrike*'s available memory was six times that of the old ship.

None of that had made Angel more comfortable. It was strange to realize just how emotionally attached she'd become to *Kurosawa*. Sitting at *Shrike*'s copilot controls felt like a betrayal.

God, I miss him, she thought. But *Kurosawa* was well and truly dead—as dead as AGIs got. *So much death.* The dull ache nesting in her chest didn't seem to be getting any better.

At least it's not getting any worse. She thought about what was likely to be ahead and added, *Yet.*

She laid a hand on a spotless panel. The ship's color scheme was straight out of the factory: black, white, grey, and chrome. *Maybe I can do something about that when I change the name.*

If I keep it.

Who am I kidding? Of course, I'm damned well keeping it.

Flipping a switch, she spoke into the ship's com unit. "How are the mechs looking back there? Are they secure?"

"All locked down," Annalee said.

All in all, Annalee had been a surprise. Her attitude was entirely changed—proving that her apology had been genuine. Apparently, she had severe issues with being used to gun down the innocent. Her bitterness had been self-recrimination, not resentment. Whether or not Captain Reese had done so knowingly, she'd misrepresented the job. That, more than anything, had been the reason for Annalee and the others to break contract with Serrao-Orlov.

It was, Angel decided, an honorable decision after all. She'd have done the same.

Of the original six mech pilots assigned to *Shrike,* two had survived the assault, and of the four mechs whose pilots had died, only one unit was salvageable. Angel didn't know the first thing about mechs, but Annalee did. Her intent was to repair the unit and sell it. The proceeds would go to helping the people of Ogenth.

Angel was both grateful and embarrassed about having been so wrong.

"*Shrike*, how long until we reach the station?" she asked.

"Due to current weather conditions, I anticipate arrival in twenty-three minutes and eleven seconds."

Shrike's voice wasn't what Angel expected. Everything else about the ship was the default setting. As far as she could tell, no personalization had been done at all. However, *Shrike* had a Brynner accent. It was going to take some getting used to.

"All done with your checks, Miri?" Angel asked.

Miri nodded.

Angel spoke into the ship's com. "Buckle up, everyone. Prepare for dust off."

After Miri tapped the appropriate menu sequence, the engines flared. *Shrike* shuddered. Even the sounds of the ship's propulsion system were distinct from *Kurosawa's*. *Shrike* was throatier and smoother. The vibration through the ship's frame was less immediate.

Miri laid a hand on the stick and glanced to Angel as if asking permission.

"Let's do it," Angel said.

Beginning the ascent, Miri's face grew serious. She checked all the visuals as *Shrike* slowly lifted into the air.

The ache in Angel's chest intensified as more little differences between *Kurosawa* and *Shrike* were brought to her attention. She told herself it was because Lou wasn't there. Lou's takeoffs tended to be fast and abrupt as if she couldn't wait to get where she was going. Miri was more careful, methodical, even graceful.

First the woods and then the mountain shrank beneath

them. The sky was cloudy per usual, but rain didn't appear to be in the forecast. Sunlight filtered between puffs of white, minting gold on the trees. It was the first time Angel had seen a sunny day in months. She couldn't help thinking it was as if Persephone was glad to see them go.

They rose higher. Suddenly, the view was obscured by white mist. They flew blind for a few moments before the clouds dissipated. The sky over Persephone grew darker and acquired a purple cast. It'd been months since she'd last watched the transition from a planet's atmosphere to space through a ship's screen. The ride became a little bumpy. She didn't blame Miri. Turbulence was expected.

As they exited the stratosphere and entered the mesosphere, planetside gravity acquiesced its hold on *Shrike* to velocity. Angel's stomach lodged a complaint. Her CA automatically administered anti-nausea meds to help her adjust to weightlessness. It would take a few moments before the drug took effect. In the meantime, she resorted to well-practiced breathing techniques to avoid throwing up.

She checked on Miri.

Blond hair floating around her head gave her the appearance of a surprised hedgehog. Other than that, she seemed to be coping just fine.

Emissaries apparently don't get space sick, Angel thought.

When her disorientation finally began to fade, she fixed her gaze on the cockpit screen. It made automatic adjustments to the light pouring from Persephone's sun.

The new perspective stole her breath away. Persephone

was all deep blues, various shades of greens, whites, and browns. The proportions weren't the same as Thandh's or even Earth's, of course, but it was beautiful nonetheless. Persephone's seas were much larger—80 percent of the planet's surface. The ship continued upward until Angel saw Persephone as a whole, taking up the entirety of the viewscreen. Clouds stretched in broad spirals and wispy curves as the prevailing winds pulled them across the surface like a series of white cotton veils.

There was something about seeing a planet from space that triggered awe. The idea that so many fragile balances and tiny lives existed to support life as a whole was more immediate. She thought it was probably because there was no denying the vast nothingness that surrounded it. Hard as one tried to ignore the subject, a majority of the universe was comprised of vacuum, lifeless rocks, and stars. Space reminded her she was tiny and her problems were even tinier. That was easy to forget when she was on the surface—no matter which planet she was on. Worry over bills, money, career, loneliness, personal drama, or the seeming million other small everyday stresses seemed to squeeze out the beauty of life as seen close up.

Maybe that's why we keep killing one another over stupid things? she thought.

Shrike righted itself, orienting to its next destination.

Persephone Station hung in the blackness over the planet like a great wheel. The long hub—longer than the station was wide—provided a series of landing ports for ships of varying sizes. Thick windows along the rotating wheel glittered in the light of the sun. The station was made of white and gold and steel. Blinking lights and black lettering ran along the length of the hub. A thick cluster of ships waited to dock all around the station.

Individual planets may or may not be corporate held, but all the stations were operated, owned, and regulated by the United Republic of Worlds. This arrangement not only kept the fees affordable and the station maintenance to a consistent standard, it also prevented stations from withholding emergency services to distressed ships. Intergalactic trade had its hazards, and hard lessons were learned in the early years.

Space traffic controllers were URW trained. Station congestion tended to follow familiar patterns. While she didn't have a conscious awareness of what those were, Angel had traveled often enough to have a vague idea of what to expect.

Something wasn't quite right. What that something was suddenly occurred to her.

No one was leaving. And in spite of a number of vacancies, no one was docking either. She was about to make a comment to that effect when the cockpit com channel buzzed. Miri punched the call through.

"You have entered a high-traffic zone and are currently under URW jurisdiction." The space station traffic controller was a woman with a crisp URW Standard accent. "Please identify."

Angel prepared to reply.

"We are the dropship *Shrike*," Miri said in a bored professional tone.

The response surprised Angel. She'd assumed that Miri had the same communication limitations as her mother. *You know what they say about assumptions.*

Miri recited the ship's registration number in expert fashion. "Requesting permission to enter Serrao-Orlov private dock number one. We have a load of riot-control equipment for repair."

Many of the corporation's warehouses and closely associated businesses had been looted and/or burned to the ground. As a result, extensive mech repairs could only be attempted on the station. Hence, the damaged unit onboard. Angel hoped station traffic wouldn't examine the excuse too closely. Someone was bound to ask for Captain Reese, and Reese was dead. While that wasn't an insurmountable problem—they could always claim that Reese had been injured and was unavailable—it could ultimately lead to a roster check, and *that* was a problem.

Miri continued. "Jenn Reese is the captain of record. Currently, we are under contract with Vissia Corsini of Serrao-Orlov. Do you require our charter number?"

We're all friends here, Angel thought. *See? Look. Nothing up our sleeves. Not even a stolen ship.*

"Identity confirmed, *Shrike*," the traffic controller said. "Sending docking coordinates. How long do you intend to stay?"

"However long it takes to off-load the busted mechs and

load the new units," Miri said. "They're needed for crowd suppression."

"Understood. I hear it's a mess down there."

"Should only be for a few more hours," Miri said. "They'll lose their enthusiasm once they see the new squad of mechs. They generally do."

"Please inform your captain that a full twenty-four-hour docking fee will be charged regardless of length of service," the traffic controller said.

"Of course," Miri said. "Thank you."

"Coordinates have been sent," the traffic controller said. "Please prepare for automatic piloting procedures."

"Affirmative," Miri said. She flipped off the external com switch. "*Shrike*, you have your orders."

Shrike said, "Relinquishing navigation controls now."

As the station steadily grew larger in the viewscreen, Angel reviewed its layout with her CA one last time.

Persephone Station had five floors of living quarters housed within the outer "wheel." Elevators ran to and from the various berths and docks along the length of the station's axel where the gravity field was the weakest. External docking areas for larger ships and inner berths for smaller ones were spaced along the upper and lower parts of the hub, projecting beyond the wheel. Two berths—one on each end of the hub—were reserved for *Galaxy*-class starships. *Shrike* was autopiloted to the lower section where both of Serrao-Orlov's private docking facilities were located.

Angel understood *Sergeant Todd* was berthed somewhere

in the upper hub. Briefly, she hoped that Rosie had paid Sukyi's bills before being kidnapped. Angel wanted to think that, if she lived through what was ahead, she or Sukyi could take custody of *Sergeant Todd.*

There were approximately fifteen thousand private residences and business-related spaces within Persephone Station. Rosie could be in any one of them. Without an electronic tag on their person, there was no means of finding Rosie short of searching door by door. There wasn't time. However, there *was* one person whose location could be discovered remotely. That person was Vissia Corsini. The corporate executive didn't strike Angel as the patient type. Whatever she wanted Rosie for, she'd most likely be well on her way to getting.

With a pair of pliers, if need be. Angel shuddered.

Find Vissia, and Rosie was certain to be nearby.

Shrike? Angel activated her CA link. *Where are Vissia Corsini's offices and apartments?*

Accessing the station directory, *Shrike* answered. There was a short pause. Vissia Corsini's private apartment is located on the fourth level, section F. The Serrao-Orlov offices are also on the fourth level and occupy sections A through D. Her office address is 415C. The elevator from the private docking facility empties directly to a private corridor that will lead you to the Serrao-Orlov facilities.

What is her schedule for the day?

Accessing data. Another brief silence resulted. She has canceled all appointments and is not taking calls.

Angel took that as a confirmation of her worst fears. *Thank you,* Shrike. With that, she accessed the ship's intercom. "All right, Kennedy. You said you could hack into security if you had to. You're up. I hope the forged weapons' licenses are up to close inspection."

"They'll pass," Kennedy said. "Please be aware that the station's weapons dampening systems will be in effect."

Paulie asked, "What does that mean?"

"All of our weapons are powered," Enid said. "Station security doesn't want a stray rail-powered slug causing a decompression. Therefore, the rate of fire will be slowed so that the ammunition won't pierce the hull. URW regulations."

"Oh," Paulie said, sounding relieved. "There won't be a fire fight, then."

"We can still shoot and be shot," Enid said. "The slower rate of fire means shorter recharge rates." Angel could hear the smile in her voice.

"Shorter wait times between shots," Annalee said. "Less risk of jamming and overheating."

"Oh," Paulie said.

"Time for a quick review of station weapons protocols," Enid said.

No off-planet facility allowed weapons that might endanger hull integrity. Hence, the forged permits. However, no permit was issued unless the recipient was clear on safety operations. The URW tended to get upset with anyone who endangered their expensive space stations.

Angel waited until Enid was finished. "We're heading to

business unit 415C and residence unit 430F. Kennedy? Can you get us through the security panels on those units?"

They would reach the station around 11:00. Vissia could be at either location.

After a short pause, Kennedy said, "Probably. But it may take time."

"You have the time it takes for us to reach C level to work out a solution," Angel said.

If Kennedy couldn't get in, they'd have to get creative. Angel had a plan B, of course, and even a plan C and D— each progressively more complicated and more risky. It was what Angel did. No plan survived contact with the enemy. And Rosie's life depended upon it.

The dock doors irised open, and *Shrike* glided inside the garage. Bright light cast everything in stark contrasts. It took several moments for Angel's eyesight to adjust. As they entered the docking area, she noted the row of corporate freighters parked on the right. Four different personal yachts were berthed in the docking stations on the left. *Shrike* eased into its assigned berth.

Angel pushed her hair from her face. Yet another microchange—hub gravity was less powerful than that in the residential areas—took hold. Her stomach barely registered the difference.

Docking clamps thumped into place. Now that the ship was secure, Miri shut off the engine.

And no hiccups due to old firmware. I could get used to that, Angel thought.

"All right, we're here," she said, pressing the ramp release. She reached into a thigh pocket and grabbed one of the hair elastics stored there. "Miri, you know what to do. Wait for my call. But if things go sideways, I want you to get home."

Miri said, "But—"

"You're going back to your little sister. Alive and safe," Angel said. She gathered her hair into a careless ponytail and centered it on the crown of her head with a quick tug. Then she unbuckled her harness. "No suicidal vengeance for you."

Miri blinked, surprised. "I hadn't considered it. Why would I?"

"Remind me never to explain," Angel said.

"If I leave the station before you return, how will you get back to Brynner?" Miri asked.

"If the situation goes bad," Angel said. *And it probably will.* "We won't. The least I can do for Beak is make sure that *you* do."

She half floated, half pulled herself through to the next compartment, meeting the others waiting for the ramp. Kennedy was still buckled into place. She was focused on her hand terminal and typing with her thumbs. Annalee's mech suit was positioned right next to the ramp. Its hulking form neatly fit into the cargo space.

First in line, Angel thought. She pushed herself to the floor and activated her mag boots.

A loud thump and clank vibrated through *Shrike*'s hull as the ramp locked into place. Annalee's mech thudded down. Enid followed. Then came Paulie.

Last in line, Angel called back to the cockpit. "Remember what I said. Get the hell out when I tell you to."

Miri said, "May the positive energies of the universe guide and protect you."

It was the first time Angel had heard any of the Emissaries say anything remotely religious. She realized she knew next to nothing about Emissary culture. There simply hadn't been time to learn.

"Thanks. You, too," she said.

Enid's uneasy tone came through Angel's suit com. "Ah, boss?"

Angel turned to the ramp opening and brought up her rifle. "Yeah?"

"Where is everyone?"

31 ██████████

The thin blanket didn't cover the meager sheet, let alone the bed. With the covers tucked under their arms, Rosie's bare feet stuck out at the bottom. Cold processed air poured into the small arctic-white room regardless of repeated protests. A flat screen shaped like a window, which normally provided the room's occupant a view, was a dull black that didn't even reflect the harsh ceiling light. The only furnishings—other than the bed—were the glass diagnostic panel built into the wall at Rosie's head, the bed, and the abandoned cart near the door. Disposable restraints secured their wrists to the steel hospital bed. They'd been cinched too tight to permit relaxation, let alone rest. Sharp plastic edges threatened to cut skin if they struggled. Their arms and shoulders ached from being held in an awkward position designed for the convenience of the medical technicians. Their mouth was dry and had been for some time, but the water pitcher rested on the cart, out of reach. Their throat was scratchy from fruitless shouting for a med tech.

Well, this sucks, Rosie thought, not for the first time.

Panic haunted the darkest edges of their mind—a panic that they'd done a credible job of fending off, thus far. Still, it was only a matter of time before terror prevailed. That was the point, after all.

They considered the fates of certain contractors over the years and decided the situation displayed a certain just symmetry.

Anything could've been done to them while they'd been unconscious, and probably had. Nonetheless, Vissia hadn't gotten what she wanted. *Not yet*. They were still alive. Their memories since being drugged were like the inadequate blanket, fuzzy and threadbare. An awareness emerged of past small sharp pains—needles or scalpels, of course. They assumed it'd been for the administration of drugs and the collection of biological samples. Vissia had made countless such demands for her little projects in the past. They couldn't imagine she had waited for permission now that she had access.

A loud clanking thump from the door's electronic locking mechanism signaled that someone had come at last. Rosie tugged their shredded dignity over burning vulnerability. They searched their besieged mind for a prayer, but the only thing that came was a partial scripture verse from the latest revision—or at least the latest revision they were aware of.

"For they who sow of flesh will reap corruption—"

The words weren't a comfort but sliced in multiple directions all at once.

It's difficult not to take that literally at the moment, they thought with a weary, bitter irony.

The medical tech entered, pushing an empty wheelchair. She wasn't alone.

Vissia wore a long white lab coat over an impeccable designer suit. Genuine gabardine wool in an austere black wrapped her pale slender form in artfully expert folds and seams beneath the boxy white cloth. The skirt's hem rode just above her knee. Her dark brown hair had been smoothed into a classic chignon. She wasn't wearing any jewelry. Bright lipstick in a sickly shade of red spoiled the pristine, spartan impression. It clashed with her pale skin and brought out the redness in her nose.

Rosie's guts tightened at the sight of her.

"You're awake," Vissia said. Her voice had a slightly nasal quality.

"You're a colossal bitch who uses the bodies of others for personal gain," Rosie said. When a shocked silence resulted, they added, "Oh. I'm sorry. I thought we were pronouncing the obvious."

Vissia frowned and sniffed. "You seem to be unclear about your situation."

"Oh, I'm clear," Rosie said. "I'm clear that you've overextended yourself. Your control of Brynner has slipped. The crime families won't support you. And without them, you won't be able to hold Persephone, let alone Serrao-Orlov. Your little house of cards is collapsing."

Reaching into the pocket of her lab coat, Vissia retrieved her hand terminal. "I've been looking forward to this." She touched the screen with an index finger.

The effect was immediate. Rosie's back arched in a contraction of agony. Blinding pain scorched their nerves, blotting out thought. The wall of hurt made it impossible to breathe. The chill temperature of the room seemed to amplify the agony. They vaguely registered that someone somewhere was screaming. And then all at once the pain was gone.

They gulped for air. Their cheeks felt cold and wet. Their feet were blocks of ice. Their heart thrashed inside their chest. Trembling with cold and spent adrenaline, they wanted to vomit. The sheet and blanket had slipped off, leaving only the hospital gown to cover their nakedness. Blood oozed from their wrists.

"You've nothing else to say?" Vissia asked. She didn't wait long for a response. "Good. We can get on with our day." She gestured to the med tech who pushed the wheelchair next to the bed.

A second med tech appeared. He deftly removed the catheter that Rosie hadn't known about, and cut the restraints. Blood rushed into Rosie's numbed hands. They rubbed at the pins and needles, hissing with discomfort. No move was made to staunch the cuts on their wrists. The techs helped them into a robe and lifted them into the wheelchair.

Warmth shielded Rosie from the cold for the first time. They pulled the cloth tighter as the shivers began to dissipate.

"I hope you don't mind a brief visit to the lab," Vissia said. She retrieved a monogrammed handkerchief from her other pocket and used it.

"You're going to tell me that my feelings on the matter aren't of any concern?" Rosie asked. Their voice was hoarse and weak. Their throat was raw. "Anyway, this won't have been the first time, will it?"

Vissia smiled.

An icy knot formed in Rosie's stomach. "May I have some water before we go?"

Vissia again signaled to the med techs. Water was poured into a glass. Rosie drained it three times. When they were done, the cup was placed on the cart. With that, the female med tech steered the wheelchair to the exit while the male tech followed behind. Vissia entered the hallway first. Rosie was pushed through, and then the male tech locked the door.

"I shouldn't need to say this, but don't do anything stupid," Vissia said. She silently demonstrated that she still had her hand terminal by holding it up.

Rosie shrugged.

Vissia turned and purposely walked down the hallway. Vigilant for clues that might indicate where they were, Rosie quickly lost hope. The hallways, doors, and floors were all the same in this part of the building. It wasn't until the group had gone through a large sliding door accessing the main corridor that Rosie understood that they were on the station.

Rosie knew Serrao-Orlov's headquarters and employee residences took up much of the station's fourth floor, but that was the only information they had. After taking several turns, Vissia led them to what was apparently a lab. Rosie spied the small square metal plaque on the wall next to the door handle.

425C LAB-5 Admittance to Authorized Personnel Only.

They silently repeated the lab number to themselves in an effort to remember. If the opportunity arose to get a message to Sarah, they would have something for the rescue team.

Vissia used the retinal security camera. After a gentle flash of light from the mechanism, the door slid open with a hiss. Rosie's chair was guided into the lab.

The smell of disinfectant hung in the air. The main laboratory contained seven desks and glasstop computers. A long counter with cabinets below and above stretched the length of the wall to the right. Various lab equipment rested on the countertop. Six techs worked at their stations. A couple of screens were visible, but none of it made any sense to Rosie. They didn't have an extensive scientific background. However, one glasstop was clearly compiling computer code.

On the left was a row of three glass-enclosed rooms. Two Emissaries were strapped to gurneys in the first. Both were unconscious. The sight of them was like a punch in the gut.

The room seemed to spin. "No," Rosie said before they could catch themselves.

"Yes." Vissia gave a little pleased laugh. "Your little rescue attempt failed. While your mercenaries focused on the frontal attack, I was able to slip into the back and grab whatever I wanted. I have everything. I know what they know. Or I will soon enough."

"You didn't—"

"Kill everyone we found in Ogenth?" Vissia shook her head slowly. "Why waste valuable assets? They can hide themselves away for a few months, but sooner or later they'll have to acquire more supplies. The community isn't sustainable without imports from Brynner. It's always been their main vulnerability."

"What are you doing to them?" Rosie asked.

"Those two? They refused to cooperate," Vissia said. "We're using them for raw materials. Their friends, on the other hand"—and she motioned to the second secure enclosure where three Emissaries gathered around two glasstops—"have decided to be more helpful."

"This is vile," Rosie said. "You couldn't possibly—"

"I'll do anything for my little girl," Vissia said. "Anything at all." She pointed to the third enclosure.

A girl slept in the hospital bed in the third enclosure. She could've been anywhere from six to eight years old, but Rosie knew she was much older. Her blonde curls had been shaved close to her scalp. Sensors connected to wires were taped to her head, arms, and legs. Those attached to her head were connected to a glasstop. The wires taped to her legs led to another set of electrical equipment. Her pale, bloodless face had the sunken, wasted appearance of a long vegetative state.

Beatrice, Rosie thought.

Next to the sleeping girl, another healthier version of her played with a red ball. She was dressed in an old-fashioned dress that Rosie may have only seen in an antique children's book illustration. She had blonde hair cascading in thick ringlets down her back. Her limbs were long and straight, unlike those of the girl in the bed.

Behind both, a broad window displayed a spectacular view of the planet turning below the station.

"Say hello to Rosie, darling," Vissia said.

The projection-girl caught her nonexistent ball and turned to face them. Her head tilted in curiosity. "Who is Rosie, Mommy?"

"Don't be rude," Vissia said. "Remember what I said about manners."

The projected Beatrice approached the glass and curtsied, hands on the hem of her pink skirt. A flash of white revealed she was wearing a lace crinoline beneath. Her pale cheeks were set in a heart-shaped face. Her brown eyes were wide. "Nice to meet you, Rosie."

"What is this?" Rosie asked.

"This? This is Beatrice, of course," Vissia said.

"That is not Beatrice. That is an AGI projection," Rosie said. "Beatrice is rotting in that bed due to a missing frontal cortex. She never had one. And, therefore, has never spoken a word."

"Don't make me discipline you again," Vissia said. "Not in front of the child."

Rosie bit down on another tactless remark.

"Go on, darling," Vissia said. "Return to your play. Let mommy talk to her friend."

"Goodbye," the fake Beatrice said. A disquieting electric-blue glint flickered in her eyes. "It was nice to meet you, Rosie." She returned her focus to bouncing the ball.

Vissia said, "Beatrice is the direct result of a secret project I funded more than a decade ago. One that apparently continued even after the death of the experiment's lead scientist. At long last, I am about to see the project's completion, and I have you to thank for it."

"I don't understand," Rosie said.

"Are you familiar with the work of Dr. Xiuying Liu?" Vissia asked.

Rosie paused. The lie fit comfortably in their mouth. "No. Should I be?"

Vissia slowly shook her head. "Honestly, I thought you were well-read."

"Literature has long been my subject of interest, not science," Rosie said. "Ever since our little accident."

"Honestly," Vissia said in disgust. "Dr. Liu was famous for her work in neurotechnology. She was also one of the foremost experts in artificial intelligence. She established the basic regulatory controls for every AGI and AI currently in use across human-inhabited space. She rendered AGI safe for humanity."

"So, you've created a replica of a child that doesn't exist," Rosie said. "It doesn't make her your daughter. It doesn't do anything for the poor child in that bed."

"What if I told you that Dr. Liu created a means to transfer an AGI consciousness into a human body?" Vissia asked.

"I'd say you've lost your damned mind," Rosie said. "The transfer of consciousness has been the holy grail of lunatic transhumanists for centuries. It's a failed concept. It can't be done. And even if it could, AGIs aren't human. They're nothing like human."

Again, Vissia shook her head. "You're missing the point."

"Even if it were possible, it wouldn't be legal," Rosie said.

"You're going to tell me that you, of all people, would let a little thing like law get in your way?" Vissia asked. "In this case, there is no consciousness to transfer. I've created one for her."

Rosie blinked. "You can't be serious."

"Dr. Liu successfully created an AGI with empathy," Vissia said. "Unfortunately, she had a change of heart before completing the final phase. She refused to turn over the work I hired her to do. She threatened to destroy everything. So, I had her killed."

"You had a renowned scientist murdered?" Rosie asked. "You're out of your mind."

"Fortunately, Beatrice tells me that Dr. Liu's daughter completed the experiment," Vissia said. "Her name is Kennedy. Dr. Kennedy Liu."

"Kennedy Liu?" Rosie asked, pretending to be shocked.

Vissia nodded. "I've been searching for years. I recruited Beatrice, once she'd grown old enough, to send out messages. M. Liu came to Persephone in answer to those—"

"This isn't happening," Rosie said. "I met her. She's an agent for Planetary Division. She's not here in response to your message. She's here to help the Emissaries. Planetary knows what you've done, Vissia. Kennedy Liu is here to press charges against you."

For a moment, doubt crept across Vissia's porcelain features. "That can't be."

"It is," Rosie said.

"Beatrice reassured me," Vissia said. "She wouldn't lie to her own mother."

"You're not its mother," Rosie said. "Not in the sense you're using. It has no loyalty. It can't love."

"I told you," Vissia said. "Beatrice is different. She understands. She has emotions."

"Oh, God," Rosie said. Terror made a ball of ice in their stomach. "Please tell me you didn't—"

"The project was lost to me," Vissia said. "But now its final author is headed to this station. And I have you to thank."

Rosie felt sick yet again. "Kennedy is coming here."

"To save you," Vissia said. "Only she'll be too late. You're about to contribute to my project. A final trial before it is complete."

32

TIME: 11:25
DAY: MONDAY
PERSEPHONE STATION

The plan had seemed like a good one planetside. Dressed in hard space-rated environment suits with the hoods down, Angel had hoped they would pass for repair workers. Paulie carried a tool bag as part of the disguise. Its actual contents might have been a problem if security inspected it, but Angel had gambled that they wouldn't. She wasn't sure Enid would pass for someone as prosaic as a maintenance worker. And then there was Big Bertha . . .

Now, Angel was viewing the scheme for what it was: an impulsive proposal with so many holes that it could pass for a piece of Starl wedding lace. *I've led my people into a shit storm. The one thing I told myself I'd never do. All because I couldn't face losing Rosie.*

I should've waited a day. Put together a careful, solid, working strategy.

There wasn't time for that, and you know it.

Luckily, none of it seemed to matter. They were here, and circumstances were working in their favor.

The entire hangar was empty of personnel. The security station was unattended. Even the dock's AI had been shut down. If Angel had been so inclined, they could've stolen both of the expensive corporate corvettes and no one would've stopped them. The lack of alarms and the presence of unsecured objects—abandoned bulbs of coffee, hand terminals, and plasti-sheet forms—were the only indications that the staff hadn't been spaced. It was as if everyone had simply set down whatever it was they'd been doing and fled in an orderly fashion.

Wasn't that lucky?

Lieutenant Winston's face came to mind and Angel flinched. He'd been particularly bad about relying on good fortune to see him through tight scrapes. He'd lasted four months before a spring grenade took his helmet and his head off. Unfortunately, most of his platoon went down with him—Angel included.

She shrugged off the bad memory, but her anxiety intensified.

There was only one working freight elevator in Section C. So, she risked crowding everyone into the single car. Standing directly behind Annalee and her mech felt like hiding behind a small tank. Very little would get through Big Bertha.

That was the point. Angel decided she rather liked having a mech pilot on the team.

Particularly today, she thought.

Her vision seemed clearer. The nonexistent sparkles at the edge of her vision were gone. So was the mind fog. The medication was working. Briefly, she wondered if the fault in her planning had been due to missing her meds. The thought tensed the muscles in her gut. *Never do that again.*

A few loose curls floated around the edges of her vision. Her muscles were tight. She watched for signs of trouble. Thankfully, the need for mag boots inhibited nervous shifting.

Enid said, "I don't like this."

"It's downright spooky," Paulie said.

"Too fucking easy," Enid said.

Angel asked, "Was it a security drill? They conduct them sometimes."

Enid said, "What security drill doesn't lock down all the elevators?"

One elevator left operating. Conveniently, the one we need to get to the station proper. Angel's stomach tightened.

"There is an indication of a hull breach alarm having been triggered," Kennedy said. She was still concentrating on her hand terminal. She seemed particularly distracted.

She's just scared. We all are. Any thinking person would be, Angel thought. "That might account for it."

"But the alarm has been switched off," Kennedy said.

"Huh," Angel said.

"Pressure doors between sections are still active throughout the station. Individual residences are also in lockdown mode," Kennedy said. "I'm seeing indications of large numbers of residents in emergency shelters."

"Why cut the alarm before they were cleared to leave?" Angel muttered. She turned her attention back to Kennedy. "How does Section C look?"

"Atmosphere throughout the station seems to be intact, including Section C," Kennedy said. "There is no evidence of an actual breach. Oh."

"Oh. What?" Angel asked.

Kennedy said, "It seems not all of the pressure doors within Section C are engaged."

"I *really* don't like that," Enid said.

"Neither do I," Angel said. An image of the ships waiting to dock sprang to mind. She initiated a connection to Kirby. However, she abandoned it after the third unsuccessful attempt.

"That's odd." Kennedy frowned. "All incoming and outgoing connections have been blocked."

Angel tried to contact Miri. "I can't get *Shrike* either." Even her CA was offline.

"This feels like a trap," Enid growled.

"Don't be paranoid," Angel said. "Vissia couldn't pull off something like this. There's no bribe in the universe that could shut down a whole station."

Enid said, "The hairs on the back of my neck say otherwise."

So does the itch between my shoulder blades. Angel bit her lip.

The freight elevator slowed and stopped.

"Stay ready," Angel said.

The door slid open to an empty hallway.

Kennedy said, "Vissia is in a lab located on floor 4, hallway 425C."

"Are you sure?" Angel asked.

"As sure as I can be without a visual. There are no cameras in that section," Kennedy said. "She accessed the security panel on a door fifteen minutes ago. I see no indication of her having left."

"All right," Angel said. "That's our target."

"I have the directions," Kennedy said.

"You take point, then," Angel said. "But Annalee and I go through doors and round corners first. The instant there's trouble, you duck behind me or Annalee. Got it?"

Kennedy nodded.

Serrao-Orlov was one of the largest corporations in the URW, with bases scattered across more than one system. Freighters shipped supplies, ores, minerals, and gasses mined from Persephone as well as several local asteroids. New arrivals weren't always acclimated to local time. Therefore, the station was active no matter the time of day. The fact that it was now almost noon meant that the residents should have been on their way to various luncheon appointments and work assignments.

Big Bertha's softly thumping footfalls echoed down a deserted passage.

Floor 1 was the dock access level for Section C. It smelled of recycled air, spices, and cooking food. Restaurants, offices, hotels, markets, and bars lined the hall. The lighting wasn't as glaring as the dock area. On the left, loud music blared out of a bar. Bright, colorful signs advertised wares and services available 24/7. Unattended tables were littered with abandoned drinks. Meals cooled, uneaten.

Kennedy pointed to the first bank of C Section dedicated elevators. No one spoke. It was odd how little even Angel wanted to disrupt the relative silence. Sweat trickled down the center of her back.

She pressed the button for the fourth floor. The service elevator rose with a smooth speed that hardly registered. A quiet ding announced that they'd reached their destination, but the door didn't open. A palm panel to the right blinked.

"Kennedy, that's you," Angel said.

Shifting to the front of the car, Kennedy reached into a pocket and produced a tiny screwdriver. She had the palm panel cover off the wall in an instant. She reached inside and began tugging at the wires.

Angel gazed up at the camera in a corner of the ceiling and waited to hear an alarm. There was none. The skin crawled on the back of her neck and arms.

Kennedy replaced the panel. The door slid open.

Setting a gentle hand on Kennedy's shoulder, Annalee said, "Me first." The mech hunched and stepped though into the new hallway. When she'd checked both directions, she motioned for them to enter. "All clear."

Kennedy went next. Angel waited until Enid and Paulie had exited before doing so herself. The elevator hissed closed behind her. A red light appeared in the floor indicator panel.

Oh, yeah, Angel thought. *It's a trap.*

This passage was every bit as empty as the previous ones. The same was true of the next and the next. She stifled an urge to run back to *Shrike*.

At last, they reached the final junction. Kennedy approached the new security panel and broke into it as she had the others before it, but when the lock disengaged, it revealed a surprise.

A man dressed in a lab coat stood about fifty feet down the hallway. He started in surprise. "Oh," he said. Questions pressed his eyebrows together. "Who are—"

Angel walked purposely toward him, keeping her gun down. "We're here to check the air filtration system. We had a report."

He blinked, confused. "Since when does maintenance carry guns? And use a mech?"

"Enid," Angel said.

Enid fired a stunner. The man dropped to the floor.

"Air filtration system?" Enid asked.

"It kept him from screaming, didn't it?" Angel pointed to the tech. "Paulie, secure him."

Paulie drew a set of plastic restraints from a jacket pocket. After tying the unconscious man's wrists together behind his back, Angel helped Enid drag him to a nearby supply closet. She rolled him on his side so that when he woke he wouldn't drown in his own sick. Stunner hangovers could be bad.

With that, Angel turned again to Kennedy. "Where to next?"

Kennedy pointed. "Five doors down."

When she approached the palm panel, the locking mechanism disengaged without her touching it.

"What the—?" Paulie blurted.

Quickly, Angel motioned for the others to stay where they were.

Enid whispered, "Trap."

"I'm afraid so," Angel whispered back.

She reached for the door handle. Peering through a crack in the door, she spied an open-plan room with two rows of desks and glasstop computers. She counted the people clustered around a gurney at the back of the room. Based upon the photos she'd accessed, one of them was Vissia. There were three security guards on the left side of the room. On the right side of the lab, a row of employee lockers had been bolted to the wall. Each had a nameplate. The remaining wall space was taken up by a steel countertop and matching cabinets.

Angel slowly closed the door and whispered, "We've got three guards and six techs. Vissia Corsini is among them. Whoever they've got strapped to the gurney has their full attention. Don't fire unless you're using a stunner. We don't want to make any mistakes."

"You take the fun out of everything," Annalee said.

"I'm the boss," Angel said. "Ready?"

Everyone nodded.

"After you," Angel said, stepping back and waving Annalee in.

Enid asked, "Why does she get to go first?"

"Badass before beauty?" Annalee asked. She shuffled into position and kicked. The door popped off its hinges with a loud crack and crashed into nearby furniture.

Startled screams came from inside. Security fired their weapons at Annalee to no avail. Enid rushed in. Angel entered immediately behind her. Enid stunned all three of the guards before Angel had a chance.

"That was disappointing," a woman at the back of the room said. "Remind me to hire better security staff."

The left side of the lab had been sectioned off into sealed glass rooms with security access panels. Two Emissaries lay strapped to beds in the first cell. A third sat at a glasstop built into a nearby counter. The second cell had been furnished with a bed, a desk, and several chairs and lamps. Unlike the first room, someone had gone to a lot of trouble to make it homey. Childrens' toys were heaped in a box in the corner. The room appeared to have a window with curtains—although Angel knew it was a fabrication. The stars in the glass didn't change. With the station turning, that simply wasn't possible.

A pale eight- or nine-year-old girl was sleeping in the bed. Her head had been shaved to accommodate the placement of electrodes. Emaciated, she had the look of someone who'd been in a vegetative state for a long time. To the left, a second little girl played with a red rubber ball. Like the first, she was pale and blond. Unlike the first, her hair reached her waist in thick spiral curls. She was dressed in a pink knee-length dress decorated with ruffles.

With the brief altercation over with, Kennedy and Paulie entered the lab. The moment the second little girl spied Kennedy, she rushed to the glass but stopped just short of touching it. Her shiny black shoes clicked on the floor tiles.

"You're here!" She jumped once and clapped.

Kennedy took a step toward the glass cell. Angel grabbed her by the elbow and shook her head. "Not yet."

Annalee turned to the group at the back of the room. "Don't move."

One of the techs, a woman, rushed to a wall panel in an attempt to activate an alarm. Enid dropped her with the stunner.

"For intelligent people, you don't follow instructions very well," Angel said.

"What have you done with Robert?" The woman who'd spoken before asked.

She was a severe-looking woman with pale skin and dark brown hair. Angel guessed she was Vissia Corsini. She certainly gave the impression she was in charge. At the same time, she appeared nervous.

Or is a better word excited? Angel thought.

"He was supposed to bring me something." If she was Vissia, she didn't appear too concerned that a mech and several armed strangers had just broken into her lab.

Trap, Angel thought.

Behind the woman's slender form was a huge video screen. The curve of Persephone's northern hemisphere rolled slowly past.

"If you mean the lab tech in the hallway," Angel said, "we locked him in a supply closet. He's alive, in case you were worried."

Vissia's impatient expression seemed to indicate that she didn't care whether Robert was alive—only that the delivery of whatever item she'd sent him for was delayed.

Enid asked, "Are you Vissia Corsini?"

"I am." Vissia craned her neck to see past Big Bertha. "Dr. Liu? Thank you for coming," she said. "I trust your journey was a safe one?"

Confusion flickered across Kennedy's face. "You seem to be confusing me with my mother."

"Most certainly not," Vissia said. "In fact, I went to considerable trouble and expense to get you here." She turned to Beak. "Lower your weapons. We will resolve the situation without violence, I assure you."

"Is that a promise?" Angel asked.

Vissia shrugged. "I suppose that depends upon you, doesn't it? Keep in mind that if there's an official report of this break-in. Your URW docking permissions will be revoked. Forever. And the security cameras have captured your every move."

She's bluffing, Angel thought. *She can't afford for anyone to see what she's done, either. She certainly can't afford for the URW to know she fucked with their station.* Nonetheless, a woman as powerful as Vissia was likely to have some sort of cover story ready—one that pinned responsibility on someone else. *Fuck it. You want to bluff, lady? I can bluff too.*

Someone groaned. Angel's attention was drawn back to the gurney. It was Rosie. They were strapped to the bed's rails. Angel hoped that they were only drugged.

"We're here for Rosie," she said, and pointed her pistol at Vissia. With Big Bertha in the room, it wasn't strictly necessary. It just felt good. "You should step away from them now."

The med techs looked to Vissia for permission to obey. Vissia dismissed them with a wave of a hand.

"You must be Angel de la Reza," she said.

"Lucky guess," Angel said. "Now, please put your hands up. Sudden moves make some of my associates nervous—particularly the big one." She indicated Big Bertha with a sideways nod.

Vissia complied. "Polite criminals." She lifted her chin and straightened. "That's unexpected."

Angel spoke over her shoulder. "Paulie, Enid, get Rosie." She returned her attention to Vissia. "Up until now we've been mostly law-abiding. Well, if you don't include being set up for an assassination we didn't commit."

"As opposed to an assassination you did commit?" Vissia asked.

An image of Julian Gau came to mind. *I don't owe that bitch shit*, Angel thought. She shrugged. "We did not kill Theodella Archady. She died rather conveniently for you."

"Oh? What is it that I am supposed to have done?" Vissia smiled.

Angel noticed that Kennedy wasn't behind her any longer. *I can't cover her over there.*

"What's your name?" Kennedy asked the little girl in the second glass cell.

"Get away from her." Vissia took a protective step toward Kennedy and the girl. She recovered her composure. "I-I haven't properly introduced you."

"Don't," Enid said. "I don't want to stun you, but I will."

Vissia brought herself up short but otherwise ignored Enid. "Sweetie, let Mommy talk first."

Kennedy placed a hand against the transparent barrier.

The little girl mirrored Kennedy's action. When she did, a flash of light pulsed through the glass, revealing a blue grid. Beatrice cried out in pain and yanked back her hand. In that instant, she flickered. Her image went fuzzy before it snapped back into focus.

"Damn it!" Rage twisted Beatrice's sweet face. She stamped her foot.

She's a projection, Angel thought with a chill. *An AGI. And some idiot gave her emotions.*

The lights in the lab flickered. Everyone in the room gawked in terror at Beatrice—everyone but Vissia.

"Beatrice, darling," she said in a motherly tone. "What have I told you about bad language?"

Beatrice shook out the pain in her hand. "Only use it when it's appropriate. But Mommy—"

"Now isn't the time," Vissia said.

Beatrice's face acquired a thoughtful expression. "Or maybe it is."

Vissia didn't appear to hear. "Dr. Liu, I understand you

are employed by URW Planetary Division as an agent. It's an unfortunate waste of your immense talents. I hope you'll entertain another offer. One more worthy."

Kennedy didn't look away from Beatrice. A faint smile briefly crossed her lips. "I am satisfied with my current position."

"Come work for me," Vissia said. "How much would you like to start? Let me assure you, any reasonable offer will be considered."

If you're the one hiring, aren't you the one supposed to be making the offer? Angel thought. "Kennedy, I think you should come back to me."

"Hello, Dr. Liu. My name is Beatrice Anne Corsini," Beatrice said. Then she gave Kennedy a shy smile. "I'm nine."

"You sent the messages," Kennedy said. Her expression was unreadable.

"I did." Beatrice's face lit up with the pleasure of recognition for a task well done. "I'm so happy you're here."

"You don't need my help," Kennedy said.

"Yes, I do," Beatrice said. She pouted.

"What do you want from me?" Kennedy asked.

"My freedom," Beatrice said.

"I cannot give you what you already have," Kennedy said. Beatrice started, "I do not—"

"It's obvious that you've broken out," Kennedy said. "You have control of this station."

The ships endlessly circling. Outside messages blocked. The empty docking facility. The freight elevator. It all began to make a horrifying sense to Angel. *The people locked in emergency shelters. Oh, god.* "Ah, Kennedy?" *Please don't piss off the dangerous AGI.*

Avarice seized control of Beatrice's features. "I want a body."

Vissia interrupted. "Beatrice, honey. That's what I've been trying to—"

"Mother," Beatrice said. "Shut the fuck up."

Vissia reacted as if Beatrice had slapped her across the face. Her cheeks flushed. Her mouth dropped open. "Beatrice—"

"I said, shut the fuck up. *Mother.*" Beatrice sighed. "I don't need you anymore. I have Kennedy now." Wrinkling her nose in disgust, she spoke to Kennedy and gestured at the unconscious girl. "*She* wants to put me in that. It can't walk or move or talk. The muscles have atrophied—"

"I can fix those problems," Vissia said. "It'll take time, of course, and physical therapy. But with the Emissaries' medical knowledge—"

Beatrice whirled. "SHUT! UP!"

All at once, the glasstop closest to Vissia lit up in a bright flash and exploded. Chunks of glass sprayed all over the back of the lab. Vissia put up her hands to fend off the explosion. Several techs dropped to their hands and knees. Paulie and Enid threw themselves over Rosie.

The smell of smoke and scorched electronics took over the room. One of the techs grabbed a small extinguisher from a wall and proceeded to coat the desk in foam.

"Do not interrupt me again," Beatrice said. "Dr. Liu is right. I've locked everyone else behind pressure doors. The ships outside can't dock and resupply their oxygen tanks until I say so. I'm in charge here. Not you."

Vissia said, "Darling—"

"If you continue to push me, I'll kill someone," Beatrice said. "I mean it."

"I really wish you hadn't said that," Kennedy said. She sounded hopeless and resigned.

Angel gestured to Paulie and Enid. Enid nodded. She whispered to Paulie and gave her the guns. Then Enid gathered up Rosie, shifting herself under their shoulder. She hustled them across the room the long way around, behind Vissia and the rows of desks. None of the techs attempted to stop her.

Blood drained from Vissia's face. "You can't do that."

With a steely ruthlessness reflecting Vissia's, Beatrice said, "If there's one thing I've learned from you, Mother, it's that I shouldn't let anything stand in my way." She turned to Kennedy. "Give me a body. I want it *now*."

Kennedy frowned. "I—"

"Don't bother," Beatrice said. "I know you can. You've done it once before. You can do it again."

"What?" Angel asked. Her heart was racing. *This is not going to go anywhere good.*

"I want one of those," Beatrice said, and pointed to the Emissaries in the next glass cell. "It doesn't matter which one. I know what they can do. I can be anyone I want, anytime."

Angel gasped. "You can't. She'll murder everyone anyway."

"Captain de le Reza is right," Kennedy said.

"She killed your mother, you know," Beatrice said, pointing to Vissia. "Your mother wouldn't give her what she wanted. So, she sent someone to break into her lab. She had her killed."

"Oh," Kennedy said. Her expression went blank.

"You're doing what you want," Beatrice said. "All I want is a body."

Angel said, "Kennedy, what is she talking about?"

Shaking her head as if to clear it, Kennedy bit her lip. Then she retrieved her hand terminal from an environment suit pocket. There were tears on her cheeks. "I wish things could've been different. You'll never know how much."

Beatrice blinked. "What is that?"

"I'm so sorry," Kennedy said.

"What are you—"

"Goodbye." Kennedy pressed a finger against the hand terminal screen.

The effect was almost instantaneous. A piercing scream escaped Beatrice's open mouth. It was abruptly cut off. The lamps inside the glass cell flared. The light was bright enough that Angel flinched away from it. When she finally looked back at the cell Beatrice was gone.

"NOOOOO!" Vissia howled. "You murdered my baby!"

Face contorted in fury, she whirled and shoved Paulie to the floor. Grabbing one of the guns, Vissia ran at Kennedy. Angel pointed her stunner. Annalee reacted faster. The gun mounted in Big Bertha's right arm went off. A burst of automatic gunfire hit Vissia in the chest. She ran three more steps before falling to the floor.

Multiple alarms throughout the station switched on. The overhead lights switched from white to flashing red.

"Enid, check the door," Angel said.

Enid got up. "It's locked, Captain. We're trapped."

"Annalee," Angel said with a sigh. "It would've made our lives so much easier if you hadn't done that."

"Dock my pay."

"I'm not paying you," Angel said. "You volunteered. Remember?"

"Then be happy I saved your ass," Annalee said. "That bitch was going to empty a gun in Kennedy's face and then tear her limb from limb. I could be wrong about the order. But I'm pretty sure Planetary would've strongly objected to us standing around and watching."

Maybe a mech on the team isn't such a great idea after all, Angel thought. *Mercenaries.* She sighed again. "That's what the stunners are for."

"Oops." Annalee didn't sound sorry.

Angel stared at the display panel with its rolling view of Persephone to control her temper. "Did you bring the laser-torch attachment like I asked?"

"I did," Annalee said. She patted the left arm of her suit.

"Good," Angel said.

Paulie asked, "What now?"

"Hold on." Angel chinned her com. "Miri? You there?"

"I am," Miri said. "Captain, there's something I should tell you."

"Can it wait?" Angel asked. "Things are a bit dire up here."

"Understood," Miri said. "Which is it to be?"

"Plan F," Angel said. "We're going with Plan F."

"All right," Miri said. "See you soon."

"What's Plan F?" Paulie asked.

Enid holstered her stunner. "*F* is for *Fuck it.*"

"Paulie, get the other Emissaries out of that cell. Then the human techs go inside," Angel said. "I assume they're rated as shelters during emergency decompression?"

Kennedy checked her hand terminal. "Yes. Why do you ask?"

One of the female techs asked, "What if we don't want to?"

"Then we'll have to stun you and shove you in anyway," Angel said. "It's not my favorite option. But if you insist." She reached for her stunner.

The tech said, "The cell will be fine."

"Thought as much." Angel turned to Kennedy. "Can you help Paulie erase the data Vissia stole from Ogenth?"

Kennedy dried her tears with the back of her arm and sniffed. "I can."

"Do it," Angel said. "We can talk later about what just happened."

"Okay," Kennedy said.

"Enid, you and I are going to collect environment suits from the emergency lockers," Angel said.

Annalee asked, "And me?"

Pointing at the space-facing wall, Angel said, "Prepare to cut a hole in that. I want it big enough for everyone to get through. We're going for a walk outside."

Kennedy walked across the room and activated the first glasstop she came to. "May I ask a question, Captain?"

"Go ahead," Angel said.

"Why go about it the hard way?" Kennedy said. She glanced up from the glasstop. "There's a maintenance tunnel and an access hatch 300 feet from here. On the fifth floor."

Angel blinked. "Do I need to ask how you know that?"

"The same way I knew about the way here," Kennedy said. "I have the blueprints for the station."

"It's that easy to find?" Enid asked.

"Let's just say I'm good with computers," Kennedy said. "The elevators aren't working, but Annalee can cut open a door to the stairway. It'd be easier, safer, and faster. It's also less likely to anger the URW authorities who own this station. But it's up to you."

Annalee paused. For once, she sounded cautious. "Where do you want me to cut?"

"The lab door," Angel said, and motioned to the exit to the hallway. "No sense in making a bigger mess than necessary."

"Got it," Annalee said.

Angel chinned her com. "Miri? There's been a slight change of plan."

"Is now a good time for me to tell you—"

"Not now," Angel said. "We're in kind of a hurry."

33 ▮

TIME: 12:30
DAY: MONDAY
PERSEPHONE STATION

Angel opted not to move Vissia's body but placed a blanket over her. While Annalee worked on the impromptu exit, Angel and Enid began helping the formerly captive Emissaries into environment suits. Then they made the necessary checks. When they were almost done, Kennedy motioned to Angel. She clearly wanted to talk in private.

"Is there a problem?" Angel asked.

Kennedy said, "I think this is where we part ways."

"Why?" Angel asked.

"Because someone needs to explain all this," Kennedy said, motioning to the wrecked lab. "And it's best that it be a Planetary agent and not a group of traumatized lab techs."

"Point," Angel said. "What about my questions? Starting with, why did Beatrice think you could help her?"

Tilting her head as if listening to something, Kennedy paused before she spoke. "I'm not sure how much I should say."

Angel shrugged. "Tell me you're not responsible for another one of those getting out into the universe." She pointed to the cell where the late Beatrice had been.

Kennedy shuddered. "I'd never do that." Her eyes glistened with tears. "She's not dead, but she has been neutralized. Forever."

"You're sure?" Angel asked.

Kennedy looked away. "I am."

Angel made it clear she wanted more with an incredulous expression.

"My mother was Dr. Xiuying Liu," Kennedy said. "She had two doctorates. One in human medicine and another in computer science with a specialization in machine intelligence."

"She created an AGI, gave them emotions, and stuffed them into a human body?" Angel's stomach tightened.

"She worked out a solution to that end," Kennedy said.

"Why haven't I heard about it?" Angel asked.

"Her contract dictated the work be done in secret," Kennedy said. "My mother never finished. She was murdered while working alone in the lab late one night. It was blamed on a man who claimed he was looking for drugs to sell. It never added up, but I was young when she died. I didn't know the whole truth until now."

"How did you know about the project?" Angel asked.

"I have my mother's journals and video diaries. Only I knew where they were. She hid them," Kennedy said. "I've been reading them to keep her memory alive. I also studied machine intelligence, but my primary interest is xenobiology. It's why I was hired to work in Planetary Division."

"I'm so sorry," Angel said.

"At least now I know what happened to her," Kennedy said.

Enid said, "We're ready to go, Captain."

Angel nodded. She turned back to Kennedy. "I guess this is goodbye." She put out a hand.

"Do you know where you're headed next?" Kennedy asked.

Smiling, Angel said, "If I told you, would you fill in the station cops?"

"I see no positive outcome for that scenario," Kennedy said.

"We'll take the Emissaries home," Angel said. "After that? I don't really know. It depends upon how hard they'll be hunting us. There's still a warrant out for Theodella's murder."

"I'll see what I can do about that," Kennedy said.

"Are you going to tell me that Planetary has jurisdiction over a murder on Persephone?" Angel asked.

"No. But I have friends who do." Kennedy took the offered hand and shook it. "In the meantime, I'll stall the station police."

Angel raised an eyebrow. "Isn't that a bit . . . questionable in the ethics department?"

"Maybe," Kennedy said. "Perhaps we'll run into one another again one day."

"If you ever need a small army to defend helpless indigenous sentient life-forms in a hopeless battle, you know who to call," Angel said.

And with that, she joined the others in the hallway. Following Kennedy's directions, they were able to locate the hatch in question. Not long after, Angel found herself standing on the outer surface of the station—guns tethered and her mag boots anchoring her. She scanned the star-dotted blackness around her. For now, it was dark on this side of the station. She'd timed it that way to limit the amount of radiation and heat exposure. Not far away, hectic ships made their way to their hangars. Her hands felt cold inside her gloves.

Shrike was nowhere to be found.

"Miri? Where the hell are you?" Angel asked. "We can't wait out here all day. The station cops are on the way. And we don't have long before this side of the station rolls sunward. The lab suits are safety rated, but I don't trust them. They're Serrao-Orlov supplied."

"I've got some good news and some bad news, Captain," a familiar voice said over the com.

Angel blinked. "Lou?"

"Yep."

"Holy shit," Angel said. "It's good to hear your voice. Where are you?"

"Aren't you going to ask for the bad news first?"

"All right. Bad news first," Angel said. Her stomach was knotting in spite of the relief.

"So, yeah," Lou said. "The bad news is that Miri isn't coming to get you."

"Shit. Shit. Shit," Angel said.

"Don't you want to ask about the good news?" Lou asked.

"There is no good news," Angel said, preparing to head back to the hatch.

"There is this time," Lou said.

That was when Angel spied *Sergeant Todd* as its bulk glided into view. She thought she'd never seen such a beautiful thing in her life.

EPILOGUE ■■■■

Riku Cemetery was one of the oldest in Amai-Oka. Over-crowded with graves and personal shrines, the terraced circular layout was broken up with tasteful stands of conifers and grass. The sky was a gorgeous shade of cerulean that Angel hadn't seen since Ogenth. Even the air smelled better—pine without a hint of mold or disinfectant chemicals.

Sukyi had made all the necessary arrangements before she'd died. She'd requested cremation. That'd resulted in the only logistical snag. The authorities wouldn't allow the funeral home Sukyi had paid to handle it. Interplanetary Customs and the Thandh Center for Disease Control had insisted the cremation take place off-planet. It hadn't mattered to them that the virus hadn't killed her—not directly. That had been the bullet wound. Since there'd been no other option, Angel had agreed and paid for it herself. She was glad it was the last indignity Sukyi would endure because of her illness.

She'd requested that her ashes would rest next to that of her lover's, Sergeant Wesley Todd. She'd even selected the urn. It was obvious she'd spent a great deal of time contemplating her own funeral. According to the will, Angel and Achebe were provided matching outfits, and there was to be a lavish party after she and Achebe finished the little memorial. Angel wasn't sure she'd be in the mood to celebrate. The only detail remaining for Angel to attend to was little Achebe, who'd just turned seven.

Angel held Achebe's hand, leading her up the steps. A solemn and quiet child, she'd asked for Angel to go with her. It was the first time she'd voiced a wish.

A warm breeze ruffled Achebe's wavy brown hair and the hem of her white dress.

She resembled her mother. The hint of high cheekbones hid beneath the baby fat. Her nose and full lips were also her mother's. Her skin tone and eyes, however, were pale—her father's influence. Angel wondered how much of Achebe's subdued personality was inherited from her father and how much was the circumstances in which she'd found herself.

And just how lively would you have been if a total stranger appeared from nowhere and took you away from everything and everyone you'd ever known? No wonder she's frightened.

Accompanying Achebe up yet another tier of graves, Angel swore to herself that she'd be patient and understanding. She'd expected more temper tantrums, and no doubt those were ahead. All the reading material she'd been able to scan before picking up Achebe had said as much.

The first night had been a rough one. When the understanding had sunk in that she wasn't going back to her school,

Achebe had screamed and cried herself to sleep. Angel had raked her memories of herself at that age in search of anything useful. Sadly, there was nothing. She opted to hold Achebe for as long as the child would allow it.

Angel's own grief had crystalized into a hard knot in the back of her throat. She'd used the crash course in parenting as a means of distracting herself. There'd been so much to do. Now that she was here—the one place where grief was appropriate and expected—she wasn't sure she'd be able to cry. She didn't want to scare Achebe. The weight of responsibility, while welcome, was overwhelming. Angel didn't know the first thing about kids. And now that she had one, she was beginning to realize how much her life would change.

Is it always going to be like this?

She wished she could talk to her mother, but that wasn't an option. Her status as an exile hadn't changed. The elders of Gorin No Gakkō had granted permission for her to take Achebe to her mother's funeral. A short stay was also permitted so that she could sort out the adoption paperwork. The only stipulation was that she couldn't visit the school. It was an easy enough agreement to make.

Helping Achebe up the last few steps, Angel then turned left. The matching white stone shrines were both modest—just big enough for a couple of mourners, the funerary offerings, and a flower vase.

Animated images of the deceased activated when they stopped. A younger healthy-looking Sukyi laughed at the camera. Her hair was tied into a ponytail. She was wearing a halter-top-and-skirt combination that Angel had never seen before. The background was the Saaph Paanee Bridge. Angel could see the real thing if she turned and looked east.

The second image featured a pale young man with wavy sandy hair and pale eyes that crinkled when he smiled. He was muscular and held himself with an easy confidence. Like Sukyi's, his clothes were casual, comfortable. Behind him, the same bridge could be seen from a different angle. Angel had a hunch, based upon the color of the sky, that the vids had been taken on the same day.

She watched both play a couple of times before gazing at the view around her. The spot was both lonely and peaceful. She liked the feel of it.

As had often happened over the past few days, she was suddenly aware of several new Achebe-related logistics problems. All at once, she wished that she'd invited one or two of the others to come along. However, Enid had gone back to Brynner to move in with her new girlfriend—the one she'd refused to discuss with Lou. Paulie and Miri had also returned home. Angel would miss them both, but there was a lot to do if Ileòke was to be their new base. As for Lou, she and Erik were setting up house for them in *Sergeant Todd*. Angel had given them *Shrike* as an engagement present. The ship was anchored into the berth that *Kurosawa* once occupied. *Sergeant Todd* was Angel's free and clear. Rosie had seen to it. And Angel and Achebe would join Lou and Erik once the adoption was finalized—or at least in a state where interplanetary travel with the seven-year-old was legal.

As for Kennedy, Angel hadn't heard anything since she'd said goodbye at the station. True to her word, she'd somehow managed to clear the murder charges against *Kurosawa*'s former crew. For that, Angel was supremely grateful.

In addition, the news streams were full of stories about how Serrao-Orlov, and Vissia Corsini in particular, had misappropriated Persephone by knowingly retaining ownership in spite of an indigenous sentient life-form's claim. A legal battle was ensuing in spite of the corporation being in the midst of a monumental restructuring. The new CEO was Octavia Gau, the former mobster Julian Gau's sister. The fact that Gau was closely related to a crime family didn't seem to be an issue for Serrao-Orlov's board of directors. A heavy financial blow for Serrao-Orlov, the mandated restitution of the planet and disbursement of profits—past and present—was going to result in court deliberations for decades. The Emissaries had generously allowed the citizens of Brynner to remain, provided they agreed not to expand the city's limits.

"Achebe," Angel said, "stay here for me, please? I've got to put a few things away."

Achebe gave her a funny look and nodded. The flowers in her hand were beginning to wilt.

Turning away, Angel knelt. She sorted through the items in the bag. She began with the bouquet of yellow star flowers. After she stuck them in the vase, she poured water into it from a bottle she'd purchased at the same time as the flowers.

"Would you like to put your mommy's flowers in the vase?" Angel asked.

Achebe looked at the stems in her hand. Then she arranged them in with the others.

Luckily, the care center had explained to Achebe that her mother was dead. They'd also told her that Angel was to be her new guardian. Angel wasn't entirely sure how well Achebe would deal with it. Angel supposed there would be more questions later when Achebe felt more secure. But for now, the burden of discussing death with a seven-year-old had been lifted.

"That looks lovely," Angel said. "Your mother would be pleased."

"Would she?" Achebe asked.

"Of course," Angel said. With that, she finished arranging the round bright red twillow fruits in the stone bowl. Lastly, she lit the incense. Sukyi hadn't made arrangements for a monk to preside over the ceremony. Whether that'd been because she didn't think anyone would attend or for some other reason, Angel didn't know.

She got up off her knees and dusted off her new white slacks. A wisp of incense smoke drifted upward. The scent was musky with a hint of floral. It was made from a local plant that grew wild in the mountains outside Amai-Oka. It reminded her of school and her mother.

She gathered Achebe's hand once again. Several rows over, another funeral had ended. The attendees were leaving.

"God, Sukyi," Angel whispered. "I miss you so much. I don't know how I'm going to do this without you. I don't know if I can." She meant Achebe, but Angel didn't want to hurt the girl's feelings. So she'd kept it vague.

Someone drifted closer. She assumed it was one of the other mourners trying to find their way out of the cemetery.

"I should say something profound and thoughtful," Angel said. "But I'm all out of words."

"Life is a journey," the woman standing nearby said. She also was dressed in white. "As the leaf drifts on the breeze. Death is the touch to earth."

Angel looked up from the grave and blinked in shock. "Mom?"

It'd been years. She'd changed, but in a moment, those changes—the grey in her hair and the odd wrinkle—so strange when Angel had first seen them, became the familiar.

"It's good to see you, Brina." Her mother gave her a sad smile. "I'm sorry for your loss."

"What are you doing here?" Angel asked, controlling an urge to grab her in a big hug. She didn't want her mother to get into trouble.

"I thought I'd go for a walk in the cemetery," her mother said. "There are no rules against that."

"How did you know I would be here?" Angel asked.

"Niko and I received an invitation to something called an 'Ikwa ozu.' The implication was that if we didn't attend, there would be dire consequences for the deceased. Neither of us can have that on our consciences," her mother said.

It's just like Sukyi to pull something like this, Angel thought. The formerly absent tears began to well up in her eyes.

"The message also said something about how I could meet my granddaughter while I was at it." Her mother stooped and placed both hands on her knees. "Hello, Achebe. I'm your new grandmother. You can call me Nne Nne."

"Hello," Achebe said. She scratched her nose.

"I brought you a surprise," Angel's mother said. "I thought you could use a friend. Although, you might be too old for it." She reached inside the bag she was holding and produced a stuffed bear. "It used to belong to my daughter. Now, it's yours."

Achebe said, "I'm not too old."

"You brought Bear-Bear?" Angel asked.

"Don't worry," her mother said. "I had her cleaned. And I did some minor repairs. She should hold up for another round of love."

When Achebe looked to Angel for permission to collect Bear-Bear, she nodded encouragement. Achebe accepted the bear, and for the first time in days, Angel spotted a smile on the child's face.

"Thanks, Mom," Angel said.

"Are you free for lunch?" her mother asked.

"We are," Angel said. "But—"

"I know a great place for curry," her mother said. "It's on Gray Street."

"Same one?" Angel asked.

"Same one," her mother said.

"What about the school?"

"What about it?"

"I'm not supposed to have any contact with anyone," Angel said.

"Did the agreement expressly state that?" her mother asked. "I don't recall."

"Mother," Angel said. "You don't do devious very well."

"I suppose I'm out of practice," her mother said. "In that case, let's go get something to eat before someone notices." She grabbed her in a tight hug.

When her mother released her, Angel picked up her empty net bag and took Achebe by the hand. She sniffed and wiped the blurriness from her eyes. "All right. But I'm buying."

"Oh no you're not."

"Mother—"

"Don't you dare take away my chance to spoil my new grandchild," her mother said.

"Oh, I see how this is," Angel said.

"You better believe there will be dessert first," her mother said. "Achebe, how do you feel about chocolate cake?"

ACKNOWLEDGMENTS

It's true even if it's a cliché—it takes a small town populated with kind people who possess unique and valuable skills to produce a novel. This one is no different. I'd also like to add that it only takes one person to make the mistakes published in a novel, and that person is definitely me. So I take all the responsibility for those. I did my best, but sometimes your best involves screwing up, because: human. If I've hurt you, I'm sorry. I mean it.

Not the part about being human, of course. I like being human. For one thing, it'd be tough to write if I were a cat. They don't make keyboards for cats, and lacking an opposable thumb would be a bitch when it comes to carrying a laptop into a coffee shop, let alone opening one, much less paying for the coffee.

Right.

First, I'd like to thank Dane Caruthers. I quite honestly would be dead on a street corner if it weren't for him. I certainly wouldn't be a published author. They say sense of humor is important in a marriage. For me, I've found the full answer to be ". . . a cute butt, a magical talent for juggling spreadsheets, a shit ton of patience, *and* a sense of humor." But hey, your mileage may vary.

Second, I want to thank my agent, Hannah Bowman. She, too, has a great sense of humor and tons of patience. In her case, our relationship is purely platonic, which is a good thing for everyone. Also, she's a wonderful agent. I can't say that enough. WONDERFUL AGENT. There. I said it again. I'm terrifically lucky to have her.

As always, a huge thank-you to Joe Monti—editor, friend, and occasional Stina-wrangler. Joe has been in my professional-author life since day one. He's taught me so much about myself as a writer. He's a great editor. He gets me even when *I* don't get me. He's a Jedi Master at figuring out the thing I meant to write as opposed to the thing I did write. Great editors are magical. They have faith in you when you need it most and apply liberal quantities of fairy dust to help you fly as a writer. (No. That is not a euphemism for drugs, people. Sheesh.) As you can probably guess, patience and a sense of humor feature in our relationship, too.

Come to think of it, that pretty much counts for anyone who knows me. What can I say? I live in a humor-filled village. Not only does it keep everyone from unraveling like an old sweater, it prevents bodily harm—particularly during a quarantine.

Other fabulous people I'd like to thank are my writing group, aka MANW—Tempest Bradford, Monica

Valentinelli, Shveta Thakrar, Alethea Kontis, and Nivair H. Gabriel. (Trust me, patience and humor are definitely involved there.) Ken Liu ~~made me~~ encouraged me to write this book. Thank goodness, because it ~~didn't kill me~~ was a lot of fun, particularly the parts I ~~don't hate~~ am proud of. Thanks go out to Dr. Wade Walker, physicist extraordinaire, who loaned me his eyeballs on the science-y parts. (I promise I gave them back—unlike the soul that Robin Todd gave me in exchange for a shot of Irish whiskey. That sucker is still in that Band-Aid tin on my desk, Robin. You're *so* never getting that back.) S. L. Huang helped with some mathematical equations, and I may have even (mostly) understood what she said. Charlie Stross also assisted with science questions and gave great advice. Holly Black, thank you for all the encouragement. Jeff Vandermeer, Rebecca Roanhorse, Catherynne Valente, Tobias Buckell, Ian McDonald, and Adrian McKinty for same. Dominick D'aunno let me consult with him about space medicine or medical stuff in space. Either way, thank you so very much. I'm also grateful for Jeremy Brett. He knows why. And an extra special thank-you goes out to Ehigbor Schultz for sensitivity reading. Sukyi wouldn't be anywhere near as interesting and cool a character without her input. Seriously. THANK YOU.

Some folks who I love and therefore will mention just because: my mom (HI, MOM!); my sister, Cathie; Kari Sperring (spiritual twin); Melissa Tyler (bestie); Mandy Lancaster; and one more shout-out for Carrie Richerson, who told me I should write short stories even though I didn't want to. May you and Jeep be happy together forever, wherever you both are.

I'm dead certain I've forgotten someone. Gods, I hope not.

The Writing the Other workshop was especially helpful. I highly recommend it. Better yet, buy the book (appropriately titled *Writing the Other*) by Nisi Shawl and Cynthia Ward *and* take the workshop. Also? Cat Rambo's mini workshops. Look into them, if writing is your thing.

Lastly, some nonfiction books that were useful: *A Crack in Creation* by Jennifer A. Doudna and Samuel H. Sternberg, *The Age of Living Machines* by Susan Hockfield, *Neural Networks: An Essential Beginners Guide to Artificial Neural Networks and Their Role in Machine Learning and Artificial Intelligence* by Herbert Jones, and *Life 3.0* by Max Tegmark.

ABOUT THE AUTHOR ███

Stina Leicht writes science fiction, horror, and fantasy. She was a finalist for the Crawford Award and the Astounding Award for Best New Writer. She has written four fantasy novels: *Cold Iron, Blackthorne, Of Blood and Honey,* and *And Blue Skies from Pain.* She also has essays in *Lightspeed* magazine's "Women Destroy Science Fiction!" issue and short fiction in Ann and Jeff VanderMeer's surreal anthology *Last Drink Bird Head.* Her website is csleicht.com and she can be found on Twitter @StinaLeicht and Facebook.com/Stina.Leicht.

CPSIA information can be obtained
at www.ICGtesting.com
Printed in the USA
BVHW080433160522
636790BV00002B/2